INDIANA JONES™

COLLECTOR'S EDITION

RAIDERS of the LOST ARK
TEMPLE of DOOM
LAST CRUSADE

LUCAS BOOKS

Scholastic Inc.

New York   Toronto   London   Auckland   Sydney
Mexico City   New Delhi   Hong Kong   Buenos Aires

Indiana Jones and the Raiders of the Lost Ark, ISBN-13: 978-0-545-00700-9, ISBN-10: 0-545-00700-3. Copyright © 2008 by Lucasfilm Ltd. & ™.

Indiana Jones and the Temple of Doom, ISBN-13: 978-0-545-04255-0, ISBN-10: 0-545-04255-0. Copyright © 2008 by Lucasfilm Ltd. & ™.

Indiana Jones and the Last Crusade, ISBN-13: 978-0-545-04256-7, ISBN-10: 0-545-04256-9. Copyright © 2008 by Lucasfilm Ltd. & ™.

12 11 10 9 8 7 6 5 4 3 2   8 9 10 11/0

Printed in the U.S.A.

ISBN-13: 978-0-545-09183-1

ISBN-10: 0-545-09183-7

First compilation printing, April 2008

CONTENTS

INDIANA JONES ™

and the
RAIDERS of the
LOST ARK

Ryder Windham
Based on the story by George Lucas and Philip Kaufman
and the screenplay by Lawrence Kasdan

Thanks to Annmarie Nye at Scholastic, and Jonathan Rinzler and Leland Chee at Lucasfilm. Thanks also to the authors of Lucasfilm's official *Indiana Jones* website (www.indianajones.com), and to Dr. David West Reynolds for his extensive knowledge about the costumes, props, and vehicles in the *Indiana Jones* films.

For Anne,
who knows what belongs in a museum

*M*aking his way up along a narrow trail at the edge of the Peruvian rain forest, Indiana Jones used the back of his hand to wipe the sweat from his unshaven face. The whiskers didn't hide the thin scar that traveled across his chin, just below his lower lip — not that he cared. He'd had the scar for years, and never spent much time in front of a mirror anyway. Besides, a shaving kit would have been just one more thing to carry. As far as he knew, there wasn't any reward waiting for a man who died in the jungle with a clean shave.

Jones looked at a mountain peak in the distance to confirm he was still headed in the right direction. To protect himself from the elements, he wore a weathered felt fedora, a battered brown leather jacket, and durable high-top leatherwork boots. Under his jacket he wore a light khaki safari-style shirt. A cotton web belt held up his dark khaki pants, and a second belt, made of leather, carried his holstered revolver and coiled bullwhip. He also toted a faded green-fabric shoulder bag that contained several small provisions.

Although he looked more like a wayward cowboy than a thirty-six-year-old university professor, he was in fact a respected archaeologist who taught at Marshall College in Connecticut. His friends called him "Indy," but the seven men who followed him through the jungle were hardly his friends.

Two of the men, Satipo and Barranca, were Peruvians who wore tattered, sweat-stained jungle khakis. Indy had hired them as guides. He had met them at a remote river outpost called Machete Landing, where they had no small reputation as thieves. Unfortunately, the motley pair also had a fragment of a map and some knowledge of the route to Indy's destination, the lost temple of the Chachapoyan warriors. Indy might have eventually found the lost temple on his own, but that would have taken more time, and he was certain that at least one treasure hunter had a head start on him. Still, Indy had no reason to trust Satipo and Barranca, and knew better than to pay thieves too much money in advance.

The other five men who trailed behind Indy were indigenous Quechuans, who'd been hired on as porters for the expedition. They wore ponchos and brightly colored knitted caps, and barely made a sound as they moved through the jungle. Aided by two donkeys, the Quechuans were laden with equipment and provisions, including special tools and drinking water. The Quechuans had been reluctant to travel in Indy's group because they were afraid of the Chachapoyan temple. They believed it was cursed.

The year was 1936. A few weeks earlier, Adolf Hitler, the leader of the Nazi Party in Germany, had presided over the Games of the XI Olympiad in Berlin. Indy would always remember those games because the American track and field athlete Jesse Owens had won four gold medals. Most Peruvians were still grumbling about the notorious football tournament quarterfinals. Peru had defeated Austria 4–2 in overtime, but then withdrew in protest after Austria raised complaints about their conduct, and game officials ordered a rematch. Even Satipo and Barranca were enraged when Peru's president announced that a "crafty Berlin decision" had cost the Peru team their victory, and allowed Austria to claim the silver medal. Now, both guides hoped to console their country's loss by claiming any treasure they might find for themselves.

Indy's group proceeded deeper into the jungle. Soon, they reached an area where the donkeys could no longer maneuver between the trees, and they were forced to leave them behind. Satipo obligingly pulled on a backpack to help the porters carry provisions, but Barranca had refused to carry anything except his heavy revolver, which was already holstered at his belt.

Indy was tired. Hungry, too. But he stayed alert, keeping his eyes and ears open. He hadn't expected to hear one of the men in his party scream, but when it happened, he didn't flinch either.

The scream came from one of the Quechuan porters. While pushing away some leaves, the man had suddenly found himself staring into the glaring eyes of a massive stone face, a demon with a wide, snarling mouth. Startled birds shrieked and flew out from the undergrowth. As the panicked Quechuan ran from the monstrous statue, all the other porters followed his example and retreated swiftly into the jungle.

Indy, Satipo, and Barranca made no effort to stop the porters. Ignoring the birds that whipped around the statue, Indy pulled an aged piece of parchment from his pocket and examined it. The parchment, which he'd brought with him from the United States, was part of an old map. He hadn't told Satipo and Barranca about the parchment, but he was aware of their silence as they watched him from behind.

If this map is good, Indy thought, *there'll be a stream just east of here.* Indy looked to his left, and then moved away from the gaping statue as he tucked the map back into his pocket. Satipo and Barranca followed.

They found the stream and crossed it, and it seemed that the surrounding jungle grew even darker. A few long shafts of light, slicing down through the thick forest canopy, were the only evidence that it was still daytime. Indy lowered the brim of his hat to protect his eyes from the brilliant shafts, and searched the trees for any sign that he was still heading in the right direction.

Then he saw the dart. It was just a thin needle of wood, embedded in the otherwise smooth trunk of a tall tree. Indy stopped to pull the dart from the tree, slid his fingers over it to feel a slightly tacky substance on its tip, then dropped it and moved on.

Watching Indy's actions with curiosity, the two guides scurried over to where Indy had been standing. Satipo picked up the dart. Studying the small projectile, he said nervously, "The Hovitos are near." Satipo rubbed the dart's tip with his fingers, felt the tacky substance, and then stuck a finger in his mouth. An instant later, he spat hard. "The poison is still fresh . . . three days." He glanced back at the way they had approached the tree from the jungle. "They're following us."

Barranca snatched the dart from Satipo's hand and took a close look at it for himself. "If they knew we were here," he said, "they would've killed us already." He dropped the dart, and then both men stepped away from the tree to resume following the American professor.

Soon, the three men arrived upon a narrow river. Indy stopped and extended his open hand to Satipo. Satipo reached into a tattered pocket to remove the map fragment he had shown Indy back at Machete Landing, and handed it over to Indy. Then Indy reached into his own pocket to remove the piece of parchment that he had consulted earlier. Both Satipo and Barranca watched intently as Indy, facing the river, held the two fragments up side by side. Despite the frayed and crumpled edges, it was obvious Indy had just reunited two parts of a single map.

While Satipo watched in astonishment, Barranca silently fumed. On several occasions, the two thieves had used their partial treasure map to lure adventurers into the jungle, only to rob and kill their greedy victims. But they never knew for certain that the map was good for something beyond their scams, not until now. And the only thing stopping Barranca and Satipo from using the assembled map to find the treasure themselves was Indiana Jones.

Barranca had always been more daring and impatient than his relatively cautious partner, and he decided it was high time to kill the American. He shifted his position behind Indy, drew his own revolver from its holster, aimed it at his target's back, and thumbed back the gun's hammer.

Clack.

The mechanical sound of the gun's hammer was out of place in the jungle, and Indy's keen ears recognized it at once. His right hand dropped to the bullwhip at his belt as he spun to face Barranca. Faster than thought, the ten-foot-long whip lashed out with a deafening *CRACK*, biting into the flesh of Barranca's gun hand. The thief gasped in pain and dropped his weapon. The revolver fired as it struck a rock before it slid into the river. Staring at Indy with wide-eyed terror, Barranca clutched at his damaged wrist, then turned and ran off into the jungle.

As for Satipo, he was stunned in a different way. He could not recall Barranca ever being defeated in a fight, nor had he ever seen anyone move as fast as Indiana Jones. He knew if he fled with Barranca, he'd never see the treasure that Indy sought. Granted, he also knew that it wouldn't be easy to take that treasure away from Jones. Satipo watched without a word as the grim American recoiled his whip.

Indy sensed instinctively that Satipo was torn between fear and greed. It was only because he imagined that he might still require at least one assistant that he didn't send Satipo running, too. With some reluctance, he allowed the trembling guide to follow him away from the riverbank.

The two men turned up a muddy hill, where they found a dark, rocky outcropping covered with a thick tangle of vines. Indy pushed the vines aside to reveal the entrance to a cave.

"This is it," Indy said as he reached into Satipo's

backpack and removed an empty canvas drawstring bag. Bending down, Indy filled the small bag with loose sand from outside the cave as he added, "This is where Forrestal cashed in."

"A friend of yours?" Satipo asked.

"A competitor," Indy said. As he tied off the bag of sand and tucked it into his shoulder bag, he added, "He was good. He was very, very good."

Looking from the cave's dark entrance to Indy, Satipo said, "Señor, nobody's come out of there alive!" Fearing for his own safety, Satipo added, "Please . . ."

Indy turned Satipo around to access the man's backpack. He quickly removed a long-handled torch as he pulled the pack off Satipo, and then tossed the pack to the ground. He lit the torch, handed it to Satipo, and led the nervous thief into the cave.

Thick veils of spiderwebs stretched across the opening, and Indy pushed them aside with his coiled whip. Moving slowly and carefully, the two men made their way up an inclined passage. Soon, it opened into a larger chamber, where plant life and stalactites hung from the damp ceiling. The place was filled with the smell of jungle rot, and the echoing sounds of dripping water and skittering creatures. As Indy advanced across the chamber floor, Satipo's hoarse voice croaked from behind. "Señor —"

Indy halted and turned slowly to face Satipo, who was trying not to tremble as he held the torch. Satipo was staring at the back of Indy's leather jacket. Indy craned his neck to see three large black tarantulas crawling up his back. Once again utilizing his rolled whip, he reached back casually to brush off the tarantulas, letting them fall to the ground.

Then Satipo's eyes went wide as he noticed a tarantula moving on his own right shoulder. He was too scared to speak, but Indy heard the man gasp and saw what he was looking at. Indy raised a hand and made a spinning motion with his fingers, gesturing for Satipo to turn around slowly. Satipo obeyed, and turned to reveal that his back was covered by at least two dozen tarantulas. Tightening his grip on the lower neck of the blazing torch, Satipo audibly gulped for air while Indy flicked off the tarantulas and let them scuttle away into the darkness.

Satipo was still breathless as he followed Indy deeper into the cave. He nearly jumped out of his skin when Indy broke the silence with a single word: "Stop." Indy had noticed a shaft of bright sunlight that angled down through the ceiling and interrupted their path up ahead. Indy didn't know just how deep underground they were, but given that there wasn't any rubble on the ground beneath the light shaft, he was pretty sure that the sunlight hadn't entered by way of a random cave-in. *Might be a trap*, he thought. Glancing back at Satipo, Indy cautioned, "Stay out of the light."

While Satipo cowered and clung to the shadows against the cave's dirt wall, Indy ducked under the light shaft and moved a few feet forward. Standing just to the side of the light shaft, Indy raised his left hand into the light and felt the briefest moment of warmth against his skin, then dropped his arm fast.

There was a loud *whoosh* as a row of long, sharp spikes sprung out from the sides of the chamber, spearing the area below the light shaft. Satipo screamed, not because he had been wounded, but because there was a dead man's impaled body embedded on the spikes. Clad in a khaki safari shirt similar to Indy's, the corpse trembled as the trap's sudden, forceful motion came to an abrupt stop. Satipo screamed louder as the corpse's head involuntarily twisted to face Indy. Even though half of the man's face was gone, Indy recognized what was left.

"Forrestal," Indy muttered. It didn't give him any pleasure to see how his former competitor had met his end. Giving the corpse a last look, Indy thought, *You should have stayed home.*

After Satipo recovered his nerve, he followed Indy into the next passage, where they were pleased to find that there was enough natural light coming down through the open ceiling that they no longer required the torch. Unfortunately, they found their path interrupted again, this time by a deep, open pit with steep, vertical walls. Standing at the edge of the pit, Indy gauged the distance across the pit to be about twelve feet. Indy knew his limitations and decided to leave the long jumps to Jesse Owens.

Indy looked at the ceiling above the pit and spotted an exposed wooden beam, then swung his whip. It wrapped tightly around the beam, and Indy tugged at the whip's handle to make sure the beam would hold his weight. Keeping his grip tight on the handle, he leaped out and swung over the pit to land on the far side of the passage. Then he threw the handle of the whip back to Satipo, who caught it and repeated Indy's action. But as Satipo swung out over the pit, the beam above his head suddenly shifted, just as his feet touched down beside Indy.

Holding tight to the whip, Satipo cried out as he lost his balance and began to fall backwards into the pit. Indy lunged forward and grabbed Satipo's belt, then hauled him up to safety. Satipo threw his arms around his rescuer so tightly that Indy could feel the frightened man's heart pounding against his chest.

Indy moved Satipo away from the edge of the pit, then — leaving the whip's tip curled around the upper beam — he wedged the whip's handle between some vines that traveled up the walls. Indy didn't want to proceed without his whip, but if they had to exit the temple in a hurry, they'd have to cross that pit again. It just seemed smart to leave it there.

Indy and Satipo exited the passage and rounded a corner to find themselves in another chamber. It was a large domed room with a stone floor in an intricate design. Passing a huge brass sun against a nearby wall, Indy realized they had reached the temple's sanctuary. But the brass sun held little interest for Indy and Satipo, for both men had their eyes trained on the far side of the chamber. There, at the top of a short flight of stone steps, a cylindrical stone table stood in the middle of what appeared to be an altar. And on top of that table, resting on a circular stone pedestal just a few inches high, was a gold figurine about the size of a human skull.

Indy had come a long way from Connecticut in search of the Golden Chachapoyan idol. At last, there it was, right in front of him.

But it wasn't in his hands yet.

*S*atipo glanced at Indy, and knew at once that the gold idol was his objective. Eager to leave the temple, Satipo said, "Let us hurry. There is nothing to fear here."

Satipo began to walk fast in the direction of the idol, but Indy caught him by the shirt and practically slammed him against the wall. All it took was one wrong move to wind up like Forrestal. *Nothing to fear?* Keeping his grip on Satipo, Indy looked again at the wide open path to the idol and said, "That's what scares me."

Indy released Satipo, and then reached for an old, unlit wooden torch that hung against the wall. Taking the torch, Indy squatted down to examine a dirt-caked stone tile on the floor. He held the torch upright over the tile and used its tip to gently push away the grime, revealing a narrow gap around the edges of the tile. *Another trap*, Indy thought.

He brought the torch down upon the tile to find out what would happen if a man were to step on it. The tile sank slightly into the floor and a tiny arrow suddenly launched out from the wall, slamming into the torch. Satipo blinked in surprise. Indy followed the arrow's trajectory and saw that it had been blown out through the mouth of one of the carved masks that decorated the altar's walls. It was a nasty but effective security system.

Indy handed the torch to Satipo, then rose and said, "Stay here."

"If you insist, señor," Satipo said with a self-satisfied smile. He was happy to let Indy do all the work.

Indy rubbed his fingers together as he gazed at the idol on the far side of the altar. It looked so easy. All he had to do was walk across the chamber, climb the steps, grab the idol, and walk back the same way. The only hitch was that there were a lot of stone tiles between him and the idol, and the walls were lined with numerous stone masks, all of which had dark holes for eyes and mouths. One wrong step and Indy would be a human pincushion.

Indy made a quick study of the tiles, noting the ones that had loose dirt around them or appeared to protrude from the floor more than others, and took a cautious step forward. Then another — and another. On either side of him, the stone masks stared at him with their deadly, hollow eyes. He risked a glance forward to the gold idol, which had a snarling face and angry eyes. If Indy had been a superstitious man, he might have suspected that the idol was watching him, cursing his every step.

Indy nearly lost his balance, and he heard Satipo gasp behind him as he jumped up the stone steps, doing his best to keep his boots on the tiles that looked safe. He continued forward until he stood before the altar, then he slowly crouched down so his eyes were level with the idol's.

Indy stroked his bristly chin as he contemplated the idol and the circular stone pedestal upon which it rested. Because the temple's builders booby-trapped the floor, he figured the idol would be similarly rigged. Fortunately, Indy had come prepared.

He reached for the bag of sand that he'd collected from outside the cave. Examining the statue, he guessed that its weight was slightly less than the bag. He removed some sand, letting it slip through his fingers onto the floor beside the table, then clutched the bag in his right hand to one side of the idol while positioning his empty left hand on the idol's other side. He held his breath.

In a swift, fluid motion, Indy used his left hand to pluck the idol from its pedestal in the same split second that he rolled the sand-filled bag onto the pedestal. Then Indy froze, waiting for something to happen, but nothing did.

Indy looked at the idol in his hands, exhaled, and then grinned. *It worked!* But as he began to turn away from the table, he heard a grinding sound, and glanced back to see the pedestal descending into the center of the table.

Uh-oh.

There came a low rumble all around the altar, and then thick streams of dust and heavy stones began crashing down from the ceiling. Disregarding the rigged tiles on the floor, Indy bolted away from the table and leaped down the stone steps. Behind him, a hail of small arrows launched from the hollows of the carved masks on the surrounding walls. Indy lowered his head and kept running and felt several arrows skim the back of his jacket.

Satipo had already started running from the crumbling sanctuary, and he arrived in the passage with the deep pit before Indy did. When Indy rounded the corner to enter the passage, he saw that Satipo had used the stashed whip to swing back to the other side of the pit. Satipo held the whip by its handle, but the whip's other end was no longer wrapped around the beam, which appeared to have been further dislodged from the ceiling.

"Give me the whip!" Indy shouted.

Keeping his grip on the whip, Satipo shouted back, "Throw me the idol!" From behind Satipo, there came yet another grinding sound as an ancient mechanism began to slowly lower a wide, heavy stone to block the only exit from the passage. "No time to argue!" Satipo said as he glanced from the descending stone to Indy. "Throw me the idol, I throw you the whip!"

Without much of a choice, Indy tossed the idol over and across the pit. Satipo caught it. Then Indy shouted again, "Give me the whip!"

Satipo grinned deviously as he dropped the whip, letting it fall to the ground at his feet. "Adiós, señor," he said, before he turned and ducked under the still-descending slab of rock to escape.

Earlier thoughts of Olympic broad jumps had left Indy's mind. His only thought was to stay alive and — if possible — get the idol back from Satipo. He took three running steps forward, and then sprang over the pit.

He almost made it. He caught the pit's opposite edge with his stomach and elbows. Ignoring the pain, he dug his fingertips into the loose dirt, struggling for leverage as his boots kicked at the walls below. Glancing at the descending stone, he figured there were less than twenty seconds before it met the floor.

He spotted a vine growing out of the dirt floor in front of him. Extending his left arm as far as he could, he snatched at the vine and then seized it with both hands. Indy grinned with relief as he began to pull himself up, but then the dirt loosened around the vine, causing it to snake out of the floor. Indy gasped as he slid back into the pit — but kept his grip on the vine. Desperate and determined, he reached for the vine hand over hand until his body was out of the pit, then he dived for the rapidly diminishing gap between the floor and the base of the stone slab. As Indy rolled under the gap, he grabbed the whip that Satipo had abandoned, taking it with him as he tumbled into the passage he'd traveled through earlier, the one in which Forrestal had died.

Indy quickly coiled his whip, then heard a loud noise echo from somewhere above his position. He turned to leave the passage, but stopped fast when he nearly stumbled into Satipo.

Like the grotesque masks within the temple, Satipo's eyes and mouth were wide open. But unlike the masks, his expression was frozen with terror. Sharp spikes protruded through his body. He had ignored every caution, and his greed had led him to die just as Forrestal had.

Indy looked down at the ground at Satipo's feet. There, as expected, he found the gold idol lying in the dirt. Indy picked it up, and then turned to face the dead man one last time. "Adiós, Satipo."

Indy headed out of the passage and was only a few steps away from Satipo's corpse when he heard a loud shifting of stone and dirt from behind, followed by an increasingly loud rumbling noise. He stopped to glance back, then gasped as he saw what was coming. A huge, spherical boulder came roaring around a corner of the passage, just above Indy's position. Indy realized instantly that the boulder had been form-fitted to travel through the passage until it blocked the exit.

Indy turned and ran as fast as he could. Behind him, the boulder gained speed as it traveled down the inclined passage. Not even the stalactites that had formed over the years could slow the boulder's velocity. It smashed into them, and launched the spiked rocks like missiles in all directions.

Indy scrambled and ran faster through the twisting, tubular passage, pumping his legs harder to outrun the boulder. Up ahead, he saw a shimmer of light through a haze of thick cobwebs. He dived through the webs to reach the light, and then found himself tumbling down and out of the mouth of the cave. A moment later, the boulder slammed home into the passage's end, sealing the temple's entrance.

Gasping for air and covered with torn cobwebs, Indy was still clutching the gold idol when his tumbling body came to a stop outside the temple. But when he looked up from the ground, he realized he was not alone.

There were three Hovitos warriors in full battle paint. One warrior held a bow and had an arrow trained on Indy, and the other two held spears at the ready. Then Indy looked to his right and saw even more warriors. Some carried spears and bows, and the others had blowguns. From Indy's sprawled position, he was fairly certain there were well over two-dozen warriors, and he was their only target.

Turning his head, Indy saw even more warriors to the left. He was completely surrounded. He was also surprised to see his former guide, Barranca, standing before one of the warriors. Before Indy could comprehend the blank expression on Barranca's face, the warrior behind Barranca gave a slight shove, and Barranca's body teetered and fell forward, landing face-first against the jungle floor. There were over a dozen arrows in the dead man's back.

A shadow fell over Barranca's prone corpse. The shadow belonged to a lean man with a charming smile who was dressed in a safari outfit that included calf-high leather boots, tailored khakis, and a pith helmet. He stepped casually toward Indy, who remained seated on the ground.

Speaking with a French accent, the man said, "Dr. Jones. Again we see there is nothing you can possess which I cannot take away." The man extended his open right hand, waiting for Indy to place the idol in it. The man added, "And you thought I'd given up."

Indy knew the man. He was René Emile Belloq, a mercenary archaeologist who worked for private collectors. They'd had several encounters since the 1920s, and Indy had nothing but disrespect for him. Although Indy had never been able to prove it, he was certain that Belloq had plagiarized his paper on stratigraphy while completing his Masters in Archaeology at the Sorbonne. Since then, Belloq had made a steady and profitable career by taking advantage of other people's hard work.

Still on the ground, Indy eased his hand to his right hip and started to pull his gun from its holster. Seeing his action, all the Hovitos took a step forward, keeping their weapons trained on him. Indy glanced at the Hovitos, then slowly turned his gun handle-forward and handed it to Belloq. As winded as he was, Indy could smell something foul. He realized Belloq was wearing cologne in the jungle.

Taking the gun and transferring it to his left hand, Belloq said, "You choose the wrong friends. This time it will cost you." Belloq extended his right hand again.

Indy shifted his body slightly and drew the gold idol out from under his jacket. As he handed the idol up to the man who loomed over him, he said, "Too bad the Hovitos don't know you the way I do, Belloq."

"Yes, too bad," Belloq said with a smile. "You could warn them, if only you spoke Hovitos." Then Belloq turned away from Indy and dramatically raised the idol high over his head. Having drawn the natives' attention to the idol, Belloq snapped off a few words in Hovitos. His announcement prompted all the natives to prostrate themselves on the ground and bow their heads.

Indy didn't know what Belloq said, but knew better than to stick around and ask. With the natives bowed and Belloq's back turned, Indy took his chance to flee, sprinting toward the edge of the clearing near the temple ruins.

The natives heard Indy's receding footfalls and raised their heads to see his running form. Then they looked to Belloq, who made two sharp hissing sounds as he signaled the Hovitos to pursue the fleeing man and kill him. As the warriors ran off, Belloq held the idol out before him, gazed into the idol's eyes, and laughed defiantly.

Indy heard Belloq's laughter as he ran through the jungle. He didn't like the sound of that laugh. He wasn't crazy about the sound of the many running feet behind him either. And so he did what any archaeologist in his situation would do. He ran faster.

Indy ignored the spears, darts, and arrows that whizzed past his body. He barely glanced at the stone statue of the gaping demon as he raced past it, and didn't stop to pet the donkeys that his guides had roped off less than an hour earlier. He just kept running past the trees and down the hillside, heading back to the river where Jock, the pilot he'd hired, would be waiting with the plane.

What if Jock hadn't waited? Indy didn't even want to think about that possibility.

For a moment, Indy thought he'd lost the warriors, but then another barrage of sharp-tipped projectiles sailed past his shoulders. As his legs carried him away from a tight cluster of trees, he saw the river in front of him. Then he saw Jock's amphibious, tandem two-seat biplane on the river, and then he saw Jock, wearing his familiar short-sleeve blue shirt — the one with AIR PIRATES on its back — and a New York Yankees baseball cap. Jock was standing on one of the plane's pontoons.

There was still a lot of ground to cover between himself and the river. Not sure if Jock could even hear him across the distance, Indy desperately shouted, "Jock! Start the engines! Get it up!"

Did he hear me? Indy was still running hard, but from what he could see, Jock was still just standing on the pontoon. *What's he doing? A jig?* Then Indy noticed a slender line projecting out from Jock's arms and realized with mounting frustration that his pilot was fishing — and seemed to have something on the line.

"Jock!" Indy screamed even louder. "The engines! Start the engines, Jock!"

Jock tossed his fishing pole, abandoning his catch, and scrambled into his plane's cockpit. He fired up the engines just as Indy arrived at a rocky ledge that loomed over the edge of the river. The warriors were still right behind him, and there was nowhere left to run.

Long vines dangled down from the trees that grew around the ledge. Indy grabbed a vine and swung out into the air and over the water, then let go. He splashed down near the plane, which Jock guided closer to his position.

The warriors ran down to the river's edge, and fired their weapons in Indy's direction. Without losing his hat or his life, Indy swam for the plane, grabbed hold of the closest pontoon, and climbed into the cockpit in front of Jock. Jock increased speed as he steered his plane up the river, and he was well out of range of the warriors' weapons as the plane lifted up into the sky.

Indy sunk back into his seat and let the air run over him. Every muscle hurt. He was fairly certain he'd bruised a couple of ribs, but wasn't sure whether that happened at the pit where Satipo had left him to die or during his race from that enormous boulder. He felt even worse about the idol. It was bad enough that'd he'd lost it, but that he'd lost it to a jerk like Belloq made him feel positively lousy. But there wasn't much he could do about it, not now anyway.

Suddenly, Indy jumped in his seat. He'd felt something shift against his legs, and when he looked down, he saw a huge boa constrictor on his lap. Indy's face contorted with an expression of loathing, and he had to fight the incredible urge to jump out of the airborne plane. Squirming in his seat, he turned his head back to snarl, "There's a big snake in the plane, Jock!"

"Oh, that's just my pet snake, Reggie!" Jock responded amicably.

"I hate snakes, Jock!" Indy shouted back as he clenched his fists. "I hate 'em!"

"Come on," Jock said disparagingly. "Show a little backbone, will ya?"

The plane soared off over the dark jungle. As Reggie flopped down around Indy's ankles, Indy made a mental note: *Never fly with Jock again!*

*L*ess than a week after his adventure in Peru, Indiana Jones was back to his classroom at the prestigious Marshall College in Connecticut. His room was inside an ivy-covered brick building with high windows. On his cluttered desk, several archaeological statues and relics and a stack of old books rested beside a globe of the Earth. Behind the desk, Indy stood before a blackboard and used a stick of white chalk to write letters as he read his writing aloud.

"'Neo,' meaning 'new,'" he said, "and 'lithic' —"

Indy paused to check his spelling, which prompted giggles from the students seated behind him. "I-T-H-I-C —" he continued, "meaning 'stone.'" He underlined the word NEOLITHIC, then turned to face the class.

Wearing a three-piece tweed suit, British-manufactured eyeglasses with gold-filled frames, a fresh haircut, and a clean shave, Indy looked very much the buttoned-down professor and barely resembled the rugged man who'd so recently escaped from the temple of the Chachapoyan warriors. However, it seemed that his glasses did little to disguise his handsome features, as almost every one of his female students was gazing at him dreamily.

Indy gestured to a map he'd already drawn on the board beside NEOLITHIC and said, "All right, let's get back to this site: Turkdean Barrow, near Hazelton. Contains a central pas-passage and three chambers . . ."

Having stumbled over the word *passage*, Indy realized his mind wasn't really on the class. But he'd given this lecture before and knew it well enough, so he just kept talking, and pointed to the map on the blackboard to show where some relics had been removed from Turkdean Barrow. "Don't confuse that with robbing," he said, "in which case we mean the removal of the contents of barrow."

Just then, the classroom door opened and a distinguished-looking middle-aged man wearing a dark pinstripe suit stepped in from the hallway. The man left the door open as he moved without a word to stand against the wall, where he caught Indy's eye. Indy paused for a moment when he realized the man was his old friend Marcus Brody, but because class wasn't over yet, he returned his student's attention to the map on the blackboard.

"This site also demonstrates one of the great dangers of archaeology," Indy continued. "Not to life and limb, although that does sometimes take place. No, I'm talking about folklore. In this case, local tradition held that there was a golden coffin buried at the site, and this accounts for the holes dug all over the barrow and generally poor condition of the find." Indy pointed to a rectangular chamber on the map and added, "However, chamber three was undisturbed. And the undisturbed chamber and the grave goods that were found in another, uh . . ."

Indy was distracted by one of his female students. Like the others, she had been wearing an almost worshipful expression as she'd watched him. But as his gaze had just momentarily met hers, she'd smiled playfully and closed her eyes, and Indy saw that the word LOVE was written on her right eyelid, and YOU on her left eyelid. When her eyes flashed open again, Indy stammered, ". . . in the area, give us a r —"

Wondering if his own eyes were playing tricks on him, Indy found himself staring back at the girl. She lowered her eyelids again and held them a moment longer than the first time so the professor could clearly read the two words: LOVE YOU. Then she opened her eyes again.

"Uh . . . reason to da —" He tore his gaze from the girl with the lettered eyelids and stammered, ". . . to, uh, to-to date this, uh, find as we have."

Just then, a bell rang to signal that class was over. Still standing before the blackboard, Indy raised a hand to keep the students seated and said, "Um, any questions, then?" He was relieved when no one answered. "No? Okay, that's it for the day, then." As the students picked up their books and began filing out of the class, he pointed to another note he'd jotted on the blackboard and said, "Um, don't forget Michaelson, chapters four and five, for next time. And I will be in my office on Thursday, but not Wednesday."

A young male student, wearing a V-neck sweater and a bow tie, hung back for a moment, waiting for the other students to leave, but then he noticed that the man in the pinstripe suit had remained in the room. Marcus Brody quickly assessed that the student appeared agitated or anxious, and that he probably wanted to talk to Indy, or rather to Dr. Jones, about his grade. The student shifted nervously from one foot to the other, but when he realized Brody wasn't about to leave, he lowered his gaze and headed for the door. The student shot a quick sidelong glance at Indy as he placed a green apple on Indy's desk before he stalked off, following his classmates out of the room.

Alone in the room, Indy and Brody looked at each other. Brody walked over to the desk beside Indy and picked up the apple.

"I had it, Marcus," Indy said. "I had it in my hand." Indy held out his right hand and clutched at the empty air.

"What happened?" Brody said as he casually examined the apple.

"Guess."

Polishing the apple against the sleeve of his suit, Brody gave a slight chuckle as he looked up at Indy, then said, "Belloq?"

"You want to hear about it?"

"Not at all," Brody said with a smile as he dropped the apple into his jacket pocket. "I'm sure everything you do for the museum conforms to the International Treaty for the Protection of Antiquities."

Unable to stop thinking about his loss of the gold idol, Indy said, "It's beautiful, Marcus." Then he quickly added, "I can get it. I got it all figured out. There's only one place he can sell it: Marrakesh. I need two thousand dollars. Look —"

As Indy opened a desk drawer and removed a white cloth bag, Brody leaned against the desk and said, "Listen to me, old boy. I brought some people to see you."

Oblivious to Brody's words, Indy said again, "Look." He removed two small artifacts from the white bag. "They're good pieces, Marcus." He handed the best piece to Brody, and said yet again, "Look."

"Indiana ..." Brody sighed, realizing that Indy was completely fixated with the idea of recovering the idol. Indy handed Brody the second piece and Brody said, "Yes, the museum will buy them as usual, no questions asked." Looking at the two pieces more carefully, Brody added with obvious admiration, "Yes, they *are* nice."

"They're worth at *least* the price of a ticket to Marrakesh," Indy insisted.

"But the people I brought are important," Brody said, "and they're waiting."

Staring blankly at Brody, Indy said, "What people?"

"Army Intelligence," Brody said as he placed both of the pieces that Indy had given him into his jacket pockets, and then began walking slowly for the door. As Indy grabbed a large leather-bound book, his briefcase, and some rolled documents, Brody continued, "They knew you were coming before I did. Seem to know everything. They wouldn't tell me what they want."

"Well, what do I want to see them for?" Indy said as he followed Brody out of the classroom and into the corridor. "What am I, in trouble?"

Brody shrugged his shoulders and grinned.

A few minutes later, in a large lecture hall that was lined with oak-paneled walls, and tall, stained-glass windows, Brody introduced Indy to the two men from U.S. Army Intelligence, Colonel Musgrove and Major Eaton. Musgrove was a lean, middle-aged man with gray hair who wore a dark three-piece suit and a red bow tie. Eaton was a stout fellow with a strong handshake, a wisp of a mustache, and a receding hairline; he wore a pale blue two-piece suit and dark blue necktie. Musgrove carried a briefcase. Eaton didn't.

After the introductions were made, Brody suggested they be seated on the platform at the front of the lecture hall, where a table and some chairs had been set up for them near a two-sided blackboard. As they mounted the steps up to the platform, Eaton said, "Yes, Dr. Jones, we've heard a great deal about you."

"Have you?" Indy said as he deposited his bag and book on the table.

Eaton said, "Professor of archaeology, expert on the occult, and, uh, how does one say it? Obtainer of rare antiquities."

"That's one way of saying it," Indy said. Gesturing to two chairs beside the table, he said, "Why don't you sit down? You'll be more comfortable."

"Oh, thank you," Eaton said as he took a seat.

"Thank you," Musgrove echoed as he sat beside Eaton. Looking at Indy, he added, "Yes, you're a man of many talents."

Indy didn't know how to respond to that, but he grinned sheepishly. Out of the corner of his eye, he noticed that Brody was standing to his left, leaning against a podium that stood near the table, as if he wanted to keep some distance between himself and the seated men. Indy decided to remain standing, too.

Facing Indy, Eaton said, "Now, you studied under Professor Ravenwood at the University of Chicago."

Noting that Eaton had made a statement, not asked a question, Indy replied, "Yes, I did."

Eaton said, "You have no idea of his present whereabouts?"

"Uh . . . well, just rumors, really." Glancing at Brody, Indy added, "Somewhere in Asia, I think. I haven't really spoken to him for ten years. We were friends, but, uh . . . had a bit of a falling out, I'm afraid."

"Mmm," Eaton said.

Indy didn't like the way the conversation was going and wondered if he'd told the men too much information. He wondered if they knew about the falling-out between him and Abner Ravenwood, and what had caused it. Marcus said they seemed to know everything, so Indy guessed they probably had some idea.

Trying to put Indy at ease, Musgrove said, "Dr. Jones, now you must understand that this is all strictly confidential, eh?"

"I understand," Indy said, still wondering what the men were getting at.

"Uh . . ." Musgrove began, then cleared his throat and looked aside to confirm that no one else was in the lecture hall. Returning his attention to Indy, he said, "Yesterday afternoon, our European sections intercepted a . . . a German communiqué that was sent from Cairo to Berlin. Now, to Cairo —"

Eaton interrupted, "See, over the last two years, the Nazis have had teams of archaeologists running around the world looking for all kinds of religious artifacts. Hitler's a nut on the subject. He's crazy. He's obsessed with the occult. And right now, apparently, there's some kind of German archaeological dig going on in the desert outside of Cairo."

Musgrove removed a document from his briefcase and said, "Now, we've got some information here, but we can't make anything out of it, and maybe you can." Musgrove traced the words on the document with his finger as he read them aloud: "*Tanis development proceeding. Acquire headpiece, Staff of Ra, Abner Ravenwood, U.S.*"

Indy looked to Brody, and Brody's eyes beamed. Clearly amazed by the communiqué, Indy rapped the edge of the table with his knuckles and said, "The Nazis have discovered Tanis."

Eaton said, "Just what does that mean to you, uh, Tanis?"

Marcus began, "Well, it —"

"The city of Tanis," Indy interrupted, unable to contain his enthusiasm, "is one of the possible resting places of the Lost Ark."

"The Lost Ark?" Musgrove said with a quizzical expression that was shared by Eaton. The two men remained seated, but leaned forward with rapt attention.

"Yeah, the Ark of the Covenant," Indy said. "The chest the Hebrews used to carry around the Ten Commandments."

"What do you mean, 'commandments'?" Eaton said with a slightly impatient edge to his voice. "You're talking about *the* Ten Commandments?"

"Yes, the actual Ten Commandments," Indy said. "The original stone tablets that Moses brought down out of Mount Horeb and smashed, if you believe in that sort of thing."

Eaton eased back in his chair and glanced at Musgrove, whose wide-eyed, open-mouthed expression suggested he was either stunned or baffled. Indy said, "Any of you guys ever go to Sunday school?"

Musgrove said, "Well, I . . ."

"Oh, look," Indy interrupted, and began gesturing with

his hands as he explained. "The Hebrews took the broken pieces and put them in the Ark. When they settled in Canaan, they put the Ark in a place called the Temple of Solomon."

"In Jerusalem," Brody noted.

"Where it stayed for many years," Indy continued. "Until, all of a sudden, whoosh, it's gone."

Eaton said, "Where?"

Indy said, "Well, nobody knows where or when."

"However," Brody said, "an Egyptian pharaoh —"

Remembering the pharaoh's name, Indy interrupted, "Shishak."

Brody nodded, and then quickly continued, "Yes . . . invaded the city of Jerusalem right about 980 B.C., and he may have taken the Ark back to the city of Tanis and hidden it in a secret chamber called the Well of Souls."

Eaton raised his eyebrows. "Secret chamber?"

Brody nodded, then said, "However, about a year after the pharaoh had returned to Egypt, the city of Tanis was consumed by the desert in a sandstorm that lasted a whole year. Wiped clean by the wrath of God."

Eaton smiled slightly as he shifted in his chair, looked to Musgrove and said, "Uh-huh."

While Eaton turned to re-examine the communiqué, Musgrove gestured with his right hand to Brody and

Indy, and said reassuringly, "Obviously, we've come to the right men. Now, you seem to know, uh, all about this Tanis, then."

Indy shook his head. "No, no, not really," he said, stepping away from Brody and the seated men to stand beside the blackboard, which was covered with physics equations. "Ravenwood is the real expert. Abner did the first serious work on Tanis. Collected some of its relics." Indy turned and glanced back at Brody. "It was his obsession, really." Then he looked to Eaton and Musgrove and added, "But he never found the city."

Still looking at the communiqué on the table before him, Eaton said, "Frankly, we're somewhat suspicious of Mr. Ravenwood. An American being mentioned so prominently in a secret Nazi cable."

"Oh, rubbish," Brody said. "Ravenwood's no Nazi."

Pointing to the incriminating communiqué, Musgrove said, "Well, what do the Nazis want him for, then?"

Indy stepped over to the table and said, "Well, obviously, the Nazis are looking for the headpiece to the Staff of Ra and they think Abner's got it."

Lifting his gaze to meet Indy's, Eaton said, "What exactly *is* a headpiece to the Staff of Ra?"

"Well, the staff is just a stick," Indy said. Gesturing with his hands to convey that the staff's length might be taller or shorter than his own height, he said, "I don't know, about this big, nobody really knows for sure how high ... and it's ..." He turned to the equation-covered blackboard, rotated the board to its unmarked side, and pulled a chalk stick from his jacket pocket. "It's capped with an elaborate headpiece in the shape of the sun," he said as he drew a circle on the board, "with a crystal in the center." Dragging a line down below the circle to represent the staff, he continued, "And what you did was, you take the staff to a special room in Tanis, a map room with a miniature of the city all laid out on the floor, and if you put the staff in a certain place, at a certain time of day, the sun shone through here —" Indy drew a diagonal line from the top of the blackboard to the center of his drawing of the headpiece, "and made a beam that came down on the floor here." He extended the diagonal line down through the headpiece, and then tapped the end of the line. "And gave you the exact location of the Well of Souls."

Looking from Brody to Indy to make sure he had their information straight, Musgrove said, "Where the Ark of the Covenant was kept, right?"

"Which is *exactly* what the Nazis are looking for," Indy said emphatically.

Eaton said, "What does this Ark look like?"

Pocketing the chalk, Indy said, "There's a picture of it

right here." He moved over to the table and carefully unfastened the latches that sealed the leather-bound book he'd carried from his classroom. Opening the book, he found the page he was looking for, and then he lifted the book and positioned it on the table so Eaton and Musgrove had a better view. Indy said, "That's it."

Eaton and Musgrove rose from their seats and gazed down at the book's open pages. At the top of the right-hand page, there was an engraving, an illustration of a biblical battle. Indy had learned most of the details about the illustration from Abner Ravenwood. The picture showed a battle between the Israelites and an opposing army. At the forefront of the Israelite ranks, four hooded men carried the Ark of the Covenant, a gold chest that was crowned by two sculptured angels. The four men were not actually touching the Ark, but carried it by holding two long wooden poles that passed through rings in the corners of the Ark. Brilliant jets of light appeared to issue from the Ark, and pierced the ranks of their vanquished opposition, who were represented in various states of agony and death.

Studying the dramatic image, Eaton muttered, "Good God."

"Yes," Brody said, "that's just what the Hebrews thought."

Pointing to the streaks of light that extended from the Ark, Musgrove said, "Uh, now, what's that supposed to be coming out of there?"

Indy answered, "Lightning . . . fire . . . power of God or something."

Indy turned away from the three men who remained leaning over the book, and walked back to the blackboard to look again at his own drawing of the Staff of Ra. Behind him, Eaton said, "I'm beginning to understand Hitler's interest in this."

"Oh, yes," Brody said as Indy left the blackboard and returned to his side. "The Bible speaks of the Ark leveling mountains, and laying waste to entire regions. An army which carries the Ark before it . . . is invincible."

Brody looked at Indy. Indy looked away, chewing on his own thoughts. Abner Ravenwood had certainly believed that the Ark of the Covenant existed, though Indy had his doubts. But if it *did* exist, he didn't want it to fall into the hands of the Nazis. Not because he believed that some old chest could possess mystical, deadly power, but because historic artifacts belonged in museums, not in the collection of a crazy dictator.

Indy had another motivation. He didn't know how Abner had gotten mixed up with Nazis, but if his former friend and mentor were in a jam, then he wanted to do something about it. But would Abner want his help? Somehow, Indy doubted that, too.

Still, the more he thought about the Ark of the Covenant, the more he realized he was hooked on finding it.

*I*t was early evening as a black sedan with whitewall tires came to a stop in front of a small brick house near Marshall College. Marcus Brody, wearing a fedora, got out of the car and walked to the house's front door. Out of habit, he removed his hat before he rang the doorbell.

Indy opened the door. He was wearing an open, faded-red robe over his pants and T-shirt, and he stared hard at Brody's face. Brody's expressions often betrayed his thoughts, and from his slightly smug grin, Indy was all but certain of what had transpired since their meeting with Eaton and Musgrove earlier that day. As Brody stepped into the foyer, Indy aimed a finger at him and said, "You did it, didn't you?"

Brody smiled broadly. "They want you to go for it."

"Oh, Marcus!" Indy said, clapping his friend on the back as they walked into the adjoining study, where the far wall's built-in shelves were crammed with books and Indy's own small collection of artifacts.

Brody went to a chair in front of Indy's cluttered desk, placed his hat on it, and said, "They want you to get ahold of the Ark before the Nazis do, and they're prepared to pay handsomely for it."

"And the museum?" Indy said as he tied off his robe's fabric belt. "The museum gets the Ark when we're finished?"

"Oh, yes," Marcus said with conviction. After all, that's what Eaton and Musgrove had guaranteed.

Indy took Brody's hand and vigorously shook it. "Oh," Indy sighed, almost overwhelmed by the situation. Releasing Brody's hand, he stepped over to a coffee table where he had an open bottle of champagne and two glasses, one already filled. As he poured a glass for Brody, he looked at his friend and said with amazement, "The Ark of the Covenant."

"Nothing else has come close," Brody said as he took the glass.

Raising his own glass, Indy said, "That thing represents everything we got into archaeology for in the first place."

They clinked their glasses together, then Brody took a sip from his glass while Indy nearly downed his own in one gulp. "Mmm," Indy said, then returned his glass to the table and walked over to a closet and pulled out his battered suitcase.

Seating himself on the arm of the small sofa beside the coffee table, Brody said, "You know, five years ago, I would've gone after it myself. I'm really rather envious."

"I've got to locate Abner," Indy said as he set the suitcase down on top of a dresser and popped it open. "I think I know where to start." He walked back to the closet and grabbed his leather jacket and his coiled bullwhip. Looking away from Brody, he tossed his belongings into the suitcase and tried to sound casual as he said, "Suppose she'll still be with him?"

"Possibly," Brody said, "but Marion's the least of your worries right now, believe me, Indy."

Indy turned around to face Brody, whose gentle smile wasn't so easy to read at the moment. Indy said, "What do you mean?"

"Well," Brody said, "I mean that for nearly three thousand years, man has been searching for the Lost Ark. Not something to be taken lightly." Brody's smile faded, and his expression became gravely serious. "No one knows its secrets. It's like nothing you've ever gone after before."

Indy laughed and slapped Brody on the back as he moved past him, heading for the desk on the other side of the room. "Oh, Marcus. What are you trying to do, scare me? You sound like my mother. We've known each other for a long time. I don't believe in magic, a lot of superstitious hocus-pocus." Bending down behind the desk, he opened a drawer and removed something wrapped in cloth. Carrying the wrapped object away from the desk, he continued, "I'm going after a find of incredible historical significance. You're talking about the bogeyman. Besides, you know what a cautious fellow I am."

Indy opened the cloth to reveal his revolver, a .45 Smith & Wesson Hand Ejector, Second Model. He tossed the gun into the suitcase. As far as he was concerned, his packing was done and he was ready to go.

Traveling by a series of planes from Connecticut to California, Indy eventually arrived in San Francisco, where Pan American Airways had recently inaugurated the first passenger flights across the Pacific Ocean. The aircraft that awaited him in San Francisco's harbor was a Martin M-130 *Clipper*, a four-engine flying boat with an interior that resembled a compact luxury liner in every way. The round-trip ticket to Manila cost over $1,400, and Indy was happy to let the United States government pay for it.

Wearing a dark blue suit and his fedora, Indy walked down the pier that extended alongside the docked *Clipper*. He paid no special attention to the man in the gray trench coat who preceded him past the uniformed steward and onto the plane. The steward, who'd met Indy on a previous flight, saw Indy approach and said, "Nice to see you again, Dr. Jones."

"Thank you," Indy said. Keeping his hat on, he boarded the plane.

Indy climbed the circular staircase that led up to the passenger compartment, which had two seats on each side of a narrow aisle. The ceiling was low enough to prompt him to duck his head. As he made his way to his seat, the steward re-emerged with a tray of drinks. Indy would have responded by saying, "No, thank you," but the noise from the plane's engines was so loud that he just shook his head as he lowered himself into his seat by a window on the starboard side.

Indy looked out the window. Even though he was traveling as fast as the government's money could carry him, it would still be days before he reached his destination. The *Clipper* would make overnight stops at Hawaii and Wake Island before reaching the Philippines, and then he would proceed to Nepal. Bracing himself for the long trip, he loosened his necktie, slouched back in his seat, tilted his hat down over his forehead, and closed his eyes.

A few seats behind Indy, the man in the trench coat lowered his copy of *Life* magazine. Narrowing his gaze through wire-framed eyeglasses, he looked in Indy's direction. The man had been keeping track of Dr. Jones for most of the day. It hadn't been easy getting a ticket on the *Clipper* on such short notice, but the man was most resourceful.

He was a Nazi spy.

*T*he renowned archaeologist Abner Ravenwood had done a fine job of making Nepal sound good to his daughter, Marion. He had described the beauty of the Himalayas, and told her they would be staying in Patan, which was widely considered the most beautiful of the three royal cities in Nepal's Kathmandu valley. But as events had turned out, they found their way to the wilder outskirts of Patan, where Abner purchased The Raven, a rough-and-tumble saloon and inn made of rickety wood and a few crumbling stone walls.

At first, it wasn't all that bad. Abner had arrived with numerous objects from his own collection of ancient artifacts, some of which he used for barter. The Raven certainly wasn't a dull place, what with the colorful locals, hikers, and shady characters who stumbled in. There were even a few customers who paid their tabs regularly, just so they could sit on a bench at one of the half dozen tables to warm themselves around the open fireplace and have a drink of the locally brewed *chaang* or distilled *rakshi*.

But then Abner had left Marion in charge of the place while he went off searching for clues and relics that might lead him to the Ark of the Covenant. Instead, he died in an avalanche, and Marion wound up inheriting a saloon that no one else wanted to buy in a country that was land-locked between China and India.

In other words, Marion Ravenwood was stuck in Nepal.

And so it was, on a frigid, windy night in 1936, that Marion found herself sitting in The Raven after closing time, staring at the remains of the evening's drinking competition. A burly, overconfident hiker named Regan had wandered into the bar at nightfall, looking for a challenge, and Marion spotted the chance to supplement her meager income. It wasn't long before Regan's friends were dragging his unconscious body out the door, leaving Marion with the winnings — and a tabletop littered with glasses to clean.

Marion counted the crumpled bills in her hand while The Raven's silent, brawny bartender, Mohan, went outside to collect firewood. The cash would keep The Raven running for another few weeks, but wouldn't get her to the nearest seaport, let alone back to the United States. Not that anyone was waiting for her to come home.

She pocketed the money, then picked up a pair of cold glasses and held them against her temples as she squeezed her eyes shut. Although the drinking contest hadn't affected her disposition much, it had given her a throbbing headache. Standing with her eyes closed and her back to the door, she did not see a man's shadow fall across the far wall as he entered The Raven.

"Hello, Marion," said a deep, familiar voice from behind her.

Still pressing the shot glasses to her temples, Marion turned to face Indy. He was wearing his fedora and leather jacket, and the stubble on his face suggested that he hadn't shaved for at least five days. The Raven's fireplace was blazing behind him, which accounted for his shadow on the wall as well as the warm glow that seemed to radiate from his back. Marion stared at him for a moment, then flung the two glasses away from her head so they smashed against the floor.

Indy didn't flinch.

Then Marion sighed and smiled, as if she were slightly embarrassed by her reaction at seeing Indy after so many years. "Indiana Jones," she said in a sardonic tone. Moving her hands to her hips, she continued smiling as she said, "Always knew someday you'd come walkin' back through my door. I never doubted that. Something made it inevitable."

Indy smiled sheepishly as Marion approached slowly. She was still beautiful, although a bit harder looking now. He was glad to see that she didn't seem at all angry with him. As she came to a stop in front of him, she said, "So what are you doing here in Nepal?"

Turning his face away from Marion, Indy glanced around The Raven. "I need one of the pieces your father collected." But when he looked back to Marion, her right fist was already flying and, before he could duck, it connected hard against his jaw.

Indy's head snapped to the side as he took the hit. He rocked on his feet but didn't fall as his own right hand came up reflexively to stroke his chin and make sure nothing was broken. Because of the way Marion had smiled at him, he'd actually forgotten for a moment that something had already been broken a long time ago: her heart.

"I learned to hate you in the last ten years," Marion spit out as she moved away from him, stepping closer to the fireplace.

Lowering his hand from his bruised jaw, Indy said, "I never meant to hurt you."

Marion snapped, "I was a child. I was in love. It was wrong and you knew it."

Indy was unable to meet her intense gaze. As he stepped over to the bar and leaned against it, he said, "You knew what you were doing."

"Now I do!" Marion snarled. "This is my place! Get out!"

Just then, The Raven's door opened, allowing a sudden blast of wind to enter along with Mohan, who backed in with an armload of firewood. In Nepalese, Marion spoke to Mohan, who placed the wood beside the open door before he stepped outside again, shutting the door behind him.

Despite Marion's command, Indy made no move to leave. Turning to look her straight in the eye, he said, "I did what I did. You don't have to be happy about it, but maybe we can help each other out now."

Turning her back on Indy, Marion walked over to the table that supported what was left of the evening's activities. As she began gathering up the empty glasses and loading them onto a tray, Indy continued, "I need one of the pieces your father collected." Gesturing with his hands as he spoke, he said, "A bronze piece about this size, with a hole in it, off center, with a crystal. You know the one I mean?"

"Yeah," Marion said as she carried the glasses-laden tray to the bar. "I know it."

This conversation is going nowhere, Indy thought. Impatient, he said, "Where's Abner?"

Averting her gaze from Indy, Marion said, "Abner's dead."

For a moment, Indy was speechless. He felt as if he'd

been punched again, only this one hurt more than the one that came from Marion's fist. After all, bruises heal, but dead people stay dead. Moving to the bar, he leaned close beside Marion, who still wouldn't look at him. He said, "Marion, I'm sorry."

Marion shook her head. "Do you know what you did to me, to my life?"

"I can only say I'm sorry so many times."

Marion jerked the tray she'd been gripping and the glasses went flying and crashing onto the bar and floor. Turning to glare at Indy, she snapped, "Well, say it again, anyway."

As Marion carried the tray back to the table, Indy said, "Sorry."

"Yeah, everybody's sorry," Marion said as she picked up the remaining glasses. "Abner was sorry for dragging me all over this Earth looking for his little bits of junk. I'm sorry to still be stuck in this dive." Returning to the bar, she added, "Everybody's sorry for something."

Hoping to get Marion off the subject of her anger and sorrow, Indy said, "It's a worthless bronze medallion, Marion. You going to give it to me?"

"Maybe," she said. "I don't know where it is."

"Well, maybe you could find it," Indy said as he reached inside the breast pocket of his leather jacket and pulled out a thick wad of paper money. Holding it up so Marion could see it was American currency, he said, "Three thousand bucks."

Marion eyed the money in his hands. "Well, that will get me back," she allowed, "but not in style." She turned her back to Indy again.

"I can get you another two when we get to the States," Indy said. Irritated by the way Marion was deliberately ignoring him, he grabbed her upper arm and spun her around to face him. "It's important, Marion," he said. "Trust me."

Either Marion didn't trust Indy or she just wanted to belt him again, for her hand suddenly lashed out toward his face. This time, Indy caught her wrist, and he gently placed the money into her hands. "You know the piece I mean," he said. "You know where it is."

Marion wrapped her fingers around the bills and laughed. Smiling at Indy, she said, "Come back tomorrow."

Cautious, Indy said, "Why?"

"Because I said so, that's why." She feinted another jab at Indy's chin, and he caught that one, too. Taking the money, she turned and sat down at the edge of a table.

"Ha!" she said as Indy headed for the door. "See you tomorrow, Indiana Jones."

Indy paused for a moment after he'd opened the door, and then stepped outside. After he'd gone, Marion walked over to another table that was littered with empty glasses that encircled a candlestick that had been carved from a twisted branch. She sat down on a bench beside the table, then slipped her fingers into her blouse to remove the circular bronze medallion she wore on a chain around her neck.

A single candle burned in the candlestick on the table, and its flame danced in the drafty saloon while Marion examined the medallion. A winged bird dominated the design, with the bird's head positioned slightly above the center. An inset crystal took up most of the bird's head, and Egyptian letters ringed the outer edge. Marion knew that this piece was the headpiece of the Staff of Ra, at least that's what her father had believed. For some reason, she hadn't wanted to sell it off after her father died, maybe because she knew it was one of his most prized pieces. Or maybe just because it reminded her of him.

She still missed her father. Every lousy day since he'd died.

Holding the headpiece in one hand and her money in the other, Marion grinned. If she wanted to, she could sneak off with the money *and* the headpiece. As far as she was concerned, that would serve Indy right. However, she doubted that she'd be able to hide for long. If he could find her in Nepal, he could find her anywhere.

She studied the headpiece again. Why was Indy so interested in it, anyway? To her surprise, she suddenly felt torn over the idea of selling it, especially to Indy. Fortunately, she had the night to think it over. She didn't really want to part with the last tie to her father, but she didn't want to stay in a stinking saloon in Nepal for the rest of her life either. If it served as her ticket back home, then at least one of her father's relics had been good for something.

Lifting the headpiece by its chain, Marion draped it over the carved candlestick and got up from the table. She carried the three thousand dollars to the bar, where she found the cigar box that served as The Raven's cash register, and placed the bills into the box. Then she reached into her pockets to remove her winnings from the drinking contest and put those notes into the box, too.

Marion had just lowered the lid on the cigar box and was stepping away from the bar when The Raven's door swung open with a loud thud into the wall. Pausing midstep, she turned to see four men standing in the doorway. Two of the men wore black hats with matching leather trench coats and gloves; one wore round wire-frame eyeglasses, and the other had a black mustache. Marion knew these two weren't locals. The other two looked vaguely familiar: a Nepalese in ratty-looking clothes and a tall, broad-shouldered Mongolian. It was the bespectacled man in black who had pushed open the door. Although he wasn't a remarkably tall man, he was the most looming presence among his group.

"Good evening, *Fraülein*," said the bespectacled man as he stepped into the saloon. His German accent was unmistakable. And like the man on the Pan American *Clipper* who had tracked Indiana Jones to Nepal, he was a Nazi agent.

lthough the bespectacled man with the German accent did not introduce himself to Marion Ravenwood, his name was Arnold Toht. He was a top agent of the Gestapo, the official secret police of the Nazi Party, and his mission was to secure the headpiece to the Staff of Ra on behalf of the *Führer*, Adolf Hitler. Toht was skeptical of the supernatural, and had no idea whether the headpiece would lead to the Ark of the Covenant, or whether the Ark would help the Nazis defeat their enemies. However, Toht was also a most devoted Nazi, and he would do anything to please the Führer, especially if it allowed him to use his skills as an interrogator. For when it came to getting information out of people, Toht was considered something of an expert.

"The bar's closed," Marion said dismissively to the four men who stood in The Raven's doorway. She could sense that they were a dangerous bunch, and the bespectacled man's accent didn't score points with her either.

But the men ignored her and stepped into the saloon. A smile twitched across Toht's pale face, and his words tumbled out in a shivering stammer. "We . . . we are . . . not thirsty."

Marion wasn't sure if the German was genuinely shivering or if he always talked that way — as if he were trying not to giggle at some incredibly sick joke. On some dim instinctive level, she wanted to run, but she refused to let anyone frighten her in her own bar. Without displaying a trace of fear, she walked casually toward them and said, "What do you want?"

"The same thing your friend Dr. Jones wanted," Toht said as Marion lit up a cigarette. "Surely he told you there would be other interested parties."

"Must've slipped his mind," Marion said.

"The man is . . . nefarious," Toht said between shivers as he came to a stop before Marion. Then, as if he had finally warmed up, he added smoothly, "I hope, for your sake, he has not yet acquired it."

Marion said, "Why, are you willing to offer more?"

"Oh, almost certainly," Toht said. "Do you still have it?"

Marion blew smoke straight into the German's face.

Irritated, he responded with a low cough. Stepping away from the man and moving behind the bar, Marion said, "No. But I know where it is."

The big Mongolian began to follow Marion. She saw his movement out of the corner of her eye and knew he was moving up behind her, but she kept her gaze on the bespectacled German on the other side of the room.

Ignoring Marion, Toht moved toward the small pile of flaming logs in the open fireplace, which consisted of four baked-brick columns that supported an exposed stone chimney that rose up through the ceiling. Bending down to inspect the logs, Toht said, "Your fire is dying here." He removed his right glove, then reached out with his bare right hand for the iron poker resting at the edge of the fireplace. "Why don't you tell me where the piece is right now?"

"Listen, Herr Mac," Marion said in a low voice as she leaned against the bar. "I don't know what kind of people you're used to dealing with, but nobody tells me what to do in my place."

"*Fraülein* Ravenwood," Toht said as he pushed the tip of the poker against a burning log, "let me show you what I am used to."

Toht snapped off a monosyllabic command, and the Mongolian grabbed Marion from behind. "Take your hands off me!" Marion shouted as he lifted her off her feet. Glasses shattered as the brute shoved her over the bar, where the Nepalese was waiting for her on the other side. "Take your lousy hands off!" The Mongolian moved quickly around the bar, then took Marion from the Nepalese and pinned her arms behind her back with one vise-like hand.

And then Marion noted that the German with the creepy voice had stepped away from the fireplace. He was holding the smoldering poker, and its tip glowed bright orange. He wasn't smiling anymore. The other man in a black trench coat — the one she assumed was also German — stood off to the side, staring at her blankly.

"Wait a minute," Marion said, and heard the fear in her own voice as the man with the poker stepped toward her. "Wait," she gasped. "I . . . I can be reasonable."

"That time is past," Toht said flatly. As he moved closer to Marion, she saw that his face was now covered with sweat. It seemed as if the fireplace had not only warmed his features, but thawed his evil nature.

"You don't need that," Marion said as her eyes went wide and she trembled in the Mongolian's grip. The man with the poker moved closer to her, so close that she could smell his foul breath. She gasped, "Wait . . . I'll tell you everything."

"Yes," he said, leaning even closer, "I know you will." He raised the poker so that its tip was just inches from Marion's face. She kept her eyes open and focused on the tip, and Toht had no doubt that she knew what he was about to do, that the red-hot poker would be the last thing she ever saw before she died.

But Toht was wrong.

From out of nowhere, there came a loud cracking sound. Toht felt a sudden jolt along his arm as the end of a bullwhip wrapped around the poker. He reflexively opened his fingers as the whip yanked the poker aside and flung it across the saloon, where it landed beneath a heavy curtain against the far wall.

Toht moved fast, grabbing Marion and shielding himself with her body as he turned to face his unseen attacker. He found himself staring at Indiana Jones.

Indy held his bullwhip in his right hand and his revolver in his left. His hands were now covered by leatherwork gloves, and there was a thin layer of snow on the brim of his hat. Keeping the barrel of his gun leveled at the man in the black trench coat who was holding Marion, Indy said, "Let her go."

Behind Indy, the heated poker suddenly caused the curtain to ignite and burst into flames. Toht's eyes flicked to the fire, then back to Indy.

Indy heard a ratcheting sound as the other guy wearing a black trench coat raised a machine gun. Indy spun fast and shot at the man with the machine gun. The machine gunner stumbled back, pumping bullets into The Raven's ceiling, but he didn't go down. Marion wrenched herself from Toht's grip, then dived for cover beside the bar.

Indy fired at the machine gunner once more, then rapidly switched his revolver to his right hand and shoved his whip into his jacket as he scrambled for cover. Indy threw himself into a stone-walled alcove that ended at the saloon's back door as a hail of bullets hammered at the walls and ricocheted past his body. But leaving through the back door was not an option he could consider — not with Marion still in danger.

The bullets were still flying as Indy poked his head and gun arm out fast to fire three more rounds back at his attackers. He only managed to hit some bottles on the bar, which exploded and sent glass flying everywhere, but he quickly noted the positions of the four men as well as Marion before ducking back into the alcove to reload his Smith & Wesson.

Marion was crouched down beside the far end of the bar. The Mongolian and the machine gunner had both moved behind the bar, and the fiend who'd been holding the poker now held a pistol that he'd pulled from the depths of his trench coat. The Nepalese was still out in the open, with just the open fireplace between him and Indy.

Indy risked more bullets and another glance from the alcove to see the Nepalese grab hold of a wooden table and flip it onto its side so he could use the tabletop's thick planks as a shield. The Nepalese's action sent more glasses and bottles crashing to the floor, as well as the candlestick around which Marion had left the headpiece.

From her crouched position beside the bar, Marion saw the headpiece hit the floor. No one else had taken notice of the bronze relic amidst the shards of broken glass and spilled liquor, but she knew there was no way she could reach it without getting caught in the crossfire.

Then Marion saw a machine gun sail over the bar and land in the Nepalese's waiting hands. She realized the Mongolian must have tossed it to him. She wanted to shout out and warn Indy, but if anyone else heard her over the roar of gunfire, she knew they wouldn't hesitate to turn their weapons and cut her down.

While the Mongolian began firing a machine pistol in Indy's direction, the Nepalese lowered himself behind the overturned table. Bracing the machine gun's barrel on the tabletop's edge, he fired a stream of bullets into the wall near Indy.

Indy ducked back into the alcove to avoid the barrage. Several agonizing seconds later, the Nepalese stopped firing, and Indy guessed the machine gun had jammed or run out of bullets. As good as Indy was with a gun, he was pretty sure he couldn't get a straight shot at the Nepalese as long as he was behind the overturned table. So when Indy leaned out fast from the alcove and fired two precisely aimed rounds, he didn't aim for the Nepalese. He aimed for the stack of logs in the fireplace.

Struck by Indy's bullets, the burning logs tumbled out of the fireplace and onto the floor in front of the overturned table. The logs ignited the puddle of spilled liquor around the table, and the Nepalese dropped his machine gun as his liquor-soaked clothes caught fire. Suddenly engulfed in flames, the Nepalese rose screaming from behind the table.

From the doorway, Indy saw he now had a clear shot at the Nepalese. He fired, killing him instantly. Marion screamed as the Nepalese fell to his knees and collapsed in front of her. The other machine gunner and the Mongolian continued firing at the far doorway, keeping Indy pinned in the alcove.

There were now several small fires burning in the saloon, and all were spreading fast. Glancing around to make sure she wouldn't be spotted, Marion reached out from beside the bar to grab the non-burning end of one of the logs that Indy had launched from the fireplace. Moving slowly, she held the log with one hand as she raised her head to peek over the bar. Sure enough, the Mongolian was still firing at Indy. As bullets continued to whiz overhead, Marion edged her way along the floor behind the bar.

Still braced in the doorway, Indy winced as one of the machine gunner's bullets creased the left sleeve of his leather jacket. Indy stumbled back and tucked his body into a smaller alcove to the left of the back door. Because of his position, Indy was forced to transfer his revolver to his left hand to return fire. But just as he prepared to squeeze off another round, the door behind him swung open and slammed against his outstretched arm. Indy groaned as the door met his arm and he accidentally fired at the ceiling. Then he felt a pair of massive hands grab him from behind and slam him into the stone wall beside the doorway.

The man who had burst through the door to attack Indy was a hulking, bearded Sherpa, even larger than his Mongolian ally behind the bar. At the sight of the Sherpa, the Mongolian and the machine gunner held their fire.

As Indy was being beaten by the Sherpa, Marion — still clutching the smoldering log — stealthily moved up behind the Mongolian. She raised the log with both hands, and then brought it down hard over the back of the Mongolian's head. The big man slumped forward, then collapsed unconscious to the floor.

Toht and the machine gunner didn't see the Mongolian

fall or notice Marion duck back down behind the bar —
their attention was on the Sherpa and Indy. They stepped
away from the burning walls as the Sherpa lifted Indy off
his feet and carried him toward the bar.

Dazed from the beating and the smoke that now filled
The Raven, Indy somehow managed to hang on to his gun
with his left hand even as the Sherpa slammed him into
the bar. As Indy let out another pained groan, the Sherpa
forced his head down so that his left cheek was pressed
upon the countertop, which was slick with spilled alcohol.

Out of the corner of his eye, Indy spied Marion down
behind the bar, fumbling with the Mongolian's fallen
machine gun. The Sherpa hadn't noticed her — he had his
head turned to gaze down the length of the bar. Indy followed the Sherpa's gaze and saw the machine gunner
standing beside the bald, spectacled man.

There was a single unbroken bottle of liquor resting on
the countertop near Toht, who had picked up a small,
burning stick from the floor. He deliberately knocked
the bottle over as he held out the burning stick, and the
liquor caught fire as it flowed across the bar's surface
toward Indy.

Indy knew it was only a matter of seconds before the
creeping flames reached his head. Craning his neck to face
Marion, he wriggled the fingers of his right hand as he
ordered, "Whiskey!"

Without hesitating, Marion snatched a bottle of whiskey from the counter near her head and handed it to Indy. He grabbed the bottle by the neck and twisted his body toward the Sherpa, gaining just enough leverage to smash the bottle against the Sherpa's head.

The Sherpa fell back from the bar, pulling Indy away from the flames that now covered the bar's surface. Indy still clutched his revolver in his left hand and tried to angle it at his opponent, but the Sherpa pinned Indy's left arm with one hand and wrung his neck with the other. Indy gasped for air as the Sherpa leaned over him, forcing him down on top of a nearby table.

Toht and the mustachioed machine gunner stepped forward. Apparently, Toht did not trust that the Sherpa would kill Indy, or maybe he just wanted to be rid of the Sherpa as well, for he tilted his head to the machine gunner and commanded, "Shoot them. Shoot them both."

The Sherpa must have understood Toht's words or sensed that he had been betrayed, for his grip slackened on Indy as he turned his gaze to the two Germans. As the machine gunner stepped forward and prepared to fire, the Sherpa suddenly pushed Indy's gun arm forward, allowing Indy to squeeze the trigger four times in quick succession.

Toht jumped aside as Indy's bullets slammed into the machine gunner. As the gunner toppled to the floor, the Sherpa pulled Indy from the table. For a moment,

Indy thought he had at least a temporary truce with the Sherpa, but then he realized the Sherpa was trying to wrestle the revolver from Indy's hand. They tumbled to the floor, punching and kicking.

Trying to stay out of range of the fighting men, Toht trotted over behind the overturned table that the Nepalese had used earlier as a shield. It was then that Toht caught sight of the bronze medallion that rested in a tangle of glass and splintered wood beside the table's charred surface. He knew at once that it was the headpiece of the Staff of Ra. While Indy and the Sherpa continued their fight, Toht reached forward, wrapping his fingers around the headpiece. He was so eager, it hadn't occurred to him that the bronze headpiece might be hot.

There was a sickening searing sound as Toht lifted the metal medallion and smoke issued from his palm and between his fingers. His face contorted with intense pain and he screamed in agony as he released the sizzling bronze, letting it fall back to the floor. He continued to shriek as he clutched his wounded hand and — wanting nothing more than to escape the burning saloon and find relief in the snow — ran straight for the nearest window and dived through it, breaking glass as he went.

Back in the saloon, the fight for the gun had taken Indy and the Sherpa to the floor beside the fireplace. Indy managed to shove the Sherpa's arm into nearby flames, forcing him to release his grip on the gun. A moment later, Indy was on his feet, but so was the Sherpa, his right sleeve now ablaze.

There was a whoosh of flame as the Sherpa swung his burning arm at Indy's head. Indy ducked and drove his fist into the Sherpa's face. The Sherpa's head tilted back slightly from the hit, so Indy hit him again. Harder.

The Sherpa stumbled. Seizing his chance, Indy grabbed a heavy table, lifted it high off the floor, and swung it down over the Sherpa's back. The table broke apart, and the Sherpa fell in a heap.

Remembering Marion, Indy turned toward the bar. But instead of Marion, he found himself facing the Mongolian that Marion had clobbered earlier. Given the angry glare on the Mongolian's face and the pistol he had aimed at Indy, it appeared that Marion hadn't clobbered the man hard enough.

Indy flinched as he heard the gunshot. He knew the Mongolian couldn't have missed him, not at such close range, so he was surprised when he didn't feel the sudden pain of a gunshot wound. But then he saw the blood trickle out of the Mongolian's mouth, just before the man's body went limp and he collapsed for the very last time ever. And as the Mongolian slid down behind the bar, Marion was revealed, standing at the back of the bar with a gun in her hands.

Indy smiled and cocked his head. As the saloon burned all around them, Marion lowered the pistol and yelled, "My medallion!"

She found the headpiece of the Staff of Ra on the floor, and used a balled-up handkerchief to pick it up. Then Indy grabbed her and pulled her through the front door of The Raven, or rather what was left of it. Less than three minutes had passed since Indy had used his whip to make the German drop the red-hot poker, and now Marion's saloon was reduced to burning timbers.

The wind howled and tore at Indy and Marion as they stumbled away from the fire. Indy glanced around, searching for any sign of danger. As far as he could see, it was just Marion and he outside.

"Well, Jones," Marion shouted over the wind, "at least you haven't forgotten how to show a lady a good time!"

He reciprocated, shouting back, "Boy, you're something!"

"Yeah?" Marion shouted back. "I'll tell you what! Until I get back my five thousand dollars, you're going to get more than you bargained for!" Holding out her medallion for Indy to see, she said, "I'm your partner!"

*I*ndiana Jones and Marion Ravenwood didn't talk much on the Air East Asia flight that carried them from Nepal to Karachi, the major port and capital city of the Sind province, and both of them slept during most of their subsequent flight from Karachi to Baghdad. But after they left Baghdad, Indy told Marion a little more about his plan and about Sallah, the man they were going to meet in Cairo.

Sallah was a professional excavator who had worked with Indy on previous archaeological digs. He had a large family, was beloved by his friends, and had a fondness for the music and lyrics of Gilbert and Sullivan. It was easy for Indy to talk about Sallah, and Marion found herself eager to meet him.

Sallah did not disappoint. He stood six-foot-two, weighed over 220 pounds, and had a baritone voice that somehow made him seem even larger. With open arms, he welcomed Indy and Marion into his home, and introduced them to his wife, Fayah, and their children. There wasn't an unhappy face in the house. Just as Indy had expected, Marion liked Sallah and his family immediately.

After Marion changed into a clean white blouse and skirt, she and Fayah followed Indy and Sallah up to the balcony on the roof of Sallah's house. It was warm outside, too warm for Indy to wear his leather jacket, which he had left inside along with his weapons and his hat. Most of the balcony was open to the bright sun, but there was also a shaded area with wicker furniture under a canopy, where Sallah's children were huddling around a table.

While Indy hung back near the canopy, the other adults carried their drinks to the edge of the balcony, which overlooked the rooftops of the city. Gesturing dramatically at the whitewashed buildings that surrounded his own, Sallah said, "Cairo! The city of the living. But a paradise on Earth!"

What a ham, Indy thought as his mouth broke into a broad smile. He was always glad to see Sallah.

A burst of giggles escaped from the table nearby. Indy turned, looking toward the children, their giggles now transformed into peals of squealing laughter. Fayah stiffened as she approached the table. "Silence!" she said. "Why do you forget yourselves? What is this?"

The children parted. On the middle of the table,

beside a bowl of fruit, stood a Capuchin monkey wearing a red vest. The small monkey chittered as it looked up at Fayah.

Fayah gasped. "Where did this animal come from?"

Marion and Sallah joined the group and watched as the monkey played with the fruit. When the monkey rolled on its back and knocked over a drink, Marion smiled as she leaned over the monkey and said, "Oh . . . oh, no."

The monkey leaped for Marion. She laughed nervously as it scrambled up her arm and onto her shoulders. As it wrapped a furry arm around her cheek, she glanced at Indy and said flatly, "Cute. What an adorable creature."

Fayah smiled and said, "Then it shall be welcome in our house."

"Oh, well, no," Marion responded quickly as the monkey tugged at her hair and hugged her neck. "You don't have to keep it here just because of me!" The monkey was still hugging her when she noticed Indy. He was smiling fondly as he looked at her.

Indy thought, *I can't believe I'd forgotten how beautiful she is.*

Marion smiled back, and then she turned, carrying the monkey away from the table. Remembering their manners, the children became suddenly orderly as they followed Marion to sit and play with the monkey beside the canopied area, leaving the wicker chairs for Indy and Sallah.

As Fayah poured more wine for the men, Indy picked up a lemon from the fruit bowl and began peeling it with a small knife. He looked across the table to Sallah and said, "I knew the Germans would hire you, Sallah. You're the best digger in Egypt."

"My services are entirely inconsequential to them," Sallah said without modesty. "They've hired or shanghaied every digger in Cairo. The excavation is enormous! They hire only strong backs and they pay pennies for them. It's as if the pharaohs have returned."

Still working on the lemon, Indy said, "When did they find the map room?"

"Three days ago," Sallah said. "They have not one brain among them." He paused. "Except one. He is very clever. He's a French archaeologist."

French? Indy looked up from the lemon he'd been cutting. He said, "What's his name?"

"They call him 'Bellosh,'" Sallah said.

Indy laughed at this, and Sallah looked at him curiously for a moment before he joined in. When the laughter ended, Indy leaned back in his chair, looked at Sallah and said, "Belloq. Belloq."

"The Germans have a great advantage over us," Sallah

said gravely. "They are near to discovering the Well of Souls."

"Well," Indy said as he reached into his pocket, "they're not going to find it without this." He pulled out the headpiece to the Staff of Ra and held it up for Sallah's inspection, letting him see the symbols etched into its surface. As Indy handed the headpiece to Sallah, he asked, "Who could tell us about these markings?"

"Perhaps a man I know can help us," Sallah said as he examined the piece closely. Then, and somewhat hesitantly, Sallah added, "Indy . . . there is something that troubles me."

"What is it?"

Sallah leaned forward and planted his elbows on the table. "The Ark," he said. "If it is there, at Tanis, then it is something that man was not meant to disturb. Death has always surrounded it. It is not of this Earth."

Not of this Earth? Because Indy wasn't superstitious, he didn't know how to respond to that. For all he knew, the stories about the Ark of the Covenant were just folklore. He wanted to put Sallah at ease, but the truth was that there did exist a great deal of danger surrounding the Ark that *was* of this Earth, namely that Belloq and the Nazis were searching for it, too.

Indy remained determined to find the Ark before the Nazis. But if anything bad happened to Sallah, he would never forgive himself.

While Sallah went to meet a man and find out about the markings on the headpiece, Indy and Marion agreed to go do some shopping. Marion changed into a white blouse and red, loosely fitted trousers that were gathered at the ankle. Leaving his leather jacket at Sallah's house, Indy put on his hat and gun belt, tucked his whip beneath his shoulder bag, and went out with Marion into the crowded streets of Cairo. They didn't go alone.

"Do we need the monkey?" Indy said as the little creature jumped from the back of his neck to Marion's. "Huh?"

Walking alongside Indy past the vendors who were selling everything from food and brass goods to rugs and jewelry, Marion grinned. "I'm surprised at you, Jones. Talking that way about our baby." She patted the monkey as it shifted to her right arm, then she added, "He's got your looks, too."

"And your brains," Indy grumbled.

"I noticed that," Marion said, smiling at the monkey, which she realized was actually female. "She's a smart little thing." Turning to Indy to make sure he'd heard her, she repeated, "*Smart.*" Then she laughed as the monkey tugged at her ear.

Without warning, the monkey leaped from Marion's arm, landed on the cobblestone street, and began to scurry away on its hands and feet.

"Hey!" Marion shouted after the fleeing monkey. "Wh-Where're you going?!" The small monkey darted past the feet of some other shoppers, then vanished from sight.

"She'll be all right," Indy said, happy to be rid of the monkey. As Marion stared off down the street, trying to sight the monkey, Indy held a small, open bag in front of her and said, "Have a date."

Marion glanced at the bag, and then removed a small piece of the dried fruit without looking at it. Her attention was still focused on down the street, where she'd last glimpsed the monkey.

"Come on," Indy pressed. He wasn't about to spend the rest of the day chasing down the animal, so he tugged Marion by the arm and repeated, "Come on."

"Okay . . ." Marion said, still looking away from him for some sign of the monkey.

"Marion," Indy said as he gave another tug.

Marion suddenly noticed the dried fruit in her hand. Having been preoccupied when she'd taken it from Indy, she now looked at it and said, "What's this?"

"It's a date," Indy said. "You *eat* 'em."

Indy and Marion moved on without the monkey. They were among the few people on the street who weren't wearing long white or black robes. Most men's heads were wrapped in *keffiyeh*, folded square cloths that were the traditional headdress of Arab men, and the women wore shawls called *hijabs*. But as the man in the fedora and the woman in red trousers found themselves relaxing slightly in each other's company, it didn't occur to either of them how much they stood out in the crowd.

Not far from where it had abandoned the two Americans, the runaway monkey made its way around the corner of a building. There was a bearded man sitting on the building's front steps. The man wore a turban and a black patch covered his right eye. The monkey climbed up next to the man and tugged at his arm.

To his employers, the man was known simply as the Monkey Man. He was a mercenary spy who hired himself out to the highest bidder. And right now, the Monkey Man and his Capuchin accomplice were working for the Nazis.

Carrying his monkey on his shoulder, the Monkey Man stepped into a nearby building where he found two men wearing tan suits. The men were Germans, Nazi agents. Seeing them, the Monkey Man raised his left hand and rasped, "Sieg heil!"

One of the Germans raised his right hand and said quietly, "Ja."

Seeing the German's casual salute, the monkey snapped its own right arm up and squawked. Without thinking, the German found himself raising his right hand again, returning the monkey's salute, as the other German muttered, "Heil Hitler."

"Sieg heil!" the Monkey Man rasped again, then he pointed past the two Germans, directing them to the area where Indy and Marion were headed. With that gesture, his clandestine meeting with the Germans was over.

While the Monkey Man and his monkey ran off to catch up with Indy and Marion, the two Germans went to an upstairs room with a balcony that overlooked the busy street. Inside the room, a group of robed men, their heads wrapped in black *keffiyehs*, waited for the Germans. The men had already been provided with a description of the American couple. After the Germans sighted Indy and Marion walking along the street below, one of them turned from the balcony and nodded.

The waiting men filed out of the room and building, taking their swords with them.

*M*oving on without the monkey, Indy and Marion continued their tour through Cairo's narrow, dirt-covered streets. Soon, Indy's arms were loaded with small cloth bags filled with various goods. They exited an arched passage that led to more vendors, and were walking past a horse-drawn cart that was loaded with straw when Marion said, "How come you haven't found some nice girl to settle down with, raise eight or nine kids like your friend Sallah?"

"Who says I haven't?" Indy said.

"Ha ha! I do!" Taking another date from the bag she now carried, Marion said, "Dad had you figured out a long time ago. He said you were a bum."

"Oh, he's being generous." Indy had been joking, sort of, but as soon as the words were out of his mouth, he regretted them. Abner Ravenwood *was* being generous, and Indy hadn't completely absorbed the fact that his former friend and mentor was dead.

"The most gifted bum he ever trained," Marion continued, oblivious to Indy's embarrassment. Stopping in front of a table that displayed cooking pots, an assortment of handmade figurines, and rugs, Marion said, "You know, he loved you like a son. It took a whole lot for you to alienate him."

"Not much," Indy said. "Just you."

Suddenly, Indy sighted three white-robed men running fast from the nearby arched passage. They wore black *keffiyehs*, which they had wrapped around their heads so only their eyes were visible. The man in the lead drew a long dagger from the sash at his waist as he ran straight for Indy. The one at the rear held a sword.

Indy dropped the packages, letting them fall to the ground between him and Marion. Unaware of the rapidly approaching men, Marion stooped down to pick up the fallen bags. Just as she crouched, the man with the dagger sailed over her stooped form and into Indy.

Dodging the dagger, Indy grabbed his attacker's weapon hand, and then shoved him hard, knocking him into the guy with the sword. As both men fell, Indy turned to help Marion, who'd been seized by the swordsman. Indy belted that guy in the face, and he, too, went down.

As the surrounding shoppers and vendors backed away to watch the fight, Marion just stood there for a moment, looking stunned. But when she saw that the man who had grabbed her was trying to get up again, she picked up a fallen metal container and began beating him over the head.

Another dagger-wielding, face-concealed attacker leaped into the fray. He lunged at Indy, who blocked the attack and struck back, sending the man crashing against the nearby merchant's table. As Indy turned, the other men he had just knocked to the ground were up again, and joined by yet another man. One of them came at Indy with a length of wood, but Indy jumped back as the fiend's swing went wide and smashed into one of the other fighters. Indy socked the guy with the wood, knocking him into the man behind him.

Before any of his attackers could get up again, Indy spun around to see that Marion was still pounding the metal container against the head of the man who'd grabbed her. As that man finally collapsed beside the merchant's table, Indy seized Marion by the shoulders and turned her to face him as he shouted, "Marion, get out of here!" Then he gazed past Marion's head and his eyes went wide.

"Duck!" Indy shouted, pushing Marion down in front of him as he threw a punch over her head. An instant later, his clenched fist smashed against the nose of still another masked attacker, who had been coming up behind Marion with a sword raised high over his head. The surrounding onlookers gasped as the Arab dropped the sword and fell backward onto the street.

Marion stood up, looking even more stunned. Indy wanted to get her out of harm's way, but as he saw one of the fallen attackers begin to rise, he realized the fight wasn't over yet. He shoved Marion aside, then turned and kicked hard at the Arab's stomach.

So far, Indy had counted at least six masked men. Before he could wonder if there were more on the way, he felt a seventh slam into him and found himself being thrown against a nearby fruit stand. Indy pushed himself away from the stand and threw his elbow hard into the man's face. There was an ugly sound at the impact, and the seventh attacker fell.

Two more masked swordsmen lunged, quickly taking his place. Indy threw himself back toward Marion, and one swordsman accidentally drove his sword straight through the other's stomach. As Marion grimaced at the carnage, Indy grabbed her wrist and yanked her after him.

As the astonished crowd shouted, Indy and Marion ran back up the street, toward the arched passage where the straw-filled cart remained parked. Indy threw Marion into the back of the cart, and then reached for the bull-whip that was coiled behind his shoulder bag.

Uncoiling the whip as he turned away from the cart, Indy saw two of the masked Arabs coming at him. He let the whip loose with a loud crack, forcing the men back. But when he cracked the whip a second time, it got the atten tion of the horse that was hitched to the cart. The horse shot forward and the cart suddenly lurched away through the passage behind Indy, taking Marion along for the ride.

The horse and cart picked up speed as they traveled out the far end of the passage, with Marion feeling every bump on the road as she flopped against the straw and tried to right herself. Because the cart's wooden sides were higher than Marion's head, she could see only the road behind the cart, and was unaware that she was being watched from the street by two men: a German agent in a tan suit, and a bearded man who wore an eye patch and had a familiar monkey sitting on his shoulder.

The moment that the cart slowed, Marion jumped out and started to run back for the arched passage. She'd run only a short distance when she saw a man sprinting straight toward her. Although he wasn't wearing a black *keffiyeh*, she could tell from his angry, determined expres-sion that he was after her. Marion dashed to the front of the nearest building, where a merchant had hung a net displaying metal pots and pans. The merchant stood speechless as Marion plucked a frying pan from his display and turned to confront her pursuer.

Marion held the frying pan and readied to swing, but her pursuer stopped in his tracks a short distance away. Then he reached behind his back and pulled out a knife, laughing menacingly as he held it out at Marion, who looked aghast.

Then Marion smiled brightly. "Right," she said, before turning on her heel and running with the frying pan still held tightly in her hand.

The attacker continued to chase after Marion, following her into a nearby alley and then through a dark doorway. But a moment after he stepped over the threshold, there was a loud *clang* as Marion whacked him in the head with the pan. He fell back out through the doorway, where he took a second hit as the back of his head struck the cobblestones.

Marion hastily grabbed the unconscious man's ankles and hauled him into the building so his body wouldn't lead his friends after her. But when she ran back into the alley, she saw two white men in suits followed by several masked Arabs approaching from an adjoining alley.

Some large rattan baskets were stacked up alongside a nearby wall. Hoping to elude the approaching men,

Marion lifted the lid to an empty basket, climbed inside, and then quickly repositioned the lid over her head.

Her heart was racing as she heard the men run past the baskets. As much as she wanted to go help Indy, she was tempted to stay in the basket until she fully recovered her breath. But a moment later, she heard a strange scratching sound outside her basket, and then something screeched from atop the lid above her head.

It was the little monkey. Though Marion had wanted the monkey to return to her, she wished it had picked a different time. It continued screeching and raising such a ruckus that Marion pressed up against the basket's lid and tried to dislodge the monkey as she whispered loudly, "Shhh! Shhh!"

But the monkey just shrieked louder, which prompted the men who had just ran past Marion's basket to stop and turn around.

Clutching his coiled bullwhip in his right hand, Indy was drenched in sweat by the time he found the cart that had carried Marion away from him. The cart and its horse were resting in the middle of the street, and there were plenty of people walking around, but there was no sign of Marion.

Indy jumped up onto the side of the cart to get an elevated view of the area. Scanning the surrounding streets and the robed pedestrians that flowed over them, he shouted, "Marion!"

No response.

Indy jumped down from the cart. He wondered if Marion had gotten away, and if she were now trying to make it back to Sallah's house. Uncertain of his next move, he'd only taken a few steps away from the cart when the people around him suddenly dispersed.

Sensing trouble, Indy looked to his left and found himself staring across a short expanse of vacated ground at a massive swordsman. The swordsman was clad in black robes and had a scarlet sash around his waist. In his hands, he held an immense scimitar. Facing Indy, the swordsman grinned as he raised his curved blade. His laughter came out in a low rumble, like approaching thunder.

The surrounding expectant crowd went silent.

By Indy's eye, the swordsman stood about twenty feet away from him, which was ten feet beyond the reach of his ready bullwhip. Indy watched closely as the swordsman quickly transferred his scimitar from one hand to the other, chopping at the air and whipping the blade expertly around his body.

Show-off. Indy had no doubt that the swordsman intended to kill him, but he sure was taking his sweet time about it. Worried about Marion, and exhausted from fighting in the oppressive heat, Indy thought, *I don't have time for this.* While the swordsman continued to demonstrate his deadly prowess, Indy wearily shifted his bullwhip to his left hand, then lifted his gun from its holster and fired.

The crowd roared as the swordsman dropped his scimitar and collapsed to the ground. A young man picked up the fallen scimitar and lifted it high above his head as other people danced around him and cheered. Apparently, no one thought Indy had fought unfairly. If the swordsman had been foolish enough to pick a fight with a gunslinger, his death was his own fault.

Looking away from the fallen swordsman as if he had been just a minor distraction, Indy returned his gun to its holster and squinted as he tried to see past the jubilant crowd that surrounded him.

Marion, he thought. *Where are you?*

And then, incredibly, he heard her voice.

"Help!" Marion called out. "Over here, Indy!"

Her voice was muffled — it seemed to be coming from a rattan basket that was being carried on the shoulders of two men who were just beyond the surrounding mob.

The men under the basket were wearing black *keffiyehs*.

"Get out of the way!" Indy snarled as he pushed his way through the crowd. "Move! Move it!" He couldn't be sure why the masked men had attacked him at the market, but given what had happened back in Nepal, he had a feeling Germans were involved.

Indy chased the two basket-carrying men into an alley. He nearly lost sight of them, but then he heard Marion shout again, "Help me! You can't do this to me! I'm an American!"

Indy followed the voice and sighted the men and the basket again. He ran faster. From the basket, Marion cried out, "Indy!"

Indy was only ten strides behind when they turned a corner into another alley. But when he reached the corner, they were gone. Indy stopped, listening intently. A moment later, Marion's muffled voice echoed off the alley walls: "Indiana Jones! Help me, Jones!"

Hoping he was going in the right direction, Indy chased the echoing voice to the end of an alley, where it emptied into a busy intersection. And then he stood there, gaping.

Everywhere he looked, Indy saw men carrying baskets exactly like the one Marion was trapped in. There were literally dozens of them, maybe over a hundred, and they were all moving in different directions. Some of the basket-carriers wore black *keffiyehs*; others wore white. The difference hardly mattered to Indy now. He ran out into the street and knocked the nearest large basket out of the hands of the men who carried it. When that basket's lid slid off and revealed that it contained nothing but folded fabric, the basket's carriers began shouting at Indy. Indy ignored them as he moved fast to upset another basket along with another group of men. That basket yielded more fabric, which tumbled onto the street, so Indy ran to knock over another basket, and then another and another.

Most of the baskets held clothing and fabric. As dozens of angered basket-carriers began shouting at Indy, he suddenly heard Marion's muffled voice again: "Jones!"

Her cry had come from behind, beyond the ring of outraged merchants and laborers that now encircled him. Indy turned and shouted, "Marion!" Thrusting out his elbows, Indy broke past the angry throng at a full run, just in time to sight Marion's basket-carrying captors dart off between two buildings and into another alley.

He bolted after them. Despite their load, the men moved swiftly through the twisting alley, but their unburdened pursuer ran faster. Indy kept his eyes forward as he hurtled over the narrow cobblestone street, and saw the men turn left when they reached an intersecting alley. He followed them, but when he ran out into the intersection, he was greeted by a rapid burst of machine-gun fire.

Bullets hammered into the cobblestones at Indy's feet. He came to a sudden stop, reflexively lifting his arms to shield his body from the bits of stone that the bullets sent flying. He had just a brief glimpse down the length of the street before he spun and doubled back into the alley for protective cover. The glimpse registered that the machine gunner was another man wearing a black *keffiyeh*, and that Marion's captors were carrying her basket toward a truck that was parked outside a small shop. Indy thought he also saw a pair of white men who wore tan suits and fedoras, but he couldn't be sure.

More bullets tore at the buildings around Indy as he drew his revolver and braced himself against the wall in the alley. When the gunfire ceased, he risked a glance down the street and saw the Arabs loading Marion's basket into the back of the truck. And he'd been right — there *were* two men in tan suits. He wondered, *Who're* those *guys?*

Indy was about to make a run for the truck when he felt hands grabbing at him. A group of beggars, apparently oblivious to the gunfire as well as the revolver held high in Indy's hand, began yammering at Indy, asking him for money. With his free hand, Indy dug into a pocket, grabbed some loose coins, and threw them away from himself, down the length of the alley. As the grateful beggars moved away from him, Indy heard a man's voice yell from the parked truck around the corner. "*Los! Schnell! Schnell!*"

Germans!

Indy heard the truck's engine start. He jumped out of the alley and faced the truck, which was now moving toward him and picking up speed. The masked machine gunner stood on the running board outside the driver's door.

Standing his ground, Indy took careful aim and fired three times at the machine gunner. The gunner screamed as he was hit and fell from the moving truck. As the driver threw the wheel hard to the right to steer away from Indy, Indy took aim again and shot the driver, too.

As the driver's body went slack, his body dragged the wheel further to the right at the same time that his foot jammed down on the accelerator. Out of control, the truck careened down the street before it swerved onto a steep embankment beside a building's loading platform. The truck's right tires traveled up the incline, and then the entire vehicle flipped over onto its side and skidded to a stop.

Indy was still running for the crashed truck when it erupted into a massive fireball. The blast knocked Indy off his feet, and he groaned as he was tossed back against the outer wall of a nearby building. He realized the truck must have been carrying explosives. As he turned his gaze to the burning truck and rising cloud of black smoke, he also realized something far worse.

"Marion . . ."

He stumbled forward, and then began to run, heading for the truck. But then he stopped running. The explosion and fire had already reduced the truck to a smoldering skeleton of twisted metal. No one could have survived it.

No one.

*I*ndiana Jones sat at a table on a patio. According to the painted letters on the wall behind him, he'd found his way to the Marhala Bar. The Capuchin monkey in the little red vest lay in front of him on the table, right next to Indy's glass and a bottle that was only a couple of pours away from being empty. Indy didn't remember his walk to the bar or ordering the bottle, and couldn't recall whether he had found the monkey or the monkey had found him. None of that seemed to matter very much, not since he'd seen that truck explode.

He knew that the blazing truck must have attracted the local authorities, but he hadn't bothered to stick around and wait for them to show up. Even if they weren't corrupt, they could no sooner bring Marion back from the dead than he could. And so he had just walked away, drifting through the streets and alleys of Cairo until he somehow wound up at the bar. With the monkey.

Marion liked the monkey.

The monkey tugged at Indy's fingers and then sat up. Indy looked down at the animal's upturned face and thought he saw concern in its eyes. He stroked the monkey's little hand with his thumb and thought, *I'll bet you're wondering where Marion is.* Unfortunately, Indy knew the answer to that question.

It's all my fault, he thought for the hundredth time. *If I hadn't gone to Nepal, and then let Marion come to Cairo with me, she'd still be alive.* He'd allowed her to get dragged into this mess, and he hadn't been fast enough to save her life. He had failed her. It was as simple as that.

A shadow fell over Indy's table. He looked up to see two men. One wore a tan jacket to match his pants, the other was in his shirtsleeves and wore glasses. Indy had never seen either of them before.

"Dr. Jones," said the man in the jacket. Then, speaking in German, he told Indy that another man wanted to talk with him inside the bar.

Indy grimaced, and felt a rush of rage sweep over him. He hadn't forgotten the other two men in tan suits he'd seen earlier, by the truck that had carried Marion to her death. One of those men had spoken German, too. Had those men died along with Marion? Indy didn't know. Were the two men who now stood beside his table Nazis? He wouldn't bet against it.

Indy glanced at the German who had just spoken to him. The man held his left arm at an angle so that his fingers brushed against the lapels of his jacket. Indy had no reason to doubt the man was carrying a gun.

Indy's own revolver was in its holster at his hip. Angered as he was, he made no move for his weapon. Instead, he decided to play along with these men and see where they took him. If they made trouble for him, he was prepared to give it back in spades.

Without a word, Indy rose from the table. He scooped up the monkey and his nearly finished bottle and walked slowly toward the bar's open entrance. The man in the jacket followed close behind.

The smoke-filled bar was a series of white-walled rooms connected by arched doorways. The only signs of modernity were the electric fans that dangled and spun from the ceilings. Most of the patrons were Arabs who sat in small groups around tables and on chairs that were lined up along the walls. A few of them stole cursory glances at Indy as he and the German moved deeper into the bar.

The German guided Indy over to a column where a glowering man stood. Glaring at him, Indy said, "You looking for me?" But the man just laughed in his face and walked away. Then, to Indy's surprise, the German walked off, too, leaving him standing alone with his bottle in one hand and the monkey on his shoulder.

Indy turned around slowly and found the man who had summoned him. The man wore a white suit and a black-banded Panama hat, and was seated at a table, examining a cheap pocket watch.

"Belloq," Indy said.

"Good afternoon, Dr. Jones."

Moving closer to Belloq's table so that he loomed over his adversary, Indy muttered, "I ought to kill you right now."

Belloq shrugged as he put the pocket watch down on the table. "Not a very private place for a murder."

Surveying the other men in the bar, Indy said, "Well, these guys don't care if we kill each other. They're not going to interfere in our business."

"It was not *I* who brought the girl into this business," Belloq said petulantly. Gesturing to an empty chair at the end of his table, he continued, "Please, sit down before you fall down. We can at least behave like civilized people."

Indy put his bottle on the table and sat down in the offered chair. The monkey crawled down from his shoulder, slinked off of his right arm, and then vanished below the table. Watching the monkey's progress, Belloq said, "I see your taste in friends remains consistent."

Seated beside Belloq, close enough to reach out and strangle the smug Frenchman, Indy kept his eyes forward, refusing to meet his adversary's gaze. Indy never felt the talented monkey remove his revolver from its holster, nor saw the animal carry the gun over to the Monkey Man, who stood with some men on the other side of the bar.

Watching Indy intently, Belloq said, "How odd that it should end this way for us, after so many stimulating encounters. I almost regret it. Where shall I find a new adversary so close to my own level?"

"Try the local sewer," Indy said.

Belloq let out a small laugh. "You and I are very much alike," he said as he gave an appreciative nod to Indy. "Archaeology is our religion, yet we have both fallen from the purer faith. Our methods have not differed as much as you pretend. I am a shadowy reflection of you. It would take only a nudge to make you like me, to push you out of the light."

Keeping his eyes averted from Belloq, Indy snarled, "Now you're getting nasty."

"You know it's true," Belloq said with a smooth, confident smile. "How nice. Look at this." He held up the pocket watch he had before him, and dangled it by its chain. Indy gave it a slight glance out of the corner of his eye. "It's worthless," Belloq continued. "Ten dollars from a vendor in the street. But I take it, I bury it in the sand for a thousand years, it becomes priceless . . . like the Ark. Men will kill for it. Men like you and me."

"What about your boss, *der Führer?*" Indy said with obvious disgust. "I thought he was waiting to take possession."

At Indy's mention of the Nazi leader, Belloq's eyes shifted to the nearby Arabs. If they'd understood Indy's words, they didn't seem to care. Returning the watch to the table and his gaze to Indy, Belloq said, "All in good time." Then he leaned close to Indy and added, "When *I* am finished with it. Jones, do you realize what the Ark is? It's a transmitter. It's a radio for speaking to God. And it's within my reach."

Indy had heard enough. Turning his head to stare directly into Belloq's eyes, he said, "You want to talk to God? Let's go see Him together. I've got nothing better to do."

Indy shoved the table forward with his left hand as his right reached for his holster. In the same instant that he discovered that his revolver was gone, there suddenly came from all around him the ratcheting and clicking sounds of dozens of guns being readied, as the surrounding Arabs and even the German in the tan suit whipped out their concealed weapons and aimed them at Indy.

Fortunately, there came another sound, too. "Uncle Indy," a child's voice cried out, "come back home now!"

"Uncle Indy!" another child cried. And while Belloq and the astonished Arabs looked on, a group of smiling children came running into the bar and swarmed over Indy, throwing their little arms around him.

Indy grinned. The children were Sallah's.

Good old Sallah. As bad as the surrounding cutthroats were, Indy doubted that they would fire on a bunch of innocent kids. When the men angled their weapons away from the children and started laughing, Indy was certain of it.

The children held tight to Indy as he rose from his chair. He tossed a defiant glare at Belloq, who said, "Next time, Indiana Jones, it'll take more than children to save you."

Sallah's children maintained their tight cluster around Indy as they escorted him past the laughing Arabs. As they moved toward the exit, Indy found the Capuchin monkey sitting on the edge of a table. He reached out and the monkey climbed up his arm and returned to his shoulder.

Walking away from the Marhala Bar, still surrounded by Sallah's children, Indy saw Sallah himself approaching from his parked blue pickup truck. Looking at Indy, Sallah said, "I thought I would find you there." Then he gestured to his children and said, "Better than the United States Marines, eh?"

Indy picked up the monkey and lowered him through the truck's open window and onto the driver's seat. As he gave one of Sallah's daughters a boost into the back of the truck, he said to Sallah, "Marion's dead."

"Yes, I know," Sallah said gravely as Indy lifted another daughter into the truck. "I'm sorry." Then he added, "Life goes on, Indy. *There* is the proof." With a tilt of his chin, he indicated his children, who were now giggling in the back of the truck.

Neither Indy nor Sallah noticed the monkey peer through the truck's open window. The Monkey Man sat on his motorcycle, which was parked about thirty feet behind Sallah's truck, on the other side of the street. The Monkey Man made a hand signal, commanding his small accomplice to stay with Indy for the time being. The obedient monkey ducked back down into the truck.

"I have much to tell you," Sallah said as he placed his hand on Indy's shoulder. Gesturing to his children again, he said, "First we will take them home, and then I will take you to the old man."

Sallah climbed into the driver's seat while Indy got into the back with the children. Behind them, the Monkey Man started his motorcycle's engine. He would keep a discreet distance as he followed the truck to its destination.

* * *

The "old man" that Sallah had mentioned was an astronomer, priest, and scholar in his seventies. Served by a small apprentice named Abu, Imam had a long, gray beard, and lived in a house that was filled with exotic artifacts, hanging lanterns, and wind chimes. The house had a large, open hole in one of its walls that offered a sweeping view over the neighboring rooftops, and allowed Imam to train his antique telescope on the stars that now twinkled in the night sky above Cairo.

The air had grown cool since sundown, cool enough that Indy now wore his leather jacket. He stood in Imam's kitchen and peered out through the back door's intricate latticework to view the alley behind the house. Ever since he and Sallah had left the Marhala Bar, he had the feeling that they had escaped Belloq's clutches just a bit too easily. He didn't think anyone had followed them to the house, but he figured it wouldn't hurt to check the alley anyway. Nothing moved, and all was quiet.

Sallah had promised Indy that he would find a replacement for the revolver that had been snatched from him back at the bar. As capable as he was with a whip, there were times when only a gun would do. Indy wasn't especially sentimental about his old Smith & Wesson, but if he ever caught the thief who'd taken it, he would make that louse pay.

Turning from the back door, Indy saw Abu standing at the sink, rinsing some dates in a colander. After the dates were thoroughly rinsed, Abu tilted the colander and poured the dates into a wooden bowl that he had placed beside a decanter on a round tray on the edge of a nearby table. Indy left the kitchen for the adjoining room, where he found the vested Capuchin monkey now perched on Sallah's shoulder while the old man examined the head-piece to the Staff of Ra. Then Abu followed after Indy, leaving the dates behind.

Lurking in the shadows of the alley outside the kitchen, the Monkey Man watched the figures leave, and then he made his move. He pushed open the back door without a sound and removed a small red bottle from beneath his robes as he stepped over to the kitchen table. He quickly emptied the bottle's clear liquid contents over the bowlful of dates, and then — hearing footsteps approach — turned fast and slipped out the back doorway. He had been inside the kitchen for barely fifteen seconds.

Abu returned to the kitchen carrying two glasses. As he placed them on the tray, he felt a breeze at his back, then turned and saw that the back door was not closed. Had the visiting American left it open? Abu could not recall. He stepped over to the doorway, peeked outside, saw no one, and shut the door.

Abu picked up the tray that held the dates, decanter, and glasses, and carried it into the adjoining room. There, Imam was seated at a low table near his telescope, and used a magnifying glass to inspect the markings on the headpiece.

"I can't figure out how Belloq did it," Indy said to Sallah. "Where'd he get a copy of the headpiece? There are no pictures, no duplicates of it anywhere."

"I tell you only what I saw with my own eyes," Sallah said while the monkey — seeing Abu approaching with the tray — scampered down from his shoulder and onto the floor. Gesturing to the bronze in Imam's hands, Sallah continued, "A headpiece like that one, except 'round the edges, which were rougher. In the center, the Frenchman had embedded a crystal, and . . . and surrounding the crystal, on one side, there were raised markings, just like that one."

Abu had placed his tray on a table near Sallah. Indy stepped over to the table, reached into the bowl, and picked up a date. Holding it in his hand, Indy turned away from the table and said, "They made their calculations in the map room?"

"This morning," Sallah confirmed as he moved after

Indy. "Belloq and the boss German, Dietrich. When they came out of the map room, they gave us a new spot in which to dig, out away from the camp."

"The Well of Souls, huh?" Indy said.

Sallah nodded. Neither noticed that the monkey had climbed up onto the table and picked up a date.

Unexpectedly, Imam looked up from his seat at the low table and exclaimed in his high voice, "Come, come look . . . Look here . . . look." There was excitement in his wise old eyes. Pointing to two chairs on either side of him, he said, "Sit down. Come, sit down."

Reaching into his pocket, Indy pulled out his glasses and put them on. As he took his seat beside Imam, he said, "What is it?"

Pointing to one side of the headpiece, Imam said, "This is a warning, not to disturb the Ark of the Covenant."

"What about the height of the staff, though?" Indy asked. "Did Belloq get it off of here?"

"Yes," Imam replied. "It is here." He dragged a bony finger over the headpiece to indicate the markings in question. Tapping at the markings, he said, "*This* was the old way, *this* mean six kadam high."

"About seventy-two inches," Sallah calculated.

Indy was still holding the date that he'd removed from the bowl and was about to pop it into his mouth

when Imam looked at Sallah and said, "Wait!" The single
word suddenly left Indy holding his breath as he waited
for Imam to continue, and he unconsciously lowered the
date away from his mouth as he watched Imam rotate
the headpiece to show him the markings on the other
side. Translating the markings, Imam read aloud, "*And
take back one kadam to honor the Hebrew God whose Ark
this is.*"

The translation left Indy and Sallah looking stunned.
As a wind blew in through the open windows and made
the chimes tinkle, they rose slowly from their chairs and
stepped away from Imam. Indy removed his glasses,
and then grinned as he looked to Sallah. "You said their
headpiece only had markings on one side. Are you absolutely sure?"

Sallah nodded.

"Belloq's staff is too long," Indy said.

Then, at the same time, both Indy and Sallah said,
"They're digging in the wrong place."

Sallah laughed, and then clapped Indy's shoulders.
Smiling broadly, Sallah began to sing from Gilbert and
Sullivan's *H.M.S. Pinafore*, "*I am the monarch of the sea. I
am the ruler of the —*"

While Sallah sung, Indy tossed the date high into the
air, tilted back his head, and opened his mouth. But before

the date could fall back down and into his mouth, Sallah's hand darted out and caught it in midair.

Surprised, Indy looked at Sallah, and then followed his friend's gaze to the rug on the floor, where the little monkey lay dead beside the bowlful of poisoned dried fruit.

"Bad dates," said Sallah.

CHAPTER TEN

Archaeologists believed that the ancient city of Tanis, located in the Nile Delta, was originally founded over 4,000 years ago. Various evidence indicated Tanis had been a commercial city and the northern capital of Egypt for centuries, but had been abandoned in the 6th century C.E. when Lake Manzala threatened to flood the area. The city was indeed flooded, and when the waters dried, most of the structures were buried under silt. Although a few European archaeologists collected statuary from Tanis during the 19th century, most of the site remained unexcavated until 1936, when René Emile Belloq arrived.

Belloq was assisted by numerous German "associates," gun-toting soldiers and guards who maintained a constant watch over the laborers who were hard at work shoveling dirt and sifting through sand. It was a massive operation, and the Germans had set up many tents to accommodate the men and vehicles. In an effort not to draw too much attention to their presence in Tanis, the Germans wore drab uniforms that were without any ornamentation that might reveal their affiliation with the Nazi Party.

Under the command of the Germans, the laborers had already moved tons of dirt. Although Belloq had found the ancient map room, and the Nazis had obtained a representation of at least one side of the headpiece to the Staff of Ra, the Well of Souls remained undiscovered.

Carrying a map of the area that he had rolled into a long, tight tube, Belloq was wearing an open-necked shirt and khaki slacks as he conducted his morning inspection of the excavation site. He was accompanied by Colonel Dietrich, the tall, blond German Wehrmacht officer who was in command of the operation at Tanis, and Dietrich's aide, a younger dark-haired man named Gobler. As the two uniformed officers followed Belloq past a group of laborers, Belloq yelled over his shoulder, "I told you not to be premature in your communiqué to Berlin. Archaeology is not an exact science. It does not deal in time schedules."

"The Führer is not a patient man," Dietrich snapped from behind. "He demands constant reports, and he expects progress! You led me to believe —"

"Nothing!" Belloq exclaimed. "I made no promises. I

only said it looked very favorable. Besides, with the information in our possession, my calculations were correct."

Because most of the laborers wore similar garments, neither Belloq nor the German soldiers thought anything unusual of the two men dressed in white robes and *keffiyehs* walking past the metal rails that had been set up for carts to transport loads of sand. One of the men was Sallah, who carried a shovel over one shoulder, and who was officially on payroll for the excavation. The other man was Indiana Jones, who carried a long wooden staff that he used like a walking stick.

Indy surveyed all the activity around them and commented, "Boy, they're not kidding, are they?" Indeed, the laborers seemed intent on leaving no grain of sand unexamined. As Sallah led him over yet another set of rails, Indy said, "What time does the sun hit the map room?"

"At about nine in the morning," Sallah said.

"Not much time then," Indy noted. "Where are they digging for the Well of the Souls?"

"On that ridge," Sallah said, indicating the ridge with a discreet tip of his shovel's handle. Then, tilting his chin to a small hilltop at their right, he added, "But the map room's over there."

Eager to reach the map room, Indy said, "Let's go, come on."

Sallah and Indy climbed up the hill where they had to step over the low barbed wire fence to reach an exposed ring of cut stones that encircled a wide hole: the entrance to the map room. Indy stopped at the edge of the hole, peered down into it, and glanced around to make sure that he and Sallah were not being watched. Then he casually held his wooden staff over the hole and let it fall until it clattered against the floor of the underground chamber.

Sallah tied off one end of a long rope to a metal pole that served as a post for the wire fence, then handed the remaining length to Indy. While Sallah braced himself at the edge of the hole, Indy lowered himself down the rope.

The air was cool in the subterranean interior of the map room, which was lined with elaborate wall coverings and frescoes, all lit by the bright stream of sunlight that flooded in through the hole above Indy. After reaching the floor, Indy gave the rope a tug to let Sallah know he was okay, and then he picked up the wooden staff that he had tossed down. He moved forward into the chamber to examine its most remarkable feature: a meticulous stone model of the city of Tanis as it had appeared thousands of years earlier, when it was still in its glory. On one of the miniature buildings, some inconsiderate German had used red paint to scrawl *nicht stören*, which Indy knew translated as *do not disturb*.

That's where they're looking for the Ark, Indy thought. *Fools.*

Sallah didn't see the two German soldiers approach until they were right behind him. He pretended to ignore them as he moved away from the hole, but when they began shouting and he realized they weren't about to go away, he decided he would have to create a diversion to keep them from discovering Indy.

Because he couldn't very well leave the rope dangling down the hole, where it could only arouse more suspicion, Sallah dragged the rope along after himself as he smiled nervously and stepped over the low barbed wire fence. Then, moving down the hill with the Germans, he deliberately stumbled and rolled to the bottom of the slope, where more soldiers watched him from beside their parked car.

Back in the map room, at the base of the architectural model of Tanis, Indy found a long, flat tablet. The tablet's tiled surface was marked by a series of evenly spaced slots.

Indy used his hands to sweep aside the layer of sand that had accrued over the tiles, and he found symbols that indicated the time of year.

He removed a small brush and notebook from his robes, and gently removed more sand from the tiles as he studied the symbols and checked them against his notes. When he found the correct slot for that time of year, he turned his gaze back to the sunlit hole in the ceiling and he grinned. It was now only minutes away from 9:00 A.M., and he was that much closer to finding the Well of Souls.

Reaching into a pocket, Indy removed the headpiece to the Staff of Ra and carefully mounted it onto his staff. As sunlight continued to stream down from above, he positioned the base of the spear into the designated slot on the tiled tablet. And then he waited.

It wasn't long before the sunlight touched the headpiece. Focused through the crystal at the headpiece's center, the sunlight generated a red beam that projected from the crystal to the miniature city. As the seconds ticked by, Indy watched as the red beam traveled slowly across the miniature. When the beam moved over the surface of the building marked *nicht stören*, he realized he'd been holding his breath. He deliberately gulped at the air to avoid getting lightheaded.

The red beam continued to move over the miniature until it reached the center of a high-walled rectangular structure. By some trick of ancient artistry, this one replica seemed to respond to the projected beam, for it suddenly glowed brightly. Beams of unearthly, golden light radiated outwards, illuminating the entire map room. Indy's eyes went wide with amazement as he beheld the radiance.

When the golden light faded, Indy was almost trembling with excitement. Recovering his nerve, he stepped away from the staff, leaving it standing in its slot, and removed a measuring tape from his pocket as he walked over to the miniature buildings. Stretching the tape from the replica that had been so brilliantly illuminated to the one that represented the area where Belloq's men were digging, Indy quickly calculated the actual location for the Well of Souls.

After scribbling a few last notes, Indy removed the staff from its slot and returned the headpiece to his pocket. Then he broke the staff over his raised, bent knee.

Finished with the map room, Indy angled his head to face the hole in the ceiling and whispered, "Sallah." When no response came, he whispered louder. "Sallah!"

Wondering what was keeping his friend from lowering the rope, Indy moved forward so he was standing directly below the hole. A moment later, his head was struck by what felt like a bundle of laundry. He reached to his head to clutch a piece of red fabric that had wrapped around his head and shoulders. As he unfurled the fabric, he was surprised to find a thick black swastika emblazoned in the middle of it. It was a Nazi flag, and it had been knotted to bits of clothing, tunics, and robes to form a makeshift rope.

Looking up, Indy saw Sallah peering down through the hole. Indy knew better than to ask questions. He climbed out of the hole.

Sallah quickly informed Indy of what had transpired while Indy was in the map room. It had taken a good deal of Sallah's cunning to extract himself from the German soldiers, enter a tent filled with various supplies, and steal the fabric necessary to make a new rope. It had also taken some nerve to sneak *back* to the hole outside the map room. Indy was relieved — and grateful that he had a partner as resourceful as Sallah.

As they made their way back across the excavation site, they neared a group of German soldiers dining at a long table. Although Indy's jaw was covered with stubble, he hardly had the swarthy features that characterized most of the Arab laborers, and knew his disguise wouldn't hold up under close inspection. So he lifted the edge of his *keffiyeh* and wrapped it across the lower half of his face.

One of the soldiers stood up beside the table and

began yelling in German at Indy. Indy shrugged and pretended that he didn't understand them, but the soldier shouted again, and then another soldier tried to grab Indy's wrist. The soldiers wanted Indy to serve them.

Indy's *keffiyeh* slipped, exposing his face. Although none of the soldiers recognized him, he didn't want to invite their attention either.

Realizing Indy's predicament, Sallah faced the shouting German and said obligingly, "Please, my friend, what is the matter? I fetch the water. I shall get it for you."

Indy didn't want to proceed without Sallah, but he couldn't just stand around the table. Pushing his *keffiyeh* back over his face, he slunk away from the seated soldiers. As he moved off, he heard Sallah tell them, "If you want water, I will get you water. No problem, no problem,"

Indy was still struggling with his *keffiyeh* when four soldiers came marching toward him. Hoping to avoid another confrontation, he turned to his left and ducked into a large striped tent. He had no idea what or who was in the tent, but because its striped exterior was an Arabic design, it seemed like a safer option than other nearby tents, which were standard German military issue. He certainly didn't want to walk into a tent full of soldiers.

Inside the tent's spacious interior, he found a young woman seated on the ground, with her back leaning up against the pole that served as the tent's central support. A knotted handkerchief gagged her mouth, and her wrists were twisted behind her back, binding her to the pole.

Much to Indy's astonishment, the woman was Marion Ravenwood.

...TRAVELING THE WORLD...

...TRACKING TREASURE...

Afri

...FIGHTING FOR HIS LIFE...

...OR AVOIDING SNAKES...

INDIANA JONES MEANS ADVENTURE!

G agged and bound inside the tent, Marion was still wearing the same white shirt and red pants that she'd had on when the Arabs abducted her the day before. The knotted handkerchief bit into the edges of her mouth as she twisted her head to glare at her visitor. There was genuine fear in her eyes, for she did not recognize the man, as his face was mostly obscured by his *keffiyeh*. She struggled against her bonds as he dropped to his knees beside her and tried to hug her. Marion released a muffled scream.

Pulling away from Marion, Indy lifted the end of his *keffiyeh* aside to reveal his awestruck expression. Despite the gag across her mouth, Marion beamed.

"I thought you were dead," Indy gasped as he reached behind her head to untie the gag. "They must have switched baskets." After he removed the gag, he was unable to stop himself from leaning forward to kiss Marion fully on the mouth. She returned the kiss, and then Indy pulled back again to ask, "Are you hurt?"

"No," Marion answered breathlessly. "You have to get me out of here, quick. They're gonna be back any minute." She saw Indy pull out his pocketknife and said, "Cut me loose. Quick."

As Indy reached behind Marion and was about to cut the rope that bound her wrists, she continued, "They keep asking about you. What you know."

Indy leaned back from Marion's bonds. Marion noticed a strange, distant look in his eyes, then felt a pang of panic as he folded the blade back into the handle of his knife and slowly returned it to his pocket.

"What's wrong?" Marion said. "Cut me loose."

Looking into Marion's eyes, Indy said gravely, "I know where the Ark is, Marion."

Surprised, Marion said, "The Ark's here?"

Indy nodded.

"Well, I'm coming with you, Jones," Marion said, wriggling against her bonds. With mounting nervousness, she blurted out, "Get me out of here! Cut me loose! You can't leave me here!"

Indy tried to keep his voice calm, but wound up rattling off quickly, "If I take you out of here now, they'll start combing the place for us." He hoped Marion would understand his reasoning. Unfortunately, she didn't.

"Jones, you've got to get me out of here!" Marion said as Indy picked up the handkerchief he'd only just removed from her face. "Come on, Jones, are you crazy?!"

"Marion, I hate to do this," Indy said as he wrapped the gag back around Marion's mouth, "but if you don't sit still and keep quiet, this whole thing is going to be shot." Marion was still breathing hard but had stopped struggling as he promised, "I'll be back to get you." He kissed her forehead, and then rose quickly to exit the tent.

Marion tried to shout after him, but Indy had tied the gag well, and her cry was muffled.

Shortly after leaving Marion in the tent, Indy reunited with Sallah and informed him that Marion was still alive. Much as Sallah wanted to help Marion, too, he agreed that a premature rescue effort would likely end in their own capture — or worse.

At Indy's request, Sallah procured a tripod-mounted transit, a small rotatable telescope used in archaeological fieldwork to measure angles and distances, and survey structures and areas of land. Although the Germans had a reputation for manufacturing high-quality optical equipment, Sallah pointed out with some amusement that the transit had been cobbled together from an old American model. Indy figured the Nazis had probably stolen the transit's pieces.

Indy kept clear of the German soldiers as he climbed up a hill that offered a good view of the entire excavation site, and also placed him at an elevation that was approximately the same as the top of the distant, dune-like mound that housed the map room. He set up the transit, and then consulted the notes he had taken in the map room.

Indy peered through the scope and centered it on the barbed wire-surrounded hole that was the map room's entrance. He adjusted the scope's focus, and then slowly swiveled the scope to the left, focusing on the area where Belloq's men were searching for the Ark. He took a reading from the transit, referred once again to a note from the map room, then swiveled the scope again to the left, letting the sights pass over more dunes until he saw what appeared to be a large, undisturbed mound of sand and rock. He checked the readings, readjusted the scope's focus, and confirmed that this particular dune was devoid of any laborers or soldiers. It had completely escaped Belloq's attention.

Indy stood up behind the transit and gazed at the unexcavated dune. He smiled and said, "That's it."

Belloq practically had to push his way through the thick atmosphere of dust that drifted over the excavation site. Leading Dietrich and Gobler past the many men who were hard at work digging or carrying dirt away in baskets and carts, Belloq said, "Who knows? Perhaps the Ark is still waiting in some antechamber for us to discover."

Neither Belloq nor the Germans noticed Sallah walk by. Following Indy's instructions, Sallah had set off to round up a group of trustworthy diggers. Sallah heard Belloq's comment, and struggled to suppress a smug grin as he moved on, away from the other men.

"Perhaps," Belloq continued, "there's some vital bit of evidence which eludes us." Pausing to gaze at the workers, he said, "Perhaps —"

"Perhaps the girl can help us," Gobler interrupted, referring to Marion.

"My feeling exactly," Dietrich said as Belloq turned with an annoyed scowl. Dietrich continued, "She was in possession of the original piece for years. She may know much if properly motivated."

Keeping his eyes fixed on Dietrich, Belloq said evenly, "I tell you, the girl knows nothing."

Dietrich chuckled. "I'm surprised to find you squeamish. That is not your reputation. But it needn't concern you." Turning away from Belloq, Dietrich looked to an approaching figure as he added, "I have the perfect man for this kind of work."

Belloq followed Dietrich's gaze. Through the rising

dust, he saw a man walking toward them. The man wore a black hat, suit, and heavy leather trench coat. Belloq imagined the man must be impossibly hot in such clothes. The man wended neatly around the many diggers until he arrived before Belloq and the two German officers.

And then Arnold Toht, peering at the men through his wire-frame glasses, raised his right hand and said, "Heil Hitler."

Belloq winced at the sight of the dark-suited man's open palm. It displayed a hideous scar, a souvenir from the red-hot headpiece to the Staff of Ra that Toht had momentarily clutched in Nepal. The headpiece had seared Toht's flesh, leaving an imprint from which the Nazis were able to make a mold, and from that mold construct a replica of the headpiece. Although the replica — like the scar — showed only one side of the original headpiece, it had enabled Belloq to enter the map room in Tanis and pinpoint the location of the Well of Souls. Or so Belloq had thought.

Toht smiled at Belloq. As much as Belloq wanted to find the Well of Souls and the Ark of the Covenant, he didn't like the idea of unleashing Toht on Marion Ravenwood.

Indy and Sallah led ten men, all carrying shovels and picks, away from the main excavation. They walked past the dunes to arrive beside the one that Indy had surveyed earlier. While Sallah and his crew waited below, Indy scrambled up the dune to stand at the top and scan the area. He was literally a stone's throw from several diggers near the base of the dune, and in plain sight of many more laborers and soldiers stationed on and around the dune where Belloq believed they would find the Ark. With so many hundreds of people at work and all the rising dust, Indy — who was still wearing his robes and *keffiyeh* — didn't draw any attention whatsoever. He felt like the proverbial needle in a haystack.

Turning away from his view of Belloq's dig, Indy held his fingers to his lips and released a sharp, quick whistle. His signal brought Sallah and his crew up to the top of the dune. As a precaution against inquiring soldiers, they positioned a tripod-mounted transit and some other surveying equipment at the upper edge of the dune, which served to make their operation appear to be official, should any soldiers question them.

Sallah and the ten men watched as Indy plunged his own shovel into the dune's sandy surface, and then they did the same. Despite his concerns about Marion's safety and the risk of being discovered by the Germans, Indy couldn't help but be excited — he was so close to making the archaeological discovery of the century. He didn't just *think* that the Well of Souls was directly under their feet. He was certain of it.

They worked all the rest of that day without incident. Progress was slow but steady, and the men sometimes sang as they shoveled and chipped away at the top of the dune. The nearby soldiers never gave them a second glance.

The sun was setting and the winds were picking up when Indy looked away from his dune to see that most of the soldiers were returning to their camp for the night. Emboldened by the approaching darkness, he removed his *keffiyeh* and robes. He had been wearing his own clothes underneath the robes all day, and it felt good to air out. Then he put on his fedora, and he felt even better.

As darkness fell, Sallah's crew set up a few low torches around their work area so that they could keep working through the night. But as the hours passed, and the winds became stronger and ominous clouds appeared over the desert, some of the workers grew uneasy with their task. A few began muttering prayers.

Indy looked away from the dune and saw a sudden flash of lightning in the distance. When another series of bolts rippled across the sky, even he began to reconsider whether they should continue the dig. His apprehension had nothing to with superstition. Any former Boy Scout knew it was downright dangerous to be out in the open during a lightning storm. But the excitement of being so close to finding the Ark overwhelmed any thoughts of safety.

Sallah called out, "Indy! Here! We've hit stone!"

Indy ran over to Sallah, kneeled down on the ground beside him, and began pushing the sand back with his fingers. Under the sand, Indy felt the smooth, hard surface of cut stone. "Clear it off!" he ordered the crew. "Come on, find the edges!"

All the men dropped to their knees and began pushing the sand back, searching for the edges of the stone slab. Seconds later, they found the narrow grooves that revealed the slab was a large, expertly cut rectangle.

"Good, good, good!" Sallah said when he saw the full rectangle revealed. "You see, Indy? You see?"

Overhead, thunder rumbled. Indy was now oblivious to the noise. "Okay," he said, "bring the pry bars in!"

Flashes of lightning illuminated the dune as the men grabbed their long metal pry bars and wedged them down into the groove around the slab. Sallah shouted, "As a team, boys! As a team!"

When Indy saw that all the men were ready, he yelled, "Push!"

The men pressed against their pry bars. Sallah felt the muscles in his arms and legs straining, but then he heard the satisfying sound of grinding stone as the great slab began to shift.

"Get 'em in there," Indy urged the men with the pry bars. "Get 'em under." As the slab began to lift from its recessed position, he continued, "Good, good, that's it. Watch your toes!"

The winds became fiercer. As the slab lifted higher, a jet of dusty air blasted out from underneath it. A moment later, the slab lay at an angle across a dark, rectangular opening. Sallah directed his men to lay down their pry bars so they could grab the edges of the slab with their hands and lift it aside. As they moved the slab away from the opening, Sallah gasped, "Carefully! Carefully!"

When the opening was fully exposed, Sallah grabbed a torch and kneeled down beside Indy to look down into a deep, dark chamber. Before their eyes could adjust to the darkness, lightning flashed, and both men found themselves looking into the eyes and gaping maw of a monstrous head.

Sallah screamed and recoiled. Indy didn't flinch. He saw the monstrous head for what it was: the top of an enormous statue of Anubis, the Egyptian god of the dead, who had a human body and a jackal's head.

Recovering himself, Sallah said, "Sorry, Indy." He adjusted the angle of his torch and looked down again. The chamber below appeared to be about thirty feet deep. The enormous statue of Anubis was one of four, all of which faced toward the center of the ceiling and stood with their arms raised to support the roof. At the far end of the chamber, there was a stone altar, an elaborately carved platform on which rested a large stone chest covered with Egyptian hieroglyphics. The chamber's floor was covered by some kind of dark carpet, and after studying it for a moment, Sallah said, "Indy . . . why does the floor move?"

"Give me your torch," Indy said.

Sallah handed Indy the torch, and Indy dropped it into the chamber. As the torch landed on the floor, the area around it erupted into a sudden chorus of hisses and slithering sounds.

The entire floor was blanketed with thousands of snakes.

Indy slowly rolled his body away from the edge of the opening. "Snakes," he muttered. "Why'd it have to be snakes?"

Sallah studied the distant snakes. "Asps," he observed. "Very dangerous." Looking to Indy, he said encouragingly, "*You* go first."

till bound, gagged, and seated on the sandy ground under the striped tent, Marion had fallen asleep against the tent's central support pole. But when she felt someone's hands against the back of her neck, she awoke with a start and let out a muffled scream.

The hands behind Marion belonged to Belloq, who had crouched down to untie the gag and ropes. Marion glanced from Belloq to another man in the tent, an attendant, who had just placed a tray of food and a pitcher of water on a nearby table. As Belloq stood up and tossed the gag onto another small table, Marion — too sore to stand up right away — wriggled away from the pole and crawled fast toward the tent's open flap. She got only as far as the edge of the tent when a tall German guard suddenly appeared in front of her, blocking her exit. The guard held a rifle.

"If you're trying to escape on foot," Belloq said casually, "the desert is three weeks in every direction." He gestured to the food on the table and said, "So please, eat something."

Still on her knees, Marion glanced from Belloq to the guard, and then turned and crawled back into the tent, heading for the table. As she crawled, the attendant walked past the guard and exited the tent. When Marion arrived beside the table, she quickly brushed the sand from her hands, then picked up a piece of bread and began gobbling it up.

Belloq said, "I must apologize for their treatment of you."

With her mouth full of food, Marion said, "Yeah? Whose idea was it? No food, no water. What kind of people are these friends of yours?"

"At this particular time and place, to do my work, they are necessary evils. They're not my friends." Belloq turned to pick up a cardboard box, placing it on his lap as he sat down in a chair across from Marion. "However," he continued, "with the right connections, even in this part of the world, we are not entirely uncivilized."

Belloq reached into the cardboard box and held up a delicate white dress. Marion, still working on the food, gave the dress a dismissive glance, but shrugged and said, "It's beautiful."

Staring into Marion's eyes, Belloq said, "I would very much like to see you in it."

"Ha!" Marion laughed. "I'll bet you would." But then she seemed to soften slightly under Belloq's gaze, as if she were reconsidering her situation. Tossing an uneaten bit of food onto the tray, she stood up and said, "All right." She reached for the dress and practically yanked it out of the box. As she held the dress up against her body to see that it looked like it would be a perfect fit, Belloq reached into the bottom of the box and pulled out a pair of matching high-heeled shoes, which he handed to her.

Marion took the shoes. As she turned and carried the dress and shoes behind a tall screen, she said, "What do you got to drink around here?"

Belloq set the empty box on the floor and rose from his chair. "We don't have much time," he said as he stepped over to a bureau where he kept his cologne. The bureau had a small round mirror on top of it, and Belloq dabbed his neck and jawline with cologne. He removed a bottle from a bureau drawer and said, "Soon they will come to harm you, and I will not be able to stop them, unless you are able to give me something to placate them. Some, uh, piece of information . . . which I can use to protect you from them."

"I've already told you everything I know," Marion said from behind the screen. "I have no loyalty to Jones. He's brought me nothing but trouble."

When Marion emerged from behind the screen, she

smiled at Belloq. The dress was made of silk and satin, very expensive, and was decorated with fabric roses. Like the dress, the shoes also fit perfectly. If Marion felt any discomfort walking across the sandy floor in high heels, her radiant smile didn't betray her, and she even managed a fashion model-like turn.

"Marion," Belloq said smoothly, "you are beautiful."

Belloq didn't seem to notice that Marion was clutching her old clothes. As she moved back to the dining table, she tossed the clothes down on the edge of the table, beside her plate, to conceal the silver-plated knife that she'd placed there only a minute earlier. She had taken the knife from the tray of food when Belloq had turned to pick up the box that contained the dress, and she wanted it within reach when she was ready to make her move.

Keeping her eyes and smile on Belloq, she picked up the bottle he'd placed on the table and said, "I don't think we need a chaperone."

Belloq made a sweeping hand gesture to the guard stationed at the tent's exit. The guard stepped away from the tent, leaving Marion alone with Belloq.

Clinging to a long rope, Indy dangled in the air above the snake-covered floor of the Well of Souls. Above him, Sallah guided the other men to lower Indy slowly. Sallah had made good on his promise to replace Indy's Smith & Wesson Hand Ejector, Model 2, but Indy took little comfort in the gun that now rested in the holster at his right hip. As grateful as he was to Sallah, the revolver would be about as useful against thousands of snakes as a peashooter in a lion's den.

"Steadily ... steadily ..." Sallah urged his crew, but then the rope began to slip and Indy suddenly dropped a few feet. "Whoa!" Sallah yelled.

Indy's grip tightened on the rope as he came to a jerking stop in front of the nearest jackal-headed statue. Looking below, he saw that the statue was poised with its left leg forward, and that he would have to descend carefully or he'd bump into its skirt. He planted the soles of his boots on the jackal's carved teeth, and then kicked out to clear the statue's torso as the crew above resumed lowering him.

"Down ..." Sallah ordered. "Down — whoa. Carefully, carefully!" Sallah looked below to see that Indy was about halfway down now, swinging slightly back and forth in the space between the statues. "You all right, Indy?"

Indy gave no reply as his eyes scanned the ground below. He had tossed down fifteen torches in advance, which served to illuminate the chamber's interior and also created a clear zone, as they drove back the snakes from the small area directly below the opening in the ceiling. However, the torches also illuminated the legions of snakes throughout the rest of chamber. The sight of this subterranean landscape of slithering forms, bared fangs, and snapping jaws left Indy mute with fear.

"Now gently, boys," Sallah's voice echoed down from the opening. "Gently, gently!"

Without warning, the crew lost their purchase on the sandy roof, causing Indy to fall the few remaining feet. He grunted as he landed on his side and rolled onto his stomach, and when he lifted his head, he was face-to-face with a large cobra.

The cobra's head was raised, poised to strike. Indy just gaped at it. Behind him, the rope swung back and forth, brushing against the backs of his extended legs.

Sallah peered down through the opening and saw Indy's form at the edge of the clear zone. Unaware of Indy's proximity to the cobra, Sallah smiled and shouted down, "I told you it would be all right!"

Indy's lower lip trembled. He wanted to tell Sallah to be quiet but was so afraid that he could barely breathe. The cobra hissed, and then its head swayed slightly, bobbing in front of Indy like a deadly, hypnotic pendulum. Indy kept his eyes fixed on the cobra as he slowly pushed himself away, inch by inch.

When he was a full four feet away from the cobra, Indy tried to get himself under control. He felt nerveless and completely exposed to the snakes. Then he remembered the supplies that he had already lowered into the chamber: a metal bucket, a small pump with an attached hose, and a cylindrical can of gasoline. He focused on these objects and tried to ignore the snakes. It wasn't easy.

Rising from the floor, Indy kicked at the sand to drive back some nearby snakes. As he lifted the can of gasoline, he looked up to the opening at the ceiling. In a shaky voice, he shouted, "Sallah, get down here!" Then he turned and poured the gasoline into the bucket.

While Sallah prepared his own descent, Indy placed the pump into the bucket. He held the end of the hose with one hand as he worked the pump with the other, spraying gasoline onto the snakes that were between him and the chamber's altar. Some snakes hissed and moved away as the spray met their bodies, but most just continued to wriggle and slither around the perimeter of the clear zone.

Lousy snakes, Indy thought. After he'd sprayed a good amount of gasoline, he lowered the hose and pump, stepped away from the bucket, and picked up a blazing torch. Then he tossed the torch at the gasoline-covered snakes. There was a loud *foom!* as the gas ignited and created a wall of flame.

*   *   *

Seated across the small dining table from Belloq in the tent, Marion eyed the bottle that stood beside their empty glasses. Wearing her most alluring smile, she said, "You pour."

Belloq removed the bottle's cork and poured a small amount into each glass. He bowed his head slightly and smiled at Marion as they raised their glasses and clinked them together, and then he took a small sip from his glass.

Marion lifted her eyebrows playfully, and then tossed her drink down in one gulp. Seeing this, Belloq's eyes went wide with surprise. Marion maintained her smile as she gazed challengingly at Belloq.

Belloq looked at the remaining contents of his own glass, then tossed his down in the same manner. A moment later, he let out a sharp, dry cough.

Marion grinned as she refilled their glasses.

With Sallah now by his side in the Well of Souls, Indy carried a torch as they walked slowly over the snake-free path they had cleared to reach the altar. A short flight of stone steps led up to the top of the ornate platform that supported the hieroglyphic-covered stone chest. Taking a moment to study the hieroglyphics, Indy confirmed that the Egyptian pharaoh Shishak had commissioned the Well of Souls to contain the Ark of the Covenant, just as the legends had told.

After climbing the steps, Indy placed his gloved hands on the surface of the thick slab of stone that was the chest's lid. A thin layer of sand covered the lid, and Indy brushed it aside to see that the lid was free of ornamentation. It appeared that the snakes had never nested on or around the platform and chest. Indy could only imagine why.

He reached to the outer, lower edge of the lid to find his grip, and then motioned to Sallah to move to the other side of the chest. Gripping the lid at the same time, they bent their knees and pushed up. The lid outweighed Indy and Sallah combined, and both men clenched their teeth as their muscles tensed and the slab began to rise. Seconds later, they'd lifted the lid clear of the chest, but with no one else to help them, they had few options for where to place it.

Indy and Sallah let go of the stone lid. It cracked and crumbled as it tumbled down the platform's steps.

Even though the lid had been undecorated, it also had been an archaeological treasure, as was every other artifact within the Well of Souls. But Indy had to live with the fact that he didn't have the time or the resources to stop the Nazis from eventually finding and seizing the ruined lid, the hieroglyphs, the towering statues, or anything else that they would claim after his work here was done. The only thing that mattered was his objective, which was now fully revealed to him as he and Sallah peered into the open stone chest to see the Ark of the Covenant.

The Ark gleamed. Although its box-shaped body was made of acacia wood, it was overlaid with gold. Its top was adorned with an elaborate gold crown, and two golden, winged cherubs who faced each other with bowed heads. Indy estimated the Ark was about four feet long, two and a half feet wide, and two and a half feet high. When he noticed the gold carrying rings that were attached to each corner, he realized it was time to stop staring at the Ark, and time to start getting the Ark out of the Well of Souls and into Sallah's waiting truck.

Sallah's crew had already finished building a makeshift winch to hoist the Ark out. Indy hoped to cover their trail, but he imagined the Nazis would find the Well of Souls within the next day or so. If all went well, the Ark of the Covenant would be long gone by then.

However, Indy had another problem: Marion. He had no intention of leaving her behind, but hadn't figured out a way to rescue her either. Right now, all he could do was hope that she was safe.

Marion and Belloq were both laughing in the tent. Marion laughed so hard she fell out of her chair.

"Whoops," Belloq said, and then they were both off laughing again.

Now seated on the ground beside the table, Marion reached up for her glass and quickly drained it. She laughed some more as she reached for the nearly emptied bottle, studied its label, and said, "What is this stuff, René?"

Taking the bottle and holding it proudly, Belloq chortled, "I grew up with this. It's my family label."

This made Marion laugh even harder. She took the bottle back from him and tried to pour some more into her glass, but she missed. Belloq found this quite amusing, laughing as he took the bottle back from her and filled her glass himself. This made them both laugh, too. But when Belloq put the bottle down, Marion stopped laughing and made her move.

Her hand darted out for the knife that she'd concealed earlier. Snatching the knife by its handle, she brought it back in front of her, the tip of its blade angled at Belloq. She was still on the ground, and all she had to do was spring forward to drive the blade into his chest.

Belloq's smile fell as he looked from Marion's blazing eyes to the knife in her grip. And then, because he knew she had no serious chance of escaping, he burst out laughing again.

Playing along as she had been the whole time they'd been in the tent, Marion laughed, too. "Well . . ." she said through the laughter, "I have to be going now, René." As she backed away toward the open tent flaps, she added, "I like you, René, very much. Perhaps we'll meet someday under better circumstances."

Marion was still backing up when she bumped into someone behind her. She whirled fast with the knife, but the man who had just entered the tent caught her wrist in his black-gloved hand.

It was Arnold Toht. His leather trench coat was draped over his back like a black cape, which somehow heightened his nightmarish appearance.

Marion's eyes went wide. Toht said, "We meet again, Fräulein."

Recovering fast, Marion tried to stab the fiend, but he held tight to her wrist. "You Americans, you're all the same," Toht said as he increased his pressure on her wrist, forcing her fingers to open and drop the knife, which fell to the sandy floor. "Always overdressing for the wrong occasions."

Marion broke free from Toht's grasp and ran back to Belloq, who had remained seated at the table. Marion huddled beside Belloq as she returned her gaze to Toht.

Dietrich and Gobler entered the tent. Gobler carried a black leather bag, which he handed to Toht before he took Toht's trench coat.

Toht reached into his bag and removed a set of three black metal rods, which were linked together by thin steel chains. Toht held the rods out before him, then gave them a slight jerk that produced a sudden snap as the connecting chains went taut. Belloq's body tensed in response to the noise, and Marion gasped in horror as she imagined what Toht would do next.

Then Toht made an adjustment to the device, flipping one rod over the other to transform it into a coat hanger. He held it out to Gobler, who placed Toht's coat on it before he took the hanger and coat back.

Both Marion and Belloq breathed a sigh of relief.

Toht moved away from Gobler and Dietrich, and then sat down in the chair that Marion had previously occupied. Facing Marion, who now cringed behind Belloq, Toht leered and said, "Now . . . what shall we talk about?"

*I*t was dawn when Indy and Sallah slid two long, wooden poles through the Ark's gold carrying rings. Standing on opposite sides of the exposed stone chest, they slowly raised the poles, lifted the Ark out, and proceeded to carry it carefully across the floor of the Well of Souls.

A few of the torches that lay on the floor had already gone out. Indy noticed that the snakes seemed to be getting restless. He could only imagine whether they were anxious about the morning sky, which could be glimpsed through the ceiling's rectangular opening, or the Ark's imminent departure from their dark lair, but he would be glad to put all the snakes behind him.

When Indy and Sallah reached the area directly below the ceiling's opening, they lowered the Ark into a wooden crate that Sallah's crew had sent down by ropes earlier. After they secured the crate and made sure the ropes would hold, Indy picked up a torch and signaled to the crew above. "All right!" he said. "Take it up!"

The crated Ark began to rise away from Indy and Sallah. Holding the torch with one hand, Indy kept his other hand on the side of the crate, steadying it, until it lifted above his head. "Easy!" he said.

A snake hissed near Indy's feet. He swung the torch over the snakes, driving the snake back. He knew it would take just a couple of minutes for the crew to hoist the crate out through the opening, and then he and Sallah could make their exit, too. As more snakes started to slither toward him and Sallah, Indy found himself wishing the crew would move just a bit faster.

The sun had just begun to rise over the desert when Colonel Dietrich and Toht followed Belloq out of the tent where they'd left Marion, who hadn't told them anything that they didn't know already. As the three men walked across the compound, passing the slumbering forms of Arab laborers who had been forced to sleep wherever they could under the open sky, Dietrich jutted his square jaw at Belloq and sniped, "You're as stubborn as that girl."

Toht giggled and added, "You like her too much, I think."

Ignoring Toht, Belloq glanced at Dietrich and said,

"Your methods of archaeology are too primitive for me. You would use a bulldozer to find a . . . china cup."

Distracted by something he saw off to his right, Belloq slowed, and then came to a complete stop. The other two men stopped, too, and then watched Belloq as he ran over to a nearby wooden ramp and jumped up on it for an elevated view. Following Belloq's gaze, Dietrich and Toht saw what he was looking at: A group of laborers, silhouetted against the dawn sky, were already at work on top of a nearby dune, and it appeared they had utilized a few long poles to construct a rudimentary winch. The silhouette of a large box rested near the winch.

Turning to Dietrich, Belloq shouted, "Colonel! Wake your men!"

Keeping close to the rope that dangled down into the Well of Souls, Indy and Sallah watched each other's backs while the snakes slithered toward them. They held their torches low and waved them back and forth to keep the snakes at bay. Glancing at the other torches that they'd placed around the clear zone, Sallah commented, "Indy, the torches are burning out."

Indy reached for Sallah's torch and took it, so he was now holding one in each hand. "Go on," he said, "get out of here."

Sallah turned for the rope. While he began climbing up, Indy swung and jabbed the two torches at the nearest snakes. When Sallah was about halfway to the opening, Indy realized the torch in his left hand was about to fizzle out. He held tight to the torch in his right hand as he dropped the other, leaving his left hand free to grab the rope.

Neither Sallah nor Indy heard the rifle-toting German soldiers who came running up the dune above their heads. Just a moment after Sallah clambered out through the ceiling, the entire length of rope slipped down through the opening. Seeing the rope land in a heap near his feet, Indy raised his head to the ceiling as he yelled, "Sallah!"

"Hello!" a voice called from above. It wasn't Sallah who looked down at Indy from the high, rectangular opening. It was Belloq.

"Hello," Belloq repeated as he held his Panama hat and waved it at Indy. "Why, Dr. Jones, whatever are you doing in such a nasty place?"

Despite a momentary shock, Indy shouted back, "Why don't you come down here? I'll *show* you!"

"Thank you, my friend," Belloq said, kneeling at the edge of the opening, "but I think we are all very comfortable up here." Belloq looked away, and then said, "That's right, isn't it?"

From below, Indy saw two German officers step up

beside Belloq. Indy guessed one of the officers was Dietrich, the ringleader that Sallah had told him about. He hadn't heard any shots fired, so Indy hoped Sallah was all right. He backed up slightly, and saw that the Ark was right behind Belloq. He also saw more soldiers.

Returning his gaze to Indy, Belloq continued, "Yes, we are very comfortable up here. So, once again, Jones, what was briefly yours is now mine. What a fitting end to your life's pursuits. You're about to become a permanent addition to this archaeological find. Who knows? In a thousand years, even you may be worth something."

Rattled and infuriated as Indy was, he responded with bravado. He smiled broadly, and then laughed before muttering a curse under his breath. A sudden hissing to his right prompted him to look away from Belloq for a moment as he swung his torch at some more snakes.

"I'm afraid we must be going now, Dr. Jones," Dietrich said casually. "Our prize is awaited in Berlin. But we do not wish to leave you down in that awful place all alone."

Hearing this, Belloq appeared baffled and concerned as he glanced at Dietrich. Before Belloq could say anything, he saw Toht and Marion approach from behind the armed soldiers who had encircled the top of the dune and captured Sallah and his crew. Marion was still in the white dress and shoes that Belloq had given her, and Toht gripped her arms tightly from behind. As Toht pushed her past the soldiers, Marion shouted, "Slimy pig, you let me go! Stop it!"

And then Toht shoved Marion straight toward the rectangular opening.

"No!" Belloq shouted as she tumbled forward and screamed.

Though the soldiers had their rifles leveled at Sallah, he bravely lunged for Marion, but his outstretched hands met empty air. Fortunately, Marion's own hands caught something else.

"Marion!" Indy shouted as a white, high-heeled shoe landed in a tangle of snakes. He looked up to see Marion clinging to the carved teeth in the lower jaw of one of the Anubis statues. Her right shoe was still on, and her bare legs kicked at the air below her shimmering white dress. Indy had already dropped his torch and he ignored the snakes as he held out his arms and moved below Marion's dangling body. "Hang on! Don't —"

"Indy!" Marion cried. The statue's teeth had not been constructed to support weight, and the tooth that she gripped in her right hand began to crumble.

"Don't fall!" Indy shouted. "Marion! I got you!"

The statue's tooth broke away from its jaw and Marion screamed again as she fell. The carved skirt that jutted out over the statue's slightly extended knee broke her fall, and she landed in Indy's waiting arms. He gasped and his knees buckled as he caught her, then they both collapsed to the ground.

"You traitor!" Marion shouted as she twisted against Indy's leather jacket and pushed herself free from his arms. "You get your hands off of me!" She rolled away from him, landed on her stomach, and lifted her head at the same moment that another creature raised its own to face her. It was only then that Marion realized that she and Indy weren't alone in the chamber.

Marion had landed beside several dozen snakes, and a cobra's elevated head was only an arm's length away. Marion stared at the cobra with wide-eyed fear and pulled away fast. The cobra snapped at her, but missed. Marion yelled as she scrambled back to Indy and jumped on top of him, clinging to his back as he struggled to stand.

"Snakes!" Marion gasped as she wriggled to straddle Indy's back. "Oh. Oh, at your feet!"

Indy sidestepped another group of snakes as he tried to keep his balance, which wasn't easy. The way Marion was climbing him, she seemed to have forgotten that he was a man and not a tree.

Belloq had seen Marion's landing from the edge of the opening above, but now shifted his gaze to Dietrich. With obvious outrage, Belloq said, "The girl was mine!"

"She's of no use to us," Dietrich replied sharply as he

stepped beside the crate that contained the Ark. "Only our mission for the Führer matters. I wonder sometimes, monsieur, if you have that clearly in mind."

As Dietrich left to prepare his report to Berlin, Belloq gazed back down through the opening. He saw Marion sitting in Indy's arms, with her own arms wrapped around his neck. Sounding somewhat regretful, Belloq called down, "It was not to be, chérie!"

Now cradling Marion in his arms, Indy turned so that they could both look up and face Belloq. "You rats!" Marion shouted back. "I'll get you for this!"

Belloq said, "Indiana Jones . . . adieu." He gave a slight wave with his Panama hat, and then stepped aside as the German soldiers forced Sallah's crew to lift the stone slab that lay at the edge of the opening.

Sallah watched helplessly as his men began to slide the stone slab back over the opening. The only person who was actually enjoying the situation was Toht, who leered and began to giggle as he walked off after Dietrich.

Staring at the diminishing rectangle of daylight above her, Marion screamed, "Nooooo — !" Her long cry was cut off to the outside world as the slab fell into place, leaving her and Indy trapped within the Well of Souls.

*I*ndy put Marion down on the ground beside him, where she stood awkwardly in her one high-heeled shoe. As the snakes began to move in, Indy snatched up the two torches that appeared to have the most life left in them. Handing one of the torches to Marion, he said, "Take this. Wave it at anything that slithers."

"Thank you," Marion gasped as she seized the torch. Sweeping the torch over some nearby snakes, she muttered, "This whole place is slitherin'."

Indy stepped a short distance away from Marion to wave his own torch at some other snakes. As he moved, Marion saw a serpentine shape shift against Indy's left hip. "Indy!" she shouted as she quickly jabbed her torch at Indy's leg.

"Ow!" Indy yelled as he jerked away from the flames. Glaring at Marion, he turned his body so she could plainly see that she had mistaken his coiled whip for a snake.

If it occurred to Marion that she should apologize, that thought vanished as more snakes slid toward them. As she returned her attention to the snake, Indy leaned in close beside her and tugged at the sleeve of her white dress. "Where did you get this?" he said in an accusing tone. "From him?"

"I was trying to escape!" Marion snapped back. "No thanks to you."

"How hard were you trying?" Indy said as he kicked sand at some snakes.

"Well, where were you? You —"

"Watch it, watch it," Indy interrupted, motioning to Marion to keep her torch away from him. Without explanation, he dropped to one knee beside Marion, grabbed the hem of her dress and began tearing at it.

"What are you doing?!" Marion screamed as the lower half of the dress ripped free from around her legs.

"For the fire!" Indy shouted, as if his answer was obvious. He wrapped the fabric around his torch.

Knowing that a few strips of fabric wasn't going to keep them alive indefinitely, Marion said, "How are we going to get out of here?"

"I'm working on it! I'm working on it!"

"Well, whatever you're doin', do it faster!"

Indy saw movement against a nearby wall that was covered with hieroglyphics. Snakes were slithering in through cracks and holes that had formed in the wall over the centuries. Seeing the way the snakes were entering the Well of Souls, Indy realized there must be another chamber on the other side of the wall.

"Ah ..." he said with a smile as he turned away from the wall and stepped over to the base of one of the towering statues.

Seeing Indy's movement, Marion said, "Where are you goin'?"

"Through that wall," Indy said, pointing to the wall where snakes continued to spill out from the cracks and holes. "Just get ready to run, whatever happens to me."

"What do you mean by that?" Marion asked as she waved her torch at some snakes. But when she glanced back at Indy, he was already clambering up the legs of the jackal-headed statue.

Although Indy's torch was dying, it was still burning enough to help him see the statue in the darkness. To keep both of his hands free, he placed the torch in his mouth, biting down on its grip so that the burning end was well away from his face. After he shimmied up over the statue's knee, he reached for his whip. Indy drew back his arm, then flung the whip up so that its end wrapped tightly around the statue's lower jaw. Then he tugged at the taut whip to make sure it would hold, and began scaling the statue's torso.

"Indy!" Marion shouted from below. "Don't you leave me down here by myself!"

Still holding his torch between his clenched teeth, Indy was lifting himself up past the statue's open mouth when he saw a coiled snake nestled between the statue's long, sculpted teeth, just inches from his face. The snake gazed back at him as its tongue darted out of its mouth. Unable to use his hands without losing his grip, Indy turned his head quickly to swing his torch's burning end directly into the snake.

The snake emitted a screaming hiss as it jerked away from the flames and tumbled out of the statue's mouth. The snake's body landed on Marion's shoulders. Marion screamed and shook the snake off and threw an angered glare at Indy.

With some dismay, Indy saw that his torch was now extinguished. Seeing Marion looking up at him, he opened his mouth and let the torch fall. Marion caught the torch's grip in her free hand, and then began swinging both torches at the snakes, using the extinguished torch like a club.

Indy quickly found his footing, removed his whip from the statue's jaw, and climbed up onto the back of the statue's head. Bracing his own arms and back against the ceiling, he pushed out against the statue with his legs. The ancient statue shifted slightly, and dust came raining down from its body. Indy grimaced with exertion as he continued to push. More dust rained down and there was a crumbling sound as the statue began to break loose from the ceiling.

"Indy!" Marion yelled as the statue started to sway under Indy's strain. The snakes were all around her now.

"Here we go!" Indy shouted from atop the statue. "Get ready!"

"Indy, the torch is going out!"

The statue's left forearm snapped in half and the entire figure began to topple. Indy wrapped his whip around the statue's shattered left arm as he jumped down from its head, neatly tucking his body against the statue so he could ride it as it fell. Just as he'd planned, the statue smashed hard into — and through — the targeted wall.

Marion had narrowly missed being struck by the falling statue, and lost sight of Indy amidst the crumbling stones and flying dust. But when she saw that the crash had created an opening in the wall that led to another chamber, she scrambled over the rubble, moving carefully to avoid any snakes. When she realized that she was holding her remaining high-heel shoe in one hand, she tossed the useless thing aside and continued on barefoot.

As she moved into the dark, adjoining chamber, her hands touched upon an object and she gripped it to steady her balance. She said, "Indy?"

She didn't know that her hands were on a decrepit mummy until it tumbled from its resting place and into her arms. Marion screamed as she shoved the mummy aside and backed away from it. Unfortunately, she backed straight into another mummy. She yelled again, but her next move revealed that foul-smelling mummies were everywhere, with their bony arms extended and waiting to snatch at her. As she shrieked and stumbled through the catacombs, she saw a large snake slither through the remains of a human skull, and she screamed even louder.

"Marion!" Indy shouted as he pushed his way through the catacombs. His hat and jacket were covered in dust, but he was uninjured. Finding Marion had been a breeze. He had just followed her screams. Taking her by the arm, he said, "Look. Look." He pushed through some cobwebs and led her into a narrow, stone-walled chamber. At the end of the chamber, just beyond the rubble-covered floor, sunlight peeked through between the blocks of stones in the wall.

Indy knew an exit when he saw one. While Marion got her breath back, he stepped over the rubble and began pushing against the blocks until he found a loose one. Pressing his weight against it, he shoved it until it budged some more, and then kept pushing until he sent it clear out of the wall. Indy slumped over the newly opened space while the heavy block landed with a loud thud on the ground outside.

Looking ragged and covered with dirt, Marion came up behind Indy and followed him through the opening. They had emerged outside some weathered ruins overlooking an area that the Germans had set up as an airfield bordered by a few small buildings and a spindly-looking watchtower. Several soldiers, a few military vehicles, and a gasoline tanker were visible, along with a single aircraft: a strange-looking plane that was essentially a large fixed wing without a fuselage or tail section. At the front of the plane, there was a cockpit with a glass canopy that offered the pilot maximum visibility. Opposite the cockpit, a glass-domed gun turret was positioned at the aft area of the wing between two large propellers. The plane was adorned with Nazi swastikas. Indy had heard that the Nazis had been working on the development of such a "flying wing" configuration, but had no idea that any had gone into production. For all he knew, this one was a prototype.

The Flying Wing's engine was already running and its propellers spinning as Indy and Marion snuck away from the ruins to hide behind some barrels near the airfield. From this position, they watched the pilot raise the cockpit canopy, allowing the pilot to stand upright while he checked the controls. As a light-armored car sped away from the airfield, Indy realized what the Germans were preparing to do with the Ark. "They're gonna fly it out of here," he said. Thinking quickly, he added, "When that Ark gets loaded, we're already gonna be on the plane."

Because the Germans finally possessed the Ark of the Covenant, the laborers were informed that their work was done. They gathered around the perimeter of the camp, waiting to be paid and watching the armed soldiers warily.

Belloq stepped out of the German Command Tent to find Colonel Dietrich seated in a chair, his boots resting on an adjacent table. A short distance away rested the wooden crate that contained the Ark. A soldier was busily stenciling the words *EIGENTUM DER DEUTSCHEN WEHRMACHT*, and a Nazi emblem onto the crate, just in time for the arrival of the light-armored car that had traveled from the nearby airfield.

Dietrich had already sent his radio message to Berlin, notifying his superiors about his acquisition of the Ark, and as he poured a glass of cognac, he looked very pleased with himself. Seeing Belloq step up beside him, Dietrich said, "Ah, monsieur. Let us toast our success in the desert." He held out the glass to Belloq and said, "To the Ark."

Ignoring the offered glass, Belloq replied petulantly, "When we are *very* far from here. That will do." He stepped over the crate to inspect it before it was loaded into the waiting car.

While Marion remained concealed behind the barrels, Indy trotted out from their hiding space and dashed toward the Flying Wing. The pilot was still in the cockpit, but was so focused on checking and adjusting the plane's instruments that he didn't see Indy dart under the plane. Indy kept a careful distance from the plane's rotating propellers, but was relieved that the engines were already running. They were so loud that he didn't even have to run quietly.

The pilot had left the cockpit canopy open, leaving him exposed from behind. Indy planned on sneaking up from the back of the plane, but as he climbed onto the aft section of the wide wing and began to crawl toward the cockpit, he suddenly heard someone shouting over the noise of the engines. Turning his head, he saw a German mechanic standing just behind the plane. *Uh-oh.*

*T*he mechanic was about Indy's size, and wore a green T-shirt and khaki pants. Indy knew the man must be a mechanic because he was holding an extremely large wrench. Indy lifted his own hands to show they were empty, and turned slowly toward the mechanic. Feinting that he was about to step down from the back of the plane, Indy suddenly kicked the mechanic in the jaw.

The mechanic fell backwards, but held tight to his wrench as he rolled to the ground. Although Indy was carrying a gun, he didn't want to shoot the mechanic — gunfire might alert the pilot and other soldiers. Indy leaped after the fallen mechanic, but the mechanic sprang to his feet and swung his wrench at Indy.

Indy dodged the swing and launched his fist into the mechanic's jaw, knocking him to the ground again. The tough mechanic jumped up and resumed his attack with the wrench, swinging at Indy and forcing his opponent back toward one of the spinning propellers.

Neither man noticed Marion had snuck below the Flying Wing to crouch down beside the landing gear. They were also unaware that their fight had attracted the attention of another German soldier: a bald, hulking brute who had just emerged from a nearby building. The bald man enjoyed boxing, and wasn't about to let one of his fellow soldiers get beaten up by some scruffy-looking interloper. Eager to join in the fight, he began removing his shirt as he walked slowly toward Indy and the mechanic.

Indy grabbed the mechanic and pushed his arm toward the propeller. There was a bright flash as the rotating blade snapped the wrench from the mechanic's hand. Indy yanked the mechanic away from the propeller and threw a powerful punch at his opponent's jaw. The mechanic stumbled backwards and struck his head on the side of the plane, collapsing in an unconscious heap below the Flying Wing.

Indy glanced toward the cockpit. The pilot, still adjusting the controls, was oblivious to the fight that had just taken place behind him.

Leaving the mechanic where he was, Indy climbed back up onto the back of the plane. Unfortunately, his intended journey to the cockpit was interrupted once again, this time by menacing laughter from behind. Then a German-accented voice bellowed, "Hey, you now . . . Come here!"

The voice got the attention of the pilot as well as Indy. Both men turned to see the hulking German soldier standing behind the plane. He was now shirtless, and he pumped the air with his massive fists as he waited for Indy to join him on the ground. Like Indy, he was unaware that Marion, at that moment, was removing two wedge-shaped blocks that held one set of the plane's tires in place.

Looking exhausted, Indy slowly climbed down from the back of the plane. It was obvious that the German greatly outweighed him, and the way he held his fists, there was no question that he was an experienced boxer. With those odds against him, Indy knew he wouldn't stand a chance in a fair fight. That's why Indy had no intention of fighting fairly.

He stood before the German and bravely raised his own fists, but then let his gaze drift from his opponent's eyes to something on the ground between them. In fact, Indy wasn't looking at anything in particular, he was just trying to distract the big man. It seemed like a good idea at the time, and as the German followed Indy's gaze, Indy thought it might even work.

While the German was distracted, Indy violated every rule of sportsmanship by kicking his opponent below the belt. Although such a kick would have leveled any ordinary man, the German merely hunched his shoulders at the impact, and fixed Indy with a slightly annoyed look as he waited for Indy to make his next move. With some alarm, Indy thought, *I may as well have kicked a redwood!*

Indy followed with his best punch, but the German ducked it and the punch sailed past him. The German responded with a left jab that caught Indy square on the chin and mouth, knocking him off his feet. Indy landed hard on the seat of his pants, and a moment later, he tasted blood. The German's jab had cut his lower lip.

The German wasn't done with him. The big man urged Indy to get up, and seemed to become infuriated when Indy continued to sit on the ground with a dazed expression on his face. But when the German bent over and grabbed Indy to haul him up to his feet, he suddenly howled in pain as Indy sank his teeth into the man's bare forearm.

The German tossed Indy aside, sending him under the back of the plane. Indy fell against the plane's landing gear, but as the German reached for him, he crouched and ran under the wing, emerging just below the open cockpit. He had assumed that the pilot had remained in his cockpit, but did not expect the pilot to be standing up on his seat with a pistol in his hand. Indy ducked back under the plane as the pilot turned and fired at him. The bullet missed and slammed into the ground.

Unfortunately, the burly German had followed Indy under the plane, and Indy ran straight into the man's fist. The punch sent Indy spinning out from below the Flying Wing, leaving him exposed to the armed pilot. The German moved after him and launched another punch that sent Indy to the ground.

Seeing Indy materialize from beneath the plane, the pilot aimed his pistol at Indy. But before the pilot could fire, the bare-chested German stepped up beside Indy's prone form, blocking the pilot's shot. The pilot raised his pistol's barrel away from his fellow German.

Still on the ground, Indy grabbed a fistful of sand and flung it up into his opponent's face. The German shouted with rage as the sand met his eyes, and then Indy was on his feet again.

As Indy moved away from the big man, the watchful pilot took aim at Indy again. The pilot was about to fire when something struck him from behind and he collapsed into the cockpit. Indy glanced up to see Marion standing on the plane, just behind the cockpit, holding the wedge-shaped blocks that she had removed from the plane's tire. As evidenced by the unconscious pilot, Marion had found a new use for the blocks.

Suddenly, the pilot's body slumped forward onto the controls and throttle. The engines roared louder, revving up, and the plane began to move, rotating around its one still-blocked set of tires. The bare-chested German ignored the roaring engines and punched Indy in the stomach.

Hoping to pull the pilot off the throttle, Marion quickly jumped down into the cockpit. But as she moved, her shoulder bumped into the cockpit's raised canopy, and the canopy slammed down, sealing her inside.

Marion tugged at the pilot's shoulders, but she couldn't budge him. Staring through the canopy's forward window, she saw Indy and the big German, still fighting. She shouted, "Indy!"

The German's fist sank into Indy's stomach again, this time with such force that it lifted Indy off the ground. Gasping for air, Indy wasn't sure how much more he could take. So far, there hadn't been one moment during their fight that the German wasn't practically on top of him, forcing Indy to defend himself with his hands and preventing him from reaching for his whip or gun.

As the plane rotated on the ground, Marion saw a German troop truck drive onto the airfield. Six soldiers rode in the back of the open truck, and when they saw the two men fighting beside the Flying Wing, they reached for their rifles.

Inside the Flying Wing, a small passage led from the cockpit to the glass-domed tail gun. Marion scrambled through the passage, seized the grips on the maneuverable double-barreled machine gun, and took aim at the incoming truck. The soldiers had already begun firing when Marion squeezed the machine gun's triggers. Marion winced at the staccato bursts of gunfire and at the sight of her bullets riddling the truck along with the men on it.

She didn't get them all. One soldier jumped away from the ravaged truck and began firing his own machine gun in Marion's direction as he ran for cover. As the Flying Wing continued its slow rotation on the airfield, Marion felt a mild bump as the starboard wingtip struck the gasoline tanker and knocked a hole in its side. But she kept her attention on the elusive soldier, shooting him down just a moment before he would have moved out of range, and failed to notice the gasoline that was spilling out from the ruptured tanker.

Although Indy heard all the gunfire, he didn't see the wingtip tear through the tanker because the big German was still using him as a punching bag. As Indy went sprawling under the rotating plane, he saw the plane's tires moving toward him and had to roll away fast to avoid getting crushed. As he rolled, his revolver accidentally slid out of its holster and onto the ground. Indy saw the fallen gun and tried to reach for it, but the big German moved in close to the landing gear and Indy instinctively backed away. He nearly stumbled over the still-unconscious mechanic.

Marion thought she had shot all of the soldiers from the truck, but when she spotted another one making a run for it, she swiveled the tail gun after him. The stream of bullets cut down the soldier, but also hit a stack of barrels that were filled with gasoline. As the soldier fell, the barrels exploded with a colossal *boom!* and sent a bright yellow and orange plume of fire into the sky.

The explosion was loud enough to awaken Colonel Dietrich, who had dozed off in his chair outside the command tent. Belloq heard the noise, too, and came running out of the tent to stand beside Dietrich. Both men watched a thick cloud of black smoke rise up from behind a nearby hill, and realized the explosion had come from the airfield.

As Dietrich gaped and rose from his chair, Belloq looked to the crated Ark, which still rested on the ground near Dietrich. Glaring at the soldiers who stood near the crate, Belloq shouted, "Stay with the Ark! Stay with the Ark!"

Dietrich began shouting orders to his men, directing them to the airfield.

Marion was still seated in the domed turret at the Flying Wing's aft when she saw Indy emerge from below the rotating plane and unintentionally move toward one of the spinning propellers. She shouted, "Look out!"

Indy saw the propeller just in time and turned around

fast, crouching below the plane as he ran past the landing gear to avoid the big German who pursued him. When Indy came out from under the plane, he looked past the cockpit to see the gas barrels that Marion had shot, which were now blazing away. Then he saw the gas spilling out of the ruptured tanker. The gas was spreading rapidly, flowing across the ground beneath the plane and toward the blazing barrels. As the gas swept under the Flying Wing, the smell was so noxious that it revived the fallen mechanic, who was fortunate to have escaped the path of the plane's tires. With the front of his clothes suddenly soaked in gas, the mechanic began to push himself up, and then ran for safety.

Marion saw the gas and the fire, too. She gasped, "Oh, no!"

"Marion!" Indy muttered.

"In here!" Marion yelled, the enclosed turret muffling her cry. "Up here!"

Moving just below the cockpit, Indy pulled himself up onto the front of the plane and climbed up onto it. As he scrambled over the wing toward the aft, Marion yelled again from inside the turret, "Indy, come on!"

"Hold on!" he shouted back.

"Move up!" she cried as he bent down beside the turret and tried to open it. Watching the gas spread closer to the barrels, Marion cried, "It's gonna blow up!"

Indy was gripping the top of the turret and trying to tug it open when he saw the big German climbing up onto the wing. As the German lunged at him, Indy rolled away from the turret and got up onto his feet. Standing on the wing, he threw his right fist at the German, but the German caught the punch and delivered his own to Indy's jaw. Indy collapsed, slid off the wing, and landed hard on the gas-drenched ground.

"It's stuck!" Marion cried as she fumbled with the turret's opening mechanism. "Indy! I can't push it off!"

Ignoring Marion, the German jumped down after Indy, who remained crumpled beside the plane. The German lifted Indy to his feet, held him at arm's length, and then belted him in the face. Indy reeled but kept his balance, then took another punch to the jaw. The German hit him again, and again.

The gas inched closer to the burning barrels. As bad as Indy hurt, he knew he was Marion's only chance to get out of the Flying Wing. He locked his gaze on the German's nose and threw his right fist into it with everything he had.

There was an ugly crunch as blood suddenly spurted from the German's broken nose, and then Indy launched his left fist at the same target. Indy wasn't aiming at the man's nose so much as he was aiming through it. The German wobbled only slightly on his feet as Indy delivered two more roundhouse punches to his head.

But then the German struck back, slamming his meaty fist into Indy's jaw. Indy saw stars as he toppled to the ground. Rolling onto his side, he looked up at the German, who was now urging him to get up and finish the fight.

The German's eyes were filled with rage, and he kept them fixed on Indy as he pumped the air with his fists. His rage only grew when his opponent looked up at him from the ground and smiled broadly.

Indy kept smiling as he shifted his weight slightly, angling his body so that the German would make another step toward him. Although Indy appeared to be keeping his eyes on the German's face, he was also monitoring the slow rotation of the plane, and the whirring propeller that was closing in behind the big man who stood over him.

Knowing what was about to happen, Indy suddenly flattened himself to the ground and shielded his head with his arms. At first, the big German thought Indy was just trying to distract him again, but then he felt a rush of air against his back. He turned and shouted once before the propeller whipped through him.

Scrambling away from the carnage, Indy found his revolver, snatched it up, and jumped back onto the plane. He looked to the blood-spattered gun turret, saw that it was empty, and thought for a moment that Marion had gotten out. But then, remembering how Marion had moved from the cockpit to the turret, he glanced to the cockpit and saw Marion there, trying her hand at the locking mechanism again.

"It's stuck!" Marion cried.

Carrying his gun in one hand as he ran across the top of the Flying Wing, Indy lowered himself beside the cockpit. He pointed to a crank at the inner edge of the sealed canopy and shouted, "Turn it! Turn it!"

"It's stuck!" Marion repeated.

Pointing to the other end of the crank, he said, "Turn it there!" Before Marion could try, he slapped the canopy window with his hand and snapped, "Never mind! Get back! Get back!"

A split second after Marion threw her body against the far side of the cockpit, Indy fired two bullets directly into the canopy's lock. The lock shattered and Indy threw the canopy open. Just as he reached down to grab Marion's arm and tug her out of the cockpit, the spilled gasoline reached the burning barrels and ignited.

A wave of flame traveled across the airfield as Indy and Marion leaped down from the plane and ran for their lives. They had barely cleared the airfield and were still running side by side when the tanker truck exploded into flames. Barely three seconds later, another explosion rocked the Flying Wing and launched burning debris in all directions.

The debris was still falling when Indy and Marion came to a stop behind a dune. They paused for only a moment to catch their breath. Indy knew the Germans would be swarming all over the airfield within minutes, maybe even sooner.

They had to go back to the camp and find Sallah, and they had to do it fast.

y the time the German soldiers and Arab laborers arrived at the airfield, they found nearly every structure and vehicle reduced to smoldering ruins. Smoke still poured from the wreckage of the Flying Wing, and the tanker was nothing but a skeletal frame of black, twisted metal.

"Get the Ark away from this place immediately!" Colonel Dietrich snapped at Gobler as they walked with Belloq past the debris. "Have it put on the truck. We'll fly it out of Cairo." As the three men came to a stop a short distance from the airfield's watchtower, Dietrich glared at his first officer to add, "And Gobler, I want plenty of protection."

Just then, the fires reached some gas barrels that had been carelessly placed near the base of the watchtower. The three men flinched as the barrels exploded and the watchtower burst into flames.

Recovering quickly, Dietrich and Gobler stormed off to direct the soldiers and laborers. Belloq glanced at the burning watchtower, and then surveyed the ruins of everything around him. He didn't have to wonder who was the cause of so much destruction. He *knew*.

"Jones," Belloq muttered harshly.

A few minutes after Dietrich had barked his orders to Gobler, Sallah left the main compound and ran to the airfield. Many laborers had gathered around the ruins of the Flying Wing, and Sallah wanted to see for himself what had happened. But as he ran past a small canvas tent, he was distracted when somebody whistled at him.

Stopping in his tracks, Sallah peered into the tent's dark, triangular opening. He could barely believe his eyes when he saw that Indy and Marion were inside. "Holy smoke, my friends," he said as he ducked to enter the tent and grip Indy's hand while Marion stood in the shadows behind Indy. "I — I'm so pleased you're not dead!"

Then Sallah hunkered down beside Indy and continued, "Indy, Indy, we have no time. If you still want the Ark, it is being loaded onto a truck for Cairo."

"Truck?" Indy said. "What truck?"

Staying out of sight of the soldiers, Indy and Marion stuck close to Sallah as he led them from the tent to a

dune that overlooked the compound. When they reached
the top of the dune, they kept their heads low and looked
to the crated Ark outside the Command Tent, which was
surrounded by watchful laborers and soldiers. Two long
wooden poles had been secured lengthwise to opposite
sides of the crate, and the poles' ends served as handgrips
to the four soldiers who picked it up and carried it to the
back of a canvas-topped Mercedes troop truck that was
parked behind a black open-topped convertible sedan.

The truck's metal tailgate was lowered, and there was
an unexpected outcry from the laborers as they saw the
soldiers load the Ark onto the truck. From his vantage
point, Indy got the impression that the laborers were suddenly eager to prevent the Germans from taking the Ark.
A moment after the laborers began shouting and moving
toward the truck, a soldier responded by sending a rapid
burst of gunfire into the air. Discouraged by the warning
shots, the laborers immediately dropped to their knees or
sat on the ground, defeated.

As seven soldiers climbed into the back of the troop
truck and raised the tailgate, Belloq and Dietrich walked
past the truck and got into the back of the convertible.
Turning his head back to face the truck's driver, Belloq
waved his arm forward and shouted, "Let's go!" A moment
later, Toht's black-clad figure slipped into the front passenger seat beside the uniformed driver.

Behind the truck, Gobler strapped on his driving goggles and climbed behind the wheel of a light-armored military car that carried two other men and a turret-mounted machine gun. Behind Gobler's car, a motorcycle with an armed sidecar completed the German convoy.

As the drivers started their vehicles and began to pull away from the compound, Indy glanced at Sallah and Marion and said, "Get back to Cairo. Get us some transport to England — boat, plane, anything. Meet me at Omar's. Be ready for me. I'm going after that truck."

"How?" Sallah asked.

"I don't know," Indy said as he got up to leave. "I'm making this up as I go."

After slipping away from Marion and Sallah, it took Indy less than a minute to find his transport: a magnificent white Arabian stallion that was standing in the shade under a tent. The stallion already had a blanket on its back and leather reins at the ready. Indy climbed on and launched the horse out of the tent. Two Arabs had been sitting on the ground outside, and they jumped up and shouted at Indy as the stallion carried him away.

The stallion was a very different creature than the type of horse that Indy had learned to ride when he was a boy. So fast and powerful, it seemed less like an animal than a force of nature. Indy held tight to the reins as he guided the stallion across the compound, heading for the road that led past the Command Tent. Beside the large tent, about two-dozen astonished soldiers and the many seated laborers saw Indy's approach. Before the soldiers could even think of taking aim at Indy, their view was blocked by the laborers, who jumped to their feet and shouted as the mounted figure flew past them.

Leaving the compound behind, Indy avoided the dirt road the convoy had taken and went cross-country. He guided the stallion up a steep, rocky hill that brought him to the top of a long ridge. From this point, he had a wide view of the area, allowing him to see not only the rising dust that indicated the convoy's wake but a shortcut that would allow him to catch up with the Germans.

Indy pressed his heels into the horse's sides, and the horse bolted forward along a ridge that traveled parallel to the road. When he looked down to his left, he could see the convoy itself.

Reaching a curve, Indy brought the stallion to a halt. He could see that it was a steep descent to an area where the road below veered off to the left, but he had to trust that his mount could make it. Glancing down at the moving vehicles, Indy's mind raced. He knew that if his timing was right, the horse would carry him down to the road and right behind the canvas-topped truck. Not allowing himself to think what would happen if his timing was off, Indy tightened his grip on the reins and sent the horse down.

Sand and small stones shifted under the stallion's hooves as it managed a skidding run down the slope, but the brave animal followed Indy's commands without fail. When they reached the area where the road curved, the horse ran onto the road directly behind the truck, just as Indy had planned.

The soldiers in the truck shouted in surprise. Their shouts were loud enough that the passengers in the lead vehicle, the convertible, heard them over the noise of the rumbling convoy. From the convertible's rear seat, Belloq looked back over his shoulder.

Because of the way the road twisted through the rocky terrain, Belloq couldn't see anything unusual at first glance, but a moment later Indy and his stallion came into view, trailing alongside the truck. At the sight of his nemesis, Belloq felt a combination of rage and panic.

Directly behind Indy and his stallion, in the military car driven by Gobler, the soldier who manned the gun turret swung his weapon in Indy's direction and opened fire, launching bullets over Gobler's head. The bullets missed Indy, but several pinged off the truck, nearly hitting the soldiers and the crate in the truck's back. The outraged soldiers yelled at the gunner to stop shooting.

The gunner held his fire, allowing Indy to maneuver the galloping stallion up along the truck's right side. When he was close enough to the truck, he leaned out, grabbed at the canvas top, and pulled himself off of the horse's back and onto the side of the truck. The horse whinnied, then began to slow its pace as the truck pulled away with Indy still on it.

As the military car and motorcycle passed the abandoned stallion, Indy quickly shifted his body forward along the truck's side until he stood on the running board that ran below the front passenger door. A soldier sat beside the driver in the truck's front compartment, which was backed by a sheet of solid metal that lacked a rear window. Although the two men had heard the shouts and shots from behind and seen Belloq, Dietrich, and Toht turn their heads in the convertible in front of them, they had neglected to glance at their own rear-view mirrors, and both were unaware that a man had just jumped onto their truck.

In a fluid motion, Indy threw the truck's door open, grabbed the soldier on the passenger side of the long seat, and yanked him out of the truck. The soldier screamed as he tumbled out of the truck and rolled to the side of the road. Then Indy launched himself into the truck and onto the driver. The driver gasped as Indy slammed into him.

Indy wrapped his left arm around the driver's neck as he grabbed at the steering wheel. Wrestling for control of the truck, Indy let his right hand fly from the wheel to the driver's face. The driver snarled as he tried to keep his own grip on the wheel and shove Indy off of him.

Indy elbowed the gearshift as he kicked at the driver's feet and stomped on the brake pedal. He braced himself as the truck abruptly decelerated and let gravity carry the driver's forehead into the dashboard. A moment later, Gobler's car slammed into the back of the truck.

Indy hit the accelerator and the truck lurched forward, causing the crated Ark to slide suddenly toward the back of the truck and into one of the soldiers. The soldier screamed as the crate smashed into his legs and launched him clear over the tailgate. Gobler's car was still directly behind the truck. The falling soldier's head struck and shattered the car's windshield as his body landed hard on the hood.

Indy and the truck driver continued their battle for the wheel as they followed the convertible toward a small village. The convertible's driver was so distracted by the swerving truck behind him that he accidentally steered toward a two-story tall building that was being worked upon by Arab laborers who stood on rickety wooden ladders and scaffolding. When Toht saw that they were headed straight for the construction site, he shouted at the driver, who swerved to stay on the road.

Unfortunately, when Indy and the truck driver saw the construction site, they were less than agreeable about which way to turn. Indy winced as they plowed straight into the scaffolding and sent the laborers leaping to safety. One laborer landed on the truck's hood and gaped for a moment at Indy and the driver through the windshield before he leaped from the truck and rolled to the ground.

Both Indy and the driver were amazed that they had made it past the building without killing anyone. Indy exhaled with relief and grinned at the driver. Despite their situation and the that fact that they were enemies, the driver grinned back. The first to remember their present predicament, Indy's face went grim and he belted the driver in the jaw.

Indy threw the driver's door open and shoved him out of the truck, letting him fall down a steep hillside. Then Indy pulled the door shut and focused on the black convertible in front of him. He could see Belloq in the back of the car. Belloq looked scared, and Indy couldn't help but feel good about that.

Indy accelerated and rammed the convertible, forcing it off the road. Alongside the road, there was a crude aqueduct, a scrap metal conduit that was elevated by long wooden poles to transport water across the village. The convertible swerved around and under the aqueduct. Indy was keeping his eyes on the convertible, but when it swung out from below the viaduct and shot out at a sharp angle across the road in front of him, he suddenly saw that both the road and the viaduct curved suddenly up ahead.

Indy twisted the steering wheel hard to the side but collided with the wooden poles that supported the viaduct. As the metal conduit broke away and clattered against the truck, it sent water splashing against the windshield.

Regaining control of the truck, Indy followed the convertible away from the village. The road became a series of twisting turns that traveled through a forest of palm trees. Indy glanced to the truck's side-view mirrors to see the car and motorcycle that followed. They were gaining on him.

While the soldiers in the back of the truck watched nervously, Gobler maneuvered his car up along the right side of the truck. At the gun turret behind Gobler, the gunner angled his weapon toward the front of the truck, waiting for the moment he would have a clear shot at Indy.

Indy saw the car coming, and gave the wheel a quick jerk to the right that forced the car off the road. Gobler gnashed his teeth as he steered his car between the trees and over bone-jarring bumps, but managed to get the car back onto the road, a short distance behind the motorcycle.

Thinking the car was no longer a concern, Indy grinned. The grin vanished when he saw the motorcycle and the machine gunner in its sidecar appear in his side-view mirror. But when the motorcycle drew up along the right side of the truck, Indy gave the wheel a jerk to repeat the maneuver that had sent Gobler's off the road. The truck smacked against the sidecar, and the motorcycle spun out and rolled into a deep puddle beside the road. The grin returned to Indy's face.

The motorcyclist and gunner were bruised but otherwise uninjured. As they struggled to their feet beside their ruined vehicle, Gobler's car raced past them.

The forest yielded to a more open, rocky area, and the black convertible raced onward. Indy stayed right behind it, watching Belloq and the outraged Nazis squirm in their seats. Then he saw Gobler's car reappear in his side-view mirror. Annoyed, Indy thought, *Don't these guys know when to quit?*

The car drew up on the left side of the truck. The machine gunner aimed at Indy and began firing. Ignoring the bullets that pinged off the truck's hood, Indy kept his eye on his side-view mirror, waited for the right moment, and then jerked the wheel to the side yet again.

The truck collided against the car, only this time, there weren't any trees to drive into, or anything else for that matter, for the road had brought the vehicles near the edge of a high cliff. Gobler and the two other men screamed as the car plunged from the cliff, carrying them to their deaths.

Indy kept driving after the convertible. As tempted as he was to deal with Belloq and his companions in some harsh fashion, he had not forgotten that his first priority was to deliver the Ark to Sallah in Cairo. He also knew it was only a matter of time before the soldiers in the back of the truck tried something foolish.

He didn't have to wait long.

*I*n the troop compartment behind Indy, the five remaining German soldiers looked at each other anxiously. They could hardly believe that a lone man had managed to overtake their truck and dispose of both Gobler's car and the motorcycle escort. But the soldiers' commanding officer, a tough-looking sergeant, wasn't about to let the American get away with it. Snapping off orders, he instructed four of his men to climb out over the tailgate and make their way up to the front of the truck.

The truck followed the black convertible around a bend, and Indy saw that they were heading through another palm-tree forest. Glancing at his side-view mirrors, Indy saw two soldiers had climbed out onto the left side of the truck, and another two were on the right. Each soldier was hugging the truck's canvas top, clinging to the metal frame below the canvas with one hand as their other hands held their pistols at the ready.

Indy threw the wheel hard to the left. The soldiers tightened their grips on the canvas top as the truck swerved along the edge of the tree-lined road. The overhanging branches and thick leaves of the palm trees whipped at the two soldiers on the left side of the truck, and they screamed as they were knocked from the moving vehicle.

Then Indy swerved to the right, trying to shake off the other two soldiers. They held tight only slightly longer than their left-side comrades, but the combination of Indy's driving and the whipping palm trees was too much for them, too. When Indy heard their cries as they fell from the truck, he smiled with satisfaction.

Indy didn't know that one of the falling soldiers had torn off a large section of canvas from the right side of the truck. The hole in the canvas allowed one of the remaining soldiers to slip out to the side quickly and move up beside the passenger door before Indy could see him coming. Like his predecessors, the soldier clutched a pistol. He landed on the running board and shoved his pistol through the open passenger window.

Indy saw the soldier out of the corner of his eye and moved fast, twisting his body to launch a kick at the passenger door. He wasn't quite fast enough. The soldier fired his pistol and there was a spray of blood as the bullet tore through Indy's leather jacket and hit his shoulder. Indy winced at the sudden pain in his arm, but he still managed a powerful kick that knocked the door open, causing the soldier to swing out and away from the truck.

Gripping the wheel with his left hand, Indy reached for his wounded shoulder with his right. His shoulder hurt like blazes, but he was pretty sure it was just a flesh wound.

The passenger door swung back toward the truck, carrying the soldier with it. The soldier still clutched his pistol, but was using both arms to hang onto the door.

Holding tight to the wheel, Indy shifted his body again to deliver a harder kick to the door and sent the soldier swinging out again. The door's upper hinge snapped off and the entire door bent down and away from the truck.

The soldier clung desperately to the door as his dangling legs dragged against the dirt road. When he glanced up, he saw his sergeant lean out through the hole in the canvas to look at him with a helpless expression.

Indy's vision blurred for a moment, and he blinked his eyes, trying to stay focused on the convertible in front of him. Glancing to his right, he saw the soldier pulling himself back up onto the damaged door. The soldier had his gun out again.

Indy kicked the door for all he was worth. The door bent further out from the truck, and the soldier wailed as he was dragged along the road. Then the door snapped off.

From the troop compartment, the German sergeant

saw his last man tumble away with the broken door. Determined to succeed where his men had failed, the sergeant stepped over the tailgate and hauled himself up onto the top of the truck. He kept his body low as he gripped the canvas covering, working his way up toward the front of the truck. Directly above the driver's compartment, there was a tubular metal rack for holding cargo. The sergeant grabbed hold of the bar, and then swung his lower body down through the open window of the driver's door and straight into Indy.

Indy grunted in pain as the sergeant's boots slammed into his injured shoulder and shoved him across the long seat, nearly sending him out through the doorless passenger side. As the sergeant slipped down behind the truck's controls and seized the wheel, he saw Indy clutching at his wounded shoulder in pain. Bracing his knee against the wheel to keep the truck on the road, the sergeant grabbed Indy's arm and began punching his shoulder. Then he seized Indy by the back of his leather jacket and shoved him headfirst into the windshield.

Indy's hat was hardly a protective helmet, but it absorbed some of the impact as he smashed through the windshield and hurtled onto the hood of the moving truck. He bounced on the hot, hard metal and as he slid over the front of the hood, he grabbed at the hood ornament, a circular ring of steel with an inner lambda, the Mercedes logo. The ornament bent and snapped, and Indy fell onto the cargo rack that was set above the bumper in front of the truck's grill.

In the convertible, Dietrich, Belloq, and Toht saw Indy's fall, and they smiled with morbid expectation.

Facing into the truck, Indy clutched desperately at the vertical metal bars on the cargo rack. They bent under his weight, and he threw himself to his right so his stomach landed against the fender of the truck's right front tire. Indy wrapped his arm around the lamp atop the fender and felt the heels of his boots hit and drag against the road. His legs were splayed on either side of the tire. If he lost his grip, he would be flattened.

The sergeant saw the top of Indy's hat above the fender and considered stopping the truck so he could kill the man with his bare hands, but then he noticed Dietrich waving to him from the convertible. Dietrich was gesturing for the sergeant to keep driving, and bring the truck straight up against the convertible's rear bumper. Imagining Indy being crushed between the two vehicles, the sergeant grinned. Then he shifted gears, stomped on the accelerator, and raced toward the convertible.

Realizing what the driver was attempting, Indy shifted his body back in front of the grill, and then lowered himself down from the cargo rack, and past the bumper so that his legs stretched out and dragged under the truck.

The rocky ground hammered against the back of his leather jacket as he faced the bottom of the truck and struggled to keep his legs straight. While the truck continued to speed after the convertible, Indy reached up to find a new grip on the undercarriage.

Seeing Indy's action, Dietrich and Belloq waved again at the sergeant, motioning for him to maintain speed by keeping his distance from the convertible.

Indy ignored the pounding that his back was taking and quickly moved hand over hand to reach the truck's rear axle. He nearly lost his grip when he snagged his whip around the axle, but recovered, moving both hands onto the whip. Still clinging to the secured whip's handle, he slid out from under the rear bumper and let out a pained groan as the whip went taut and dragged him after the truck.

Indy rolled onto his stomach and began pulling himself up along the extended whip. He could hardly see what he was doing because of all the sand and dust, but he kept his hat on and stayed focused on the rear bumper as he hauled himself closer to the truck.

When he reached the bumper, Indy pulled his battered body up onto the back of the truck, leaving the whip to trail like an angry snake behind the vehicle. Every movement hurt, but he continued to block out the pain as he scrambled over the tailgate and into the troop compartment. The truck hadn't slowed, and neither did Indy. Moving past the crate that held the Ark of the Covenant, he climbed through the torn canvas and out onto the truck's right side.

Belloq sighted Indy and pointed to the side of the truck as he shouted, "He's there!"

The sergeant looked to his right at the same moment that Indy swung his legs through the space formerly occupied by the passenger door and into the driver's compartment. Indy's boots connected with the stunned sergeant's face, and then Indy shoved the man aside and leaped over him to land behind the wheel. The sergeant looked angry and dazed as Indy grabbed the back of the man's neck. Furious at the way the sergeant had nearly killed him, Indy rammed the sergeant's head into the dashboard before belting him in the jaw. Indy could have shoved the sergeant out through the side of the truck, but in his rage, he gave the man a taste of his own medicine by seizing him with both hands and throwing him out onto the hood.

The sergeant tumbled down past the grille and caught hold of the cargo rack. The bars on the rack bent under his weight, and the sergeant screamed as he fell away and the truck's tires barreled over him.

Indy gnashed his teeth. His entire body felt like a mass of exposed nerves, but he was fueled by his fury at Belloq and the soldiers, as well as by his determination to get the

Ark out of Cairo. He stomped on the accelerator and aimed for the black convertible.

The road now stretched past rocky dunes. The convertible's driver tried to veer away from the approaching truck, but Indy swerved hard to the side and forced the convertible off the road. As Belloq's car rolled to a dusty stop, Belloq stood up in the backseat and saw the truck heading off. Turning his gaze to the convertible's driver, he shouted, "Idiot! Idiot!"

The rattled driver put the convertible in reverse and returned to the road. Less than a minute later, Belloq and the Germans were following the truck as it headed to Cairo. But Indy had a good lead on them, and he wasn't about to stop until he reached his destination.

Indy steered the battle-damaged truck through the narrow streets of Cairo until he arrived at Omar's Square, the cul-de-sac where he had arranged his rendezvous with Sallah. There were lots of people in the square, and all of them looked up with excitement as the truck swept past them and headed for the wide-open doors of Omar's Garage. Thanks to Sallah, they were expecting Indy.

Indy guided the truck straight into the garage's shadowy interior, and the moment he brought the truck to a stop, the men outside closed the garage doors, dropped an awning over the doorway, and wheeled a large fruit cart in front of the building.

Mere seconds after Indy had delivered the truck into the garage, the black convertible raced into the square. Because the square was a terminus without any outlets, the driver steered the car into a tight circle before he brought it to a stop. Belloq stood up in the back of the car and surveyed the square. As far as he could see, there were only merchants around, and no sign of Indy.

One young merchant stepped up to the back of the convertible and held out some melons to Dietrich, who had remained seated. He sneered as he snatched a melon from the merchant and hurled it into the road. Fuming and apparently defeated, Belloq sat down beside Dietrich. The convertible took off.

After the black car had left the square, the crowd cheered. They didn't know why Sallah had asked them to conceal Indy and the truck from the Germans, but they had been happy to help Sallah.

Night had fallen and a thick mist had risen over the waterfront when Marion and a very weary Indy walked onto the pier where an old tramp steamer, the *Bantu Wind*, was docked. Indy had his arm wrapped around Marion's shoulder not only out of affection but because he was so sore that he could barely stand, let alone walk.

Sallah walked up to them and grasped Indy's hand. Sallah said, "Everything at last has been arranged."

"The Ark?" Indy said.

"Is on board," Sallah answered. "Nothing is lacking now that you're here." Seeing how stiffly Indy was walking, Sallah added, "Or what is left of you."

A gangplank extended down from the steamer to the pier. Indy glanced at the shifty-looking crew of the *Bantu Wind*, then faced Sallah and asked, "You trust these guys?"

"Yes," Sallah said. He looked to his right to see a lean man standing a short distance away. The man's dark skin contrasted sharply with his white sweater and captain's hat. The man looked away from Sallah as he lit a cigar. Sallah said, "Mr. Katanga."

Simon Katanga was the captain of the *Bantu Wind*. After lighting his cigar, he spat onto the pier before he turned and walked over beside Sallah. Sallah gestured to Indy and Marion, and said, "Mr. Katanga, these are my friends. They are my family. I will hear of it if they are not treated well."

Katanga smiled. "My cabin is theirs," he said graciously. "Mr. Jones, I've heard a lot about you, sir." Surveying Indy's unshaven face and rumpled clothes, he added, "Your appearance is exactly the way I imagined." Katanga glanced at Sallah and both men burst into laughter. Katanga was still chuckling as he headed for the gangplank.

Stepping away from Marion, Indy shuffled over toward Sallah, extended his right hand, and said, "Good-bye."

Ignoring Indy's hand, Sallah threw his arms around Indy and embraced him in a bear hug. Indy grimaced in pain as Sallah said, "Look out for each other. I am already missing you."

Indy pulled gently away from Sallah. Managing a smile, he said, "You're my good friend."

Then Marion stepped up to Sallah and took his hands in hers. "Sallah," she said, and then stood up on her toes to kiss his left cheek. "That is for Fayah . . ." she said, and then she kissed his right cheek and said, "that is for your children, and this is for you." She kissed his mouth, then looked up into his eyes and said, "Thank you."

Sallah was so moved by Marion's words and gesture that he was initially speechless as she and Indy headed for the gangplank, where Katanga stood waiting for them. But a moment later, Sallah burst into song: "*A British tar is a soaring soul, as free as a mountain bird. His energetic fist should be ready to . . . a dictator . . .*"

The other men on the pier smiled and laughed as Sallah, still singing, headed for home.

Indy and Marion boarded the steamer. Indy took

comfort in knowing that he had finally recovered the Ark, and that they would soon be on their way to meet his contacts in England. He thought that his worst troubles were behind him.

Unfortunately, he was wrong.

The *Bantu Wind* had left Cairo and was on open water under a moonlit sky. Indy was still wearing his hat and dirty clothes as he stretched out on the bunk in Captain Katanga's cabin. He could see the moonlight through the venetian blinds that covered the two portholes that were set above the bunk. Most of the cabin's furniture was built-in, but one eccentricity was a cheval glass, a long mirror mounted on swivels in a frame, which stood near the bed. This particular cheval glass had a mirror on each side of the frame, but Indy didn't need to gaze into either to know he looked awful. He was too tired and worn out to care.

The cabin's door opened and Marion walked in. She had a red blanket wrapped around her upper body and was carrying two metal bowls and some neatly folded white towels.

Indy carefully raised his aching body to sit on the edge of the bunk. Looking at Marion, he said, "Where did you go?"

"I'm cleaning up," Marion said as she placed the towels and bowls on a wooden table beside the bunk. One of the bowls was filled with water, and the other held washcloths and some small bottles of medicine. She shrugged off the blanket and tossed it onto the bunk beside Indy, revealing that she was wearing a white satin nightgown.

Eyeing the nightgown, Indy said, "Where'd you get *that*?"

"From him."

"Who him?"

"Katanga," Marion said as she soaked a washcloth in water. "I got a feeling I'm not the first woman ever to travel with these pirates."

"It's lovely," Indy muttered.

"Yeah?" Marion said, surprised by Indy's compliment.

"Yeah." Indy winced as he tried to sit up straight.

"Really?" Marion said as she placed the washcloths in a bowl and stepped over to the cheval glass to inspect her reflection in the mirror opposite Indy.

"Yeah," Indy said again, but with more conviction, as he shrugged out of his jacket. He leaned forward and peered into the mirror on his side of the cheval glass. There was what looked like a slight abrasion on his forehead, just above his left eyebrow. Indy touched the abrasion with the tip of his finger. Despite appearances, it stung fiercely. Indy winced yet again.

Marion couldn't see her reflection clearly because the mirror on her side of the cheval glass was marred by long smudges. She tried wiping a smudge away with her hand, but that only made the smudge worse. Hoping to get a clearer look, and unaware that Indy was leaning close to the glass on the other side, she pushed down on the top of the frame to flip the glass. The action caused the frame's base to swing up and slam hard into the bottom of Indy's chin.

Indy let out a muffled howl.

Peering around the glass to see Indy stroking his injured chin, Marion said, "What'd you say?"

Indy ignored the question and began taking off his shirt. This proved to be something of a challenge. His muscles were so knotted and his fingers were so numb that he couldn't tell what was going on behind his back as he tried to shrug the shirt down past his elbows. Marion left the cheval glass and sat down beside Indy.

"Wait . . ." Indy said as he felt Marion's fingers gently tugging off his shirt. "I don't need any help."

"You know you do," Marion said.

Indy saw his shirtless reflection in the smudged mirror that now faced him. A strip of white cloth was wrapped around his upper left arm where the bullet had grazed him. Following his pained gaze, Marion said, "You're not the man I knew ten years ago."

"It's not the years, honey, it's the mileage."

Indy shifted his weight and tried to lie down. He still had his hat, pants, and boots on. Seeing that he was having trouble raising his legs up onto the bunk, Marion reached down and lifted his ankles. She said, "You are —"

"Please," Indy interrupted as he lowered his head back against a pillow. "I don't need a nurse. I just want to sleep."

"Don't be such a baby," Marion said. She began cleaning Indy's chest with a damp towel.

"Marion, leave me alone," Indy said as he pushed her hand away.

"What is this here?" she said, touching a bruise on his abdomen.

"Go away," Indy said, and then quickly added, "Yes, it hurts."

Marion moved the damp towel up to Indy's neck. Indy said, "Ow!"

"Well, gosh, Indy," Marion said, flustered, "where *doesn't* it hurt?"

Scowling, Indy pointed to his left elbow and said, "Here."

Unexpectedly, Marion leaned forward and kissed his elbow.

Indy pointed to his forehead, above his right eyebrow. He said, "Here."

Marion removed Indy's hat and tossed it behind her so it landed on the red blanket at the foot of the bunk. Then she leaned down and kissed Indy's forehead.

Marion pulled away. Indy thought for a moment, then reached up to rub the top of his right eyelid. Speaking softly, he said, "This isn't too bad."

Marion kissed his eyelid.

Indy slowly dragged his finger up to the left side of his mouth. As if he weren't entirely certain, he said, "Here?"

Marion kissed Indy's mouth, careful not to press too hard against the split in his lower lip. Indy's head eased back onto the pillow.

Raising herself to look at Indy's face, Marion said, "Jones..."

Indy's eyes were closed.

"Jones?!"

Indy was asleep.

Although the crated Ark had been secured in the hold of the *Bantu Wind*, the hold's locked doors did not prevent a visit from some unwelcome passengers: a group of rats that had snuck on board while the steamer had been docked in Cairo.

As the rats scampered past the crate, they became

suddenly agitated. They could sense that the crate radiated some kind of danger, something so powerful that it made their whiskers tremble.

The painted swastika on the side of the crate began to burn, sending out blue flames and smoke. A moment later, the flames went out, leaving a charred, black area where the swastika had been.

The nervous rats squeaked and scurried away.

Daylight was sifting through the venetian blinds in the captain's cabin when Marion awakened with a start. It hadn't been the light that caused her to wake up but the sound of Indy loading his gun. She opened her eyes to see Indy standing in the middle of the cabin. He was fully dressed and tucking his gun into his belt.

"What is it?" Marion asked.

"Engines have stopped," Indy said. "I'm going to go check."

Leaving Marion in the cabin, Indy proceeded through a corridor and up a series of metal stairways on the steamer's port side to reach the bridge. On the bridge, he found Katanga, who was returning a corded intercom to its wall mount. Indy said, "What's happening?"

Katanga gestured to the bridge's starboard windows and said gravely, "We have most important friends."

Indy looked out the windows. "Oh, no," he muttered. There was a long, gray submarine in the water, a Nazi U-boat, and a small boat carrying German soldiers advancing on the *Bantu Wind*. Indy picked up a set of binoculars and trained them on the German soldiers who stood atop the sub's conning tower. He didn't recognize any of the soldiers, but it was an easy guess that Belloq and Dietrich were with them.

"I sent my man for you," Katanga said. "You and the girl must disappear. We have a place in the hold. Come on, go, go, go."

Indy wore a stunned expression as he lowered the binoculars.

"Come on," Katanga urged, "go, my friend, go."

Moving fast, Indy left the bridge. But just as he rounded a corner to descend a flight of stairs, he saw another boatload of soldiers had already boarded the *Bantu Wind*. The soldiers were brandishing rifles and machine guns, and Indy realized he'd have to try a different route back to the captain's cabin or risk being sighted by the soldiers. Indy slunk off into another corridor, hoping that he could make it back to Marion before the Germans found her.

The soldiers began searching every room and chamber. They threw open a hatch to find a hold full of pirates who raised their hands in surrender. None of the pirates revealed any information about Indy or Marion, so the soldiers kept looking.

Indy pulled his gun from his belt as he arrived at the end of the corridor that led to the captain's cabin. Running quickly but quietly, he was but a few strides from the cabin's door when he heard a man's German accented voice from within. "Where is Dr. Jones?" the man demanded.

"What's the big idea?" Marion answered. "Let go!"

Indy's mind raced. Knowing he wouldn't be any use to Marion if he were captured, too, he ducked into an empty vestibule to conceal himself. A split second later, a German soldier shoved Marion out of the cabin, and she struck the corridor wall hard with her shoulder.

Marion was still wearing her white nightgown. She leaned against the wall as three German soldiers stepped out of the cabin and into the corridor. Each soldier gripped a machine gun. Marion glared at the soldier who'd shoved her and jabbed his chest with her finger as she said, "Don't you touch me."

The soldier grabbed Marion by her upper arm and escorted her out of the corridor.

Indy heard Marion and the soldiers walk past his hiding place. Knowing that the soldiers would come back looking for him, he tried to think of a better place to hide. He found a hatch that led to a tubular ventilation shaft and climbed up into it.

Indy saw light at the top of the shaft, and poked his head up to peer out through an air-scoop ventilator. The ventilator was positioned beside the abaft funnels that vented gases from the steamer's boiler. A German soldier stood near the ventilator, facing away from Indy's position to survey the deck, where other soldiers were herding the *Bantu Wind*'s subdued crew out into the open.

A winch was suspended over the open hatch of the main hold, and Indy saw the Germans hoisting the crated Ark up through the hatch. And then he saw Marion, who was bracketed by a pair of soldiers.

Stepping onto the deck, Marion saw Dietrich and Belloq standing among the soldiers who had apprehended the crew. As Dietrich turned slowly to face her, Marion felt her rage boil over at the sight of the man who'd shoved her into the Well of Souls. Marion stepped boldly away from her escorts and raised her hand to punch Dietrich.

Katanga saw Marion's approach and he reached out fast to catch her wrist, and then pulled her away from Dietrich and held her in front of him protectively. Seeing the fire in Marion's eyes and how their captain had stopped her from striking Dietrich, Katanga's crew burst into laughter. Even Belloq found himself chuckling.

Dietrich lifted his angry gaze to four soldiers who stood above the deck on the bridge and shouted, "What about Jones?!"

"There's no trace yet, sir!" one soldier answered.

"Jones is dead," Katanga said.

Surprised by Katanga's claim, Dietrich turned to face Katanga, who still held Marion in front of him. Katanga continued, "I killed him. He was no use to us."

From inside the air-scoop ventilator, Indy heard Katanga's words. The soldier who stood near the ventilator lit a cigarette, and Indy winced as the smoke drifted back into his face.

"This girl, however," Katanga continued, "has certain value where we're headed. She'll bring a very good price." Katanga stroked Marion's hair and lifted it as if he were inspecting something of exceptionally fine quality. Smiling at Dietrich, Katanga said, "Mmm? Herr Colonel, that cargo you've taken . . ." Katanga tilted his chin to the crated ark. "If it's your goal, go in peace with it, but leave us the girl. It would reduce our loss on this trip."

"Savage!" Dietrich snarled at Katanga, who made no response to the Nazi's insult. "You are not in the position to ask for anything," Dietrich continued. "We will take what we wish." Grabbing Marion by her upper arm, he added, "And then decide whether or not to blow your ship from the water." Dietrich pulled Marion away from Katanga.

Indy ducked fast as the nearby soldier turned and tossed his cigarette butt into the ventilator. Indy felt the still-burning butt land on his shoulder and he wriggled silently to snatch it up and extinguish it before lowering himself out of the vent.

As Dietrich escorted Marion from the deck, Belloq stopped them and said, "The girl goes with me." Facing Dietrich, he continued, "She'll be part of my compensation. I'm sure your Führer would approve." Belloq turned his attention to Marion. As he removed his jacket and draped it over Marion's shoulders, he said, "If she fails to please me, you may do with her as you wish. I will waste no more time with her now." Then he faced Dietrich again and said dismissively, "Excuse me." Belloq wrapped his arm around Marion and guided her away from Dietrich.

After the Germans and Belloq left with Marion and the crated Ark for the waiting submarine, Katanga stood at the rail on the *Bantu Wind* and faced the sub. A crewman moved up beside Katanga and said, "I can't find Mr. Jones, captain. I've looked everywhere."

"He's got to be here somewhere," Katanga said, letting his gaze drift from the sub to his steamer's bridge. "Look again."

A moment later, the crewman said, "I found him."

"Where?"

The crewman pointed to the sub and said excitedly, "There!"

Katanga followed the crewman's gaze to see Indy swimming beside the German sub. The sub's engines had just started when Indy grabbed hold of its hull and pulled his dripping body onto the deck.

In his haste to reach the sub, Indy had left his hat, jacket, and other gear on the *Bantu Wind*, but managed to tuck his whip into his safari shirt. As he caught his breath and pushed himself up from the sub's deck, he heard the steamer's crew cheering for him across the open water. He waved to the crew, and then ran quickly toward the sub's conning tower and climbed up onto it.

What now? Indy wondered. The sub's upper hatch was sealed from the inside, and he wasn't about to knock and let the Germans know he was still alive and had hitched a ride. Indy had no idea where the sub might be headed, but if it completely submerged, he'd be in deep trouble. As resilient as he was, he could only hold his breath for so long.

The submarine moved away from the *Bantu Wind*, carrying Indy with it.

*T*he German U-boat was named *Wurrfler*, and Indiana Jones was fortunate that the sub's periscope remained above the water's surface as it traveled across the Mediterranean Sea. He was even more fortunate that he'd brought his whip, for he used it to tie himself to the periscope, and relieve his aching arms and hands from the task of hanging on as the sub sped to its destination. Still, by the time the sub began its approach to an island north of Crete, Indy was cold, tired, and soaked to the bone.

The sub's conning tower lifted from the water as the sub steered toward the base of a high, rocky cliff. As Indy untied himself from the periscope and recoiled his whip, he saw what at first appeared to be a cave at the cliff's waterline, but then he saw lights inside the cave, and realized it was a submarine pen. Indy knew there were probably some German lookouts stationed at the mouth of the pen, so he moved cautiously down from the sub's conning tower, and then eased himself off the deck and into the cold water. He clung to the side of the sub, letting it carry him toward the pen.

He heard a clang from above, and realized some members of the sub's crew had opened the upper hatch and were stepping onto the deck. Indy kept his head low, and then released his grip on the sub. He stealthily swam after the sub and into the pen.

The sub pen was a long, narrow chamber with high stone walls that were decorated with Nazi banners and flags. Two elevated platforms ran the length of the pen on either side of the man-made canal that allowed the U-boat to float in. Indy spotted a ladder that traveled up from the waterline to the platform on his right. He seized the bottom rung of the ladder and began to haul himself up.

Keeping to the shadows, Indy snuck past a group of German soldiers who stood on the platform, watching the sub's arrival. The sub was still floating to a stop when Indy found a convenient hiding place behind some tarpaulin-covered ordnance.

Indy wanted to get closer to Marion and the Ark. To accomplish that, he realized he needed to disguise himself in a German uniform. He ducked down behind the tarp as three soldiers walked toward his position. While two of the soldiers continued walking, one came to a stop and turned his back to Indy so he could face the sub.

Two soldiers were visible on the sub's conning tower, and more soldiers were standing on the opposite platform. All of them had a clear view of the tarp that shielded Indy, but they were focusing on the sub. Indy tried not to think about them. He didn't want to miss what might be his best or only chance to get a uniform. He took a couple of deep breaths, and then leaned out from his hiding spot.

Indy grabbed the nearby soldier by the back of his jacket, and yanked him off his feet and over the tarp. The soldier was so startled that no sound left his mouth as Indy slammed him to the platform floor. Indy belted the soldier and knocked him out cold.

Raising his gaze from the unconscious soldier, Indy peeked out from his position to see Marion emerge on the deck of the sub. Her escort was a soldier who had his machine gun leveled at her. Indy saw that the soldier's head was bandaged and his left arm was in a sling. Belloq and the Nazi in the black hat and leather trench coat — Indy didn't know his name — followed Marion and the wounded soldier onto the deck. Indy hoped that Marion was responsible for the soldier's injuries, but for all he knew, the soldier may have been one of the guys that he'd shaken off the troop truck during the trip from Tanis to Cairo. In their olive drab and khaki uniforms, the German soldiers had started to look alike to Indy.

But less than a minute later, he learned that the soldiers

were definitely not all alike, or at least that they came in different sizes. He had removed the unconscious soldier's uniform shirt as well as his own safari shirt, but as he sat with his back to the tarp and tried to pull on the soldier's jacket, he realized he was unable to button it. It was simply too small for him. He thought, *Of all the rotten luck!*

While Indy turned his head to see if any other soldiers might be standing nearby, he heard a voice speaking from almost directly above him. Still seated, Indy turned and looked up at another soldier who had walked up to him from out of nowhere, and who now loomed over him, speaking in rapid German.

Wearing an embarrassed, sheepish smile, Indy rose from the platform and stood before the soldier. Indy didn't understand German very well, but could tell that the soldier was reprimanding him for his unkempt appearance. Indy pulled a comb from his pocket and dragged it through his hair while the soldier prattled on with additional criticisms and reached out to adjust the collar of Indy's ill-fitting stolen jacket. Indy was no expert on German soldiers, but he knew two things about this one in particular. First, he was a fool. Second, he was about the same size as Indy.

Indy brought his knee up fast into the soldier's abdomen. The soldier doubled over, and Indy used his other knee to clip the soldier's jaw. The soldier's cap sailed up in front of Indy, who caught it as the soldier collapsed at his feet.

Indy put the cap on his head. It fit just right. So did the rest of the soldier's clothes.

While Indy changed, the crated Ark was hoisted out from the U-boat and placed on the deck near Belloq. As Dietrich walked past Toht and the captive Marion to arrive beside the Frenchman, a soldier stepped out onto the opposite elevated platform, gazed down at Belloq, and said, "The altar has been prepared in accordance with your radio instructions, sir."

"Good," Belloq replied. "Take the Ark there immediately."

The soldier nodded and walked off.

Belloq stepped over to the crated Ark and looked at the crate's scorched surface. He didn't think there was anything unusual about the way the German lettering and Nazi emblem had been burned away. He assumed that either Indiana Jones or the crew of the *Bantu Wind* was responsible, that they had just been trying to erase evidence that they had taken the crate from the Nazis. He checked the ropes that wrapped around the crate to make sure they were secure.

Stepping close to Belloq, Dietrich said, "Monsieur . . . I am uncomfortable with the thought of this . . . Jewish ritual." The racist Dietrich said *Jewish* with obvious distaste. "Are you sure it's necessary?"

Belloq pursed his lips in mild irritation. He had explained to Dietrich that opening the Ark required the recitation of Hebrew prayers, and that he would wear elaborate ceremonial robes for the occasion. As the winch began to lift the crated Ark from the sub's deck, Belloq replied, "Let me ask you this: Would you be more comfortable opening the Ark in Berlin, for your Führer? Finding out, only then, if the sacred pieces of the Covenant are inside? Knowing, only then, whether you have accomplished your mission, and obtained the one true Ark?"

Not surprisingly, Dietrich offered no response. He didn't even want to think of what might happen to him if he failed his mission.

Belloq walked up a gangplank and onto the elevated platform that bordered the port side of the docked U-boat. As he walked past a stack of oil barrels, his shoulder connected hard with a German soldier who walked from the opposite direction. The soldier did not stop to apologize to Belloq but averted his gaze as he kept walking toward the barrels. Belloq wondered if the soldier had deliberately bumped into him, but because he had more important things on his mind, he moved on.

Standing beside the oil barrels, the disguised Indy glanced at Belloq's departing form. There had been no smart reason to bump into Belloq, but Indy had just felt like it. When the time was right, he hoped he'd have the opportunity to bump Belloq right off the planet.

Indy looked up to see an automated winch carry the crated Ark across the sub pen. Indy had overheard the soldier tell Belloq that an altar had been prepared for the Ark. He had no plan for saving Marion or getting them both off the island, but he knew he had to do whatever he could to make sure that the Ark never reached that altar.

Belloq and Dietrich led a procession that included Marion, Toht, and two-dozen German soldiers through a steep, sandy canyon that traveled away from the secret U-boat pen. Marion, still wearing the white gown that Katanga had given her, was followed by Nazi flag bearers. Behind them, four soldiers carried the Ark of the Covenant, which had been removed from its scorched crate and was now draped under a dark blue sheet to protect it from the harsh sunlight. Toht removed his black hat and used a handkerchief to mop the top of his sweaty head.

At the very rear of the procession was Indy, who walked quietly and tried not to draw any attention. Although his stolen uniform fit well enough, his unshaved face was definitely not in keeping with the other soldiers.

He had been unable to obtain any weapons when he left the sub pen, so when the procession flowed past tall stacks of crates that contained military supplies, he fell back and then darted between the crates.

Indy had hoped to get his hands on a machine gun, but in the first crate he opened, he found something even more devastating, and also astonishing. It consisted of a long metal tube with an explosive warhead attached to the end of it; from an illustration on the inside of the crate, Indy realized that it was an anti-tank weapon, an expendable preloaded grenade launcher. Remembering the Flying Wing back at the Tanis site, Indy wondered, *What will the Nazis think up next?!*

Indy slung the grenade launcher over his shoulder and then scrambled up a steep slope. When he reached the top of the ridge, he kept moving until he arrived at the top of a cliff that overlooked the canyon. Seconds later, Belloq, Dietrich, and Marion came into view along with the rest of the procession. From above, the Nazi in the leather trench coat looked like a moving black blot against the sand.

"Hello!" Indy shouted.

The startled soldiers stopped and turned, raising their guns. The soldiers who had been carrying the Ark gently placed it on the ground so they could draw their own weapons. Marion, Belloq, Dietrich, and Toht turned and looked up, too. They all saw Indy on the cliff, aiming the grenade launcher at the Ark.

Belloq and Dietrich gaped. Marion beamed.

"Jones?" Belloq gasped. Then he stepped forward and shouted, "Jones!"

Indy answered, "I'm going to blow up the Ark, René!"

The sight of Indiana Jones made Toht feel queasy. He shuffled away from the soldiers and sat down on a low rocky ledge.

Marion bolted away from Belloq and Dietrich, but was immediately seized by two soldiers who held her fast near the ledge where Toht sat.

"Your persistence surprises even me," Belloq said to Indy. Then he muttered, "You're going to give mercenaries a bad name."

"Dr. Jones," Dietrich said, stepping forward. "Surely you don't think you can escape from this island?"

"That depends on how reasonable we're all willing to be!" Indy answered, keeping the grenade launcher trained on the Ark. "All I want is the girl!"

Still in the clutches of the two soldiers, Marion beamed more brightly.

Dietrich glanced at Belloq, who was using his hat to fan his face. Belloq shook his head. Returning his gaze to Indy, Dietrich said, "If we refuse?"

"Then your Führer has no prize."

Belloq looked to the soldiers who stood around the Ark and said, "Okay, stand back." He shook his hat at them, motioning them to move aside. "All of you, stand back. Get back."

The soldiers obeyed. Then Belloq placed his hat on his head, walked over to stand beside the Ark, and said, "Okay, Jones. You win. Blow it up."

Shocked by Belloq's words, Dietrich mumbled a command under his breath. The troops responded by moving toward the Ark to defend it, but then Belloq snatched a machine gun from a soldier and leveled its barrel at the others. The soldiers looked at him uncertainly, but something in Belloq's eyes convinced them that he was the one in control of the situation.

Tearing his gaze from the soldiers, Belloq glared at Indy and shouted, "Yes, blow it up! Blow it back to God. All your life has been spent in pursuit of archaeological relics. Inside the Ark are treasures beyond your wildest aspirations." Belloq smiled. "You want to see it open as well as I," he continued as he lowered the machine gun. "Indiana, we are simply passing through history. This . . ." He gestured to the Ark. "This *is* history."

All eyes were on Indy, wondering whether he would pull the grenade launcher's trigger.

Belloq said, "Do as you will."

Indy felt his stomach churn. He hadn't been operating with much of a plan, just trying to stay alive and keep one step ahead of the bad guys as usual. But he hadn't expected Belloq to call his bluff either. He felt disgusted that Belloq knew him well enough to know that he never had any intention of destroying the Ark, and felt even worse because he had failed Marion.

Utterly defeated, Indy lowered the grenade launcher.

Four soldiers had worked their way up to Indy's position. They moved in behind him, their machine guns aimed at his back. When they took the grenade launcher from him, he didn't offer any resistance.

*N*ight had fallen by the time the Nazis had finished preparing their makeshift altar for the Ark of the Covenant and Belloq's ritual. The site was a remote area of the island, where wide, staggered stones served as a stairway up to a natural amphitheater, an open space surrounded by high, rocky walls. The soldiers had set up a portable generator to power a series of klieg lights that were positioned around the altar, and also a motion picture camera to record the ritual for prosperity.

Indy and Marion were tied back-to-back to a tall lamp pole that jutted up from the ground at the outer edge of the amphitheater. They craned their necks and watched as two soldiers removed the blue sheet from the Ark and then lifted the Ark up the stone steps to the altar, where Belloq, Dietrich, and Toht awaited. The soldiers set the Ark down in front of Belloq, and then stepped back.

Belloq wore a turban and ceremonial robes with a

jeweled breastplate, and held an ornate staff that was decorated with a sculpted ram's head. Indy thought Belloq looked ridiculous. Blasphemous, too.

In a low, solemn tone, Belloq began reciting a Hebrew prayer. When he was done, he gestured to the two soldiers who had remained standing on either side of the Ark. The soldiers moved toward the Ark and slowly removed its lid.

Dietrich and Toht moved up on either side of Belloq to peer inside. The anxious soldiers who stood below their position took a few cautious steps forward, hoping that they, too, might be able to see the Ark's contents.

It was Dietrich who leaned down to reach into the Ark. When he lifted his hand, he was holding nothing but sand, which was all that remained of the sacred Ten Commandments.

As the sand filtered through Dietrich's fingers, a stunned looking Belloq lunged forward to catch the sand in his own hand. Dietrich sneered as he threw the sand down in disgust and turned away from the Ark. The realization that the Ark contained nothing but sand prompted Toht's face to crease into a sick smile, and then he began to laugh. Toht turned away from the Ark, too, leaving Belloq clutching at sand.

Indy grinned. He hadn't imagined the possibility that the Ten Commandments had been long reduced to dust. Belloq may have obtained the Ark, but it appeared that history itself had stopped him from trying to use its contents for some supernatural purpose. Not that Indy believed in that sort of thing.

Suddenly, there was a strange vibration and a whirring sound in the air, and bright blue-white sparks began flying from the power generator. One by one, the klieg lights started exploding, spraying bits of glass at the surprised soldiers. The generator flung more sparks, some of which struck the soldiers' rifles. The soldiers reflexively dropped the hot metal to the ground.

Indy felt the wind begin to pick up.

A low, growling sound seemed to emanate from the open Ark. Clutching the ram's head staff, Belloq peered into the Ark again. A light appeared to glow from deep within the Ark's dark interior, so deep that Belloq wondered if the Ark had somehow opened an access to an ancient well, or some more mysterious place.

A strange, luminescent white mist rose up from inside the Ark and spilled out over the altar. The mist began flowing down the stone steps, moving over the soldiers and the surrounding rocks, past Marion and Indy.

Indy wasn't sure what was happening, or what was about to happen, and that made him nervous. Despite his repeated claims that he wasn't superstitious, something inside him told him that an unknown force *had* been unleashed.

Indy's mind raced as he strained at the ropes that bound him and Marion to the lamp pole. *What if the stories about Tanis weren't just myths?* he thought, casting his mind back to his meeting with Brody and the Army officials. What was it Brody had said about the lost city? "Wiped clean by the wrath of God"—just like Sodom and Gomorrah. Thinking of Lot's wife, who had been turned to a pillar of salt when she looked upon God's destruction of Sodom, Indy turned his head away from the Ark and the soldiers and tried to relax his body against the pole as he spoke in a voice so low that only Marion could hear: "Marion, don't look at it. Shut your eyes, Marion. Don't look at it, no matter what happens."

Marion looked up at the sky, where dark, ominous clouds had suddenly appeared. Then she closed her eyes.

The mist continued to pour out of the Ark. To the amazement of Belloq, Dietrich, Toht, and the watchful soldiers, long wisps of light appeared to extend from the mist, and then transformed into unearthly apparitions. Some of the apparitions resembled cloaked, ghostlike beings. The apparitions flew rapidly through the air, circling the soldiers.

Some soldiers just stood speechless as they watched the apparitions and ducked away from them. Others twisted uncomfortably as the apparitions passed through their bodies. When one apparition whipped past Toht, the Nazi regarded it with an openly bemused expression.

Belloq gazed at a cloaked apparition that flew before him and sighed. A moment later, the apparition lifted its head to reveal what appeared to be a lovely, female face.

"It's beautiful!" Belloq cried out in wonderment.

The apparition turned and lifted its head to Toht. Toht's lips twitched as he eyed the apparition skeptically through his glasses. And then, unexpectedly, the apparition's face transformed into a sneering death's head.

Toht screamed.

Indy heard the scream. So did Marion. As the wind and mist whipped about them, Marion shouted, "Indy?!"

"Don't look, Marion!" Indy repeated. "Keep your eyes shut!"

Belloq's eyes went wide as he returned his gaze to the nether regions of the Ark's interior. A bright light shimmered up from within the Ark and swept over Belloq's head and torso. Then his eyes blazed, and twin bolts of bright energy streaked out from his eyes and into the soldiers. The soldiers jerked as the bolts struck and then passed through them, tearing out from their backs and into the neighboring soldiers. It happened so fast that none of the soldiers had time to scream, let alone make any effort to flee. One blast of energy tore straight through the motion picture camera — destroying the film within — and the head of the soldier who had been operating it. The rippling energy radiated from Belloq's eyes until each soldier was struck. The soldiers' knees buckled, and they collapsed to the ground.

But the light from within the Ark wasn't through with Belloq. As his head blazed with energy, Dietrich's eyes went wide and a horrified moan escaped from his gaping mouth, and Toht shrieked louder. Belloq screamed as he raised his hands to the sides of his head. Then Dietrich and Toht began to literally melt, screaming in agony as the intensity of the blazing energy boiled the flesh off their skeletons.

Belloq howled, and then his entire body exploded.

Moving like a massive wave, a wall of flame and smoke surged away from the altar, crashing over the dead soldiers and cremating them instantly. Still tied to the pole, Indy and Marion felt the heat rush past them, but kept their eyes shut as they screamed and braced themselves for death.

And then, the wave of flame surged back toward the altar, as if the Ark were now inhaling the destruction it had just exhaled. Then the Ark sent a column of fire straight up into the night sky, so powerful that it launched the Ark's lid spinning into the air and created a hole in the clouds that hung over the island.

The fire carried the Ark's lid high up beyond the

clouds, but then the fire arced back toward Earth. The Ark's lid came down, too, and landed back in its place atop the Ark with a resounding thud, which was followed by a distant, thunderous boom.

Indy listened to the thunder, and sensed that the danger had passed. He opened his eyes tentatively, and then turned his head to look down at his right arm. With some surprise, he lifted his wrist to see the smoldering remains of the rope that had bound him to the pole.

Brushing the rope from his wrist, he reached around to touch Marion's shoulders, turned her to face him and said, "Marion."

Marion's eyes were still closed, and she was trembling. A moment later, she cautiously opened her eyes, and then threw herself into Indy's arms. Neither one of them was entirely certain of what they had survived, but both were glad to be alive.

When they ended their embrace, they looked to the altar. There wasn't any sign of Belloq or the Germans, but the Ark of the Covenant rested exactly where the soldiers had placed it.

Indy remembered seeing some radio equipment among the stacks of military supplies outside the sub pen. He hoped some of that equipment still worked, or it was going to be a long swim home.

CHAPTER TWENTY-ONE

Shortly after returning to the United States with Marion and the Ark of the Covenant, Indiana Jones — clean shaven and wearing a decent suit — and Marcus Brody were sitting around a conference table with the two men from U.S. Army Intelligence, Colonel Musgrove and Major Eaton, in a large oak-paneled room in the War Office building in Washington, D.C. A fifth man, a rotund fellow who wore a cheap sportcoat, thick rimmed glasses, and a humorless expression, listened silently to the others as he leaned against a nearby file cabinet. Musgrove and Eaton hadn't introduced the man, but the way the conversation had been going, Indy and Brody hadn't seen any point in asking who he was.

"You've done your country a great service," Musgrove said to Indy.

Puffing at his pipe, Eaton added, "And we, uh, trust you found the settlement satisfactory."

"Oh, the money's fine," Indy said, trying to remain calm. "The situation's totally unacceptable." He couldn't believe Musgrove and Eaton had lied to him and Brody. They'd *never* planned on allowing the Marshall College Museum to keep the Ark of the Covenant.

Ignoring Indy's comment, Eaton said, "Well, gentlemen, I guess that just about wraps it up."

In a measured tone, Brody said, "Where is the Ark?"

"I thought we'd settled that," Eaton said petulantly. "The Ark is somewhere very safe."

"From *whom?*" Indy said.

As Eaton tossed an irritated glance at Indy, Brody said, "The Ark is a source of unspeakable power, and it has to be researched."

"And it *will* be, I *assure* you, Dr. Brody," Eaton said in his most placating tone, then turned to Indy and added, "Dr. Jones. We have top men working on it right now."

Indy leaned forward in his chair, stared hard at Eaton, and said, "*Who?*"

Eaton held Indy's gaze and repeated slowly, "Top . . . men."

After his meeting with Musgrove and Eaton, Indy could hardly wait to leave the War Office building. Marion had been waiting for him at the top of the grand stairway in the lobby, but he brushed past her as he put on his hat and started down the steps, heading for the exit.

"Hey, what happened?" Marion said as she ran down the steps to catch up. "You don't look very happy."

"Fools," Indy muttered. "Bureaucratic fools."

"What'd they say?"

Stopping on the steps, Indy turned to face Marion. "They don't know what they've got there," he fumed.

Smiling at Indy, Marion said, "Well, I know what I've got here. Come on. I'll buy you dinner."

Indy looked down at his shoes. Marion reached up to lift the brim of his hat.

Indy looked at Marion. She was wearing a pale tan jacket with a matching skirt and a broad-brimmed hat. She really was lovely.

Indy turned away from Marion, but then stuck his left elbow out. Marion linked her arm around his, and then they proceeded down the steps. As Indy wondered about the fate of the Ark, he cast one last glance over his shoulder before they left the building. This adventure may have been over, but a new one would surely be coming.

The Ark of the Covenant wound up in a new wooden crate, custom built for its dimensions. After the crate's lid was lowered and nails sealed it shut, a stencil was slapped on the side of the crate so that black paint could indicate:

TOP SECRET
ARMY INTEL. 9906753
DO NOT OPEN!

The last "top man" to see the Ark was a little old man who worked in a warehouse in a government building. After he nailed the crate shut, he loaded it onto a metal hand truck and pushed it down an aisle that was lined by stacks of similarly marked crates. It was a long aisle because there were a lot of crates, some stacked five or six high. How many crates were there? More than the old man had ever cared to count.

In fact, after all his years of government employment, he really had no idea how many crates were stored in the warehouse. He didn't even know anything about the contents of the crates. He was only paid to put things into storage, not remember what was in them, and that was good enough for him. But if he had to guess, he would have estimated there were thousands of crates in the warehouse.

Maybe more.

INDIANA JONES
and the
TEMPLE OF DOOM

Suzanne Weyn

Based on the story by George Lucas and Philip Kaufman,
and the screenplay by Willard Huyck & Gloria Katz

Princeton University, 1935

*I*ndiana Jones, professor of anthropology, known to his friends and enemies alike by his nickname, Indy, walked into his father's office in the medieval division of the history department at Princeton University. He put down the battered satchel that carried his traveling clothes.

He settled into a high-back leather chair to wait for his father, Dr. Henry Jones, Sr. As he stretched out, he sighed contentedly.

Indiana Jones was no stranger to worldwide travel. In fact he'd spent most of his life traipsing around the globe, first as a boy accompanying his parents on the many lecture tours his scholarly father gave in various countries, later as a young Allied soldier and spy during World War I. And these days he traveled in his role as a professor of archaeology. He participated in only the most fascinating digs for ancient treasure, and sometimes sought these treasures for private collectors.

He rose from the chair and paced around the office. Where was his father? Indy couldn't stand waiting. He was restless and impatient by nature. It was the reason he could never settle down to the safe life of a full-time professor at a university, despite his vast knowledge of the exotic, strange treasures of the ancient world. Usually, he'd teach for a few semesters — he was both a professor of archaeology and linguistics, specializing in ancient tongues—and then things would seem too quiet, even boring, and he'd yearn for a new adventure.

Still . . . the adventurous life could be exhausting. It was certainly dangerous. He was looking forward to a little rest and relaxation now.

He glanced fretfully at his watch. It annoyed him to sit around doing nothing.

He'd taken a chance on catching his father between classes. But obviously, he'd diverted from his usual schedule, perhaps he'd taken a meeting or left to attend a colleague's lecture. Indy knew he could be waiting a while. Luckily, there was always something interesting to read in his father's office. He glanced around the room, checking out the books and manuscripts: the older, the better.

But on his father's wide desk, he spotted something decidedly modern. It was a pile of unopened mail — his mail. Indy had almost forgotten his request that the post office forward everything to his father while he was in the South Pacific. He checked the stack and, sure enough, all the letters were addressed to him.

Well, it wouldn't be as interesting as leafing through an old text, but as long as he was waiting, Indy figured he might as well do something useful. He began to sort through the various correspondences. Bills. Bills. Some scholarly journals, one of which contained an article he had written on ancient Chinese artifacts of the Tsang Dynasty. It was a subject that had come to fascinate him lately.

He came to a letter that particularly intrigued him and he put the others back on the desk. Its foreign stamps, postmark, and return address indicated that it had come from Shanghai, China.

He had a number of friends and acquaintances in Shanghai; one of his closest associates was a man named Wu Han, with whom he'd worked on various archaeological adventures. But he didn't recognize the writing as belonging to any of the people he knew.

Burning with curiosity, he tore open the letter. *Dr. Jones,* it began. *Your reputation is known to us. We require your services. We are in possession of the Eye of the Peacock, which we offer to you as payment, though you must promise not to inquire how we came to possess such a prize. If these terms are agreeable to you, be at the observation deck of the Empire State Building at sundown on July 6.* The letter ended there with no signature.

The Eye of the Peacock! He'd come so close to obtaining the magnificent diamond years ago, only to have it slip through his fingers. Was it possible that this collector really had it in his possession — and, if he did have it, that he was willing to part with it? It sounded too incredible to be true.

Who could possess this mythical diamond without the world knowing about it? It had to be owned by some sort of underworld black-market dealer in antiquities, a thief, or a mobster of some kind.

It would be safer to steer clear of having someone like that as an employer. Who knew what kind of danger it could lead to?

And yet . . . if it was *true*, how could he pass up the chance to actually get his hands on the Eye of the Peacock diamond? It was a rare treasure that the entire world had the right to see.

He glanced at the calendar on his father's wall. July 6 was today! If he left immediately, he could get to the Empire State Building by sundown.

Snapping up his satchel and leaving the rest of his unopened mail behind, he was quickly out the door.

CHAPTER ONE

Shanghai, China, December 1935

I ndiana Jones stopped at the top of the stairs and peered down at the elegantly dressed patrons of the opulent, art-deco style Obi Wan night club. The international assortment of lavishly coiffed women wore glittering evening gowns and their equally intercontinental partners were in black tuxedos from the city's finest tailors.

Indy was dressed to fit right in, decked out in his new white tuxedo jacket with contrasting black pants and vest. The Shanghai tailor who had sold it to him had said that this year everyone would be wearing this style. "It's the latest from Paris," he'd insisted. "For 1935, it is the style to have."

Since coming to China months earlier, he hadn't worn his trademark leather jacket and snap-brim hat much. There had been little need to dress for action. Most of his digging had been through the dusty back rooms of Chinese museums and the musty, crumbling scrolls of antique archives. Except for a mercilessly bouncy yak ride over the Himalayas where he and his companions Wu Han and Short Round had been beset by nomadic thieves and the relatively minor matter of having to escape from a band of mountain-dwelling rogue monks who had tried to imprison him . . . it had been a fairly uneventful time.

Indiana spotted the stylishly dressed men he'd come to meet sitting together at a table not far from the stage. They were Shanghai's notorious crime boss Lao Che and his two thuggish sons, Chen and Kao Kan.

Lao Che turned out to be the "private collector of valuable antiquities" who had written to him. Just as Indy had guessed, he was one of Shanghai's most notorious crime lords. Undoubtedly, he had come into possession of the Eye of the Peacock Diamond through underhanded means, but he had not asked Indy to do anything illegal. And now Indiana felt he would be undoing any wrong Lao Che might have done by bringing the diamond to a world-class museum. He would charge a fee, of course, but it would only be fair considering all the work he'd done to bring this spectacular diamond to the world.

Lao Che and his sons didn't notice Indy because they were watching the show on the stage with rapt attention. Following the intent focus of their gazes, Indy surveyed the act. A beautiful blond singer wore a red gown covered in shimmering beads that sparkled with her every flowing gesture. She glided across the stage crooning Cole Porter's latest hit, "Anything Goes," in what Indy considered to be pretty good Mandarin. It would be tempting to let this bedazzling singer hypnotize him with her violet blue eyes, blond curls, and a voice like liquid gold, but he had other things on his mind at the moment.

At the bottom of the stairs, Indy's friend and helper, Wu Han, crossed in front of him disguised as a waiter. "Be careful," he murmured under his breath so that only Indy could hear him.

Wu Han was there as backup in case the deal between Lao Che and Indy turned nasty. They already had good reason to believe that it would. In the months since Indy had been in China, he'd seen how the crime chief operated, and Indy fully expected that Lao Che would soon be up to his old tricks.

Indy had done some planning, just in case his worst fears were realized. Wu Han and Indy's junior assistant, Short Round, would be there to help if things went south. They had worked out a course of action in scrupulous detail. With this plan in place, Indy was reasonably sure that he'd make it out of there — even if things went terribly wrong.

Crossing the crowded club filled with tables of rambunctious, fun-loving patrons who watched the show while they popped champagne corks, Indy took a seat at the table across from Lao Che and his sons. He greeted them in Shanghainese, one of the Chinese Wu dialects he spoke fluently. While he talked, two of Lao Che's men frisked him for any concealed weapons but found none.

"You never told me you spoke my language, Dr. Jones," Lao Che commented.

"Only on special occasions," Indy replied politely. This wasn't entirely true. He often spoke the dialect most used in Shanghai whenever he was in the city. But he wanted to underscore the fact that tonight was a momentous occasion. It was the end of the line, the final moment in the undertaking that had brought him halfway around the world.

"So, is it true, you found the Nurhachi?" Lao Che inquired, a bright eagerness coming to his dark eyes. He leaned forward attentively, barely controlling his excitement.

A sneer curled Indy's lip. "You *know* I did," he responded disdainfully. His eyes bore into those of Lao Che's son, Chen. "Last night one of your *boys* tried to get Nurhachi without paying for him."

Chen lowered his bandaged hand below the table and glowered at Indy. Just the night before, he had broken into Indy's apartment with three other of Lao Che's thugs and tried to steal the Nurhachi, the prize Lao Che had commissioned Indy to procure. Indy had suspected that Lao

Che would try something like this and was ready for them. He'd broken Chen's hand as he twisted the gun away from him. It was one of the reasons he'd asked Wu Han to watch his back tonight.

"You have insulted my son," Lao Che barked angrily.

Indy kept cool. "No, *you* have insulted *me*," he insisted levelly. "*I* spared *his* life."

Lao Che's other son, Kao Kan, rose from the table, cursing in Chinese, ready to spring at Indy. Lao Che motioned for him to sit.

Indy kept his eyes on the three crime lords sitting across the table from him. He was dimly aware that the blond singer from the stage show had come to the table, but this was no time to let himself become distracted.

She draped her red satin, elbow-length gloved hand over Lao Che's shoulder. "Aren't you going to introduce us?" she asked Lao Che. Her voice was warm and flirtatious. From her accent, he placed her as being decidedly Midwestern American.

Lao Che kept his eyes on Indy as he spoke. "This is Willie Scott," he said with the slightest nod toward the woman at his shoulder. "This is Indiana Jones, the famous archaeologist."

Willie smiled and her pearly teeth shone between her shining red lips. She slid into a seat between Indy and Lao Che.

Excellent, Indy thought, adjusting his plan to suit the new development. She was exactly where he wanted her.

"Well," Willie said smoothly, looking him over appreciatively. "I thought archaeologists were always funny little men searching for their mommies."

"You mean, *mummies*," Indiana corrected, not sure if she had been joking.

He assessed her quickly, not letting his eyes wander from his adversaries for more than seconds at a time. Under all that exotic makeup and the slinky dress, she was a classic American beauty. She must have seen some rough times to have landed in Shanghai, singing in a nightclub, the moll of an unscrupulous crime lord like Lao Che. He wondered what unfortunate circumstances had brought her here.

"Dr. Jones found Nurhachi for me," Lao Che explained to Willie. "And he's going to deliver him . . . now!"

Indy was aware that Kao Kan was holding a pistol under the table and aiming it right at him.

"Say, who is this Nurhachi?" Willie asked.

Before anyone could answer her question, Indiana pulled Willie over to him, grabbed a carving fork from a nearby tray and jabbed it into her side. She tried to squirm away from him, her eyes wide with fright, but he had a firm hold on her waist and pulled her closer.

It was exactly what he'd been planning since he realized Kao Kan was holding a gun on him. The moment Willie had sat beside him, Indy saw the chance to turn the tables. "Put the gun away, sonny," he growled at Kao Kan.

Kao Kan looked to his father uncertainly. Lao Che nodded for him to put the gun away.

Indiana kept his hold on Willie, but took the fork from her side. He didn't really want to hurt her, but he'd had to make it look real. For that to happen, Lao Che had to see true fear on her face. "Now I suggest you give me what you owe me, or anything goes," he threatened.

Around them, the patrons of the club were still unaware of the scene unfolding at Lao Che's table. They popped more champagne corks and laughed, oblivious to the explosive situation threatening to erupt in their midst.

Beside him, Willie whimpered and gazed at Lao Che, silently, her eyes imploring him to hand over Indiana's payment so he would release her. At a signal from his father, Chen reached into his pocket and set a small, velvet pouch on the revolving tray at the table's center and spun it toward Indy.

As the pouch swung into position in front of him, Indy could feel his excitement growing. The diamond was so close he could touch it! But he controlled himself, refusing to touch the pouch. Who knew what trap they had set for him?

He nudged Willie closer to the table. "Open it," he demanded gruffly.

With trembling hands, she poured ten gold coins onto the revolving tray. Only ten gold coins! He should have known this would happen!

"The diamond, Lao," Indiana snarled, enraged but not surprised. "The deal was for the diamond!"

He wouldn't have gone through all the difficulty of getting Nurhachi, wouldn't have dealt with Lao Che at all, if he hadn't been promised the enormous Eye of the Peacock.

Lao Che reached into his pocket and placed another pouch on the revolving tray beside a glass of champagne. Grunting unhappily, he spun it over to Indiana.

Once again, Indy nudged Willie to open the pouch. Her eyes widened and his mouth was agape at the sight of the spectacularly brilliant, luminous diamond inside. It was priceless: larger than a walnut and beautifully cut. "Oh, Lao," she murmured, awestruck. Sighing, she wrapped her fingers around it possessively.

Indy jabbed her once again with the carving fork, this time harder than before. A short, sharp, high-pitched shriek erupted from her lips.

Scowling fiercely at him, she released the diamond into his outstretched palm.

Indiana smiled. The job was over and everything had come off as he'd hoped. He lifted the champagne from the tray, relieved.

He'd left his junior assistant, Short Round, with instructions to book all three of them on a flight to Bangkok that very night. In a half hour, Short Round would come to collect Wu Han and Indy to drive them all to the airfield.

From Bangkok, they would fly to London. He'd already contacted a colleague at the British Museum who had expressed great interest in obtaining the diamond for their Far East exhibit. *Maybe I'll visit friends at London University,* he thought, twirling the stem of the champagne glass in his fingers, but not drinking. He had taught at London University for a time and had enjoyed it very much.

Yes, life was looking good. "To your very good health," he toasted Lao Che, raising his glass and feeling very pleased indeed.

He released his hold on Willie's waist, and she instantly leaped away from him. "Lao," she shouted angrily, "he put a hole . . . he put two holes in my dress from Paris!"

Indy tensed. How much did Willie Scott mean to Lao

Che? Would he retaliate if his girlfriend insisted on it? Was he in for more trouble?

"Sit down!" Lao Che barked at her and Indy relaxed once again. Willie Scott would not be a threat to him.

Willie plunked back down into her seat, but slid her chair well out of Indy's reach. She wasn't stupid and clearly had no intention of becoming his hostage again.

"Now you bring me Nurhachi," Lao Che demanded smoothly.

Indy grinned at him and nodded. "My pleasure." He beckoned to Wu Han, who lingered nearby, still pretending to be a waiter.

"Who on earth is this Nurhachi?" Willie asked, bewildered and aggravated at being kept in the dark.

Before anyone could answer her, Wu Han approached and presented a tray. On it was a six-inch high carved jade urn. Indy placed the urn on the table's revolving tray, turning it toward Lao Che. "Here he is," he announced.

Willie turned to Lao, still completely puzzled. "This Nurhachi is a real small guy," she remarked, her brow creasing in confusion.

"Inside are the ashes of Nurhachi, the first emperor of the Manchu Dynasty," Lao Che explained solemnly. He lifted the urn with two hands, turning it reverently.

Indy sat drinking his champagne and watching Lao Che. Having this dead emperor's ashes obviously meant a lot to him. *Strange*, he thought. Did owning an emperor make him feel important — like he was also an emperor, too, ruler of his own crime-infested world? Possibly.

Whatever Lao Che's reasons were, Indy had to admit, at least to himself, that he'd enjoyed the challenge of finding the urn containing Nurhachi's ashes. Years earlier, it had been smuggled out of China and sold on the black market. Through rigorous research and with steely determination, Indy had tracked the urn to a tiny, dark pawn shop in Istanbul where it had been sitting unopened for years.

Indiana toasted Nurhachi. "Welcome home, old boy," he said, draining the last drops from his glass.

Lao Che, Chen, and Kao Kan began to chuckle giddily with delight. "And now give the diamond back to me," Lao Che said.

It was Indy's turn to be puzzled. "Are you trying to develop a sense of humor or am I going deaf?" he asked. Surely he hadn't heard Lao Che correctly. The man couldn't be serious!

Indy squirmed uncomfortably in his chair, though he tried to hide it. He didn't like being the only one not in on their little joke. It didn't seem to him that these guys had much of a sense of humor. The only kind of joke they would find this funny was one in which the joke was on him.

The three men broke into gales of even more uproarious

laughter, practically falling off their chairs as they convulsed. Kao Kan pounded the table. Chen could barely
breathe and clutched his sides as his shoulders shook with
merriment.

Suddenly the smile faded from Lao Che's face. He
held up a vial of vivid blue liquid.

"What's that?" Indy asked.

"Antidote," Lao Che replied, suddenly quite serious.

Indy didn't like the sound of that. "To what?"

"The poison you just drank, Dr. Jones," he said.

Indy swirled his finger around the inside of the champagne glass. It came out covered in a filmy, white residue.
There had indeed been something more than champagne
in his glass. Indy cursed his carelessness: He should have
expected something like this.

Swallowing, he realized he was suddenly nauseated
and his throat was swelling. He'd begun to sweat, and his
hands had picked up a slight but uncontrollable tremor.
This wasn't fear — it was the poison taking effect.

Lao Che smirked at him. "The poison works fast, Dr.
Jones," he said, deadly serious now.

Indy knew he had to hold on somehow and stay as
calm as possible. He couldn't afford to have his heart rate
get any faster. It would only send the poison coursing
through his bloodstream with greater speed. If he was

going to get out of this on the winning end, he had to think quickly and not let the poison take him down.

The time to act was now — while he still could.

Willie squealed as he lunged for her. Digging her high heels into the floor, she tried to slide away from him, but her chair tipped almost spilling her onto the floor. Once again, he grabbed her waist and jabbed the fork into her side.

"Lao!" she shouted.

"Lao . . ." Indy growled at the same time, his voice overlapping Willie's.

He didn't really want to hurt Willie, but he hoped Lao Che didn't know that. Indy just hoped he cared enough to save her.

Unfortunately, Lao Che was unfazed. "You keep the girl," he said. "I'll find another."

The room seemed to be spinning and the voices all around became garbled. This was bad. How much longer could Indy hold himself together? He might not have much time left. He had to force himself to think clearly.

Letting go of Willie, Indy shook his head, breathed deeply, and felt his mind clear slightly. Scanning the room, he was relieved to find Wu Han among the crowd. With a wave of his hand, he signaled his friend.

Wu Han arrived at the table holding a drained

champagne glass on the same silver tray he had brought Nurhachi on earlier. This time, though, he raised it ever-so-slightly to reveal that it concealed the pistol he was aiming at Lao Che.

Indy smiled at Wu Han. "Good service here," he remarked with a grin. With Wu Han by his side, armed, things were looking a lot less hopeless.

"That's not a waiter!" Willie gasped.

"Wu Han's an old friend," Indy told her. Wu Han nodded at him confidently, keeping the three mobsters in his steely sight. Indy knew Wu Han was an excellent shot.

"Game's over, Lao," Indy said, rising as best he could from the table.

All around them, patrons continued to laugh and open champagne bottles which popped loudly when the corks were pulled. The pops masked the shot when Kao Kan fired his pistol at Wu Han.

A look of profound puzzlement swept over Wu Han's face. At first, he didn't even understand what had happened. He saw the shattered glass on his tray and then noticed the red bloodstain slowly spreading across his white shirt. Moments later, the pain registered with him. "Indy!" he cried, clutching his chest.

Indy grabbed hold of Wu Han, easing him onto a chair at the table. He hadn't heard the shot, either. It took his clouded mind a minute to realize what had happened to his friend.

Looking around, he saw that the muffled shooting had still not attracted any attention and the nightclub's activity was continuing as usual. It gave the situation an air of unreality. How could this be happening in the middle of all these people with no one noticing?

"Don't worry, Wu Han," Indy said to his friend. "I'll get you out of here." No matter how badly the poison was affecting him, he had to come through. If he had to crawl out, dragging Wu Han behind him, he would do it.

Wu Han gazed up at Indy, his visage pale with pain, his voice fading. "Not this time, Indy," he said, smiling bravely even though his eyes were rapidly clouding over. "I've followed you on many adventures, but into the great Unknown Mystery, I go first, Indy." He'd barely gotten the words out when he slumped to the table.

Indy lunged forward to feel Wu Han's pulse — but found none. No! It couldn't be! When he'd asked Wu Han to back him up, he knew there might be trouble, but he never expected his friend to end up dead.

"Don't be sad, Dr. Jones," Lao Che sneered. "You will soon be joining him."

Stunned with grief, Indy's gaze drifted over to Lao Che's smirking face. Beside him, Chen continued to giggle and the murderous Kao Kan gloated triumphantly.

Indy burned with rage. Normally he would have tried to avenge Wu Han's murder, but the room was lurching erratically now as the poison continued to course through his veins.

Impulsively, he staggered angrily toward Lao Che, but was thrown off balance by the affects of the poison. He gripped the table for support.

"Too much to drink, Dr. Jones?" Lao Che taunted.

Summoning all his energy, Indy righted himself but then stumbled backward as the room spun yet again. He collided with a waiter who had just set a row of Cognac-soaked skewered pigeons on fire at a nearby table.

The dish was a delicacy, a specialty of Club Obi Wan, but to Indy it was something else — a weapon. Grabbing one skewer, he hurled the long spear of flaming pigeons at Kao Kan.

At the same moment, Kao Kan fired at Indy, but missed. He screamed as the flaming, improvised spear pierced his chest.

This — a man being wounded with a flaming row of cooked birds — was finally something the other patrons of the club could not miss!

Screams erupted.

People leaped to their feet and began to flee the club in terror.

Lao Che bolted up, bellowing threats at Indy in Chinese. Indy threw himself across the table with abandon, desperate to get hold of the vial of antidote in Lao Che's hand.

Willie stood nearby, now holding the diamond. When Indy charged past, the diamond was knocked from her hand! It slid across the floor into the crowd of panicked, escaping patrons, stampeding for the nearest door. With a cry of anguished disappointment, Willie plunged into the onrushing crowd—and risked being trampled — to retrieve the fabulous gem.

Lao Che sprang away as Indiana barreled into him, grabbing for his wrist. In the struggle, the vial flew into the air and was soon sliding and being kicked across the room along with the diamond.

Indy crawled across the floor after the spinning vial — the diamond could wait. If he didn't get the vial, though, it would probably mean the final end of all his adventures. He'd encountered various poisons in his travels but never one this fast-acting or potent.

The nightclub was in an uproar as people trampled one another, pushing and shoving to get out. The rolling vial was kicked underfoot, making it impossible for Indy to get hold of it. Several times it was almost in reach when it was knocked across the room by a stampeding patron.

As Indy crawled across the floor, he saw that Willie was also on her hands and knees, pursuing the diamond. If she got hold of it, she would probably disappear with the fortune it would bring. For a moment, he considered going after her to be sure she wouldn't run off with his payment. He couldn't though. All his remaining energy had to be spent getting that vial before it was too late.

Unaware of the scene going on in the audience, a line of tapping show girls began to dance onto the stage, beginning the next show. At the same time, Lao Che's army of tuxedo-wearing hoods raced into the club. The chorus girls screamed and fled the stage when they saw them.

Lao Che barked orders at his men in Chinese. Reaching into their formal jackets, they produced small but deadly sharp axes. And they didn't pause before hurling them all in Indy's direction. He lunged for cover behind a life-sized female statue near the stage, but now he was trapped there as the axes whizzed past the statue or bounced off of it.

He saw that Willie was still out crawling on the floor, seemingly oblivious to the flying axes. She cursed and stomped the floor with her delicate fists as buckets of ice on stands were accidentally toppled, sending cubes everywhere and making it nearly impossible to find the diamond among them.

Indy continued watching from behind the statue and noticed Willie reaching out for the vial of antidote that came skidding past her through the ice. Its blue liquid sparkled. She plucked it up and tucked it into the bodice of her gown.

That was good. She would certainly be easier to keep in sight than a little vial of blue liquid.

Now all he had to do was find a way to get to Willie Scott!

*I*ndy jumped out from behind the statue, ducking and covering his head to avoid the flying axes. In the confusion, someone released hundreds of balloons that had been bound up in nets in the ceiling.

The sea of bouncing balloons covered everything, making it impossible to avoid the ice cubes on the floor. Everyone began sliding, colliding with furniture, and crashing into each other.

Darting and weaving through the crowd and Lao Che's henchmen, Indy didn't know how much longer he could last. Passing an abandoned glass of champagne, he threw it in his own face just to keep from passing out.

Before Indy could reach Willie, Chen spotted him. He snapped up a machine gun and began firing, not caring that he was shooting into the crowd.

As bullets sprayed around him, Indy sailed across the room, throwing himself behind an immense, round, brass gong for cover. Darting out just long enough to grab a large broadsword from the hands of a nearby warrior statue, he brought the sword down on the cords that fastened the huge gong to its stand.

The immense gong bounced from its stand.

C-r-r-as-s-sh!

It hit the floor and began to roll across the room on its side.

Indy ran along behind it, using the gong as a moving shield as Chen continued to fire at him. The rapid-fire bullets ricocheted from the gong, clanging ceaselessly as the huge metal disc rolled across the room, gaining momentum and traveling ever faster.

Peeking around the side of the gong, Indy observed Willie heading for an exit. Her eyes widened in terror when she turned to see the gigantic gong rolling toward her.

Indy reached out and once again wrapped his arms around her waist, pulling her to him. "Come on," he yelled. He knew she had the antidote, which meant he couldn't let her out of his sight.

"I don't want to go!" she shrieked. She demanded in loud tones that Indy release her as he pulled her along behind the gong toward a tall, stained-glass floor-to-ceiling window. Indy anxiously tightened his hold on her waist.

The gong was about to crash through the third story

window and they would have no choice but to go out with it!

"One ... two ... three ..." he counted down.

Willie clung to him, screaming wildly as they smashed through the window with the gong, their bodies plummeting into the night.

The gong flew away from them, spinning off into the darkness. They hurtled downward, shouting in terror, their arms and legs flailing wildly.

At the second floor they crashed through an open awning with a deafening ripping sound of torn fabric assailing their ears.

Landing hard on the first-story awning, they bounced up and came down again near the awning's edge. Another bounce would send them pounding down onto the pavement below.

Before that could happen, Indy hooked his foot onto the edge of the awning and grabbed hold of Willie, pulling her back down. They slid along the awning for several feet, but were both able to grip the rim and hold tight.

Willie and Indy hung there, their feet dangling six feet above the ground. "Who *are* you?" Willie asked, panting breathlessly, amazed at what had just happened. Indy wanted to grin and say something witty in reply, but his head was more clouded than ever and bouncing out a third story window hadn't helped any.

In the next second, a canvas-topped car careened around the corner of the neon-lit street below them. It was a car Indy couldn't have been happier to see.

"Jump," he told Willie as he let go. She also released her hold on the awning rim and the two of them fell, tearing through the car's roof and landing in the car's spacious backseat.

Behind the wheel was an eleven-year-old Chinese boy, a street urchin named Short Round, Indiana's bodyguard and junior assistant. "Wow! Holy smoke!" he cried. "Crash landing!"

"For cryin' out loud, there's a kid driving the car!" Willie cried when she got a good look at Short Round and realized how young he was.

"Short Round, step on it!" Indy instructed urgently. He tried to calculate how long it would take Lao Che's men to scramble down three flights of stairs. In his current blurry-headed state, he couldn't do the math, but he knew they'd be right behind.

"Okey, dokey, Dr. Jones," Short Round replied.

A block of wood strapped to his feet enabled Short Round to reach the car's pedals. With a no-nonsense scowl, he yanked the bill of his New York Yankees baseball cap to the back, hunched forward, and stomped down on the gas pedal. "Hold onto your potatoes," he shouted gleefully, zooming off.

The car's tires squealed. Willie and Indy were thrown abruptly back against the seat. "Oh!" Willie cried in distressed surprise as her head hit the seat hard.

The car raced past the entrance to Club Obi Wan just as Lao Che and his thug army raced out. Lao Che instantly recognized Indy's car and ordered his men to chase after it. The armed thugs piled into a black sedan and revved the engine. Peeling out into the crowded Shanghai street, they zoomed off after Indy, Short Round, and Willie.

As Short Round drove faster and faster to escape the sedan, Indy knew he didn't have much time left. "Where's the antidote?" he asked Willie urgently.

She batted her eyes at him, feigning bewilderment. He didn't have time for this little game! He asked again and when she didn't answer, he lunged at her. "Let me have it," he shouted, shaking her.

"Ohhh, I hope you choke," she snarled, handing the vial to him.

Indy didn't waste a second. Throwing away the stopper, he guzzled down the blue liquid. He hoped it was the real thing and not another one of Lao Che's double crosses.

"Hey, Dr. Jones, we've got company," Short Round informed him as gunfire shattered the rear window glass.

Willie ducked, terrified in the back corner of the seat. "No shooting!" she insisted.

Indy ignored her and shot back at their pursuing attackers through the broken back window while Short Round continued his lunatic drive through the crowded streets. After several rounds of gunfire, Indy needed to reload. He handed his gun to Willie while he went for the bullets he knew were in the glove compartment.

The gun was red hot. Willie juggled it, tossing the searing metal from one hand to the other. Finally, she couldn't stand it any longer. Not knowing what to do with it, exactly, she tossed the gun out the window. At the same moment, Indy reached out for her to hand the gun to him.

When he turned back to find out why she wasn't giving him the gun, he saw that it was gone. "Where's my gun?" he shouted. "Where's my gun?"

"I burnt my fingers and I cracked a nail," she whined.

Indy fought down the anger rising inside him. He could see that Willie Scott was going to be no help to him whatsoever.

Finally, Short Round screeched onto an airfield on the outskirts of Shanghai. He wheeled the car past a small terminal and proceeded to the cargo area.

Out on the field, a tri-motor plane revved its engines. The car squealed to a stop and Indy leaped out, followed by Willie. Short Round caught up to them, carrying the knapsack packed with a few essentials they'd need for the trip ahead.

At the boarding gate, a very proper airline official ran out to meet them. "Ah, Dr. Jones," he greeted Indy in a clipped British accent. "I'm, ah, Weber. I spoke with your . . . uh . . . *assistant*," he added, glancing at Short Round curiously, slowly realizing he had been talking to this child.

Short Round simply nodded seriously, silently acknowledging that he was, indeed, Indy's assistant.

"We've managed to secure three seats," Weber continued. "But there might be a slight inconvenience, as you will be riding on a cargo full of live poultry."

"Is he kidding?" Willie asked shrilly.

Weber caught her in an icy glare. "Madame, it was the best I could do at such short notice." Suddenly his stern expression melted and he smiled eagerly. "Heavens!" he cried, "Aren't you Willie Scott, the famous American female vocalist?"

Willie bestowed one of her full wattage smiles on Weber.

They rushed toward the passenger steps of the waiting plane when the black sedan carrying Lao Che and his men pulled up to the gate. They sprang out of the sedan and hurried toward the plane.

But Indy knew they were too late. The three propeller engines were already turning. They'd be in the air in minutes.

Indy realized that he was feeling like his old self again. The antidote had worked!

He stood at the plane's doorway and shot his enemies a heroic mock salute. "Nice try, Lao Che," he called, triumphantly taunting his nemesis.

Turning, Indy pulled the door shut behind him as he entered the plane.

He did not see the pilot wave conspiratorially at Lao Che while the plane taxied down the runway. Nor did he hear Lao Che chuckle as he whispered, "Good-bye, Dr. Jones." And, most importantly, he didn't see the logo written on the plane door he had so quickly pulled shut behind him: LAO CHE AIR FREIGHT.

CHAPTER FOUR

Once they were in the air, Indy opened the cockpit to greet the pilots. They were two short, chunky men who smiled warmly and assured him that everything was fine. They would reach Bangkok in several hours.

With a satisfied nod, Indy left them to fly the plane. He rubbed the back of his neck and yawned. What a crazy night. He thought about Wu Han, but there was nothing he could do to help his old friend now. When he got to Bangkok, he'd wire money to help Wu Han's family. He wished he'd gotten hold of that diamond; he'd have been able to send them a lot more if he had.

Indy stepped into the plane's restroom, peeled off his tux, and donned more familiar and comfortable attire. It felt great to pull on his canvas pants, work shirt, and leather jacket. Kicking off his fancy dress shoes, he sighed as he slipped his feet into the comfort of his well-worn leather work boots. Good old Short Round. He'd packed everything just as Indy had instructed.

Plunking his favorite fedora hat onto his head, he stepped out from the restroom with his tux draped over his arms. He made his way to the front of the plane where Short Round slept and Willie sat pouting, looking extremely unhappy.

All around them, crates of chickens clucked with agitation at being airborne. Feathers flew everywhere and the stench was overwhelming. On the ceiling overhead, nets rocked back and forth, loaded with fruits and vegetables. Burlap sacks of rice were piled three-sacks deep and five high all along the walls. The cargo hold was packed so tightly that only the narrowest of aisles remained to walk up and down.

Willie looked up and surveyed Indy's change of outfit. She raised her eyebrows skeptically as he put down his tux and hooked his coiled bullwhip over a crate. "So what are you supposed to be — a lion tamer?" she taunted him snidely, pulling his tux jacket over her shoulders for warmth.

Indy sneered back at her. She was really starting to get on his nerves. "I'm allowing you to tag along, so why don't you give your mouth a rest? Okay, doll?" he snapped at her. He'd just about had it with her wisecracks and complaints.

Willie jumped to her feet, her hands on her hips. "What do you mean, *tag along?*" she demanded indignantly. "You're the one who *dragged* me along on this insane escapade!"

He shrugged indifferently. Those were the breaks. She was probably better off getting away from Lao Che, anyway, even if she didn't realize it.

"And as for *allowing* me to tag along," she went on, a superior tone creeping into her angry voice, "ever since you got into my club you haven't been able to take your eyes off of me."

Everything she'd said was true, but Indy wasn't about to admit to it. She was beautiful. And it was true, too, that she hadn't had much choice about coming along. Still, he didn't like having it all thrown back in his face the way she doing now.

"Oh, yeah?" he said laconically, settling into a corner beside Short Round and pulling his hat down over his eyes. He'd show her just how unable to keep his eyes off her he was. In fact, his eyes were beginning to close on their own. It was a perfect time for a nap.

Indy dreamed that he was home at Marshall College, where he was a professor of archaeology. In his dream, he was doing research in the high-ceilinged library. But from somewhere in the aisles among the shelves of books, he could hear Willie Scott's voice. She was crying out, her voice becoming more agitated with every moment. "Oh, no! Oh, NOOOO!" she wailed.

And then suddenly he was shaking uncontrollably. He didn't know why. Was it an earthquake?

Indy's eyes snapped open. Willie had grabbed him by the collar and was bouncing him up and down. "Mister! Oh, Mister!" she shouted into his face.

"You call him Dr. Jones," Short Round told her sleepily, awakened by her shouting.

"Okay. Dr. Jones! Dr. Jones!" she shouted frantically. "Wake up! Please!"

Befuddled with sleep, Indy struggled to come fully awake. "Are we there already?"

"No!" Willie shouted. "No one is flying the plane!"

This unbelievable news instantly snapped Indy awake. In a second, he was on his feet. Willie pulled him to the cockpit and flung open the door.

"I went into the restroom to change into your tux pants and shirt and when I was done I thought I'd say hi to the pilots . . . but when I opened the door, there was no one to say hi to," she explained in a high-pitched wail.

Indy rushed past her into the cockpit. "Oh, boy," Indy muttered when he saw the two empty seats. Much as he'd like to deny it, this plane was too small for them to be hiding anywhere.

The pilot and co-pilot had obviously bailed out, leaving them there to crash!

"They're all gone!" Willie wailed, her voice climbing hysterically as it echoed his desperate thoughts.

There was no time to stand there gaping in dismay, so Indy jumped into the pilot's seat. Below him was a range of snow-covered mountains. He didn't know exactly where they were, but he was pretty sure this wasn't the way to Bangkok.

"You know how to fly, don't you?" Willie asked hopefully.

He surveyed the plane's many dials and switches. He'd always meant to learn to fly but somehow had never gotten around to it. There was no sense in lying to her. "No," Indy admitted. "Do you?"

She threw her hand over her mouth, gagging with fear. Willie's eyes went wide in terror. "Oh, no!" she cried, sinking into the jump seat behind him.

"How hard can it be?" Indy asked philosophically. He'd been in tighter spots than this before. At the moment he couldn't think of any, but he must have been.

"I'm going to faint!" Willie moaned.

The secret was to stay cool. Those pilots hadn't looked like geniuses. If they could navigate the dials of this flying crate, so could he. "Altimeter: okay," he checked. "Airspeed: okay. Fuel . . ."

The fuel gauge didn't appear to be working.

It read E . . . for EMPTY.

He tapped it and a red light came on.

Indiana swallowed hard. Apparently it really was empty.

At the same moment, the engine began to sputter. Looking sharply to his right, he saw one of the propellers stop turning.

Through the front windshield, he could see that they were dipping ever lower over the snow-covered mountains. The remaining two propellers conked out and the plane nosed downward even more sharply. "I think we've got a big problem," he told Willie, realizing that this was something of an understatement. "Look for parachutes, Shorty," Indy called to Short Round at the back of the plane.

The boy frantically dug through an equipment bin, but came up empty. He turned toward Indy, shaking his head.

Indy left the cockpit and came up behind Short Round to survey the bin's contents. It did indeed appear to be lacking in parachutes. Obviously the pilots had seen to that.

Pulling out a large box, Indiana read the cover and began to break the box open. "Shorty, come on. Give me a hand," he instructed. Inside was an inflatable raft. Not exactly ideal for escaping from a plane about to crash land in the snow-covered mountains, but it wasn't as though he had much else to choose from.

Working fast, they unpacked the bright yellow emergency life raft, spreading it flat on the floor of the plane. "Shorty, get our stuff," he told the boy as he slid open the cargo bay door. Instantly, a fierce wind flattened him against the side of the door.

Gripping the doorway, Indy peered out. Below, the snowy mountains loomed ever closer. It would be a matter of minutes before they crashed.

Short Round arrived with their knapsack of supplies and tossed it on top of the flat, deflated raft. Together they dragged it to the door.

Willie fought her way to them, her hands raised against the wind blasting into the cabin, her blond hair blowing wildly around her head. "A boat?!" Willie shouted when she saw what they were doing. "We're not sinking! We're crashing!"

Indy ignored her and turned to Short Round. There was no time for arguing or explaining his plan. She was a grown woman. If she didn't want to take part in his plan, he wasn't about to force her. "Grab on, Shorty! Grab on!" he instructed as he stepped into the boat. Short Round leaped in with him and grabbed Indy around the neck.

The mountainside seemed to be rushing up to meet the downward spiraling plane. Indy knew he had to wait until just minutes before they crashed for his plan to succeed. It was time to go!

Willie screamed, jumping on just as Indy yanked the inflation cord and propelled the raft out of the plane by pitching his weight forward and pulling against the door's frame.

Willie and Short Round hugged Indy from behind while he kept a white-knuckle grip on the sides of the raft. The wind beat at him mercilessly, but he couldn't let go — no matter what. All their lives depended on his not losing his grip on the raft. Indy just hoped that the rubber seams were tough enough not to come ripping apart under the pressure of the fierce wind and their speed. After all, it hadn't exactly been built for this kind of punishment.

Below them, the plane crashed into a snowbank, sending up a spray of snow. They watched in horror as it exploded in a ball of fire, with metal and other debris shooting in a million directions.

Their raft descended more slowly through the air, buffeted by the roaring wind all around. Nonetheless, they were jolted when it landed, bouncing hard against the mountainside before rocketing down the slope at tremendous speed.

"Slow it down!" Short Round pleaded, clutching Indy's neck so hard he was afraid he'd choke.

There was no way to slow the raft, but Indy felt it

losing velocity as they covered ground. Eventually it would slow to a stop. His mood soared as he realized that they'd made it. His crazy plan had worked and they were going to be okay!

Smiling, he glanced over his shoulder at ashen-faced Willie and grim Short Round. "That wasn't so bad, was it?" he asked jauntily.

He wasn't expecting the look of sheer terror that swept over their faces.

Turning swiftly back toward the front, he saw what they were seeing.

The yellow raft was sailing out into the open air off the end of a sheer cliff!

For a second it seemed to hang in mid air, and then it plummeted, falling downward until it landed with a huge splash in a raging torrent of white water.

The raft bounced over rocks in the river, twisting and turning helplessly through narrow gaps and sudden drops. The wild spray soaked them as they desperately clung to the raft.

Waves of white foam crashed over the side of the raft, soaking them to the bone. More than once, Indy was sure they would be thrown up against one of the many jagged rocks in their path. He had to stick his legs outside the raft to push them away from slippery boulders.

Indy was a strong swimmer, but getting out of this powerful current alive would be tough. And he didn't know if Short Round or Willie could swim at all. If he had to swim with one of them under his arm, he wasn't sure if he could make it.

"Put on the brakes!" Willie shrieked. "I hate being wet! I hate the water! And I hate you!"

"Good!" Indy shot back. "Good!" What did he care if she hated him? He had bigger problems to worry about!

CHAPTER FIVE

*F*inally, the raft slowed its mad, rushing ride and drifted from the main part of the river into a narrower tributary. The current flowed more gently there, swirling the raft in its languid eddy.

As the raft glided toward a clearing, Indy finally breathed a sigh of relief and relaxed against the side of the raft. On the other side of him, Willie stared out glumly, watching the river go by. Short Round sat between them creating a buffer. "All right, Shorty?" Indy asked him. "You okay?"

Short Round nodded and Indy smiled at him. What a great kid he was; brave as could be. And he never complained — unlike a certain unpleasant person sulking on the other side of the raft.

"Where are we, anyway?" Willie asked, still staring out onto the river.

The raft floated to a gentle stop in a pool of slowly

swirling water. Indy wasn't exactly sure where they were; though he wasn't about to admit that to Willie. He'd keep his eyes out for any landmarks.

They first thing he had to do was check what rations Short Round had packed. They were pretty thin — after all, he had only anticipated needing enough snacks to last them until they settled into a nice hotel in Bangkok. It didn't look like there were *any* hotels near their current location.

Short Round and Willie both gasped loudly. Indy swung around to see what had caused their alarm.

A very tall, old man stood on the nearby shore, studying them with a piercing gaze. His long, receding white hair made a halo around his dark face. He wore many strands of heavy beads over a rough, flowing robe. There was something dignified, almost mystical, in his somber demeanor.

Indy immediately knew where they were. He recognized this man as a shaman, a high priest, from the mountains of India. In a silent greeting, he placed his palms together and moved his hands up to touch his forehead.

Silently, the shaman led Willie, Short Round, and Indy down a narrow path through desolate mountainous terrain to his village. All around them, the earth was scorche spiky, charred remains of tree trunks were all that remained of a forest that had once stood there.

Soon they came to a village at the base of a mountain. A single road ran to it and the villagers stared with awed curiosity at the newcomers as they entered. It was a desperately poor village; the buildings were all simple mud huts. Like the path they'd just traveled, there were no trees or plants of any kind, only their burnt remains.

Indiana noticed that the villagers seemed particularly interested in Short Round, and he quickly realized that he did not see any other children around. One elderly village woman clutched Short Round affectionately to her side. Unnerved, Short Round pulled away quickly.

The shaman invited them into a thatched hut that was larger than any of the others they had seen. In the dying sunset, long shadows crossed the dim room.

Another white-haired, robed man greeted them. He seemed to be their chieftain. Sitting in half circle on a shabby rug on the floor were six other older, robed men. Indy was sure they were the ruling elders of the village. The shaman indicated that Willie, Short Round, and Indy should be seated near the elders.

The chieftain waved his hand, and three village women hurried in carrying wooden bowls filled with food, one for each of the visitors. Indy had noticed that the people were speaking Hindi and thanked them in that language.

Willie looked into her bowl, aghast at the lumpy, brown food in front of her. "I can't eat this," she hissed quietly as her face crumpled with disgust.

"That's more food than these people eat in a week," he informed her, hoping their hosts didn't speak English. "They're starving."

Willie looked around at the thin face of the woman that had given her the food and offered the bowl back to her. "I'm sorry. You can have my —"

"Eat it!" Indy interrupted her sharply.

Willie pouted at him and put down the bowl. "I'm not hungry," she stated, which they both knew was a lie.

He sympathized with her, in a way. It didn't look very appetizing. He'd taken a quick swallow and it didn't taste any better than it looked. In fact, he wasn't even sure what it was, and for him that was a new experience — normally he could identify all sorts of local cuisines. But it was all these people had and they'd offered it as a sign of friendship. The three of them were lost and stranded in these mountains and the villagers were treating them well. It was important to stay on favorable terms. "You're insulting them and you're embarrassing me," he insisted pointedly. "Eat it!"

"Eat it," Short Round echoed. Indy nodded at him approvingly. Short Round was just a kid, but he had enough sense to size up the situation and know what had to be done.

Willie picked up some of the food in her fingers, following Indy and Short Round's example. She examined it and then put it in her mouth.

Indiana continued pushing his food into his mouth and tried not to think about the taste. The sooner it was consumed, the better. If they didn't eat this food, it might be a long time before they were offered anything else and they had to save their stash of snacks for as long as possible.

He watched Willie struggle to get the food down. She grimaced and wrinkled her nose, but she was eating. He had to give her at least a little credit. She was doing what she had to do.

Wind blew through the hut as the golden glow of the sunset gave way to a growing darkness. "Bad news coming," Short Round whispered ominously, unsettled by the howls of the wind. "Bad news coming."

Indy looked to the chieftain. "Can you provide us with a guide to take us to Delhi?" he asked, switching back to Hindi. "I'm a professor. I have to get back to my university."

"Yes, Sajnu will guide you," the chieftain said helpfully.

The old shaman spoke now for the first time. His voice was raspy and low. He told them that the village was called Mayapore. "On the way to Delhi, you will stop at Pankot," he added.

"Pankot is not on the way to Delhi," Indy replied, puzzled.

"You will go to Pankot Palace," the shaman insisted.

Indy knew the old stories about Pankot Palace. He also knew those stories had ended sometime ago. "I thought the place was deserted in eighteen-fifty," he said.

"No," the shaman stated firmly. "Now there is new maharajah — and again the palace has the power of the dark light."

The old man gazed around sadly at his unfortunate people who stood at the doorway, eager to see what was happening within. "It is that place kill my people."

"What has happened here?" Indiana dared to ask.

"The evil start in Pankot," the shaman revealed. "Then, like monsoon, it moves darkness over all country."

"The evil?" Indiana asked. "What evil?"

Short Round leaned close and whispered to Indy. "Bad news," he said, nodding assuredly, grimly satisfied that his prediction was being born out by the shaman's words. "You listen to Short Round. You live longer."

Indy nodded, shushing him gently as the shaman continued his tale of woe. "They came from palace and took *sivalinga* from our village."

Willie looked to Indy. "They took what?" she asked.

"It's a stone," he explained, "a sacred stone that protects the village."

"It is why Shiva brought you here," the shaman spoke, referring to an important deity of the Hindu religion.

Indiana disagreed politely but firmly. "We weren't brought here. Our plane crashed."

"It crashed," Willie affirmed.

"No! No!" the shaman disagreed. "We prayed to Shiva to help us find the stone. It was Shiva who made you fall from the sky. So, you will go to Pankot Palace to *sivalinga* and bring back to us. You bring back to us."

Indy opened his mouth to argue. All he wanted was to travel to Delhi where they could get a good meal, sleep in a hotel-room bed, and then book a flight back to the United States. He hadn't been home in a long while and things hadn't exactly turned out as he'd hoped. The safe, steady routines of his university life seemed very attractive at the moment.

But somehow, the words wouldn't come out of his mouth. He glanced over his shoulder at the anxious faces of the villagers. These people needed help more desperately than any he had ever met.

He didn't know what to do. It might be best to decide in the morning after he'd had a chance to sleep and think about it further. He hoped that in the clear light of day, this shaman wouldn't seem so desperate. He'd become just another old man who wanted him to chase after some stone that his people had invested with a lot of silly, superstitious beliefs.

"Come. I show you place where stone was once," the shaman said, standing on his spindly, yet sturdy, legs. The chieftain and elders trailed him out of the hut. Indy, Willie, and Short Round mingled with the villagers, who also followed as the shaman led them to the very edge of their village.

Short Round tugged on Indy's jacket. "Dr. Jones, did they make the plane crash to get you here?" he asked.

"No, Shorty," Indy assured him. "It's just a ghost story. Don't worry about it."

Everyone stopped walking and circled around a crude stone shrine hacked out of a large boulder. The niche that had been carved into the rock was empty, but an indentation indicated the cone shape of the stone that had been stolen. Indy ran his palm around the inside of the place where the stone had been. "Was the stone very smooth, like a rock from a sacred river?" he asked.

"Yes," the chieftain confirmed.

"Did it have three lines across it?" Indy asked.

To this, the chieftain nodded.

"Did the three lines represent the three levels of the universe?"

Once again the chieftain nodded excitedly.

"Yes. I've seen stones like this one you lost," Indy said. "But why would a maharajah take the sacred stone from here?"

"They say we must pray to their evil god," the old shaman told him sadly. "We say we will not."

"Excuse me," Willie spoke up. "I don't understand how one rock could destroy a whole village."

The old man's eyes filled with tears that glistened against his dark eyes. He looked off into the distance and began speaking in Hindi.

As the shaman spoke, Indy translated for Willie and Short Round. "When the sacred stone was taken from the village, wells dried up and the river turned to sand," he said. "The crops were swallowed by the Earth. The animals lay down and turned to dust. Then one night there was a fire in the fields. The men went out to fight the fire. When they came back, the women were crying in the darkness."

The old shaman paused as though what he had to say next was too terrible to speak of. Indy prodded him, asking in Hindi why the woman had been crying.

Indy could hardly believe the shaman's reply. It explained why the old woman had hugged Short Round to her side so passionately. "The children," Indy told his companions. "He says they stole all their children."

That night, Indy's companions went to sleep early, completely exhausted. But his restless mind wouldn't let him relax, so he walked out into the silent, sleeping village. Under a blue-black sky studded with brilliantly bright stars, he paced.

There was so much to decide. And he felt torn in two different directions.

These people sorely needed his help. He didn't believe they had conjured him out of the sky, but he had to admit he was the perfect person for the task they required. A more well-suited recruit was unlikely to stumble upon this desolate little village. Who could be a better candidate than he — with his intimate knowledge of ancient lore and track record with valuable antiquities — to get their sacred stone back for them?

Still ... he was tired, worn out. He'd just met these people hours ago. Why should he risk his life for them? If this maharajah had managed to wipe out an entire village of strong, able-bodied men and women and stolen their children right out from under them, what chance did he have against such a formidable foe? He was only one man — a man responsible for a rambunctious kid and a spoiled nightclub singer.

No. It was nuts. *Crazy.* He wouldn't do it.

He stopped and leaned against the wall of one of the mud buildings, thinking. This was the right decision. Besides, he had to get back to Marshall. The new semester would begin in a few weeks. He'd committed to teaching three classes and he wasn't even remotely prepared.

Indy suddenly pushed himself off the wall, alert to the sound of something moving nearby. Ordinarily, he would have dismissed it as an animal scurrying through the night, but all the animals around this village were dead.

He peered into the night and saw a dark form stumbling toward him; whatever it was moved erratically, weaving and stumbling, as though it were injured, exhausted, or both. Indy squinted, moving toward the sound. The figure emerged from the darkness and he was barely able to register that it was a young boy before he collapsed into Indy's arms.

Indy saw that the boy was half-starved: emaciated, his large, black eyes exaggerated by his bony, skeletal face. The boy reached up to Indy. His fingers were bruised and cut. He opened them and released something into Indiana's hand. "Sankara," he whispered through parched lips, his voice a rasp. "Sankara."

From out of the darkness, a woman gasped and rushed to the boy. From the way the boy stretched his arms to her, Indy was certain this was his mother. He would have been touched by their emotional reunion as the joyfully sobbing woman cradled her son, but he was too distracted by the artifact the boy had just given him. It was a palm-sized piece of tattered cloth; an old fragment of a miniature painting.

Indy recognized it immediately — and it made him deeply uneasy. "Sankara," he whispered.

Awakened by the emotional cries of the village woman, people were emerging from their huts. Indy wanted to get away to examine this cloth more closely.

He climbed atop a hill just outside the village until he reached the scorched remains of a tree. Looking down at the village, he saw that all the huts were now illuminated and buzzing with activity. He couldn't get the poor kid's desperate face out of his mind.

If he'd escaped from Pankot Palace, he'd traveled a long way on his own, and probably gone without food or water for days.

Rimmed by moonlight, Short Round appeared, climbing up the hillside toward him. "The boy escaped from the evil place," he said, breathlessly confirming Indiana's suspicions. "Many other children still there. What we do, Dr. Jones?"

Indy's mouth went dry. He had no idea what to tell Short Round.

"What you think?" Short Round pressed him impatiently.

"I think that somebody believes the good-luck rock from this village is one of the lost Sankara Stones."

"What is Sankara?"

Indy wondered how he could best explain the power that the Sankara Stones allegedly possessed. It was beyond words. But Short Round was clearly waiting for an answer.

"It's fortune and glory, kid," Indiana said at last. "Fortune and glory."

*I*n the morning, the villagers provided two huge, Asian elephants with massive curved tusks for Indiana and Willie to travel on, and one baby elephant for Short Round. With a helpful boost-up from two village men, Indy easily saddled his animal, while Short Round mounted his much smaller version. Willie's ascent, however, wasn't so graceful. She slid, arms and legs unable to find a hold, sputtering and complaining all the while, as villagers labored in vain to help her up.

"Willie, quit monkeyin' around on that thing," Indy mockingly scolded, trying to suppress a grin. Begrudgingly, he had to admit — if only to himself — that she had a game spirit even though she did love to complain.

With a desperate squeal of effort, Willie hoisted herself onto the elephant's back, but pulled too hard with her right hand, causing her to spin around so that her head faced the animal's rear end!

Good enough, Indy decided, eager to get going. She was up on the elephant. It didn't really matter which direction she faced; a village guide named Sajnu walked beside her and would guide her elephant wherever it needed to go.

Indiana gave the lead guide the signal to move out. Together, the elephants, along with five other village guides on foot, began their journey.

"Oh, wait a second, Indy," Willie wailed pitifully, struggling to hold on while traveling backward. "I can't go to Delhi like this!"

"We're not going to Delhi," he informed her. "We're going to Pankot Palace."

He'd made his decision at dawn. He couldn't get the escaped boy's starved, desperate eyes out of his mind; there was no way he could refuse these people who needed his help so much. It just wouldn't be right.

"Pankot?" Willie shrieked. "I can't go to Pankot. I'm a singer. I need to call my agent! Is there a phone? Anybody? I need a phone."

Indy heard her hollering, but like the distant buzz of a mosquito, he paid no attention to it. Instead, he was looking down at the villagers who had come to see them off. He waved as he took in their hopeful expressions. They were all counting on him. He just hoped he would prove worthy of their trust.

As the sun rose, the day grew increasingly warm and

steamy. Indy was on the lead elephant but Willie soon passed him, led by Sajnu. She had somehow turned herself forward, but still looked mightily distressed.

Indy had to smile as he watched her sniff her armpits, and then realize it was the elephant whose strong smell was disturbing her. His smile widened even more when he saw her sprinkling perfume from her back pocket all over the odorous animal — as though that would make the slightest difference. And his smile turned into a burst of laughter when the elephant's trunk swung back over its head, sniffed the flowery fragrance, and trumpeted its disgust into the air. "Oh, quit complaining," Willie yelled at the creature. "This is expensive stuff!"

Short Round and his small elephant drew up alongside Indy and, unlike Willie, he seemed to have befriended the creature. "You come to America with me and we get a job in circus," he spoke to it soothingly and Indy couldn't help but grin. "You like that? You like America? You're my best friend."

But Indy was distracted from watching Short Round by a whirring, flapping sound overhead. Gazing up, he saw a flock of large creatures whose wide, black wings obscured the blue sky.

"Oooh! What big birds!" Willie remarked excitedly.

"Those aren't birds, sweetheart. Those are giant vampire bats," Indy told her.

Willie shuddered and went pale, ducking her head.

Hah! Got ya! Indy thought, gloating triumphantly. Vampire bats were small. These large bats were flying foxes — all they liked to bite was fruit. But Willie didn't know that. He'd gotten her back for throwing his gun out the window, or maybe for all the complaining she'd done, or maybe just for saying she hated him. Now they were even, he figured.

They traversed the dense, moist jungle, moving steadily westward, until an immense red sun hung low in the sky. Indiana was beginning to feel the strain of bouncing along, rigidly upright, for so many hours. Surely the guides on foot had to be getting fatigued. Checking over his shoulder, he glanced back to see how Willie was faring.

Her blond curls were disheveled and damp with sweat. She slumped forward wearily, sprinkling the last of her perfume over her elephant's neck. The elephant snorted, protesting the strange floral smell raining down on it. "Oh, pipe down, you big baboon," she scolded the elephant. "This doesn't hurt. You know what you really need? You really need a bath."

As though it understood her words, the elephant dipped its trunk into a shallow, muddy, river running alongside the dirt path on which they traveled. After drinking deeply, it swung its trunk over its head and unleashed a torrential spray of water right on top of her.

Screaming, she slid off the elephant's side, splashing right into the river.

Short Round convulsed with laughter at the sight of Willie, sputtering and flailing in the river. "Very funny!" he cried, rocking gleefully. "Very funny! Very funny! All wet!"

Willie pulled herself into a sitting position there in the river. She didn't even try to get up. "I was happy in Shanghai," she wailed, on the edge of tears. "I had a little house and garden. All my friends were rich." She shook her head mournfully and Indy could tell this had been the last straw. "We went to parties all the time." She slapped the water and started sobbing, speaking in gulps through her tears. "I hate being outside. I'm a singer. I could lose my voice."

If only that would happen, Indy thought hopefully. Still, she looked so pitiful there, sobbing in the water, that he had to feel sorry for her. "I think we'll camp here for the night," he told the guides.

Indy slid off his elephant and went to help Willie out of the water. She got up on her own power and splashed past him, stomping onto the embankment, spraying him with water as she went. *Suit yourself*, he thought.

Indy made a fire for them in a circle of thick, vine-strewn jungle trees. The guides gave them more of the strange, brown mush they had eaten the evening before and then retreated to bed down for the night a short way off.

After eating and tending to the elephants, Willie went off to find a stream in which to wash up. Indiana and Short Round settled down to play a heated game of poker, betting with the coins in their pockets. By the time Willie returned, Indy's dripping tuxedo slung over one arm and wrapped in a blanket, they were into their third round.

"Whadda you got?" Short Round challenged Indy, holding his cards close.

"Two sixes," Indy said, showing his cards.

Short Round laughed victoriously. "Ah, ha! Three aces! I win!" He clapped his hands, his face lit with good-natured greed. "In two more games, I have *all* your money!"

Willie settled down to watch them play. She sat in front of her elephant, which stood beside a tree at the outskirts of the clearing. As she attempted to concentrate on the game, the pachyderm nuzzled her playfully with its trunk. "Cut it out!" she scolded, impatiently pushing its trunk away. After it had so rudely dumped her in the muddy river, she wanted nothing to do with it.

Indy wasn't paying attention to Willie. His mind was focused on the game. Short Round was beating the pants off him; it was true. His pride was injured and he felt determined not to be trounced by a child, even one as wily as Short Round. "It's poker, Shorty. Anything can happen," he said, feigning confidence. Short Round was good at this!

Willie stepped between them and began hanging Indiana's drenched tux shirt and pants on a tree branch. "So, where did you find your, ah, little bodyguard?" she asked with a nod toward Short Round.

"I didn't find him. I caught him," Indy answered in a matter-of-fact tone as he dealt cards.

"What?" Willie asked, perplexed by this reply.

"Shorty's family were killed when the Japanese bombed Shanghai. He's been living on the street ever since then, since he was four. I caught him trying to pick my pocket. Didn't I, Short Stuff?"

Indy remembered how stealthily Short Round had slipped his little hand right into his bomber jacket. He'd thought Indy was just another clueless tourist — an easy target. When he realized his mistake, Short Round tried to get away, and Indy had never seen anyone run so fast or amble over crates and carts with such dexterity. But Indy's bullwhip was faster, and Short Round was caught before long. It was obvious, though, that the kid was just trying to survive. And Indy had to admire his nerve. He knew he would make a perfect assistant.

While recalling his first encounter with Short Round, Indy languidly watched Willie hang clothes. She stooped to pick up the tux pants from a pile and came up holding one of the large fruit bats they'd seen earlier, holding each one of its velvety wings. At first she didn't realize what she held, absently spreading its wings wide, assuming they were the two legs of the pants.

In a second, though, she turned ashen as she beheld the creature in her hands. It hissed at her and began flapping its wings in an attempt to free itself. Screaming frantically, she tossed the bat aside and began to race around the campsite as the bat flew off into the night.

Short Round and Indy both suppressed grins while Willie continued to shriek at the top of her voice and run around flapping her arms hysterically. "The biggest trouble with her is the noise," Indy commented wryly to Short Round.

Willie shrieked again when she came face-to-face with a small monkey on a low lying branch. Whirling away from it, she ran right into a large lizard resting tranquilly on the trunk of a tree. Indy wouldn't have thought it possible for her shrieks to become any louder or more shrill than the ones he'd already heard, but when she saw the lizard, his eardrums actually *hurt*.

He tried to block out her piercing yells by focusing on the card game. But in the next moment, Short Round began shouting, too. "Hey, you cheat, Dr. Jones!" he accused, pointing at Indy's cards.

Indy checked his cards and saw that he did, indeed have four instead of three. "Oh, they stuck together," he realized.

Short Round didn't believe it. "You pay now!" he demanded. "No stuck!"

"A mistake," Indy insisted.

All the while their voices were growing louder as they shouted over Willie's screams. "I very little," Short Round yelled. "You cheat very big." He was turning red with anger. Normally, Indy respected Short Round's relentless ferocity, but at the moment it was getting on his nerves.

"Dr. Jones, you cheat! You pay money! You owe me ten cents!" Short Round continued on.

As Short Round flailed his arms in anger, Indy saw a flash of white. Deftly grabbing Short Round's wrist, he extricated a fourth card from his long white cotton shirt sleeve. "Look at this!" Indy shouted indignantly. "Look at this! You accuse *me* of cheating!"

Never one to back down, even in the face of incriminating evidence against him, Short Round continued his furious tirade in Chinese. Indy automatically made the language shift with him, shouting back in Chinese.

As the heated disagreement between Indy and Short Round escalated, so did Willie's howls of horrified terror. A startled owl, upset by the commotion, fluttered its wings in her face. Terrified, Willie stumbled backwards only to trip over the lizard who had moved down from the tree.

"You make me poor. No fun," Short Round shouted in Chinese.

He was right, Indy decided. All this fighting was definitely not fun. "I quit," he announced, throwing down his cards.

Announcing that he also quit, Short Round stomped away from the campfire and crawled into his blanket roll. Seconds later, Willie slid hers onto the dirt beside Indy, panting breathlessly. "This place is completely surrounded," she declared miserably. "The entire place is crawling with living creatures."

A slight smile played on Indiana's lips. "That's why they call it the jungle, sweetheart," he remarked.

Off in the distance, some creature snarled fiercely. "Oh my God! What else is out there?" Willie wailed.

He reached out to pat her back, attempting to calm her, but his touch only startled her once again. She leaped up with a shout and bounded to the other side of the campfire where she stood breathing heavily with fear.

He really did want to do something to help her calm down. She was getting so worked up! If she didn't relax, she'd be headed for a nervous collapse before dawn. Some friendly chit-chat might do the trick. "Willie. What is that?" he asked. "Is that short for something?"

"Willie is my professional name ... *Indiana*," she revealed a bit defensively, pointing out his own unusual name in a derisive tone, as if to say: *You of all people should not be commenting about strange names.*

Groggily, Short Round popped up from his roll of blankets. "Hey, lady, you call him Dr. Jones," he insisted loyally, their recent fight apparently forgotten.

"*My* professional name," Indy told her as he flipped a ten-cent coin to Short Round in appreciation.

Willie once again settled down, cross-legged, in front of her elephant. It instantly resumed its attempt to get her to play with it by tapping her on the head and curling its trunk around her neck. Absently, as though shooing off a persistently buzzing fly, she swatted the annoying trunk away as she spoke. "Why are you dragging us off to this deserted palace?" she asked. "Is it for fortune and glory?"

"Fortune and glory," Short Round echoed sleepily, about to drift off to sleep.

From his inside jacket pocket, Indiana carefully withdrew the scrap of cloth the escaped village boy had given to him. He pointed out the drawing of ancient figures done in red, blue, and gold with hieroglyphic writing beneath it, handing it to her. "This is a piece of old manuscript," he explained. "The pictograph there represents Sankara, an ancient priest."

She gazed down curiously at the frayed material with

its drawings of figures from long ago. As she tried to concentrate on the scene depicted on the cloth, her elephant
ran its trunk around her neck again. "Scram," she told it,
pushing it away while she studied the picture before her.

"Gently. Gently," Indy cautioned. "That material is
hundreds of years old."

"Is that some kind of writing?" she asked, pointing to
the hieroglyphs.

"Yeah, Sanskrit," he replied.

Willie nodded while slapping the elephant away. "Cut
it out!" she muttered with growing irritation.

"It's part of the legend of Sankara. He climbs Mount
Kalisa where he meets Shiva, the Hindu god," Indy
continued.

Willie located Shiva in the drawing. "What's he handing the priest?" she asked.

"Rocks. Shiva told him to go forth and combat evil.
And to help Kalisa, he gave him the five sacred stones with
magical properties."

A quizzical expression came over Willie's face. "Magic
rocks?" she questioned skeptically.

Indy nodded. The ancient texts might have described
it more fancifully, and academic terminology more for-
mally. But that's what it actually boiled down to: magic
rocks.

Willie's voice took on an unexpected softness as she

recalled a memory from her childhood. "My grandpa was a magician. He spent his entire life with a rabbit in his pocket and pigeons up his sleeve. He made a lot of people happy and died a poor man. Magic rocks. Fortune and glory."

Willie turned away, her face full of bitter disgust. Indiana could see she believed it was all superstitious nonsense leading to disappointment. But he'd seen enough in his many adventures around the globe to know that even the most outlandish tales often had a hint of truth — or at least an incredible archaeological find — behind them. It was the reason he'd made archaeology his life's work.

He'd read the tale of Sankara in the original Sanskrit years ago. He'd read accounts dating back hundreds of years by people who swore they had witnessed for themselves the staggering magical power of the magic stones.

Willie pulled her bedroll off further from the campfire. "Sweet dreams, Dr. Jones," she said with a yawn.

"Where are you going?" he asked.

She tugged her beddings even further away.

"I'd sleep closer if I were you," he advised, "for safety's sake."

She chuckled knowingly. "Dr. Jones, I'd be safer sleeping with a snake," she replied.

As she spoke, Indy leaped to his feet.

His heart raced.

The thing he feared most on the planet — the one creature that truly made his knees buckle in terror and his skin grow clammy — maybe the *only* thing that could reduce him to a sniveling mass of panic, had slithered from the tree behind Willie and was making its way around her neck.

It was a snake.

And it was gliding along Willie's shoulders.

Indiana Jones detested snakes, feared and loathed them. He fought back all the gut-wrenching memories of his encounters with the slithery demons. None of them had cured him of this phobia; they'd only made it worse.

With a trembling hand, he pointed to the creature making its way down the front of Willie's chest. He tried to warn her, but the words turned to dust on his fear-parched tongue.

She looked at him questioningly. Then she felt the snake.

Indy braced for her ear-splitting scream of terror.

But Willie mistook the snake for the trunk of the pesky elephant that been tormenting her all night. Finally fed up, she gripped it with both hands and hurled it away from her, shouting, "I said cut it *out!*"

The boa flipped end over end into a clump of nearby bushes and slithered away.

Not even realizing what she'd done, Willie shook her head woefully. "I hate that elephant!"

Indy slumped back against a boulder in relief, his frenetic heartbeat gradually slowing. He wiped sweat from his brow.

He watched Willie crawl under her blankets, oblivious to the danger she had just encountered. Indy was slowly revising his opinion of her. She might be skittish over nighttime creatures, but he had a feeling that when it mattered, she could be counted on.

He couldn't be sure. Still, his gut feelings had a habit of being right.

At dawn, they set off on their way once again. Tall, vine-covered trees swayed in the humid breeze as the elephants plowed through the dense, tropical forest. The squawks, growls, and chirps of teeming jungle life surrounded them.

After many hours of difficult travel, they came to a place where the thick jungle canopy broke, giving a glimpse of the sky. Indy gazed up and saw that the sun was still high. It was a good thing, too, because he estimated that they still had many miles to go. If what he surmised was correct, Pankot Palace was at the other end of the jungle, high in the mountains.

After another hour, they left the jungle and traversed a swampy valley. Several times, the elephants nearly became stuck in the muddy ground, trumpeting their displeasure as they struggled to extricate their thick, round legs from the muck. By the time they made it through the valley, all of the elephants were caked in mud.

Finally though, as a dusky glow suffused the sky, they began to ascend a mountain where the shrubbery was low and scruffy. The size and shape of the plant life told Indiana that they were very high up and climbing higher every minute. He tried breathing deeply, finding it was more difficult than he expected. The air was thinner at this altitude.

"Look!" Short Round cried out when they turned a bend in the path.

"I see it, Shorty," Indy replied. They were gazing at a resplendent cluster of high, dome-topped towers rising in the distance.

It seemed almost unreal sitting there so regally atop the mountain, especially after they had traveled so many hours without seeing so much as a single fabricated hut. The mogul-style palace was as large as a small city. The setting sun bounced off the inlaid gold of its many rounded rooftops, making it appear to radiate with unearthly light.

Turning, Indy looked to see how Willie was reacting to this majestic sight. She sat astride her elephant with her mouth agape, staring in awe. He understood her amazement. It was like something out of *Arabian Nights*, an enchanted place that had somehow survived from a time long ago.

As they climbed the steep path to the palace they stopped at what appeared, at first, to be some sort of roadside shrine. Indy did not want to pause for even a short break. At this point, he was eager to reach their destination before dark. But looking closer, Indy grew worried about the sight before him, an ominous statue throwing a wavering form in the shadowy dusk. He had seen this deity, a goddess of destruction and death, in ancient books and scrolls.

If he was seeing the deity he suspected, it was not a good sign. No, not good at all.

He motioned for the guides to stop. They barked commands to the elephants, which obediently halted. Indiana slid down the side of his elephant and walked toward the shrine to get a better look at the life-sized stone statue at the end of a narrow pathway.

As he had suspected, the many-armed, female deity before him was the Hindu goddess Kali. Kali the Destroyer had her positive aspects, destroying the bad as well as the good. This was a particularly sinister depiction of the goddess, suggesting, bloodthirsty, malevolent destruction.

A small and dangerous sect known as the Thuggee had worshipped Kali as representing all the dark powers of magic. Her presence was ominous and a very bad sign.

Indy was so engrossed in reappraising their situation that it took him a moment to realize what was hanging from her many arms. When he finally focused more closely, he staggered backward in horror.

Heads!

In each of her eight hands she gripped rotted human heads.

Fighting the wave of nausea that threatened to overwhelm him, he stepped closer and realized that someone had draped a garland around the statue's neck. He let out a quick revolted grunt when he saw what hung from her vine necklace: dead rodents, birds, and reptiles.

On top of that hideous adornment lay another string of blood-stained body parts — *animal or human?*

Who had concocted this gruesome warning? Who had killed these people and why?

"Dr. Jones, what you look at?" Short Round shouted up to him, getting off his small elephant and standing beside Willie, who had also dismounted.

"Don't come up here," he warned him firmly. This was something Indy would not soon forget and he didn't want the horrifying image emblazoned in Shorty's young mind.

He was about to inspect some ancient writing on the statue's base when a yelp from Willie made him whirl back around.

"No! No!" she cried, running after the guides who were

riding off on the backs of the elephants. They quickly out-distanced her, leaving her fuming on the path. "Indy! They're stealing our rides!" she shouted.

He shook his head and grinned at her misunderstanding. "The elephants can't go any further," he explained. "We have to walk from here."

He guessed that after seeing the gruesome warning, the guides had decided that this was as close as they wanted to get to Pankot Palace. He could hardly blame them.

Were Indiana, Willie, and Short Round fools to keep going? *Probably*, Indy thought as he motioned for Short Round and Willie to follow him up the mountain toward the palace.

*I*t was midafternoon by the time the trio entered the silent, foreboding outer courtyard of Pankot Palace. Two guards dressed in long white robes and crimson turbans were stationed at opposite sides of the open space with broadswords strapped to their hips. If not for their presence, Indy would have thought the place was deserted.

"Hello," Indy greeted the guards. But they did not answer or acknowledge him in any way, as though he hadn't spoken at all.

Before he could make a second attempt at communicating with the guards, a very official-looking man in a dark suit stepped out of a doorway. He was small with a pinched, officious manor. He surveyed them with an amused smirk, yet when he spoke, his tone was polite, even helpful. "I should say you look rather lost. But then I cannot imagine where in the world the three of you would look at home."

Indiana suddenly realized how the three of them must appear: a blond with a mop of messy curls dressed in a man's tuxedo, a small Asian boy in a New York Yankees baseball cap, and a grown man in a fedora, bomber jacket, and boots, carrying a bullwhip.

They were a motley bunch, to be sure!

"We're not lost," Indy explained to the man. "We're on our way to Delhi. This is Miss Scott. This is Mr. . . . Round."

"Short Round," the boy concurred, with a dignified air of importance.

"My name is Indiana Jones," Indy added.

The man's eyebrows lifted in delighted surprise. "Dr. Jones — the eminent archaeologist?" he asked, clearly very aware of and impressed by Indy's reputation.

"Hard to believe, isn't it?" Willie quipped derisively.

Indy shot her an annoyed look, but said nothing. Her mouth was likely to get them into trouble around here.

The man took no notice of Willie's remark and kept his attention on Indy. "Ah, I remember first hearing your name when I was up at Oxford," he recalled excitedly. "I am Chattar Lal, Prime Minister to His Highness the Maharajah of Pankot."

"Oh," Indy said, not knowing how to respond to this news. Until he'd crash-landed into the mountain village, he hadn't known there even *was* a Maharajah of Pankot, let alone that he had a prime minister named Chattar Lal. As far as most outsiders knew, Pankot Palace and its kingdom had been abandoned a long time ago. Obviously the old shaman had known what he was talking about.

Chattar Lal extended his hand and Indy politely shook it. Then the prime minister turned to Willie, finally looking at her, and bowed, taking her hand gallantly. "I'm enchanted," he said, suavely kissing her hand.

"Thank you very much," Willie said smoothly, charmed by his elegant manners. "Thank you very much."

Indy scowled. There was something about Chattar Lal's syrupy, cheesy, overblown manners that he just didn't trust.

Chattar Lal motioned for them to follow him into the palace. Short Round began to go, but Indy held him back and politely gestured for Willie to proceed first. He'd shown her that he could be as well-mannered as that buffoon of a prime minister, Chattar Lal.

Willie graced Indy with an appreciative nod and quick smile before following the prime minister inside. "Enchanted, huh?" Indy grumbled as he and Short Round went in behind her.

The palace might have been the most splendid place Indy had ever seen firsthand. The golden ceilings were immensely high, vaulted and supported by thick, ornate columns. Every turn revealed an obviously priceless work of art: paintings and statues of every description. The floors were inlaid with gold and studded with rubies, emeralds, and pearls that made them sparkle wherever sunlight filtered through the lavish and complex cutouts of the shuttered windows.

Chattar Lal brought them up a winding spiral of stairs laid with mosaics and showed them to two separate rooms on the same tranquil corridor. Willie's lavish room was directly across from an even larger one that Indy and Short Round would share.

The prime minister told them to refresh themselves and then invited them to be his guests at a dinner party to be held in the maharajah's pavilion that evening. If they were lucky, he said, the maharajah himself might join them.

When Willie protested that she had nothing to wear to a party — she explained to Chattar Lal that her designer gown from Paris had been lost in a horrific plane crash — Chattar Lal said not to worry. He would instruct servants to bring her fresh clothing for the event.

Willie smiled at Chattar Lal so charmingly that Indy furrowed his brow at her as she exited into her room. Not once since they had met had Willie smiled at him like that. Up until now he hadn't even known she *could* smile like that. He'd thought all she could do was to complain and scream.

Then again, Indy hadn't even been able to offer her a bath, much less a new gown.

Entering the room he would share with Short Round, Indy stretched out on the luxurious, canopied bed and sighed. He hadn't been in a bed this comfortable since . . . since . . . well, maybe never. It was certainly a drastic change from the hard ground on which he'd slept for the last two nights.

He thought of the smooth, well-dressed Chattar Lal and the way Willie had smiled at him . . . not that he cared, of course. She could smile at anyone she liked. It wasn't as though she had any taste in men. Her last boyfriend had been Lao Che, for crying out loud!

Still, it bugged Indy that she treated him with such contempt while she mooned over these lowlifes. If the village shaman was right, the people so eager to charm them now were responsible for kidnapping hundreds of children — maybe more. Had she forgotten that?

Indy hadn't seen any signs of the missing children yet, but that didn't mean the palace wasn't hiding any secrets. Hopefully, dinner would be illuminating. He had some ideas about how to turn the evening's situation to his advantage. But in order to get anything out of these royal criminals, Indy would have to look the part of the esteemed professor: the eminent Dr. Jones.

He rolled over onto his side. "Shorty," he called into the alcove where Short Round was bouncing on the chaise lounge where he would sleep. "Where are my clothes?"

CHAPTER NINE

When it was time for the dinner party, a servant came
to each room and rang a tinkling bell outside the door.
Indy examined himself in the long mirror by his bed.
He had showered, combed his hair, and donned a fresh
sports jacket, creased pants, a shirt, socks, shoes, and a bow
tie. He'd even dug his glasses out of the satchel Short
Round had packed. Indy really only needed them for
when he did a lot of reading, but they gave him a distin-
guished air.

He told Short Round to finish up. The boy was in the
bathroom, luxuriating in a large bathtub inlaid with gold.
The tub was so big that he was actually underwater, swimming in a circle. Coming up for air, he assured him that he
would hurry, though Indy thought it would probably take
a lot to get him out of the tub.

In the hallway, Indy knocked on Willie's door. She
didn't answer so he tried again. Where could she be? Was

she also submerged in a golden bathtub? Maybe she was napping.

Giving up, he went down the spiral staircase to the Pleasure Pavilion. Guards in turbans stood in front of two tall, silver doors. A third guard opened the door as he neared it.

Indiana was not the first guest to arrive. Fourteen other men were already standing in front of a dais watching swirling female dancers in colorful, diaphanous saris dance to music played by musicians dressed in traditional robes. The dancers moved together to the music, their dresses creating a fluid rainbow around their lithe, graceful bodies.

The majority of the guests also wore the traditional robes and turbans of the region, although much more elegant versions than the robes of the musicians. Chattar Lal wore no turban, but he had donned a high-collared garment. Indy identified it as a *sherwani,* a traditional style for northern Indian men. The only other guest who was not dressed in the traditional local style was an older, balding man in a uniform of a British cavalry captain.

At first, Indy went unnoticed. When he arrived, all the guests were engrossed in watching the entertainment. That was fine with him. He wanted a moment to take in his surroundings.

This room was even more spectacular than any other room of the palace Indy had seen thus far. The curtain over the dais shimmered, the golden threads softly reflecting the light from the lamps. Golden chairs lined the room, and the rug below his feet appeared to have been woven entirely from golden yarn.

When the musicians stopped playing and the audience applauded, Chattar Lal leaned close to speak to Indy. "We are fortunate tonight to have so many unexpected visitors," he said. Beside him stood a tall, middle-aged man with blazing blue eyes and thick muttonchop whiskers. He was the British cavalry captain that Indy had spotted earlier. "This is Captain Blumburtt," Chattar Lal introduced him.

The captain smiled cordially. "Eleventh Puma Rifles," he said proudly, elaborating on his specific station. "And you, sir, are Dr. Jones, I presume."

"I am, captain," Indy confirmed.

"Captain Blumburtt and his troops are on a routine inspection tour," Chattar Lal explained. "The British find it amusing to inspect us at their convenience."

Chattar Lal's smoothly pleasant tone belied the sourness of his jab, but the complaint was not lost on the captain and he reddened. "I do hope, sir, that it is not, ah, inconvenient to you, ah, sir," he sputtered in a thick English accent.

The prime minister's voice remained silkily snide. "The British worry so about their empire. It makes us all feel like well-cared-for children," he replied.

As the dancers were exiting, Short Round appeared and was nearly run over by the rush of women. He shouted at them indignantly in Chinese, but was ignored.

Willie came in right behind Short Round. Indy drew in a sharp breath when he saw her. She was stunning in a gossamer gown that appeared to have been made for an Indian princess. The lavish Mogul-style jewelry she'd been loaned sparkled on her neck and arms. She was completely refreshed and unbelievably radiant.

"You look beautiful," Indy said when she joined him.

Willie gazed around, her eyes wide as she drank in the luxurious splendor of her surroundings. "I think the maharajah's swimming in loot," she noted in a conspiratorial undertone. "Maybe it wasn't such a bad idea coming here, after all."

Indy was too mesmerized by his surroundings to pay attention to her tactless words. "You look like a princess," he told her.

"Mr. Lal," Willie said, turning toward him, "what do they call the maharajah's wife?"

"His Highness has not yet taken a wife," Chattar Lal informed her.

Willie's eyes lit with excitement and Indy was roused from his stupor. He saw at once what was in her conniving mind. The little opportunist had forgotten all about charming Chattar Lal; she'd set her sights higher. Now she was bent on dazzling the maharajah — and she hadn't even met the guy yet! Indy could practically see the wheels turning in her scheming head.

"How interesting," Willie commented, delighted at the news that the maharajah was still a single man eligible to make her his queen or maharani or whatever the term turned out to be. It wouldn't matter to Willie, Indy was sure, just as long as she got the gold and jewels.

"Well, ah, maybe the maharajah hasn't met the right woman yet," she went on, a crafty smile coming to her lips.

Indiana shook his head woefully, amazed at the obvious thought behind her remark.

A gong was sounded and the assembled guests moved into an adjoining room toward a long, low table surrounded by colorful pillows. Like everything else in the palace, the table was a study in luxury, with golden candlesticks, vases overflowing with flowers, and silverware that shone as though it were studded with diamonds.

Short Round was shown to a spot next to Willie at the far end of the table, and Indy was guided to a place near the head of the table, next to Captain Blumburtt and across from Chattar Lal. No one sat, and so Indy, Willie, and Short Round stood at their places, as well.

Everyone quieted as Chattar Lal cleared his throat, preparing to make an announcement. With an arm raised toward two solid silver doors, he intoned: "His Supreme Highness, guardian of Pankot tradition — the Maharajah of Pankot, Zalim Singh."

The doors opened as if blown by a magic wind and through them walked a figure outfitted in a spectacular, red-and-gold-brocaded, high-collared coat that came to below the knees of his legging-swaddled legs. The coat was festooned with enormous jewels, as was the ornate, shimmering turban on his head. But the most unexpected thing about the maharajah was his age; he could not have been more than thirteen!

All the guests bowed and Indy did the same.

The maharajah was a kid!

He snickered softly, amused. How was Willie reacting to this new development? He bit down on his smile as he imagined the look of disappointment and distress that must be playing across her face.

The little maharajah gazed imperiously at his bowing guests before seating himself on an array of golden pillows at the head of the table. He nodded and everyone else was free to sit. Another nod to the serving staff initiated the flow of food carried out on golden trays.

Glancing down to the end of the table where Willie and Short Round sat, he saw the servants set down a huge platter in front of them. Willie's eyes widened with panicked alarm when she saw what was on it: an enormous, steaming boa constrictor!

Did it have to be a *snake*? Indy gripped the table tight in an effort to control his terror and not make a spectacle of himself. He was glad the table was so long and hoped there would not be a similar delicacy coming his way.

Although Willie and Short Round were recoiling in horror at the dish, a fat, turbaned merchant beside Willie rubbed his hands in greedy delight as he inhaled the steam emanating from the platter. "Ah, snake surprise," he said with rapturous delight.

"What's the surprise?" Willie asked cautiously.

Indy clenched his stomach muscles to keep the insides of his belly from lurching forward when he saw a waiter slit the snake's skin and the so-called surprise erupted from inside the boa. Eels slithered out of it, flopping all along the table.

The guests stabbed them with their forks, dropping them whole into their mouths, obviously relishing the tasty treat. Indy was extremely grateful that Captain Blumburtt also displayed nothing but disgust for the creatures, swatting them off the table each time one crawled too close.

Captain Blumburtt began telling Indy some facts about the history of the palace and he was thankful for the distraction. Indy already knew most of the information, but listened intently anyway, alert for anything new he might learn that would help him understand what was going on here.

He noticed Chattar Lal listening to their conversation and looked to him politely. "Captain Blumburtt was just telling me about the importance the palace played in the mutiny," he informed him. In 1857, a revolt against the British rule of India had had its origin at Pankot Palace, though it had been suppressed by British troops.

Chattar Lal sniffed haughtily. "It seems the British never forget the Mutiny of 1857," he commented dryly, a sarcastic sneer in his voice. It was obviously a point in the palace's history that Chattar Lal was not keen to be reminded of.

Indiana figured he would learn more if Chattar Lal was in a better mood, so he turned the topic away from the mutiny. Besides, he was working on a theory, one he was eager to explore now. "I think there are other events before the mutiny, going back a century to the time of Clive, that are more interesting," he said diplomatically in his most academic, professorial tone.

It had done the trick. Chattar Lal relaxed and even

managed a tight smile. "And what events are those, Dr. Jones?" he inquired, leaning forward with interest.

Indy paused, wanting to frame his next comment just right. He had been thinking about the horrible, head-wielding statue of Kali. Its presence so near the palace surely had to mean that the ancient Thuggee cult was once again active in the area.

"If memory serves me correctly," he began in an off-handed manner, trying to sound as though his interest was purely academic, "this province was the center of activity for the Thuggee."

The Thuggee cult had been active from the 13th century all the way to the 1800's, though they had been strongest in the 1600's. Thuggee groups traveled in gangs of between ten to two hundred members. They would join wealthy travelers along the road, at first seeming helpful and friendly, and when the moment seemed right, would strangle the travelers with a yellow cloth, a symbol of their goddess, stealing the travelers' possessions. They would also assassinate anyone for money. They claimed to do all this in the service of Kali, and put aside a portion of what they stole and earned through killings in honor of their dreadful goddess.

The British encountered them when they took over India and it was the Thuggee who brought the word *thug* into the English language. In the 1830's the British began to crack down on the cult and by the 1890's these notorious killers and thieves had been mostly stamped out — but perhaps not as completely as was thought.

Chattar Lal clearly knew all about them and grew angry at the mere mention of the word "Thuggee." "Dr. Jones, you know perfectly well that the Thuggee cult has been dead for nearly a century," he snapped peevishly.

"Yes, of course," Captain Blumburtt joined the exchange. "The Thuggee was an obscenity that worshipped a Kali-like goddess with human sacrifices. The British Army nicely did away with them."

"Well, I suppose stories of the Thuggee die hard," Indiana conceded philosophically, trying to smooth things.

"There are no stories anymore," Chattar Lal insisted stiffly, offended.

"I'm not so sure," Indy disagreed. If he'd had no ulterior motive, Indy might have let the subject drop. But he needed to probe further. No matter what this phony prime minister said, he was *sure* the Thuggee had resurfaced; everything pointed to it.

It was time to stop beating around the bush. He couldn't worry about offending Chattar Lal any more. "We came from a small village," he began. "The peasants there told us Pankot Palace was growing powerful again because of an ancient evil."

*T*here! It was out on the table. Indy sat back in his chair awaiting the reaction.

"Village stories, Dr. Jones," Chattar Lal insisted. "They're just . . . fear and folklore. You're beginning to worry Captain Blumburtt."

"Not worried, Mr. Prime Minister," Captain Blumburtt said, "just, uh, interested."

Chattar Lal began to tell the captain that the Thuggee was a mere fabrication of the British who were trying to insult the people of the land they ruled. In fact, he insisted, they had never existed.

Indy's attention drifted away as Chattar Lal went on at great lengths, attempting to prove that the Thuggee was simply myth. Indy didn't want to hear a lot of empty propaganda; he knew for a fact that the Thuggee had existed, had read firsthand accounts of their sinister rituals and evil deeds.

A goblet was set in front of him: the next course. In the goblet sat the head of a monkey, its wide-opened eyes staring at him. The top of its head had been cut off revealing the brains within.

Indy did not recoil in horror. He'd eaten monkey brains before. Really, once a person got over the strangeness of it, it wasn't bad. But before digging in, he looked down the table to see how Willie and Short Round where reacting to this bizarre delicacy.

Short Round's upper lip was quirked up in an expression of utter disgust.

Willie stared, goggle-eyed in disbelief, at the monkey head in front of her.

Indy smiled to himself. He wondered how attractive life in the palace as the wife of a monkey-brain-eating, teenaged maharajah seemed to her now.

Chattar Lal continued to ramble on about how the Thuggee didn't exist and Indiana was growing weary of his lies. Once again, he went straight to the point. "You know, the villagers also told us that Pankot Palace had stolen something very valuable from them."

Chattar Lal reddened angrily. "Dr. Jones, in our country it is not usual for a guest to insult his host," he snapped irritably.

Indy could see he'd struck a nerve. "I'm sorry," he

apologized with feigned sincerity. "I thought we were talking about folklore."

"What exactly was it they say was stolen?" Captain Blumburtt wanted to know.

"A sacred rock."

This revelation was greeted by uproarious laughter from Chattar Lal. "You see, captain," he boomed when he had stopped laughing. "A rock!"

Indy leaned in to Chattar Lal and spoke to him pointedly. "*Something* connected the villagers' rock and the old legend of the Sankara Stones."

He studied Chattar Lal's face for any sign that the man knew about the escaped child who had carried the ancient cloth with him.

Chattar Lal's expression revealed nothing. In fact, his irritable demeanor had vanished and he'd regained his professional, diplomatic equilibrium. His formerly scowling visage was now an inscrutable blank. "Dr. Jones, we're all vulnerable to vicious rumors," he replied lightly. "I seem to remember that in Honduras *you* were accused of being a grave robber rather than an archaeologist."

Chattar Lal had done his homework! "Well, the newspapers greatly exaggerated the story," Indiana commented modestly, undisturbed.

The prime minister stayed on the attack. "And wasn't it the Sultan of Madagascar who threatened to cut your head off if you ever returned to his country?"

Indy chuckled at the memory. "No, it wasn't my head."

"Then your hands, perhaps?" Chattar Lal checked.

"No, it wasn't my hands," Indy assured him, still smiling. He decided not to go on with the true story since it might not seem polite, especially at the dinner table. "It was a misunderstanding."

Chattar Lal threw his hands in the air triumphantly as though Indy had just proved his point for him. "That's exactly what we have here, Dr. Jones — a most unfortunate misunderstanding!"

The young maharajah had been sitting at the head of the table, but had not seemed to be listening to the conversation regarding the Thuggee. At least, that was what Indy thought when he occasionally glanced at him to gauge any reactions he might be having and saw nothing but blankness in the maharajah's expression.

Apparently, though, Indy had been wrong because now the maharajah raised his head and had a very definite opinion. "I have heard the evil stories of the Thuggee cult," he remarked in a mature, even-keeled voice. "I thought the stories were told to frighten children. Later I learned the Thuggee cult was once real and did unspeakable things. I am ashamed of what happened here so many years ago, and I assure you, this will never happen again in my kingdom."

"If I offended you, then I am sorry," Indy told him, and this time the apology was sincere. The maharajah had struck him as an honorable, well-intentioned young man from the moment he began to speak. Indy felt certain that if there was indeed evil at work at Pankot Palace, the maharajah was not the source of it. Of Chattar Lal, he was much less certain.

*T*hat evening, after the dinner, Indy noticed that Willie and Short Round hadn't been able to eat a single thing. In the excitement of his conversation, he hadn't eaten much either. Fortunately, he was able to get a tray of fresh fruit from a servant. After he and Short Round ate a few apples and oranges, they went up to their rooms with the tray to offer some fruit to Willie. She had claimed she felt sick and had gone straight to her room after dinner.

Sending Short Round to their shared room, Indy knocked on Willie's door. Holding the plate behind his back with one hand, he loosened his bow tie with the other. He wondered if she'd noticed how dashing he looked. When Willie opened the door she was dressed in luxurious purple silk pajamas and a matching robe. Her hair hung loose at her shoulders. "I've got something for you," Indy said.

Her eyes narrowed scornfully. "There's nothing you have that I could possibly want," she replied.

"Right," he said, turning away from the door and shifting the plate of fruit to his front side. He paused long enough to take a loud, crunchy bite from an apple.

Willie was at his side instantly, grabbing the apple from him and voraciously attacking it. "Oh, you're a very nice man," she said as she ate. "Maybe you could be my palace slave."

Willie took the entire plate of fruit from Indy and walked back to her room.

In his room, Indy fumed and paced the floor, only taking a short break to check on Short Round who was sleeping soundly. "Palace slave," he muttered angrily. Who did she think she was? She'd be there knocking on his door in five minutes . . . maybe four. But the four minutes, and then five passed, and Willie did not appear. He realized that she really wasn't going to show up. He began to unbutton his shirt to get ready for bed, when he froze. Something inside his room had moved.

It was the male figure in the life-sized wall hanging in the shadowy far corner of the room.

Cautiously, he stepped toward it to get a better look. Perhaps it was just a trick of the torchlight, but he was sure he'd detected movement.

And then, all at once, there was a man standing in the

middle of the room, as if from out of nowhere. He was a very large man dressed in traditional robes and wearing a turban.

The mysterious intruder lifted a yellow silk cord over his head and advanced on Indy.

The Thuggee, Indy thought as his attacker approached and he stepped backwards away from the man. Strangulation was their chosen form of murder and yellow cord was their trademark. It was just as he'd thought! Under other circumstances it would have been gratifying to be right, but that was little comfort at the moment.

The man lunged at Indy and swiftly wrapped the cord around his neck. The huge assassin stood behind him and twisted the cord ever more tightly.

Summoning all his strength, Indy shoved his attacker back against the wall, ramming him hard into it. But the assassin maintained his death grip on Indy's neck.

Gasping for air, Indy snapped up a brass pot from the floor, gripping it by its handle, and, with the last of his strength, smashed it up into the assassin's head with a skull-crashing *clang*.

The assassin reeled back, stunned.

With lightning speed, Indy curled forward and pulled the man into a somersault, sending him flying over his back. Indy's attacker crashed onto the floor and slid next to the bed where Short Round continued to sleep soundly.

All the while, the assassin never lost his grip on the cord around Indy's neck!

The wild, thrashing battle continued right there beside Short Round's bed.

Indy grabbed anything he could reach and hurled it at the assassin. He was so completely involved in this life-and-death battle that he didn't see Short Round awaken and climb out of bed. But the next instant, his young assistant was standing beside him. "Dr. Jones, your whip!" he said, handing the bullwhip to Indy.

Indy grabbed the whip and lashed at the assassin. At last the man released his grip on Indy's throat, allowing Indy to roll to his feet. With another forceful snap, Indy was able to circle the man's neck with the whip's end. Now the tables were turned.

The big man struggled, desperate to pry the whip from his neck, but Indy held fast as his would-be killer gasped for air, his face turning red.

Just as Indy was beginning to feel confident that he'd gotten the best of his enemy, the assassin spun into a full-blown backflip that ripped the whip from Indy's grasp. The Thuggee assassin grinned at him victoriously while the whip handle was still spinning through the air.

His smile came too soon.

The handle of the whip caught in the motor of the slowly spinning fan, and began turning along with the blades. The surprised and horrified assassin was tugged upward like a fish being reeled on a fishing line. The whip twisted around the ceiling fan, pulling him higher and higher until the man's toes dangled off the marble floor. The assassin let out a last dying gasp as he hung from the fan.

Short Round closed his eyes tightly, not wanting to view the awful image of the dead man as the fan slowly spun him in a circle.

"Shorty," Indy said quietly as he slumped onto his bed, rubbing his neck. "Turn off the switch."

Opening his eyes, Short Round obeyed. Instantly the dead assassin dropped to the ground, allowing Indy to uncoil his whip from the fan.

Then he remembered Willie. Was she all right?

He dashed across the hall and burst into her room. She was lying atop her bed, awake. She smiled when she saw him.

But Indy didn't even notice her smile. He was too busy scouring the room. He looked around frantically, swung back curtains, checked under the bed. "There's nobody here," he said.

"I'm here, Indy," she told him, sitting up. "You're acting awfully strange."

Indy knew *she* was there. He was searching for anyone *else* who might be lurking around. He suddenly felt a breeze that ruffled a vase filled with dried flowers. A current of air could mean only one thing — there was some sort of secret passage or cave in this room. He followed the current of air to a statue of a woman in the far corner of the room. Giving it a push back was all it took.

The statue receded into the stone wall and an opening appeared behind it. As soon as Indy stepped through, he became aware of a painted inscription on the inside wall. Spidery Sanskrit calligraphy ran under a flaking illustration of an ancient priest bowing before a god. Indy translated the writing out loud: "Follow the footsteps of Shiva. Do not betray his truth."

Indy took out the piece of cloth he'd received from the escaped boy in Mayapore. The similarities between this picture and the one on the cloth were striking. Both depicted Shiva and Sankara.

Short Round appeared at the open passageway. He looked up at Indy with questioning eyes. "Shorty, go get our stuff," Indy told him. They had some exploring to do.

*I*ndy and Short Round entered the secret passage, moving forward slowly into the inky darkness. "Stay behind me, Short Round," Indy cautioned in a low tone. "Step where I step and don't touch anything."

One of Short Round's best qualities was his ability to follow instructions. But, outweighing this was his overwhelming curiosity about almost everything. Only minutes after Indy warned him not to touch anything, he spied a metal ring on a door embedded in the wall and gave it a forceful tug.

The door shattered!

Two mummified corpses tumbled out, falling onto him.

"HELP!" Shorty shouted.

Indy yanked him out from beneath the rotted bodies. Trembling, Short Round crouched behind Indy. "I step where you step. I touch nothing," he restated Indiana's warning in a quaking voice. From the way the boy continued to shake, Indy felt certain that this time he'd do as he was told.

Indy and Short Round continued to creep down the dark tunnel. Gradually, it grew smaller and Indy had to duck down to fit. Soon he could hear a crunching sound underfoot. "I step on something," Short Round alerted him.

Indy had felt it, too. There had been a definite crunch underfoot. "Yeah, there's something on the ground," he agreed.

"Feel like I step on fortune cookies," Short Round remarked.

"It's not fortune cookies," Indy said, feeling certain. It would be much too lucky to be true if they were simply crunching cookies beneath their feet. He reached into his jacket pocket and took out a book of matches. "Let me take a look," he said, igniting a match with his thumb and watching it flare.

They froze as a gruesome scene was illuminated around them.

The floor and walls of the narrow tunnel were an undulating mass of millions of enormous bugs: a living collection of the world's ugliest arthropods, hexapods, and arachnids!

Short Round clutched Indiana's arm when he spotted

a huge scorpion on his leg. "That's no cookie," he said in a quivering whimper, pointing to the hideous bug with a trembling hand.

"It's all right. I got it," Indy said, stooping to brush the scorpion off. As he swatted the bug away, another hopped onto him.

And then another!

He batted it off but another two replaced it!

They were jumping on faster than he could get rid of them. In another minute, they would be completely covered.

Indy reached for a bug that was crawling up his shirt when he noticed an open chamber just several yards away. It appeared to be bug-free. "Go! There! Go!" he urged Short Round, steering him toward the chamber.

Short Round wasted no time hurrying into the chamber. Indy followed him. As they entered, Short Round unwittingly stepped on a button in the floor that caused a stone door to roll shut. At the same time, another door at the opposite end of the chamber rumbled closed.

They were trapped inside!

Indy lit another of his matches. The light revealed two skeletons lying on the floor.

Wearing a horrified expression, Short Round began to cross the chamber toward him, but Indy held up a cautioning hand. "Stop," he said. It was better if they stayed still. Who knew what other traps were rigged in this chamber? "Just stand up against the wall, will ya?"

Slowly and obediently, Short Round backed against the wall. "You say stand against the wall, I listen to what you say. Not my fault! Not my fault!"

They had only one hope of getting out of there. And that meant to Indy that their chances weren't too good at all. But he had to try. "Willie!" he shouted through the smallest of openings between the boulder and the door archway. "Willie! Get down here."

When they'd gone into the tunnel, they had left her behind in the bedroom, telling her it was too dangerous for her. Indy was sure they'd travel faster and more safely without her stumbling along and shrieking at every little thing. He certainly had never expected to have to call on her to rescue him. But now he had no choice. "Willie!" he bellowed once again. "Come down here! We're in trouble!"

He waited for what seemed like a long while, though maybe he was just impatient and time was dragging. Finally, off in the distance, he heard a horrified scream and smiled, but only a little.

The scream meant that Willie had come to the crispy corpses Short Round had released from their stand-up crypt. At least she was on her way.

He slid down the wall, preparing to wait for her arrival. She was probably wearing some fluffy heeled slippers and she'd be stumbling along at her own slow pace. *Oh, well,* he thought. The important thing was that she'd heard him calling and was on her way. They were in no hurry.

He had nearly slid to the bottom of the floor when he felt something click against his back. He hoped it was nothing.

It was something.

Instantly, one of the skeletons on the floor jerked to a sitting position as deadly spikes punched up through the floor and started down from the ceiling.

Indy and Short Round began pounding on the doors. "This is serious!" Indy shouted to Willie. "Hurry!"

The ceiling was moving downward!

Soon — he had no idea *how* soon — they would be crushed like bugs in a giant pair of fanged teeth.

What was taking her so long?

Another set of wild shrieks told him that she had reached the hall with all the insects. How tough was she? How much did she care about helping them? He didn't know. He could only hope.

Finally he could hear Willie moving in the tunnel behind the boulder. She hadn't run away, after all! The oil lamp she held flickered into the moving spike-filled chamber.

"There are two dead people down here," she cried, an edge of hysteria in her voice.

"There are going to be two dead people down *in here!*" he said urgently. "Hurry!"

"I've almost had enough of you two," she whimpered unhappily as she came closer.

Indy looked up at the spikes. They didn't have long — and he couldn't be sure Willie would pull through. He needed to do *something*. So when he spotted a skull on the ground, he snapped it up and wedged it firmly between the roller and the track, jamming the mechanism. For a moment, the ceiling slowed its descent and Indy held his breath. With any luck, the gears would lock up and stall the whole thing out. But almost immediately, the skull shattered, sending the ceiling barreling toward them once more. "Willie!" he shouted.

"What's the rush?" she asked as she disgustedly swatted at the many crawling bugs that had attached themselves to her robe.

Indy glanced back at the spikes that were moving ever closer together. "It's a long story," he said quickly, "and if you don't hurry, you don't get to hear it."

She began to pound on the boulder. "Indy, let me in."

"No! Let us out!" Indy didn't have time for this! He was now stooped forward and Short Round clung to his back to avoid the moving spikes.

"Let me in!" she insisted, not realizing what was going on inside the chamber and desperate to escape the crawling bugs. "They're all over me."

The situation inside the chamber wasn't getting any better, and sweat began to bead up on Indy's brow. But he knew that if he started panicking, he'd lose his only shot at getting out of this alive. "There's got to be a fulcrum release lever somewhere," he told her, straining to keep his voice clear and level.

"What?"

"A handle that opens the door," he explained, talking faster. "Go on, look."

"There's no handle," she reported, "Just two square holes."

"Go to the right hole," Indy instructed, his patience wearing thin.

"Hurry, Willie!" Short Round pleaded. A spike now pressed against his forehead, and a look of terror was plastered all over his face.

"Ooohh, there's slime inside this hole," she complained. "I can't do it."

"You can do it," he encouraged her. "Feel inside!"

"*You* feel inside," she objected.

He was out of patience and out of time. "Do it now!" he barked.

"Okay!"

The deadly spikes were nearly poking into Indy's leather jacket. One was pressing down on the brim of his hat. He turned his head sideways and sucked in his breath in one last effort to avoid the spikes.

This was it. "We are going to die!" he shouted, finally losing his cool.

But then he heard the sweetest sound in the world. "Got it!" Willie cried triumphantly.

The spikes suddenly retracted, disappearing into the floor and ceiling, and the stone door slid back into the wall.

Short Round leaped off Indy's back and he slumped against a wall, nearly faint with relief.

Willie raced into the room, still batting bugs off her robe. "Get them off of me! Get them off of me!" she ranted, turning in a frenzied circle. "They're all over me! Get them off! They're all over my body."

She jumped up and down trying to shake off the insects that clung on. As she bent to brush off her legs, her rear end struck the same stone block on the wall that had triggered the trap.

With a rumble, the door rolled back again, sealing the doorway once more, and the spikes began to appear all over again!

"It wasn't me!" Short Round cried out defensively.

Willie screamed, not understanding what was happening.

"Come on! Get out!" Short Round urged, pointing at the rapidly closing door at the other end of the chamber.

"Go! Move! Move!" Indy shouted as they raced for the door.

They got out just in time. *My hat!* Indy thought, realizing that he was bareheaded. Without thinking, he reached back and snapped it up from the floor where it had fallen just seconds before the door crashed shut.

A DOUBLE CROSS!

A CRASH LANDING!

AND A JUNGLE JOURNEY!

EVIL DEEDS!

UNLIKELY ALLIES!

AND A NARROW ESCAPE!

IF ADVENTURE HAS A NAME, IT MUST BE INDIANA JONES!

*I*ndiana, Short Round, and Willie raced out of the spiked chamber and started down a large tunnel. After a few paces, they were flattened against the wall of the tunnel by a roaring wind that howled eerily like a note of gloomy music.

When it died down, Indy led them around the next curve, toward the light. As he moved forward, the wind howled another dramatic gale that blasted past them just as they reached the mouth of the tunnel.

He stopped suddenly, amazed at the sight in front of him. Willie and Short Round crashed into his back, before they, too, dropped their jaws, astounded by what they were seeing.

Below them, at least five stories down, a colossal subterranean temple had been carved out of a solid mass of rock. A vaulting, cathedral-like ceiling was supported by rows of carved stone columns. Balconies overlooked the temple floor and pillared halls led off to dark side chambers.

And the temple was not empty. Gigantic stone statues of elephants, lions, and scary-looking deities — half-human, half-animal monstrosities with horrible, fanged, leering faces — loomed above crowds of chanting, male worshippers dressed only from the waist down in white loincloths. The rumble of their monotone intonations reverberated against the rock walls around them, making the temple hum as though a steady motor rumbled at its core. They worshipped before an altar jutting from a stone wall in the cavern. Between the worshippers and the altar was a natural crevasse that occasionally spewed clouds of smoke.

At the altar was a statue that towered over all the others. It was similar to the one Indy had found on the road to the palace — the goddess Kali, a manifestation of death and complete destruction.

Unlike the statue at the roadside shrine, this one was even more loathsome. It bore the visage of a hideous, devouring monster, its eyes and fanged mouth dripping blood. Its dangling earrings were made from two human corpses. Many skulls adorned its neck and chest and a gigantic glowing skull sat between its legs. Skulls surrounded its stone feet. Carved serpents twisted up its leg, and around its waist hung a gruesome belt of human hands.

The statue clenched a sword in one of its four arms and a decapitated head of a giant in the other. Its other two hands were stretched forward as if encouraging the adoring throng at its feet, whose chants grew increasingly loud and impassioned.

Willie, Indy, and Short Round watched in silence as three priests in robes materialized out of the swirling smoke. They each carried an urn attached to a strap around their necks. Gray smoke billowed from each urn and they brought it toward the malevolent object of their adoration, the statue of Kali. The priests knelt at the base of the statue and bowed reverently.

"It's a Thuggee ceremony," Indy whispered to Willie and Short Round.

"Have you ever seen anything like this before?" Willie asked quietly.

"Nobody's seen this for a hundred years," he replied.

A huge drum was banged three times.

Abruptly, the chanting ceased.

The silence in the immense chamber was chilling as a sinister figure appeared from out of the smoke. Indy was sure he must be the high priest of the Thuggee cult.

The high priest's red-rimmed eyes glared from sunken sockets in his pale face. His bloodred robes made him look almost as vile and diabolical as the goddess he served. Like her, he wore a necklace comprised of animal fangs and bones. His horned headpiece appeared to have been made from a bison skull on top of which a small, screaming shrunken head had been placed.

The drum banged three more times and the high priest lifted his arms ominously.

From somewhere came a bloodcurdling scream.

All heads turned toward a man dressed only in a loincloth, who struggled violently between two priests. They dragged him, screaming and kicking, to an upright iron frame and strapped him in.

The high priest stepped toward his victim and began to intone a wild ritual chant as his hand moved slowly across the man's face and neck.

Suddenly, the high priest placed his hand over the victim's chest, sunk it into the man's body, and removed his living heart.

Willie screamed in horror, clamping her hand over her mouth to stifle the sound and falling back against the rock wall.

Short Round covered his face with his hands, cringing.

Indy felt his stomach lurch. "He's still alive," he murmured to himself quietly, not quite believing his own eyes. But a second glance told him that what he'd witnessed had indeed happened.

The sacrificial victim gazed in amazement down at his

chest, slowly realizing that he was still alive. There was no evidence of a gash on his chest, only a red mark.

As he looked in wonder down at his chest, a stone door beneath him slid open, emitting intense heat along with a rush of steam. The metal frame, on which the victim was chained, was lifted from the ground by a man operating a pulley wheel and directed by one of the priests.

The man looked down into the pit and began to thrash frantically in terror. From where they were standing, high above, Indy, Willie, and Short Round could see what the man was seeing. Molten lava bubbled crimson deep inside the pit!

The priest slowly released the lever controlling the wheel. Willie turned away as the victim was lowered into the molten pit, but Short Round and Indy watched in horror. The lava flared and spit sparks while the screaming man disappeared into it.

The high priest kept the beating heart raised high above his head while this was happening. His eyes were glazed, and the corners of his mouth turned up in a vicious smile. Indy could tell that the man was actually enjoying this!

The metal frame was raised out of the lava pit, glowing red. There was no sign of the man who had been sacrificed.

The fierce wind that had flattened Indy, Willie, and Short Round in the tunnel blew once more. Indy could tell from Short Round's sickened expression that he was appalled by what he'd just seen. His own legs weren't feeling all that sturdy, either, and Willie quivered all over, her face frozen into an expressionless stone mask.

While the multitude of worshippers chanted at a frenzied pitch, the high priest walked back to the altar and disappeared. The three priests approached the altar, each carrying something wrapped in a cloth.

Indy leaned in to get a better look at it.

The priests reverently unwrapped three cone-shaped pieces of crystallized quartz. They placed the three stones in the eyes and mouth below the statue of the goddess. As the stones were brought together they began to glow a burning, incandescent white.

"That's the rock they took from the village," Indy quietly pointed out to Willie and Short Round. "It's one of the Sankara Stones."

"Why do they glow like that?" Short Round asked.

"Shhh," Indy shushed him. If they were discovered here, they'd be in huge trouble. Speaking even more softly, he explained: "The legend says that when the rocks are brought together, the *diamonds* inside them will glow."

"Diamonds?" Willie asked in a whisper.

"Diamonds!" Short Round confirmed with a nod.

They stared down at the altar, mesmerized by the glow from inside the Sankara Stones.

After another moment, the worshippers began to disband, leaving the temple empty. Indy considered that this might be a perfect time to get a better look at what was going on down there. It was too dangerous to bring Willie and Short Round, though. "Look," he whispered to them, "I want you two to stay up here and keep quiet."

"Why? Where are you going?" Willie demanded in a slightly panicked voice.

"Down there," he said as he took the satchel Short Round had packed from the boy. He'd need something in which to carry the stone once he'd gotten back.

"Down there?!" she yelped softly. "Are you crazy?"

"I'm not leaving here without the stones," he told her firmly.

"You could get killed chasing after your fortune and glory," she said, a note of true concern in her voice.

"Maybe," he replied seriously. Then he shot her a grin. "But not today."

Emboldened by her distress, he planted a quick kiss on her lips. Then he swung around to a balcony overlooking the temple.

*   *   *

In the dark shadows of the jumping torchlight, Indy was able to move stealthily along the columns that sat horizontally over the balconies until he arrived at the end.

He peered down at the altar below. If he was going to reach the altar, he would have to find a way to climb down, and then manage to get over the crevasse in front of it.

His eyes darted to a tall column not too far from him, but still at least a yard out of reach. On it a tremendous stone elephant perched, its trunk raised and jutting out past him into the temple.

Mentally he estimated the distance between the balcony, the elephant's stone trunk, and the altar.

After a moment's thought, he decided on a bold and dangerous course of action. It was the only way.

Taking his bullwhip from his belt, he unfurled it, letting its tail drop to his side. Then, with lightning movement, he cracked it, letting it fly. The whip's end wrapped tightly around the elephant's trunk. He tugged the whip taut, took a breath, and jumped.

He swung out on the whip, arching down and over the chasm of fiery lava in a spectacular curving jump, landing lightly on his feet by the altar. Indy rewound the whip and attached it to his belt before moving toward the towering, monstrous statue. At its feet, the three Sankara Stones still glowed.

Indy was aware of their immense power and approached the stones cautiously. Tentatively, prepared to spring back at the first sign of trouble, he reached out and touched one of the stones. Despite its brilliant light, it didn't burn. Carefully, he lifted it, peering into its light, its glow reflected on his face. The diamond glow from deep inside faded as he put the first stone in his satchel and reached for the others.

As he gathered all three stones, he couldn't get over the feeling that the huge, hideous statue above him was watching. Crouching low so not to be seen, he backed away from the statue. Then, suddenly, he heard a voice. Could it be the horrible goddess? No. That was crazy.

The voice was coming from the altar.

Curious, he stepped behind the altar and came upon a column of light emanating from an enormous hole dug below its back. Listening closely, he was sure he heard the clink of metal against rock.

He crept toward the edge of the hole. The light rising up illuminated the horrified expression on his face as he saw what was below him.

Down below was a mine. Concentric paths led off into many narrow tunnels. Crawling around these burrows were scrawny, hollow-eyed children dragging sacks of dirt and rock. Other children pulled the sacks to mine cars waiting on rails.

Straining to lift the rocks into the mine cars, several of the children slipped and fell. Bare-chested Thuggee guards shouted at the enslaved children and kicked some of the ones who had fallen.

Shifting the satchel of stones on his shoulder, he considered what to do next. He could leave with the Sankara Stones now and let the villagers return to fight the Thuggee. It was probably the sensible thing to do.

He couldn't fight all these guards by himself. Could he? Of course he couldn't.

He was distracted from his thoughts by the pleading cry of a child below him. Looking down, he saw a burly Thuggee guard raise his arm and bring it down forcefully on the little slave.

Indy was enraged. What monsters could treat children like this? Anger drove caution from his mind. Indy grabbed a nearby rock and hurtled down at the guard. It crashed onto the shoulder of the Thuggee guard and bounced off, sending him staggering forward.

The startled slave children stared up at him in shock.

The Thuggee guard's head shot up. Indiana met his angry glare with a victorious smile.

His smile faded as he sensed a presence behind him — many presences. Turning slowly, he faced at least a dozen

Thuggee guards, their heads wrapped in turbans. Elaborate designs were painted on their glowering faces, bands of color outlined in white with a broad ring of black circling their eyes.

But what Indy was most aware of were the rifles and the broad, sharp swords gripped firmly in their hands.

*A*s Indy stirred to waking, he vaguely recalled being struck on the head by a heavy, blunt object. It hurt to open his eyes, but he had to. In the murky light, he realized he was in a prison cell with his hands chained over his head.

Short Round was chained to wall across the cell from him. "Dr. Jones!" he cried when he saw Indy coming to. He hurried over, his chain clanking behind him, and hugged Indy. "I keep telling you, listen me more, you live longer," he scolded affectionately. Short Round told him that the guards had also captured Willie but that he had no idea where they had taken her.

Indy nodded groggily. Did his head ever hurt! As he came increasingly awake, he noticed a young boy in rags sitting near Short Round. Through the iron bars of the cell he could see children slaving in the mine tunnels.

The boy sat and rocked. He seemed to be praying. "Please let me die," he pleaded. "I pray to Shiva, let me die, but I do not. Now the evil take me."

"How?" Short Round asked him.

"They will make me drink the blood of the evil one. Then I'll fall into the black sleep," he replied.

"What is that?" Indy asked the boy.

"You become like them," he explained. "You are alive — but like a nightmare. You drink blood; you not wake from nightmare."

Guards came and dragged Indy from the cell and chained him once more to a large rock in another chamber of the temple. This one was a terrifying gallery of the monstrous, ritualistic statues and grisly icons of the Thuggee sect.

In one corner there was yet another statue of Kali in her most bloodthirsty form. At the base were the three Sankara Stones the guards had taken back from Indy. Once again, she was draped with necklaces of real human skulls and had a belt that slithered snakes — except this time they were living snakes! Indy felt goosebumps rise on his flesh at the sight of them.

The high priest entered the chamber and walked to

Indy. In person he was even more revolting than he had been at a distance. Without his bizarre headdress, Indy saw the hate burning in his deep sunken, burning eyes.

"I am the high priest, Mola Ram," he introduced himself ominously. "You were caught trying to steal the Sankara Stones." He paused, gazing transfixed at the stones glowing at the statue's feet.

"There were five stones in the beginning," he continued after a moment. "Over the centuries they were dispersed by wars, sold off by thieves like you."

Indy sputtered at the man's audacity. "Thieves like me, huh? Ha! You're still missing two!"

"A century ago when the British raided this temple and butchered my people, a loyal priest hid the last two stones down here in the underground tunnels, the catacombs."

"So that's what you've got these *slaves* digging for, huh?" Indy realized. "They're innocent children!"

A guard entered, gripping Short Round roughly. The boy's eyes were wide with fear.

"They dig for diamonds to support our cause," Mola Ram insisted maniacally. "They also search for the last two stones. Soon we will have all five Sankara Stones and the Thuggee will be all-powerful."

"What a vivid imagination," Indy scoffed.

Mola Ram remained unruffled. "You don't believe me,"

he taunted. "You will, Dr. Jones. You will become a true believer."

The large Thuggee guard Indy had hit with the stone came beside him and loomed there menacingly. Indy winced as he attempted a smile. "Hi," he said as the guard glowered into his eyes.

The boy who had been in the cell with Short Round and Indy entered the chamber. Or was he? Indy felt certain it was the same boy — though he was very much changed. He was now dressed like a Thuggee guard.

More striking than his uniform, though, was his manner. He walked forward, zombie-like, handing Mola Ram a skull. It was the living death he had so feared!

The large guard grabbed Indy's jaw in a crushing grip and jerked his head back. Indy resisted, twisting his head as best he could against the guard's viselike grip.

Mola Ram stood in front of Indiana and tipped the skull forward, attempting to pour the poisoned liquid between Indy's lips. Indy clenched his jaw tightly but a second guard pried it open.

"Dr. Jones, don't drink!" Short Round urged him. "Don't drink! It's bad! Spit it out!"

Blood ran down Indy's chin as, helpless to resist, he had no choice but to let Mola Ram pour it in. He held it in his mouth, gagging, until he couldn't stand it another second and spit it out, spraying Mola Ram and the guards.

Mola Ram gazed down at his clothing and grew furious. As he did this, the young maharajah entered the room. The little prince's eyes glowed angrily and he hissed at Indiana.

Mola Ram spoke to the young maharajah, who stepped in front of Indiana and produced a *kryta* from his robe.

Indy instantly knew what it was. The small doll had been crudely fashioned to resemble him. Like a voodoo doll, it supposedly possessed the power to pass any injury inflicted onto the doll to the person it had been made to resemble.

Ordinarily, Indy wouldn't have been too worried by such a thing, thinking it was only silliness. But he'd already seen the power the Sankara Stones — even the incomplete set — had brought to this cult to dismiss anything. And, as he'd feared, this kryta made him writhe in agony when the maharajah thrust it into a flaming urn.

"Dr. Jones!" Short Round shouted, breaking free of the guard's grip. He jumped up and kicked the maharajah, knocking the boy prince backwards and sending the kryta flying from his hands.

The guards recaptured him instantly, but at least Indy no longer felt the searing heat of the flames.

Mola Ram still seethed with fury. He ordered the guards to turn Indy around and chain him once more against the rock.

The high priest gave orders to the huge guard Indy

had hit earlier. The guard picked up Indy's bullwhip and began to whip him, ripping through his shirt.

After several torturous lashings, Mola Ram approached Indy, the skull of blood in his hands. The guard forced his head back and Mola Ram tipped the skull to Indy's lips.

Mola Ram cackled with fiendish delight. "When the five Sankara Stones are reunited, the Thuggee will rule the world!"

Indiana was horrified by what was happening to him, but so weakened that he was helpless to resist. Still, he tried, clamping his mouth shut. But the guard pinched his nose shut so that he was compelled to open his mouth in order to breathe. The moment his mouth opened, the blood was poured down his throat.

"Dr. Jones," he heard Short Round whisper sadly.

Indy passed out.

When he awoke, Indy found himself on a slab surrounded by hundreds of burning candles. His body convulsed and he groaned in pain as the unspeakable potion took effect.

Then, all at once, his body relaxed. A strange peacefulness came over him. It was unlike any feeling he'd ever had before — being so completely at ease.

He raised his hand and examined it in wonder, as though he'd never really seen it before, never truly realized the power it held.

He was not himself. Dimly, somewhere in a tiny chamber in the back of his mind, he knew this. But, the amazing thing was . . . he didn't care.

He liked this new thing he had become. He smiled malevolently and threw his head back in uproarious laughter.

CHAPTER FIFTEEN

*I*ndiana stood before the altar dressed in a loincloth like the other worshippers who chanted to the statue of the goddess. He glanced across the chasm at them. What he had once seen as a sea of frightening faces now seemed like a brotherhood of the Thuggee, all united in their quest to please the goddess they adored.

Chattar Lal, dressed in the robes of a priest, stood beside Indy at the altar. He glanced at the mystical mark ing on Indy's forehead and his lips quirked in a pinched, approving smile.

The young maharajah sat among the worshippers, but on a raised platform. Like the other believers, the maharajah stared across the crevasse at the altar of Kali.

As he had done before, Mola Ram materialized evilly amidst the swirling smoke coming from the crevasse. Behind him, the three Sankara Stones glowed in the skull beneath the statue's legs. He began to intone in the ancient

361

language of worship, and Indy, staring blankly, translated. "Mother protect us. We are your children. We pledge our devotion with an offering."

He watched, feeling no emotion, as Willie was dragged out, struggling desperately, and dressed in the same beautiful dress she had worn to dinner. But, at dinner, he had been overwhelmed by her loveliness. This time the sight of her did nothing but make him think what a fitting sacrifice she would be.

Chattar Lal turned to Indy. "Your friend has seen and she has heard. Now she will not talk."

The iron frame on which the victim had been sacrificed the day before was brought out. Willie spotted Indy as she was dragged to the frame. "I'm not going to have anything nice to say about this place when I get back," she shouted when the guards pushed her, face first, into the metal lattice.

Craning her head, she looked at Indy questioningly. Why was he just standing there? "Help me, Indy!" she shouted. "What's the matter with you?"

Still chanting in Sanskrit, Mola Ram approached Willie and stroked her cheek. Abruptly, he turned to Indy, who remained impassive, watching Willie struggle.

"Come. Come," Mola Ram commanded Indy.

Trancelike, he began to walk to Willie. "Indy! Help me!" she cried.

Indy just looked away from her terrified face and gazed up adoringly at the statue of the hideous goddess he now served.

Turning back to Willie, Indy stroked her face as Mola Ram had done. "Please snap out of it," Willie pleaded, near tears. "You're not one of them. Please come back. Don't leave me."

She reached out to him with the only hand that was not chained. Indy grabbed her wrist and shackled it to the chain.

"No!" Willie cried, still unable to believe the change in him. "What are you doing? Are you mad?"

Indy responded by calmly closing the outside gate on the iron frame, locking her inside. Outraged, Willie spit in his face. Indy wiped the spit from his face and smiled.

Chains clinked and gears squeaked as the sacrificial frame and its victim were turned facedown and the heavy stone doors slowly opened to reveal the molten death at the bottom of the chasm.

"This can't be happening. This can't be happening," Indy heard Willie telling herself frantically. "Wake up, Willie. Wake up!" But her words did not move him. In his trance, he was there to serve the goddess. That was all he cared about.

One of the priests pushed a lever, and the frame with

Willie strapped to it began to descend slowly into the crevasse. Willie shrieked. "No! No!"

Watching in a passive fog, Indy just stood there and watched her go. In that small chamber in his mind where what remained of his old self was trapped, he heard a small voice urge him to help her, to do something. But the voice was too far away; he couldn't hear it clearly enough to take any action.

And then, suddenly, it was much clearer. It wasn't in his mind, either, but right beside him.

Short Round was there, beside him, tugging on his hand. Somehow he had managed to escape from the mines where he'd been imprisoned. "Wake up, Dr. Jones!" he begged. "Wake up!"

Indy, still in his trance, jerked his hand from Short Round's grasp, swung it back, and backhanded him, knocking him to the floor.

"Dr. Jones!" he shouted from the floor, tears in his eyes.

Recovering quickly, Short Round jumped to his feet and ran, pursued by the guards. He grabbed for a torch and yanked it off the wall. Using it as a weapon, he swung it at the guards, keeping them at bay as he scrambled over to Indy.

"Indy, I love you!" he shouted, plunging the flaming torch into Indy's bare side.

Indy screamed in pain.

"Wake up! Wake up!" Short Round shouted at him urgently.

Indy crumpled to the ground. As he fell, he saw guards rush toward Short Round and grab the torch from him. Another guard moved forward and pulled a knife from his belt.

"You're my best friend!" Short Round cried, in one last attempt. "Wake up, Indy!"

Indy rose slowly from the floor.

He turned to the guards holding Short Round. "Wait!" he told them, holding up a hand. He spoke in the monotone of the zombie-like worshippers. "He's mine." The guards willingly handed Short Round to him and he lifted the boy over his head, carrying him toward the smoking crevasse.

Short Round squirmed in terror. Indy held him out over the opening, gripping him tight.

He looked up into Short Round's terrified face . . . and winked. The boy's voice — and torch — had cut through the smoke befogging his brain and had reached him as no one else could have. "I'm all right, kid," he told him.

Setting Short Round down safely, he whirled and punched an approaching guard. Short Round also sprang into action, stopping another guard with a quick karate kick in the stomach.

Indy heard Willie's screams from down in the fiery pit

of lava. A guard ran to the lever and dropped her farther down. Indy dove for the lever and fought to stop it from descending any more.

Forcing himself to look down into the pit, he saw that the frame had come to stop only yards above the fiery lava. The heat was so intense it scorched him even from the top of the pit. Willie had passed out from fear, dangling unconscious in the extreme heat.

From the other side of the crevasse, the chanting slowly dropped away as the worshippers realized there was a battle taking place on the altar. There wouldn't be much time before Indy and Short Round were swarmed by the hundreds of men in the crowd. If Mola Ram had a way to let them across the crevasse, it would all be over.

It was important to get rid of Mola Ram, he decided. That was their only chance. So Indy grabbed a spear one of the guard's had dropped and charged toward the high priest, shouting his name.

With a triumphant laugh, Mola Ram disappeared through a secret trapdoor near the base of the statue. Seeing his target vanish, Indy tossed the spear aside and threw himself on the wheel controlling the iron frame in the pit. He cranked it furiously and the iron frame began to rise. He continued to strain mightily and before long, Willie appeared at the top of the pit.

But before he could free Willie from the frame, Chattar Lal lunged ferociously at him, pulling a dagger from his sash. He slashed at Indy, forcing him to release the crank wheel as he leaped away from the blade.

With a clank, the frame began to descend once again. And then, with a screech of chains, the frame plummeted deep into the pit.

Chattar Lal slashed again with his dagger, keeping Indy away from the crank.

Indy knew he had to regain control of the crank — and fast — or Willie would not survive. Charging toward Chattar Lal, he kicked the dagger from the man's hand and punched him in the jaw, knocking him backwards.

The gears of the crank slammed to a halt, blocked by Chattar Lal's limp body. In an instant, Indy tossed him off and began furiously winding the gears to pull the frame back up.

Short Round ran to his side, throwing all his weight onto the wheel. Together they labored, and the sacrificial frame with Willie strapped to it came back into view. This time, with Short Round operating the wheel, Indy was able to grab the frame and swing it away from the pit, over the platform. "Give me some slack!" he yelled to Short Round.

Short Round released enough chain for Indy to bring

the frame closer and begin to unstrap the unconscious woman. "Willie, wake up!" he urged her as he worked. "Willie!"

Moaning, Willie moved her head. Indy pulled her off the frame. Her head jerked up and her eyes opened as she began to cough violently. Seeing Indy there, she slapped his face hard.

"Willie, it's me," he told her. "I'm back."

Relief flooded Willie's face when she heard these words and slumped into his arms. "Oh, Indy," she murmured.

The tender moment was interrupted by Short Round, who threw Indy's satchel to him. Turning toward the statue, Indiana grabbed the three glowing Sankara Stones and shoved them inside the bag.

He snapped up Short Round's trusty baseball cap from where it had been knocked off in the struggle and placed it back onto his assistant's head. "Indy, my friend," Short Round said.

The boy reached into his own pants pocket and produced Indy's fedora, the one he'd rolled up and kept for his friend when he'd found it in the prison cell.

"I'm sorry, kid," Indy apologized for all he'd put Short Round through.

Short Round nodded, understanding. "Indy, now let's get out of here."

He held up a hand for Short Round to wait while he peered down into the adjacent mines. Down there he could still see the child slaves working.

Leaning closer, he saw a huge conveyor belt below. Children in chains loaded stones from it onto an elevator that was, in turn, lifted and unloaded by child slaves waiting on a high ledge nearby. They loaded its contents into a mining cart and then one of the children rode the cart down a track and out of sight.

Those empty cars have to go down to the mines, Indy thought. And there had to be a way to get what they found out of the mines without bringing it up through just this one opening. That meant there was a chance he could get down there and find a way to bring all the children out some other way.

There were three of them . . . and hundreds of guards. The plan was completely crazy.

But there were also hundreds of children down there, children desperate to be free.

He thought of the young boy who had made it back to the village. He'd been starved, beaten, and bruised. But his will to return and to help his friends had been so strong that he'd survived. Hundreds of children with that kind of desire could be a powerful weapon.

"Indy," Willie urgently pressed him to get going.

"Right," Indy agreed. But he couldn't leave those children down in that hateful mine. "*All* of us are leaving," he said firmly.

He waved his hand for Willie and Short Round to follow him down to the mines. They would have to lay low and avoid the guards while they searched for the fastest way out.

Willie sighed loudly, but followed Indy and Short Round down. It wasn't very long before they came to a tunnel. Lighting a match, Indy saw a carved door at the end of the tunnel. A dim light filtered through a small window at the top of the door. Indy took in the door's intricate carvings and the quality of the light. *I bet that goes right back to the palace,* he figured.

Willie caught his eye and he knew what she was thinking. They could get out through that door, sneak through the palace, and — if they were lucky — there might be no one in the way to stop them.

In the distance, a whip cracked and a child cried out in torment. Willie looked up at him and nodded. This was a rescue mission now.

*I*ndy stood in the shadows of the mining tunnel, watching the child slaves laboring under the watchful eyes of hulking guards and thinking of what to do next. Behind him, Willie and Short Round stayed close to the rock wall, trying to be as invisible as possible. The guard overseeing the nearby group of children was so close that they could smell him.

Indy had a plan — sort of. He had picked the lock of the door leading into the palace using the wire stem of one of the fake flowers on Willie's gown. It was now unlocked, a clear escape route, just waiting.

But that was as far as his plan went. How he was going to free these children under the noses of the guards was something he hadn't quite figured out — but he was working on it.

Something would come to him. It always did.

A small girl fainted to the ground and the other children

frantically urged her to get up before the guards noticed her. Clearly, they had seen the awful fate awaiting any worker who fainted. Alerted by the clamor of their voices, a burly, guard turned and glared at the fallen girl. He strode toward her and raised his whip to strike.

This was more than Indy could bear.

Plan or no plan, he couldn't let this brutality happen right in front of him. Stepping out of the shadows, infuriated, he flattened the guard with one mighty blow to his jaw.

A low gasp swept through the group of startled children. One small boy dared to cheer, which immediately set off a torrent of happy shouts.

Willie and Short Round scrambled out from hiding as the rebellious slave children swarmed around Indy, their chains clanking. Willie lost no time in finding the large gold key in the guard's jacket. In minutes, she became busy unlocking the shackles that held the children prisoner, while Indy and Short Round made quick work of pulling off their chains, which rattled as they fell to the ground.

Not long after that, the liberated kids spilled from the tunnels where they'd been imprisoned for so long. Indy directed them toward the tunnel that would lead them out of the mines and into the palace.

As they stampeded, they knocked over any of the guards that tried to stand in their path, their sheer numbers allowing the children to easily trample right over them. Looking down from a ledge, another group of kids waited with baskets of rocks. When an ascending squad of guards approached underneath them, they overturned their baskets, instantly disabling them.

Indy, Willie, and Short Round searched every fallen guard they found for more keys. Indy kept any of the guards that tried to rise in place with more well-aimed punches to the jaw. Soon they had enough keys to pass out to the freed children, who moved quickly to unlock the shackles holding more of their friends.

The swarm of excited, joyful children made it all the way aboveground to the top of Pankot Palace and exploded into the pavilion where Indy, Willie, and Short Round had dined earlier.

They ran across the banquet table and kicked aside the luxurious cushions around it. Now they could see the windows — and the light — that showed them the way out.

Yelling with happiness, they burst out the front doors into the glorious, bright sunshine that they had not seen for such a long time.

Indy, Willie, and Short Round unlocked child after child until the last one was out. Willie had just freed the last small girl, sending her scampering to meet her brother's waiting hand when a very large Thuggee guard barreled down the tunnel toward them with a raised club in his hand and a mean, determined expression on his face.

Whirling to face him, Indy grabbed a nearby sledge-hammer from the ground and hit the giant man in the stomach. The guard didn't seem to feel it. He wrenched the hammer out of Indy's hands and flung it away.

The Thuggee lifted Indy over his head as if he were no more than a doll. He slammed Indy into a mine car and then doubled him over with a blow to the stomach.

As he slid down the side of the car, he was aware that Willie was off to the side arguing with Short Round, trying to keep him out of the fight. "I gotta save him!" Short Round protested as she clutched his shoulder, holding him back from going to Indy's aid.

"He can take care of himself," she insisted, though she didn't sound entirely convinced.

As Indiana struggled with the guard, he wasn't entirely sure he could get the best of this fight, either. Suddenly, mysterious, piercing pains were shooting up and down his legs. And he was short of breath, as though his chest was being squeezed by a giant hand. Although he swung at the guard, his blows fell lightly, without sufficient force to slow the man down.

Short Round could see that Indy was losing the struggle. What was happening to Indy? He wanted to rush in and help, but Willie was holding tight to his shoulders.

Indy was grateful, and hoped she would be able to maintain her grip. Even with Short Round's spunk and all his good intentions, he didn't stand a chance against the giant of a man who was now pummeling Indy.

"He needs me!" Short Round shouted at Willie, still struggling to get free. "I gotta save Indy!"

The Thuggee guard lifted Indy once again, and spun in a circle with Indy over his head two times. Indy's strength had left him completely. He had no way to free himself when the guard turned to the mining car, about to heave Indy into it.

He looked over to Willie and Short Round helplessly, his face creased with an apologetic expression. The guard would turn his attention to them next, and there was nothing he could do about it now. He was failing them and he felt terrible about it.

He locked eyes with Willie. Her jaw dropped slowly as she realized how helpless he really was. "Okay, save him," Willie relented, letting go of Short Round.

Short Round grabbed a whip from one of the fallen guards and began to lash at the legs of the man holding Indy. "Drop him down!" Short Round insisted fiercely, still wielding his whip. "I kill you! Drop him down!"

The guard dropped Indy into the cart and scooped up Short Round instead. The boy screamed and kicked out at his Thuggee attacker, but just as Indy had predicted, he was no match for him. The large man easily tossed Short Round aside, sending him sliding along the rock floor of the cavern until he stopped beside a pool of water, nearly hitting his head on a pulley system that had been used to bring water up to the mining level high above.

When Short Round stopped sliding, a noise caught his attention and he looked up. The sound was coming from a rock balcony on the upper level, overlooking the cavern below.

On the balcony stood the malicious young maharajah — and in his hand he held the kryta doll made to look like Indy. He was staring intently, stabbing the replica doll repeatedly with a long, sharp, sapphire-tipped turban pin.

Although he was dizzy from banging his head on the edge of the cart, Indy climbed to stand once more. Gripping the sides of the cart for support, he followed Short Round's gaze and witnessed the maharajah stabbing the doll.

Indy had felt the power of this doll earlier. No wonder he couldn't fight!

Short Round leaped out over the pool, grabbing onto the big water bucket attached to chains on the pulley mechanism just as it was rising with a bucket full of water. Clinging to the bucket, he sailed upward.

Indy was distracted from watching Short Round when

the guard jumped into the cart and began pounding him with a hammer-like fist. They fought fiercely, every blow rocking the cart. They slammed against its side, their combined weight finally tipping it over and dumping them onto the wide conveyor belt behind the mining cart. All around them, large rocks were being carried somewhere by the moving belt. Their struggle continued as the belt moved them along with the rocks to some unknown final destination.

Indy threw himself into the struggle. He was dimly aware of someone running alongside of the conveyor belt. A quick glance told him it was Willie.

But he didn't have long to look: His head was roughly jerked back around. The guard's hands closed around his throat, repeatedly banging his head against the conveyor belt. Indy couldn't breathe and didn't have the strength to break the Thuggee's choke hold on his windpipe. Now he was sure that the kryta doll was the reason for his weakness.

Willie had found a heavy, metal bucket. "Here! Try this!" she shouted, pushing the bucket onto the conveyor belt beside the flailing, breathless Indy. Snapping it up, he hit the bucket over the guard's head with a resounding clang.

The guard reeled back, his eyes momentarily blank.

Indy was able to kick the guard away and scramble to his knees. But instantly, a piercing pain ran up his spine, crippling him and causing him to fall back onto the conveyor. *Get that doll, Shorty,* he thought desperately as he writhed in agony.

A loud pounding sound was coming closer to him now. What was it?

It was agonizing for him to strain around backwards to get a look, but he had to do it. Just about two yards further on, tiny pebbles sprayed through the air.

The conveyor belt carried its contents to a large, heavy, stone wheel. The rocks on the conveyor belt were being smashed to smithereens by a rock-crushing machine! If Indy didn't find a way off, he'd be next.

But the sharp pain in Indy's back made it impossible to move. All he had to do was throw himself off the conveyor belt to avoid becoming dust, but even that small movement was more than he could manage.

Nearby, the guard had rallied and was crawling toward Indy on the conveyor belt. If the guard didn't finish him off, the rock crusher would do the job!

Suddenly, the pain in Indy's back and legs stopped. Breath rushed into his lungs with a bracing whoosh of air. His normal strength and agility came roaring back.

Indiana knew what had happened: Short Round had gotten the kryta doll away from the maharajah.

And just in time!

The giant Thuggee guard was now looming over him, and the rock crusher was no more than three feet away. Indy didn't waste any time. He grabbed the nearest thing he could: a handsaw he glimpsed beside the conveyor. It wouldn't be his first choice of weapon, but it'd have to do. He swung with all his strength, hitting the guard directly in the stomach.

The guard staggered backwards and collapsed in front of the rock crusher. Coming to his senses, he rolled over, attempting to scurry away on his hands and knees, but it was too late. The long sash of his uniform was already caught! As the guard screeched in horrified terror, he was pulled into the crushing wheel!

Indy turned away, unable to watch the guard's horrific death. Then he climbed up onto a catwalk that hung above the conveyor belt. He had to make sure Short Round was safe.

It wasn't long before he caught sight of the boy trading punches with the young maharajah on the balcony. Indy picked up his pace. It looked as if Short Round could use some help.

A Thuggee guard appeared on the walkway in front of Indy, blocking him. But this time, Indy was full of restored energy and quickly flattened him with a powerful blow.

Looking back toward the fight, he watched helplessly

as the maharajah had pulled out a knife and was lunging for Short Round. Indy knew he would never reach Short Round in time to stop him.

Short Round was backed up against the wall, with nowhere to go. But he was used to tight corners, and still had a few tricks up his sleeve. During their fight, there was something in the maharajah's blank gaze that Shorty recognized. Thinking quickly, he reached for the burning torch hanging on the wall above and hit the maharajah with it, just as he had done to Indy.

The effect was the same!

The cloudiness in the maharajah's eyes lifted. He looked as though he was awakening from a long sleep. He shook his head, gazing around and obviously perplexed at finding himself in such unfamiliar surroundings.

"It was the black sleep," Short Round told him.

Indy swung onto the balcony just in time to see the maharajah wake. *Well, that explains a lot.* Indy had a good feeling about the young ruler when they'd first met, and his instinct didn't often lead him astray. He couldn't be angry with the maharajah now; not when he himself had fallen under the sinister spell.

"Shorty, quit fooling around with that kid," Indy joked as he dropped to the balcony floor.

"Okay dokey, Indy," Short Round agreed with a happy grin.

He'd made light of the situation, but they really did have to move quickly. They had won this battle, but who knew how many they had left to fight? Hundreds of Thuggee guards still stood between them and freedom.

"Please, listen," the young maharajah said. "To get out, you must take the left tunnel."

Short Round and Indy made their way along the catwalk, headed down to the lower level of the cavern to reach Willie. They'd already spotted her in the cavern below, pushing a mining car along a rickety track, trying to get it rolling.

Smart, Indy thought as they ran along the catwalk to her. A mining cart would be the fastest and most direct route out of this diabolical pit.

Suddenly Mola Ram and six Thuggee temple guards ran out onto a high platform next to an underground waterfall. At a shouted command from their leader, two of the guards pulled out pistols and opened fire.

Ducking and rolling, Indy and Short Round dodged the bullets as they made their way forward. The guards stopped shooting only when the remaining four guards appeared on the catwalk.

Indy stepped in front of Short Round to protect him. His fist flew in a blur of activity. Short Round kicked and pounded every guard who fell in his path.

A guard slashed at Indy with a sword, slicing the air with rapid movements. Indy ducked as the sword came down inches from his shoulder and sunk into the wooden railing of the catwalk. While the guard frantically attempted to yank the sword out of the railing, Indy slammed his knee up into the guard's stomach and then brought his fist down onto his neck.

From their high vantage point on the catwalk, Indy could see guards hurrying toward Willie. He nudged Short Round and pointed to a rope that reached all the way down to where Willie was still struggling with the cart and jerked his thumb, silently indicating that he wanted Short Round to go down and help her.

Short Round did as Indiana instructed, deftly leaping the short distance from the catwalk to the rope. When he was at the floor, Indy saw more guards running forward on the catwalk. "Shorty! Quit stalling!" he yelled down to the boy.

Willie had gotten the cart to a slow roll and was struggling to get into it. A guard was now racing after her. Short Round would have to be faster than the guard in order to catch up with Willie and get into the cart.

"Go! Go!" he urged Short Round as he ran toward the cart.

The cart was picking up speed. Indy wasn't sure Short Round could run fast enough to reach it. With his eyes darting back and forth between the guards approaching him on the catwalk and Short Round, the guards, Willie, and the rolling cart below, Indy knew he'd have to do some fast thinking and quick, tough fighting if they were going to get out of this one.

The guard below ran faster to get hold of Willie in the cart. With a reckless burst of energy, he leaped forward and grabbed hold of the cart's side. Willie screamed and held onto the cart's other side as the guard tried to climb in with her. But the cart had gained more speed and was moving too fast for the guard to get in. Instead, he was dragged along, refusing to let go, his legs trailing behind him.

More guards were gaining on Short Round, closing in from behind. "Shorty! Look out!" Indy shouted down to the boy. If he didn't get on that cart with Willie soon, the guards would overtake him.

Short Round had reached Willie's cart, where the guard was still being dragged along behind it. Moving as fast as his short, sturdy legs had ever carried him, he raced up the guard's legs, over his back and shoulders, and into the cart!

Even though the Thuggee guard was *still* clinging to the cart, it had begun to roll down an incline and was picking up speed at an even faster rate. It would soon outpace all the other guards. But it was the best chance of escape, and if Indy didn't do something quickly, it would speed away from *him*, as well.

He was only yards away from the end of the catwalk and guards were still coming forward, grinning satisfied smiles, sure he was trapped there. His eyes darted around, searching for some escape route and not finding any.

Out in the middle of the ceiling, a block and tackle crossbar hung balanced on a long rope. It had been used to transport rocking and mining equipment across the wide expanse of cavern. Could it transport Indy, too? It was a crazy plan, but Indy thought he just might be able to jump out far enough to reach it.

No. It was too far. If he jumped and missed, there was nothing out there but air. He would hurtle to his death on the cavern floor below.

The approaching guards were nearly to him. He glanced at them and back to the block and tackle. *It's too nuts*, he decided.

But what other choice did he have? He was a dead man once these guards reached him.

When the approaching guards were just a yard away, he took off running . . .

"Come on, Indy!" Short Round urged from the cart.

"Hurry!" Willie called.

"Hurry! Hurry!" Short Round agreed frantically.

. . . and leaped into the wide, open expanse of cavern.

Bullets whizzed past Indy as he sailed, like a parachute jumper with no chute, toward his goal.

The bar of the block quickly came closer. With a thud, one hand grasped half the bar, but his dangling weight upset the balance and pulled his fingers toward the edge. One finger slipped, then another, and suddenly, there were only three fingers between Indy and certain death.

Arms and legs flailing wildly, he kicked and reached forward with his other hand.

At last — a solid grip. Now propelled by Indy's weight, the block and tackle began to move. He was traveling on a downward path along the rope toward the speeding mining cart carrying Willie and Short Round, as well as the guard still tenaciously clinging to its back.

But Indy's troubles weren't over. He quickly discovered that the bar was greasy and hard to keep hold of. He pulled himself up with all his strength, struggling to get the bars under his arms as he hurtled forward at incredible speed.

But in moments, he was directly over the cart. He let go of the bar, dropping three body-lengths down, joining Willie and Short Round with a crash.

In this part of the mine, the tracks caused the cart to

swerve sharply around the curving cavern walls. Above and below them, the wooden tracks crisscrossed one another like an elaborate roller coaster ride.

Indy couldn't believe the guard was still holding on, but there he was, trying desperately to pull himself into the cart. *This is where you get off,* Indy thought as he gave the guard a push.

Shouts from behind alerted him that six rifle-wielding guards had jumped into another mining cart and were now chasing them, speeding down the track behind their cart. Short Round and Willie ducked low as the bullets flew.

At the same time, Mola Ram led another squad of armed guards out onto a rock ledge and ordered them to open fire.

Up ahead, Indy saw that the tracks split into two paths. One led back into the quarry and the other led out of the mine.

Indy saw a switch on the rock wall rapidly approaching. At the bottom of the cart, a shovel sat beside a rotted, old railroad tie. Thinking fast, he grabbed the shovel and, gripping its handle, he held it out toward the switch and braced for impact.

CLANG!

He hit the switch!

The cart was shunted, tipsy-turvy onto the track toward the two tunnels, racing away from the guards in the other cart. Willie cringed, her eyes shut as they barreled toward the tunnel — the right tunnel.

"Indy, it's the left tunnel!" Short Round shouted, recalling the maharajah's words. "The left tunnel, it should be the *left* tunnel!"

Willie clutched Short Round as the mine cart picked up speed and roared around a curve at top speed. Wind rushed past them and it was growing ever darker.

It was too late to do anything about taking the left tunnel now. They were speeding back into the quarry.

CHAPTER EIGHTEEN

*I*n the blackness of the quarry, Indy pulled back on the brake lever to control the cart's speed and keep it from careening off the tracks. Watching for trouble, Short Round peered over the back side of the cart.

Willie ducked, looking up as the dangerously low beams passed over their heads. Then she groaned with dread when the cart plummeted on a steep track, descending even deeper into the quarry.

A gunshot rang through the pitch blackness. Indy whirled away from its whistling song. Once his eyes had adjusted, Indy could see the black form of another cart filled with Thuggee guards swinging around a curve behind them. "We've got company!" Indy warned Willie and Short Round.

Mola Ram's gunmen had spotted them, too. They began blasting away. Bullets ricocheted erratically off the mine walls.

Short Round scurried forward beside Indiana and took hold of the brake, freeing Indy to battle the guards. "Let it go," Indy instructed Short Round.

"What?" the boy questioned, not understanding.

"Let it go!" Indy told him. Short Round didn't move, so Indy released the brake himself. The cart rocketed forward at an unbelievable velocity. "It's our only chance to outrun them," Indy shouted, gripping the side of the cart so hard his knuckles ached.

They all shouted in terror as, there in the blackness, they hit a curve so sharp that it tipped the cart precariously to one side.

The curve was so extreme and they were hurtling around it so fast that the inside wheels lifted off the track! Indiana was thrown to the bottom of the cart. Willie and Short Round tipped over, too, tumbling onto him.

Peering up over their heads into the darkness, Indy saw that the guards behind them had also taken off the brake and were racing down the track at top speed. "Shorty!" Indy said.

"Huh?" he asked.

"Take the brake. Watch it on the curves or we'll fly right off the track."

"Okay," Short Round agreed as gunfire continued to explode all around them.

As the cart dropped back onto two wheels with a thud, Indy felt for the railroad tie he recalled seeing at the bottom of the cart. Getting to his knees, he heaved the heavy beam onto the back of the cart. Then, he stood, and with a great effort, pushed it over the edge of the cart and onto the tracks.

The gunmen behind them spotted the beam in their path and began to cry out in panicked alarm.

The cart hit the beam with a roaring crash. The guards screamed horribly as the car tumbled end over end, slamming against the tunnel walls, and sending pieces of metal, wheels, and other debris shooting in every direction.

Willie and Short Round whooped with joy, but it was short-lived. More gunshots rang out and a second mining cart full of gunmen appeared behind them.

The walls of the tunnel flashed past and curves appeared in the darkness as the top-speed chase continued. Indy staggered to standing, clutching the shovel.

"What are you doing?" Willie asked in a fearful shout.

"Short cut!" he replied.

"What, Indy?" Short Round asked uncertainly.

"Short *cut!*" Indy repeated, once again reaching out with the shovel for a switch in the rock wall.

The guards behind began shooting at Indy. Their bullets clattered off Indy's outstretched shovel blade, making it nearly impossible to hold steady. Despite the gunfire, he concentrated on reaching the switch, batting the shovel blade at it as they whizzed past.

The car abruptly swerved onto a new track, throwing them all to one side.

A bullet clanged off the switch, throwing it back and diverting the guards' cart onto another, parallel track. The guards that had been behind them were now able to come alongside, raising their rifles to shoot.

Indy reached out and grabbed hold of one rifle, attempting to pull it from the guard's hand. Behind him, another guard reached forward, grabbing hold of Short Round, lifting him off his feet. Indy dropped his grip on the rifle and clutched Short Round's legs, working hard to prevent the guard from pulling Short Round into his own cart.

"Indy! Help!" Short Round hollered as he was yanked in two directions as the carts continued to career along the two, side-by-side tracks. "Indy!"

"Pull him in!" Willie shouted, joining Indiana in pulling Short Round back inside the speeding cart.

Ahead, a rock divider threatened to split Short Round in two. If they didn't pull him back in the next minute, Indy and Willie would be forced to release Short Round to avoid killing him.

As the rock divider raced toward them, Indy gave a powerful tug and pulled Short Round into his arms. The shaking boy wrapped his arms around Indy, quaking with terror.

At the divider, the both tracks rose dramatically higher and divided, so that the track the guards were on now ran above the one Willie, Indy, and Short Round rode. Peering over the side of the cart, Indy realized exactly how far above the chasm they were, the tracks held up by wooden supports that looked serviceable, but not sturdy. They certainly weren't meant to take the abuse of a high speed chase, he realized grimly.

They could hear the cart carrying the Thuggee guards rumbling above them. Indy thought hard, trying to calculate where the tracks might meet again. He didn't want to have to fight off a cart running alongside as they just had. It seemed to him that they might actually be in the clear. The track had no doubt divided to carry the carts riding on it to a different destination.

There was no way the guards could get to them now. Unless . . .

Well, there *was* one way — but he didn't believe they'd have the nerve to do it.

As if answering his challenge, one of the guards dropped down into their cart, and immediately grabbed hold of him. Willie screamed.

He had been wrong. Obviously, they did have the nerve.

The two men grappled with one another, struggling desperately. Indy knocked the man to the floor of the cart, but he instantaneously reappeared behind him, clutching Indy in a strong choke hold.

But this guard had underestimated the other passengers in the cart. Willie jumped into the fight and punched him in the jaw. He lost his grip on Indy as he flew up and over the front of the cart and tumbled off the track.

Indy turned to thank her, but his words caught in his throat. Just a couple hundred feet away, the track ended — there was a gap at least five car lengths long!

He pushed Short Round and Willie to the cart's floor and then knelt beside them as the cart flew off the track, sailing out into the air.

Would it make it?

They all cringed, hunched down in the cart, not daring to look over the sides, while the cart hurtled forward carried by nothing other than its own momentum.

BANG! The front wheels hit the other side of the track. Indy felt as though his bones were shaking and his teeth were rattling in his mouth. Then the back wheels took hold.

Yes! he thought with a long, low sigh of relief.

But suddenly, the cart began wobbling crazily. Looking down, they saw what was causing it. Mola Ram was down below with his men. The men banged at the track's wooden supports with large sledgehammers. They were trying to knock the track down and they appeared to be succeeding!

And that wasn't even the worst of it. Across from the track, an immense water tank sat on high wooden supports. They were also banging at those supports. If that tank went over, it would flood the tunnels.

Willie gripped Indy's arm as, together, the three of them saw the gigantic tank begin to list forward and topple toward the ground. The noise was deafening when it hit, sending a half million gallons of water exploding across the cavern and surging in a tidal wave toward the tunnels.

The cart continued its mad pace along the tracks. They were going so fast that Indy worried that they would fly off the tracks. "Brake," he told Short Round, who was standing beside the hand brake.

"Okay?" Short Round replied, pulling on the brake with all his weight. But it didn't slow the cart. His face crunching and reddening with effort, he pulled on it even harder. The increased force snapped the break lever completely off the cart. Short Round fell backwards, still clutching the busted lever. "Uh-oh! Big mistake! Big mistake, Indy!" he shouted.

"Figures," Willie muttered despondently, dropping her head into her hands and shaking her head. This only lasted a moment — right away, the cart tossed her across the floor. Pulling herself up onto its side, she held on for dear life.

Indy crawled toward Shorty and bent over the front of the cart as it pitched to the right and began a screaming decline into a section where the tunnel widened. He could see the brake hanging loose on the outside of the cart, so he swung himself over the front side of the cart and lowered himself as carefully as he could.

He clung onto the outside of the hurtling cart, bouncing along just inches above the rail. To him, the sparking track below his feet was no more than a blur passing beneath as he attempted to kick the brake pad back up.

And then his foot slipped! His hand clenched the side more tightly then ever as the cart dragged him along, his feet kicking the track.

With all the strength he could summon, he forced his leg from the track and felt around the undercarriage of the cart, searching for a foothold. He found one, which steadied his position a little. With his other foot, he resumed kicking the brake as hard as he could.

After five solid slams, the brake finally moved forward against the front wheel, slowing its forward motion. The wheels screeched as they rubbed against the brake. "We're still going too fast!" Willie shouted.

"Help!" Short Round bellowed.

Groaning with the effort, Indy shoved his boot against the wheel, trying to create even greater friction. Small sparks were forming under his heel and he could smell smoke.

Seeing the look of horror on Willie's face, he followed her gaze, quickly checking over his shoulder. The track ended in about fifteen yards! Beyond it was nothing but rock wall.

He *had* to slow this cart down!

Bracing himself on the cart, he applied even more pressure to the brake. The bottom of his shoe felt warm and he could smell the rubber of his soles melting, but he couldn't let up.

He wasn't sure if he was imagining it. Was the cart slowing? It seemed like it might be.

It was slowing!

But would it be enough to keep them from crashing?

The cart rolled to a stop just inches from the rock wall, pressing Indy's back up against it.

He'd done it! Gulping for air, he laughed out loud with relief. But looking down, he realized that smoke billowed up from his shoe.

"Water!" he shouted as he stomped his foot on the ground. He'd created so much friction that his shoe had ignited! There was a fire inside it, searing the bottom of his foot. "Water! Water!"

"Oh, you're on fire!" Willie shouted, both sympathetic

and frantic, as she hopped around him helplessly, not knowing what do. Where could she find water? Instead, she kicked dirt on his shoe in an attempt to smother the flame.

The dirt helped and as his pain abated, Indy slowly became aware of an ominous rumbling, getting steadily louder. Whatever was causing it was coming toward them with great velocity.

When he looked toward the sound, he froze, paralyzed with fear, yet awestruck at the sight before him. They'd survived a lot, but this had to be the end. How could they survive this?

A monster wall of water crashed spectacularly around a turn in the tunnel. This tidal wave had been unleashed when the Thuggees dumped the water tank, and it had only picked up power as it rushed through the tunnels. Now it had finally reached them. It was as though a veritable tsunami struck the tunnel walls, spewing foam and debris: an unstoppable juggernaut.

"Come on! Come!" Indy shouted, gripping Short Round by the wrist. The three of them ran faster than they'd ever moved in their lives.

The tidal wave smashed forward, booming behind them, and Indiana knew this was a race they were bound to lose.

Just then, he spotted a narrow opening in the tunnel

wall. If it led nowhere, the water would fill it and they'd drown then and there. But if it led to the outside . . .

It was a chance they'd have to take because they would never be able to outrun this crushing flood of racing water. He pulled Short Round in front of him, and shoved him into the hole. Then he steered Willie into it as fast as he could, quickly following them into the black space.

They pressed their backs against a cold wall and watched as the colossal tidal wave exploded past the opening, drenching them with its spray.

The roar of the rushing water subsided slightly and they caught their breath, panting hard, but once again relieved to be alive.

Their rest was cut short almost instantly by the sound of a loud bang. The force of the water had pushed the wave into this opening and it was once more cascading toward them relentlessly at torrential speed.

"Let's go!" Short Round hollered. They all took off, yelling with fear, down this new tunnel that led to who knew where.

As the tidal wave loomed up to annihilate them, a small speck of blue appeared ahead of them. New hope sprang up inside Indy.

A way out!

If they could only outrun the rushing tidal wave behind them!

Cold spray pelted the back of his neck as they raced toward the ever-brightening sunlight.

Willie was the first to reach the end of the tunnel — and she let out a bloodcurdling scream. Indy reached her a second later, with Short Round still in his grip. He and Short Round also let out cries of terror.

Flailing their arms wildly, the three of them faltered, trying desperately not to lose their balance.

They had come out onto the sheer face of a cliff. They teetered there precariously, looking down in horror at a three-hundred-foot drop to a gorge of foaming water below.

Swinging her arms, Willie lost her balance and began to pitch forward. Indy grabbed her, hurling her to his left onto the narrowest of ledges. He moved Short Round beside Willie just before stepping over onto an even narrower rock shelf on the right of the opening.

He'd barely gained a sure footing when an explosive torrent of water burst from the tunnel. The gusher spewed forth, sending rock and debris from the cliffside into the air.

The erupting, pressurized geyser slammed a log out through the opening in the cliff face near Indy's head. Willie screamed as another log slammed through right beside her.

"Willie! Look out!" Short Round shouted.

The ledge beneath her feet was crumbling, shaken by the eruption of water.

She moved in tiny, frightened sideways steps to a place where the crumbling rock was more solid. Looking down the steep and towering precipice, she flattened her back to the rock wall and stared skyward, terrified by the view below.

They couldn't afford to stay there long. Eventually, one of them would slip. It was only a matter of time, Indy thought, knowing that he couldn't let panic get to him. Despite the cascading water at this side and the dizzying drop below, he forced himself to survey the situation as rationally as possible, scanning the vast rock for any sort of escape route that might present itself.

A surge of new hope grabbed him as he spotted a long, narrow, rope bridge that crossed to a cliff on the other side spanning the gorge below. It was about six yards to the left of Willie and Short Round and twenty feet above them. The gusty wind made it swing back and forth. Crossing it would be harrowing, but it beat their only other alternative, which was to go straight down.

To reach the bridge they would have to traverse the narrow ledge very slowly, one tiny footstep at a time, and with the utmost caution climb the sheer face of the cliff. And more dangerous still, in order to get to it, Indy would have to find a way to cross the blasting torrent of water still spraying from the opening at full force.

"Head for the bridge!" he shouted across the water to Willie and Short Round.

Willie's head snapped to her left and then back to

Indy, her eyes wide with terror at the idea of moving even one more step. Nonetheless, she glanced at Short Round who had begun to move and crept along behind him, her back flat against the rock wall.

Drawing in a deep breath to steady his nerves, Indy turned to face the wall and dropped down so that the length of his body was below the cascading water. Painstakingly, he went from foothold to handhold to foothold, inching along under the spray until he reached the other side.

The thundering water was deafening and the further underneath it he went, the more his hands slipped and slid. He couldn't allow himself to think about what he was doing, the insane danger of it, only to consider where he might position his hands and feet next. He clung to pieces of soaked scrub brush jutting from the cliff and rested for the briefest of seconds on small outcroppings along the way.

Finally, he made it out of the water and pulled himself up onto the ledge where Willie and Short Round had stood. In a short time, he had crept along the narrow ledge and would soon join them at the bridge.

He could see them ahead, viewing the bridge with apprehension. He knew it was far from reassuring. The ropes that made up the bridge crossing the gorge must have been years old, perhaps even dating back to the original glory of Pankot Palace. Lying across the two bottom rope spans, worm-eaten and rotten boards offered risky footings. Vertical side ropes attached to the long horizontal pieces of old rope were all they would have for hand railings.

Short Round stepped out bravely onto the bridge with a small bounce. It held him. He turned to Willie with a smile. "Strong bridge," he told her encouragingly. He made another light bounce just to prove his point. "Come on. Let's go. Strong bridge."

Willie didn't budge, so Short Round bounced even harder. "Look! Strong wood! Come on!"

Suddenly, with an anguished wail of terror, he fell through the board, clinging desperately with his hands onto the bridge. "I'm falling down!" he screamed, his legs kicking.

"Shorty!" Willie cried with a gasp.

Indy quickened his steps, hurrying to reach Short Round, but he couldn't run or he would lose his footing. All he could do was to keep moving forward steadily and not let the boy's horrified squall unnerve him.

"Help! I'm falling down! Help! Help!" Short Round continued screaming.

In the water below, hungry crocodiles thrashed expectantly, eyeing the delicious morsel dangling far above their heads.

Willie crawled toward Short Round on hands and knees and gripped his arms firmly at his shoulders, slowly pulling him back up onto the bridge. "Not very funny," Short Round whimpered, his body aquiver.

Willie held him tightly until his trembling subsided. Then the two of them cautiously set out to cross the bridge, picking their way carefully and assessing the strength of each board before putting a foot down on it. Their job was made no easier by the bridge's constant swaying and heart-stopping up and down movement.

Indy watched their progress as he neared the entrance to the bridge. He was about to step onto it to follow them, when a sound caused him to glance back over his shoulder. Two Thuggee guards were rushing toward him. Yelling savagely, they swung their swords in an elaborate attack pattern.

Indy reached for the holster at his side, wanting to grab his gun, but found that it was empty. The guards were on him in seconds, flashing their swords and shouting.

Indy began to throw punches as rapidly as he could. He hit the first guard and ducked under his sword, grabbing him from behind and using the guard's sword arm to engage in a duel with the second guard.

He shoved both guards out of the way and freed his whip. In a flash, he cracked it around one of the guard's wrists, yanking the sword from his hand.

He swiftly turned the sword in his hand, studying it quickly. He had never used a weapon quite like this one before and was unsure of how best to wield it. Judging from his attackers, he figured that shouting wildly was part of the overall technique, so he let out a savage cry and charged after the guards with his new sword and his trusty whip.

He stopped short, though, when his charge brought him face-to-face with eight more Thuggee guards. His only chance was to retreat — and the only place to retreat to was the rope bridge.

Willie and Short Round were nearly at the other side. He wasn't sure if he could move fast enough to catch up with them, but he would try. He just hoped the guards would be too intimidated by the bridge's scary sway and unsafe appearance to follow him. After all, if they all charged out onto it, the whole thing might come down.

Still gripping his whip and the sword, he headed out, walking as quickly as possible across the rickety span. He kept his eyes down, judging the safety of each board until he became suddenly aware of shouting ahead of him.

Looking up sharply, he saw ten Thuggee guards and Mola Ram waiting on the far side of the bridge. Willie and Short Round were so intent on watching their every footstep that they were taken by surprise when they reached the end of the bridge and were seized by the guards.

He watched helplessly, swaying in the middle of the bridge with Mola Ram in front of him, Thuggee guards behind, nothing but the sky above, and the rocky river gorge filled with hungry crocodiles below. Wind whipped around Indy and he staggered unsteadily. "Let them go, Mola Ram!" he shouted over the howling wind.

Even from a distance, he could make out Mola Ram's diabolical sneer. "You are in a position unsuitable for giving orders," he jeered.

"Watch your back!" Willie suddenly warned urgently as she struggled in vain to free herself from her captors.

Whirling around to where he'd just been, Indy saw Thuggee guards starting across the bridge toward him.

He was utterly trapped.

It was time for a serious negotiation with Mola Ram.

He pulled the pouch of Sankara Stones from his satchel and dangled it over the gorge. "You want the stones?" he shouted. "Let them go!"

Mola Ram was unflustered, even amused by this. "Drop them, Dr. Jones," he replied with a nasty smile. "They will be found in the gorge. You won't."

"Indy!" Short Round shouted in alarm, twisting and struggling in a guard's iron grip.

"Behind you!" Willie cried out.

Mola Ram shouted a command in his ancient language and the guards closed in on Indy from both sides.

His eyes darting in both directions, Indy looped the pouch of stones around his neck and considered his predicament, muttering a curse under his breath. He was certain he'd been in worse situations than this one — but at the moment he couldn't think of any.

The guards crept closer still, brandishing their swords.

Desperate times called for desperate measures, he thought, as a plan formed in his mind.

He lifted the sword, threatening to bring it down on the bridge's rope handrail.

Mola Ram's smile faded slightly. With his dagger, he gestured for Willie and Short Round to move out onto the bridge. The guard's released them but they hesitated, not sure what his intentions were. "Go on! Go!" he demanded impatiently.

Reluctantly, Willie stepped out onto the bridge.

"Go on!" Mola Ram snapped, shoving Short Round forward. "Go on! Get going!"

Indy watched intently as Short Round followed Willie onto the bridge. "Shorty!" he shouted to get the boy's attention before switching to Chinese so no one but Short Round would know what he had in mind.

As Indy spoke to Short Round rapidly in Chinese, he carefully hooked his own leg around the webbing of the side spans of the bridge.

Short Round's face took on an expression of sheer terror but he nodded and hooked his arm into a rope stay.

Indy glanced at Willie with a meaningful expression

and a nearly imperceptible nod that said: *See what we're doing? Do the same.*

As the realization of what Indy was about to do struck Willie, she staggered back two steps. "He can't be serious!" she muttered frantically.

"Hang on, lady," Short Round told her. "We're going for a ride."

Moving rapidly, Willie wrapped a piece of frayed rope securely around her arm and squeezed her eyes shut. "Is he nuts?" she asked Short Round as Indy raised the sword over his head once more.

"He no nuts. He crazy," Short Round replied.

With the sword still poised over his head, Indy looked Mola Ram straight in the eyes and swung the sword with all his strength. It whooshed through the air and slashed clear through the top and bottom ropes!

Immediately, Mola Ram's guards started to flee in panic — but it was too late! The rope bridge was shorn in two! As it broke in the middle, both halves swung down toward opposite sides of the gorge.

The guards shrieked horribly in mid air as they fell from the bridge and hurtled toward the croc-infested river. Mola Ram pitched forward, off balance, as he clutched at the bridge's ropes and slats.

Willie and Short Round clung to the ropes they had wrapped around themselves. They fell with the bridge toward one of the cliff walls. Below them, Indy stayed latched onto his rope support and also swung with the bridge as it hit the sheer face of the cliff wall.

The bridge now hung like a ladder, with Short Round and Willie closer to the top and Indy hanging on below. But above them, Mola Ram also dangled, along with one of his guards.

Mola Ram tried to climb upward, but a slat broke in his hand. "Noooo!" he shrieked as he lost his grip and plummeted past Willie and Short Round. Flailing wildly, he managed to grab onto the rope once again, knocking another of his guards down into the gorge.

He wasn't far below Indy now, and began to climb up. The Thuggee High Priest was surprisingly strong and agile. He quickly reached Indy and was about to pass him when Indy reached out and grabbed his leg. Indy wasn't going to let Mola Ram climb and reach Willie and Short Round before they could escape to the top.

Mola Ram kicked violently, trying to break Indy's grip on his leg but Indy was determined not to let go. He yanked Mola Ram down the rope until they were face-to-face. Mola Ram stretched toward Indy, trying to reach his chest.

"Indy, cover your heart!" Short Round warned from above. "Cover your heart!"

Indy remembered what Mola Ram had done to the

sacrificial victim in the temple. He writhed away from the High Priest, more terrified than he had been even when he cut the rope bridge in two.

Still clinging to the vertical rope bridge, Mola Ram's fingers inched toward Indy's chest. Indy clutched Mola Ram's wrist, trying to keep the deadly fingers away from his heart. The High Priest simply laughed and began chanting, moving his hand ever closer.

Indiana heard Willie crying out to him from the edge of the cliff.

Slowly, using great concentration to focus all his strength into his arms, he pushed Mola Ram's hand away. But as Mola Ram withdrew his hand, he hit Indy in the face with a powerful blow to the jaw.

Indy lost his grip on the rope.

He was falling!

Reaching out as he tumbled down, Indy could see the shining triangular teeth of the crocodile below him as he hung no more than five feet above the bottom of the gorge. At the last second, he had been able to grab the rope bridge before plunging into the gorge. His heart hammered in his chest as he dangled there. When its frenetic beat slowed, he pulled himself up and began to climb.

He'd advanced only several rungs when something flew past his face and bounced off the cliff wall. He continued to climb, but an arrow splintered the wooden slat he had gripped. Looking up, he saw that more Thuggee guards had arrived on both sides of the cliff. They stood at each edge and were shooting arrows at him from large bows.

Indy heard shouting from above. "Look out!" Short Round shouted down to Willie.

"Noooo!" Willie wailed as Mola Ram climbed up below her. She kicked at him and pounded on his head, trying to keep him from reaching her.

Mola Ram lost his grip and fell once again. He reached out for Indy as he hurtled past, his fingers grabbing Indy's shirt.

It took all Indy's strength to keep from being knocked off the bridge by Mola Ram's weight. The High Priest regained his grip on the bridge and reached toward Indy's satchel, trying to get the Sankara Stones away from him. "The stones are mine!" Mola Ram bellowed.

"You betrayed Shiva," Indy countered. Speaking in Sanskrit, he repeated the ancient warning about the power of the stones. As Indy spoke the words, the stones began to glow inside the bag.

Mola Ram grabbed for them and their intense heat scorched his hands.

The stones began to spill out of the bag.

Mola Ram reached out, trying to grab them back.

Indy kept speaking the sacred Sanskrit words. The blazing stones seared Mola Ram's flesh and he screamed in pain, letting go of two stones, which dropped into the gorge. He juggled the third stone, determined not to let it slip from his grasp. But the pain was too much, and the stone fell from his hands. But this time, the stone didn't fall into the gorge. Indy thrust his arm out, deftly catching it in midair.

Thrown off balance by the burning stones, Mola Ram reared backwards. Indy watched him plummet downward until he finally crashed into the water.

The crocodiles arose, instantly eager for the meal that had just dropped in.

Indy was once again climbing toward the top of the cliff and dodging arrows when he saw the young maharajah appear on the cliff. Behind him were Captain Blumburtt and his British troops. The maharajah pointed across the chasm to the Thuggee guards on the opposite side who were still firing arrows at Indy, Willie, and Short Round.

The British took aim with their rifles and fired on the guards. It wasn't long before the Thuggees gave up and retreated into the woods.

Willie and Short Round made it to the top of the cliff first. Still climbing below them, Indy was relieved to see them standing on safe ground.

Every muscle in Indy's body ached with the effort of pulling himself up the last several feet to the top. Slowly, painfully, his face lifted above the edge of the cliff. With joyful expressions, Willie and Short Round gripped his shoulders and pulled him to safety.

Indy rolled on his back to recover for a moment. Then, he reached into the pouch that had once carried the three Sankara Stones and triumphantly lifted the one remaining stone he had managed to save. It was the one that belonged to the villagers.

CHAPTER TWENTY

*A*s Willie, Short Round, and Indy emerged from the
jungle and looked down a hillside at the Mayapore village
below, they could hardly believe the change; brilliant sunshine now shone on blossoming fruit trees and abundant
foliage, and colorful, well-kept homes.

Weary, but happy to be safe once again, the threesome
entered the village. They were not alone. Behind them followed a multitude of the village children they had freed
from the mines. Indy couldn't wait to see the faces of the
villagers when they saw that their most valuable treasure — their children — was being returned to them.

Instantly, villagers came forward to greet them. The
children rushed forward into the arms of their parents.
Cries of happiness and tears of joy filled the air; there was
laughter and crying mixed in a soaring exultation as families were reunited.

The old shaman came toward Indy, followed by the

village elders. The shaman touched his fingers to his forehead and bowed. The three travelers returned the greeting.

"We know you are coming back when life returned to our village," the old shaman said with great emotion. He swept his arms around the village. "Now you can see the magic of the rock you bring back."

The old shaman smiled wisely. Indy took the stone from the bag and handed it to him. "Yes, I understand its power now," he agreed.

The shaman took the stone reverently and bowed once again to Indy, Short Round, and Willie. He joined the elders and they walked to the village's small sacred mound. Kneeling, he replaced the stone in its niche.

Willie turned to Indy. "You could've kept it," she pointed out, her voice filled with admiration for the fact that he had not.

"Ah, what for?" he asked. "They'd just have put it in a museum. It would be just another rock collecting dust."

"But then it would have given you fortune and glory," she reminded him.

He smiled at her slyly. "We might find fortune and glory yet. It's a long way to Delhi."

Willie looked up at him with an expression that asked: *Are you crazy?* "No thanks," she declined firmly. "No more adventures with you, Dr. Jones."

Indy played at being shocked. "Sweetheart, after all the fun we've had together?"

Willie's hands went to her hips. "If you think I'm going to Delhi with you, or anyplace else after all the trouble you've gotten me into — think again, buster!"

Indy didn't really think she would travel to Delhi on her own, but he'd come to learn that despite her outward demeanor, she was tough and brave as they came. She might do anything.

"I'm going home to Missouri," she went on, "where they don't feed you snakes before ripping your heart out and lowering you into hot pits. This is not my idea of a swell time!"

Turning, she walked toward a villager. "Excuse me, sir? I need a guide to Delhi," she requested.

Indy suddenly knew he couldn't let her get away. And he didn't believe she *really* wanted to go, either.

Wielding his bullwhip with slow ease, he unfurled it, drew back, and let it out with a flick of his wrist. The whip wrapped around Willie's waist.

Willie frowned angrily as he reeled her in, pulling her toward him and into his arms.

If she had wanted to get away from him, she could have. But she didn't struggle. Instead she gazed up into his eyes and he knew that there was something special between them.

As he bent to kiss her, they were soaked with a spray of water. Jumping apart, they both looked up at Short Round sitting on the back of the baby elephant that had just drenched them and laughing uproariously at his own joke. "Very funny!" he cackled hilariously. "Very funny!"

Indy laughed along and so did Willie. Finally, they kissed — a sign that while one adventure had come to an end, more were waiting on the horizon.

INDIANA JONES™

and the
LAST CRUSADE

Ryder Windham

Based on the story by George Lucas and Menno Meyjes
and the screenplay by Jeffrey Boam

Thanks to Annmarie Nye at Scholastic, and Jonathan Rinzler and Leland Chee at Lucasfilm. Thanks to Mark Cotta Vaz and Shinji Hata, authors of *From Star Wars to Indiana Jones: The Best of the Lucasfilm Archives,* which features information and numerous close-up images from Henry Jones' diary and other props. Thanks also to the authors of Lucasfilm's official Indiana Jones website (www.indianajones.com), and to Dr. David West Reynolds for his extensive knowledge about the costumes, props, and vehicles in the Indiana Jones films.

For Dorothy and Violet,
who make every day Father's Day

*I*ndiana Jones kept his horse in line with the other mounted Boy Scouts who followed their Scoutmaster, Mr. Havelock, across the red rocks of the Utah desert. It was the summer of 1912, the year that Indiana — Indy to his friends — turned thirteen. He was excited to be a member of the Boy Scouts of America, a relatively new organization, founded just a little over two years earlier.

Except for his wide-brimmed hat, Indy didn't care much for the Boy Scout uniform. And unlike his fellow scouts, he wasn't especially eager to collect merit badges, even though he had already earned five. What he liked most about being a scout was that it kept him outdoors and away from his father.

Indy and his father didn't talk much.

The Boy Scout troop proceeded past towering buttes until they arrived at the base of an ancient cliff pueblo.

Overhead, natural arches spanned like bridges across the sky. Indy marveled at the sight and tried to imagine what life must have been like for the ancestors of the Hopi, the indigenous tribe who had once made their homes at the edges and recesses of the cliffs. His admiration was such that he had adorned his Boy Scout uniform with an authentic Hopi Indian woven belt.

Mr. Havelock brought his horse to a stop, turned to the boys behind him, and cried, "Dismount!"

The boys swung off their horses. One especially hefty thirteen-year-old scout, Herman, accidentally fell from his saddle and landed hard on his side, sending his hat off of his head.

"Herman's horsesick!" teased another scout.

Indy tossed an angry glare at the teaser. He was about to step over and help Herman to his feet when he saw Herman push himself up from the ground and put his hat back on. Herman looked embarrassed. Indy caught his eye and shrugged, letting Herman know that the fall was no big deal.

Leaving their horses, the scouts followed Mr. Havelock up along the base of the cliff. "Chaps, no one wander off," Havelock said, his voice echoing off the high cliff walls. "Some of the passageways in here can run for miles."

Indy and Herman ran off on their own, scrambling up

a steep hill to investigate a pair of big, wide-mouthed caves at the top. Herman was carrying his bugle, and it glinted in the sunlight as it bounced against his hip. After Indy chose the darker of the two caves, Herman mustered up his courage and entered first. Indy followed.

As they made their way inside, the temperature dropped several degrees. They had only walked a few yards when Herman pulled up short. "I don't think this is such a good idea."

Before Indy could argue, he heard something coming from a small passage in the wall to his right. *Voices?* He stopped and gazed into it, noticing that it sloped downward. He could make out a faint light in the darkness, and caught a whiff of burning kerosene.

Herman heard the sound, too. "What is it?"

Indy knew better than to reply. He reached forward, grabbed Herman's sleeve, and tugged the larger boy after him as he stepped down into the passage. Moving quietly, they arrived at what appeared to be a large hole in the floor. But then Indy noticed the exposed wooden beams at the edges of the opening. He realized they were looking down into a *kiva*, an underground ceremonial chamber built by the ancient pueblo.

Indy and Herman hunched down and peered into the *kiva*, where several kerosene lanterns illuminated the forms of four men. Three were filthy-looking fellows, digging with shovels and pick-axes. Indy couldn't see them too well. The fourth man wore a leather waist jacket and a brown felt fedora hat, and stood with his arms crossed as he watched the others dig.

The man in the fedora was clearly in charge. "Alfred, did you get anything yet?"

"Nothing."

"Then keep digging."

Suddenly, one of the other men said, "The Kid's got something."

"Whoo! Yee-hoo!" Indy assumed the man shouting was "the Kid." He said, "I got something, Garth! I got something . . . I got something right here."

When the excited speaker turned, Indy saw he was indeed an older kid, maybe fourteen years old, with dirty blond hair. The Kid had dug up an old box, which he carried over to the man in the fedora. The other two men laid down their tools and stepped over, too. One man wore wire frame spectacles, an unbuttoned vest, and had long black hair that flowed out from under his black hat. The other man was middle-aged with a gray mustache, and was wearing a dingy old Rough Rider cavalry uniform.

Indy and Herman watched silently as Fedora — the

name that Indy had given the man below — took the box and opened it slowly. The Kid huddled close beside Fedora and said, "Oh, look at that!"

Fedora removed a bejeweled cross from the box. The cross was made of gold, as was the long, finely linked chain attached to it.

"Whoo!" the Kid shouted. "We're rich! We're rich!"

"Shut up. Shut up," muttered the long-haired man. Because of the man's spectacles, Indy thought of him as Glasses.

"Well, we're rich, ain't we?" the Kid said.

Indy removed his scout hat and bent down to get a better view of the cross. Beside him, Herman nervously whispered, "Indy . . . Indy? What are they doing?"

Indy gazed intently at the cross and hoped that his silence would encourage his companion to be quiet. It didn't work.

"Indiana?" Herman said. "Indiana?"

"Shh!" Indy responded. Herman went quiet.

Fedora blew dust off the gold cross, and then he smiled.

Glasses didn't want to waste any more time. "Hey, we got to find more stuff to bring back." While Fedora continued to examine the cross, his three allies returned to their digging.

Leaning close to Herman, Indy whispered, "It's the Cross of Coronado. Cortez gave it to him in 1520."

A moment later, the Kid found an old ring and began whooping again. "Ah! Oh, boy! Whoo!"

Looking at the ring, Glasses said, "I'm thinkin' about raisin' my dead mama, dig down, and put it on her bony finger! Ha ha!"

Indy watched Fedora place the cross upon a stone. As Fedora stepped away from the cross, Indy whispered to Herman, "That cross is an important artifact. It belongs in a museum." Rising from the edge of the *kiva*, he shifted Herman to face him and said in a low voice, "Run back and find the others. Tell Mr. Havelock that there are men looting in the caves. Have him bring the sheriff."

As Indy spoke, Herman felt something slither over his leg. A snake. His face contorted with sudden horror, but Indy casually tossed the snake aside. "It's only a snake."

Herman was still trembling, apparently too afraid to move. Indy grabbed his neckerchief and tugged it, forcing Herman to meet his eyes, and said sternly, "Did you hear what I said?"

"Right," Herman gasped. "Run back...Mr. Havelock...the sheriff..." Suddenly realizing that the instructions required leaving Indy behind, Herman added, "What, what are *you* gonna do?"

Indy released the neckerchief. "I don't know," he admitted. "I'll think of something." He patted his friend on the shoulder, and Herman turned and began to make his way back up and out of the passage.

A rope dangled down from Indy's position to the floor of the *kiva*. Indy figured that the four looters had used the rope themselves, but he tested it to make sure it would hold his weight anyway. The looters continued to dig, their backs to him as he lowered himself down into the *kiva*.

Quiet as a cat, Indy slunk forward and picked up the gold cross. He nearly jumped when Fedora snapped, "Dig with your hands, not with your mouth." But Fedora was still focused on the other men and unaware of Indy's presence. Indy tucked the cross into his belt and returned to the rope. He cast a last glance back at the looters, smirking as he began to haul himself up the rope. He was just pulling himself up through the hole in the ceiling when his boots struck one of the exposed wooden beams. The beam was very brittle.

Crack!

Fedora and the others turned their heads in the direction of the sound, hardly believing what they saw: was that a Boy Scout scurrying away with the Cross of Coronado? The Kid was the first to react, exclaiming, "He's got our thing!"

"Get 'im!" Glasses yelled. Fedora grimaced as his three allies fell over each other in their haste to get their hands on the Boy Scout.

Indy removed the cross from his belt and gripped it tightly as he fled back through the passage and out of the cave. He bounded down the rocky slope that led up to the cave's entrance, kicking up dust and trying his best not to slip and break his neck. Stopping for a moment, he quickly scanned the area and shouted, "Mr. Havelock!"

No response.

"Anybody!"

Still no response. Indy couldn't see any of the other scouts and then he realized what had happened.

"Everybody's lost but me," Indy muttered.

"There he is!" shouted Fedora as he emerged from the cave above.

"Let's go! Let's go!" the other men hollered from behind.

Indy bolted, leaping from one rock to another until he arrived at the ledge that overlooked the area where he'd left his horse. He stuck two fingers into the corners of his mouth and let out a loud whistle. His obedient horse responded immediately, trotting over to stand at the base of the ledge, directly below his position. Indy slid the bejeweled cross back under his belt.

Then he jumped.

He'd intended to land squarely on the horse's saddle, and he might have succeeded if the horse hadn't stepped forward just as Indy's feet left the ledge. As gravity had it, Indy landed on the ground instead.

"Hey!" came the voice of one of the looters. "Hey you!"

Indy picked himself up and climbed onto his horse's back. "Hyah! Hyah!" The horse galloped away from the base of the ledge, just as Fedora and the others arrived.

"Hey!" the Kid hollered. "Come back here!"

Fedora put two fingers into his mouth and whistled. His whistle brought a pickup truck, which came roaring up, with an open-topped automobile right behind it. A man in an expensive white linen suit and Panama hat sat in the auto's passenger seat. Fedora and his men jumped into the back of the truck, and then the two vehicles sped off after Indy.

Indy kept his horse at a fast gallop as he raced away from the towering rock formations and into a wide, open area. Over the sound of thundering hooves, he heard the engines of the truck and car closing in.

The man in the Panama hat gestured to the looters in the truck, motioning for them to catch up with the elusive Boy Scout. "Come on!" he shouted. "Get him!"

Indy could feel his heart pounding as he crouched low

and leaned forward in his saddle. He knew his horse couldn't outrun the two vehicles, so he scanned the terrain, searching for some kind of escape route. That was when he saw a train in the distance, barreling down a railroad track.

Indy veered off, guiding his horse toward the train. The car and truck swerved after him.

"Hey!" the Kid shouted as he bounced in the back of the pickup. "Come back here!"

As he drew closer to the railroad tracks, Indy saw that he was chasing down a circus train. The train's brightly painted exterior and colorful banners proclaimed it to be the property of the Dunn & Duffy Circus, and big letters on the side of one stockcar promoted the WORLD'S TALLEST GIRAFFES; indeed, the two giraffes who extended their long necks up through open hatches in the stockcar's roof did appear to be quite tall.

At full gallop, Indy guided his horse up along the right side of the train until he reached the first boxcar, right behind the coal car. Indy barely noticed the laughing clown painted on the door — all his attention was focused on the built-in ladder protruding from the side. When his horse drew level with the ladder, Indy leaned out and grabbed it. The horse veered away from the train and ran off.

As Indy scrambled up the ladder at the front of the boxcar, Glasses leaped from the pickup truck to the ladder at the rear. Indy saw him climbing up — and knew his allies were right behind. Indy took his last chance to get a running start and leaped to the roof of the stockcar carrying the giraffes. Glancing back over his shoulder, he saw Glasses in pursuit, so he ran right past the giraffes and leaped to the next car, a flatcar that carried stacks of boxes under red, white, and blue tarpaulins.

But his pursuers weren't slowing down: Rough Rider was now right behind Glasses. Indy got up, scrambled over the boxes, and then skipped over the coupling to grab the ladder on the next car. There was an open window at the front end of it, and Indy climbed right through.

Less than a minute earlier, when Indy had ridden past this stockcar on his horse, he hadn't taken any special notice of the oversized paintings of snakes or the words HOUSE OF REPTILES that adorned the stockcar's side. After all, reptiles didn't scare him. So when he entered the car at its unmarked front end, he really didn't know what he was getting himself into.

The window led Indy directly onto a wooden catwalk that stretched the length of the stockcar. The catwalk was suspended by metal bars attached to the ceiling, and the clearance was so low that Indy was forced to crawl onto it.

He had no sooner started to haul himself headfirst onto the catwalk when Glasses reached in through the window and grabbed his boots. Indy struggled to shake himself free of the man's grip, which caused the rickety catwalk to shake, too. Would it hold up? Indy couldn't be sure, and glanced briefly at what lay below him. He nearly lost his scout hat when he saw what was directly above him. It was an open pen with a straw-covered floor that contained a bunch of large crocodiles.

The crocodiles wriggled and snapped at the air. Indy gasped as he kicked free from Glasses and pulled himself forward. The catwalk began to shake more violently as the old Rough Rider scrambled in after Glasses. Below the catwalk, Indy saw open-topped bins filled with squirming snakes. He'd never seen so many snakes in his life.

The combined weight of Indy, Glasses, and Rough Rider was more than the catwalk could take. Ahead of Indy, bolts began to rip from the ceiling, and the catwalk was transformed into a sudden slide. The lower end of the catwalk fell into a water-filled vat, sending Indy careening into an uncontrollable somersault.

The water erupted in a splash as Indy's legs hit the water, and then an enormous anaconda suddenly raised its head right in front of him — and hissed. Indy's eyes went wide with fear as he pulled his legs up and rolled to his left in a desperate effort to escape the deadly snake. Unfortunately, Indy's effort cost him not only his hat, which fell away from his head, but also what was left of his nerve, for he tumbled straight into one of the adjoining vats filled with hundreds of snakes.

They were all under and over him, writhing everywhere. He felt them slither and shift against his body and through his hair and across his face. He had never imagined what it might be like to be smothered by snakes. He would have screamed if he weren't afraid to open his mouth.

With trembling hands, Indy managed to push the snakes off his face. He lifted his head and gasped out a subdued howl. He gave a louder gasp as he began pulling himself up and out of the vat, and then released an all-out scream.

Indy's scream caused Glasses and Rough Rider to recoil on the ruined catwalk, but didn't reach the ears of the engineer — the train kept moving. Trying to regain his senses, Indy saw a small rectangular clean-out door at the car's rear. He gave the door a push, and it swung on its hinges. As the train continued to rumble along the tracks, he crawled through the doorway and stepped over a coupling and onto another flatcar carrying tarp-covered supplies and tied-down crates.

Realizing that Glasses and Rough Rider weren't about to give up, he quickly turned, slammed the small door shut, and threw its locking bolt into place. And just in time, too: A moment after he stepped away from the door, the two men began hammering against it from the other side.

The Cross of Coronado was still safely tucked in Indy's belt. He had taken only a few steps toward the rear of the flatcar when he felt something wriggle against his stomach. He stopped, drove his hands down into his shirt, and frantically pulled out a long snake that had slithered into his clothes. "Oh, oh . . ." Indy gasped with disgust as he tossed the snake aside.

No sooner had the snake left Indy's fingers than the blond kid came running over the top of the reptile car. He pounced and shoved Indy against the tarp on the flatcar. Indy shoved back, launching the Kid backwards. As the Kid caught hold of the ladder at the end of the reptile car, Indy turned, jumped up onto the tarp-covered supplies, and ran to the next stockcar. The Kid recovered and ran after him.

There wasn't any door at the end of the stockcar, so Indy raced up a ladder to reach its roof. On top of some crates on the flatcar behind Indy, the Kid spotted a long wooden stick with a metal hook on one end. He grabbed the stick and lifted it fast to snag Indy's foot.

Indy tripped over the hook and fell forward onto the stockcar's roof, landing with a thud. He had no way of knowing that his landing had caused an unlit lantern to shake free and fall from the ceiling inside the stockcar. The lantern crashed against the head of the stockcar's single passenger: a large — and now very angry — rhinoceros.

Indy started to rise from the boxcar's roof, but the Kid had climbed up after him, a long knife in his left hand. Indy grabbed the Kid's left wrist and fell back against the roof with the Kid on top of him.

Indy was sprawled flat on his back, with the Kid's blade just inches from his throat. It was then that the agitated rhinoceros made his presence known by raising his head and thrusting his horn through the ceiling. The horn tore straight up through the roof, just above Indy's head.

Indy and the Kid only shifted slightly as they looked at the horn with astonishment. The horn drew back into the hole it had created, but a moment later the rhino raised his head again and tore a new hole through the roof, just beside Indy's right elbow.

Indy shot a worried glance to the face of the knife-wielding boy who straddled his chest. It was fairly obvious to him that if they didn't move immediately, the rhino might impale them. But the Kid just grinned, thinking Indy was the only one in danger, and began to lower his blade.

But his grin vanished when the rhino's horn smashed up through the roof, passing up between Indy's outstretched legs and coming within two inches of the Kid's inner thigh. Both of them stared at the horn with stunned expressions.

"Holy smokes!" Indy said. He shoved the Kid, who tumbled to the edge of the roof but kept from falling off. As Indy rolled over and onto his knees, two gunshots issued from the end of the reptile car. Indy glanced past the Kid to see that Glasses and Rough Rider had blasted through the lock on the clean-out door. The two men scrambled out of the reptile car, eager for vengeance.

Indy got to his feet and saw a water tank alongside the track directly ahead. The tank's maneuverable waterspout extended out over the path of the moving train. Just as Glasses climbed up onto the rhino car's roof, Indy made a quick calculation and leaped for the waterspout.

Catching the spout perfectly, Indy lifted his legs and landed a solid kick against Glasses' chest. The train ran alongside as the waterspout swung a full 360 degrees around the tank, positioning Indy neatly over the roof of the last stockcar. But as Indy released his grip and landed on the stockcar's roof, he found himself face-to-face with Fedora.

Indy hadn't had a clear view of Fedora's face in the *kiva*, but was now close enough to see that the man hadn't shaved for a few days. Startled and off balance, Indy fell to his knees.

Fedora took a step toward the fallen Boy Scout. "Come on, kid. There's no way out of this."

Shifting his weight onto his hands, Indy edged away from Fedora. He backed himself straight over a hatch that was covered by thin wooden planks, too thin to support Indy. There was a loud crash as he fell through the hatch and landed on his back on the much more solid wooden floor that lay within the stockcar.

Indy felt the wind knocked out of him. There was a thin layer of straw on the floor, hardly enough to have broken his fall. He groaned as he lifted his head and sat up. His hair had fallen in front of his eyes, and when he pushed his hair back, he saw that he wasn't alone in the boxcar, and that his fellow traveler had an even thicker mane around his own head.

It was an African lion.

Seeing Indy, the lion rose slowly to his feet. Then he advanced toward Indy and growled.

Indy scrambled to his feet and backed away from the lion. The lion roared again and Indy raised his hands defensively and cried, "Hey!" Indy plastered himself against the wall. Looking for anything that he might use to defend himself, Indy saw a lion trainer's coiled whip hanging on a nail on the wall to his right.

The lion began walking toward him, its hungry eyes following the boy's every movement.

A low growl sounded as Indy reached for the whip. When he removed it from the nail, he realized it was heavier than he had anticipated. Swallowing hard, he threw his arm forward to give the whip a try. The whip unraveled awkwardly, and its tip flew back and hit him in the face, cutting his chin.

Indy's head jerked back at the sudden, stinging pain. With his free hand, he reached up to feel the already bleeding gash below his lower lip. Then the lion roared again — the wound would have to wait.

Holding his arm out and trying to get a better feel for the whip, Indy lashed out again. The whip cracked sharply. The lion bellowed and swatted at the air. Indy didn't want to strike the lion, only drive it back, so he took a cautious step forward and snapped the whip again. There was another loud crack, and the lion began to back away.

The Cross of Coronado had slipped from Indy's belt and lay at the center of the floor. As the lion backed up against the far end of the stockcar, Indy held the whip tight with one hand as he reached down with the other to pluck up the cross and return it to his belt.

Indy had every reason to assume the lion car's doors were locked from the outside. He wondered, *How do I get out of here?*

"Toss up the whip," a voice said from above.

Indy glanced up to see Fedora's head leaning over the ceiling's open hatch. Glasses and Rough Rider were also hunkered around the hatch. Fedora extended his right arm down toward Indy.

Indy tossed one end of the whip up to Fedora and coiled the other end around his arm. Just then, the lion advanced toward Indy. Indy gasped as the lion sprang at him but held tight to the whip. As Fedora pulled him up, Indy felt the lion's front paws brush against his legs. But it was too late — he was already being lifted through the hatch and onto the boxcar's roof.

Standing atop the boxcar, Indy faced the four looters. Rough Rider drew his revolver and aimed it at Indy, but Fedora grabbed the revolver's barrel and forced it down.

Fedora's eyes flicked to the cross at Indy's belt. With some admiration in his voice, Fedora said, "You got heart, kid, but that belongs to me."

"It belongs to Coronado," Indy said defiantly as he pulled the cross from his belt, holding it out and away from the men.

"Coronado is dead," Fedora replied sharply, "and so are all of his grandchildren."

"This should be in a museum," Indy said sternly.

Tired of the conversation, the Kid lunged for Indy. "Now give it back!"

Suddenly, Glasses moved behind Indy and grabbed his arms while the Kid tried to tear the cross from Indy's grip. Indy didn't let go, even when he felt something shift inside his shirt. It was another snake. But this time, Indy didn't squirm. He stayed perfectly still, letting it exit his sleeve and wrap around the Kid's hand.

"A snake!" the Kid hollered as he released his grasp on the cross. "Snake! Aah!"

Indy twisted out from Glasses' clutches and clambered down the end of the lion car, taking the cross with him. He touched down outside the front door to the caboose. Hoping he wasn't about to walk in on another deadly animal, Indy glanced at the letters painted above the door: DR. FANTASY'S MAGIC CABOOSE.

"Magic?" Indy said aloud as he pondered his next move. Knowing that the looters would soon be on top of him, he threw the door open and entered the car.

Back atop the lion car, Fedora put his arm out, gesturing to the others not to follow the Boy Scout. "Hold it," Fedora said. "Make sure he doesn't double back."

The caboose's interior was lined by large boxes and assorted equipment for a magic show. At the far end, there was a door with a barred window, where he could see the tracks recede behind the train. But when he tugged at the door's handle, he found it was securely locked.

Indy realized the men would enter the caboose in seconds. Glancing around, he noticed a large, ornately painted wooden box that appeared big enough to conceal him. He stepped quickly over to the box, lifted its upper lid, and discovered that the box was empty. With the cross once again tucked inside his belt, Indy climbed into the box and lowered the lid.

Fedora threw the caboose's front door open just in time to see the large box's lid settle in place. Closing the door behind him, Fedora stepped toward the box.

"Okay, kid," Fedora said as Indy's weight shifted inside the box, causing it to shake. "Out of the box. Now!"

Incredibly, the shaking box suddenly collapsed, with all four sides flopping away from its rectangular wooden base to reveal nothing but empty air. Fedora gaped, but his amazement gave way to anger, and he cursed as he ran to the back of the caboose.

The door's lock didn't inconvenience Fedora a bit. It snapped as he yanked the door open, and then he stepped out onto the caboose's balcony. He saw the Boy Scout running alongside the tracks and away from the train. Fedora cursed under his breath, but as he watched the scout running off with the cross, he couldn't help but smile. He really did admire the kid's spirit.

Indy ran all the way to the town where he lived with his father. Clutching the Cross of Coronado, he glanced back over his shoulder more than once to make sure that none of the looters were following him. He ran past the industrial brick buildings that bordered the railroad tracks and headed up a street that was lined by modest houses, most with clapboard siding. Although Indy and his father had only lived in Utah for a short time, the sun had already done a solid job of fading the painted white letters that spelled *Jones* on the wooden mailbox outside of their small house.

"Dad!" Indy shouted as he neared the house. He bolted past the mailbox and up the dirt path that led to his front porch. The house had a sun-bleached stucco exterior with green trim, and the surrounding lawn hadn't been mowed since long before he and his father moved in. Usually, the sight of the run-down house or the prospect of any conversation with his father made Indy feel depressed, but right now, he only felt elated.

"Dad!" Indy shouted again as he flung open the front door and carried the cross into the house. "Dad!"

Indy's dog, a big Alaskan malamute, was lying on the floor in the front room, just outside the door that led to Indy's father's study. The dog raised his head and barked as Indy skipped past him and threw open the door. The study was filled with books, and its windows overlooked the cruddy backyard. As usual, Indy's father was seated at his desk beside a window, with a large, open book laid out before him. He was using a pen to copy an image from the book into his own notebook.

"Dad!"

"Out," the elder Jones responded without looking up, causing Indy to stop in his tracks. His father had a deep, commanding voice, and people usually listened to it.

Ignoring his father's order, Indy thrust his arm out to display the Cross of Coronado and said, "It's important!"

"Then wait," his father said, his eyes never straying from his work. "Count to twenty."

"No, Dad," Indy said defiantly. "You *listen* to me —"

"Junior!" his father snapped, clearly outraged. Still, he did not turn his gaze to Indy.

Indy hated it when his father called him *Junior*. Every time he heard it, he felt infuriated and — even worse —

deflated. Hoping his father would eventually look his way, Indy began counting out loud: "One, two, three, four . . ."

Without turning his head, Indy's father raised his left index finger and said, "In Greek."

Indy's father was Professor Henry Jones, formerly of Princeton University and an expert on medieval chivalric code. The book he happened to be examining at the moment was a medieval-era parchment volume, which was opened to an illuminated picture that resembled a design for a stained-glass window; the design incorporated an armored knight and a series of Roman numerals. Henry Jones had recently begun work at Four Corners University in Las Mesas, which was why he and Indy had moved to Utah. Indy couldn't stand his father's habit of transforming every attempt at conversation into an educational exercise. His father had become only more insufferable over the past few months, ever since Indy's mother died.

Indy wanted desperately for his father to look up and see the Cross of Coronado. He also wanted his father to see his rumpled Boy Scout uniform and the dirt on his face and the gash on his chin that was still bleeding. Indy wanted to tell his father all about what had happened that day, but he couldn't even get the man to look away from his old book. And so Indy did as he was told, and began counting to twenty in Greek.

"Ena, dyo, tria . . ."

Just then, a bugle sounded from outside. Indy glanced out a side window to see an automobile pulling up outside his house. The town sheriff and another man were in the front seat. In the back seat, Herman held his trumpet high and blew for all he was worth, proud that he had delivered the cavalry to Indy's home.

"Tessera," Indy continued counting as he moved for the study's door. Glancing at his preoccupied father, he added, "Pente," and then exited the study, quietly closing the door behind him.

Henry Jones remained so engrossed by his work that he didn't notice Indy's departure. As he continued copying the image of the knight into his notebook, he said to himself, "May he who illuminated this . . . illuminate me."

Outside the study, Indy was halfway across the front room when the front door opened and Herman walked in, proudly blowing his bugle. Indy reached for the horn, pulling it out of Herman's mouth, which was a mistake. Herman wasn't done blowing and accidentally spat right into his face. Indy flinched.

Herman was so excited and pleased he could hardly contain himself. Smiling broadly, he pointed to the door and blubbered, "I brought the sheriff!"

The sheriff walked in, followed by the man he'd been riding with in the car. The sheriff wore a big brown hat that matched the color of his caterpillar-like mustache, but his hat's height did nothing to disguise the fact that he was several inches shorter than Indy.

"Just the man I want to see," Indy said, stepping up to look down into the sheriff's eyes. "Now, there were five or six of them —"

"It's all right, son," the sheriff said calmly.

"They came after me —"

"You still got it?" the sheriff interrupted.

Realizing the sheriff meant the Cross of Coronado, Indy smiled and said, "Well, yes, sir." He held the cross up for the sheriff's inspection and said, "It's right here."

"I'm glad to see that," the sheriff said as he took the cross from Indy, "because the rightful owner of this cross won't press charges if you give it back. He's got witnesses. Five or six of them."

The front door opened again, and Fedora, Glasses, Rough Rider, and the Kid walked right into Indy's house. The looters just stood there, staring at Indy. Unlike the other men, including the sheriff and his partner, Fedora showed some degree of courtesy by removing his hat, and then he nodded at Indy in a friendly manner.

The sheriff and Fedora are in cahoots?! Indy couldn't believe it. He felt suddenly ill and his jaw went slack.

The sheriff turned his head to look through a window. Indy followed his gaze and saw another automobile had pulled up outside his house. It was the car that carried the man in the white linen suit and the Panama hat. The man had an obnoxiously large red flower in the lapel of his jacket, and used a cane as he stepped away from the car.

The sheriff handed the Cross of Coronado to Fedora, who in turn handed it back to the Kid. He took the cross and cried, "Whoo! Yeah!" as he carried it through the door and out of the house.

Indy was speechless. His mouth twitched, and the dull pain that came with it made him realize his chin would probably need stitches. He looked through the window again, and this time he saw the Kid hand the cross over to the man with the Panama Hat. The man took the cross, examining it for a moment. Then he reached into his jacket pocket and removed a large packet, which he handed to the Kid.

Money, Indy thought with disgust. *They dug up the cross for some dirty money!* He shifted his gaze to Fedora, then his eyes flicked to the sheriff. The sheriff tilted his head to Indy and said, "Good day," and then turned on his heel to walk out of the house.

The other men followed the sheriff, but Fedora lingered for a moment, long enough to face Indy and say, "You lost today, kid, but it doesn't mean you have to like it."

Before Indy could think of a response, Fedora took his hat and placed it squarely on top of Indy's head. And that's how Fedora left Indy, standing in the dingy, book-filled house in Utah, his head adorned by a rumpled, well-worn brown fedora that was slightly too large for him.

Fedora couldn't tell what the future held, but he knew that the kid would eventually grow into that hat.

*I*ndiana Jones's hat kept some of the rain off his face, but it didn't do anything to stop the fist that slammed into his face — not that he had expected it to. The year was 1938, and among the many things he'd learned since he'd first acquired his fedora was that a hat didn't offer much protection in a fistfight, especially when one's arms were pinned behind one's back.

Indy was standing on a cargo ship, which was currently being tossed around in a storm somewhere off the coast of Portugal. His arms were held by two sailors while a third — the one who had just punched him — stood before him on the ship's rain-drenched deck. As Indy felt blood flowing from the corner of his mouth, he lifted his head and bared his teeth in a broad, defiant smile.

The sailor hit him again.

The waves pounded against the ship and Indy braced himself for another punch, but then another figure emerged onto the deck. Indy hadn't seen the man in twenty-six years, and even though they'd both aged, there was no mistaking the man he remembered as Panama Hat. He still wore a white linen suit with a red flower in his lapel and still walked with a cane. When he left the bridge and began limping down a flight of metal steps to the slick deck, the sailor who'd been hitting Indy stepped aside while the other two tightened their grip on his arms.

Moving carefully but steadily across the deck, Panama Hat limped straight up to Indy. Because he preferred dry climates and indoor saloons and routinely hired other people to do his dirty work, Indy was surprised to see the man venture onto the deck without so much as a servant carrying an umbrella by his side. When the man was close enough for Indy to smell the liquor on his breath, he came to a stop and said, "Small world, Doctor Jones."

"Too small for two of us," Indy said boldly.

As rain pounded down on them, the man pushed Indy's leather jacket aside to expose the shoulder bag that rested against Indy's hip. Panama Hat dipped his tobacco-stained fingers into the bag and removed the Cross of Coronado. Raising his gaze to Indy, he said, "This is the second time I've had to reclaim my property from you."

Indy said, "That belongs in a museum."

"So do you." He glared at the two sailors who held Indy's arms and said, "Throw him over the side." Panama Hat began moving back toward the bridge, following the sailor who'd been using Indy's head as a punching bag, and taking the cross with him.

The two sailors held tight to Indy as they maneuvered him across the deck toward the rail. Another sailor stood at the rail, and he flung open a metal gate that was normally used to access the gangplank. But there wasn't any gangplank now — just a sheer drop into the cold, stormy sea.

A thirty-foot wave crashed against the side of the ship. Held fast by the two sailors, Indy lifted his legs and kicked out at the sailor who'd opened the gate. The sailor screamed as the kick knocked him past the gate and off of the ship.

On the other side of the deck, Panama Hat heard the scream and assumed it had been Indy's. He grinned. He was so eager to get back inside the bridge and out of his soaking-wet suit, he didn't bother to glance back in Indy's direction.

Another wave blasted over Indy and his captors. One of the sailors stumbled. Indy shoved him aside, then drove his elbow into the other sailor and flipped him to the deck. Turning fast, Indy sighted his next target heading back up the steps to the bridge.

As rain and waves continued to hammer the ship, Indy scrambled past a stack of fuel drums and over to the metal steps that led up to the bridge. He tackled Panama Hat and yanked him from the steps. The man howled in pain as he landed hard on the deck. Indy grabbed the Cross of Coronado.

But no sooner had Indy reclaimed the cross than two sailors jumped him. The cross was knocked from his grasp and skidded across the deck. A fire hose was coiled on a wall mount beside the nearby steps, and Indy grabbed the hose's metal nozzle. Using the nozzle like a club, he struck his attackers, knocking them both to the deck.

As another wave swept over the ship, it struck the fallen cross and carried it to the edge of the deck. Indy leaped away from the men and snatched the cross a split second before the rushing water would have sent it into the sea.

The ship tilted sharply, sending several fuel drums sliding across the deck. Indy scrambled to his feet and dodged the sliding drums as he moved fast for the stern, where a tarpaulin covered a high stack of wooden crates.

Panama Hat recovered and began pulling himself up the steps to the bridge. Gripping a rail as he turned to see Indy running off with the cross, he shouted, "Grab him! He's getting away! Stop him!"

The sailors came at Indy. He pummeled two of them with a single punch. Turning fast, Indy saw part of the tarp slip away from the crates.

The crates were marked TNT — MUITO EXPLO-SIVO.

Glancing up, Indy saw a large stevedore's hook swinging above the crates. He quickly climbed up onto the crates, grabbed the hook, and then leaped away. He swung out over the deck, narrowly avoiding a huge wave just as it smashed into the side of the ship, and then released the hook. He fell well past the ship's port rail and plunged into the rollicking ocean, never losing his grip on the cross.

On the ship, yet another wave struck a fuel drum and sent it flying straight onto a crate of TNT. The crate exploded, causing the entire ship to blow. Indy ducked down below the water's surface as the explosion sent an enormous orange fireball into the sky.

Cinders were still falling through the air when Indy bobbed up in the water amidst the debris. Clutching the cross, he reached out his arms, desperately trying to snag some piece of debris that might keep him afloat. He could hardly believe his eyes when he saw one of the ship's life preservers drifting nearby.

Indy looped his arm through the preserver. As he clung to it, he saw the destroyed ship begin to sink into the sea.

The last he saw of it was the painted letters on the stern that spelled out the ship's name: CORONADO.

A moment later, a shredded Panama hat floated past him. *Good riddance*, Indy thought. His own waterlogged hat had somehow remained on his head throughout the ordeal.

When Indy caught his breath, he began to kick his legs. It was a long way back to shore, and there was no time to waste.

*I*t was a balmy day in Fairfield, New York, and Indiana Jones — known as Dr. Jones to his students — was back at Barnett College, where he'd been teaching archaeology since he'd transferred from Marshall College in Connecticut.

Indy stood before the blackboard in his classroom, wearing a clean shave, British-made spectacles, a tweed suit, and a bow tie. Most of his students, who watched him attentively from their rows of tiered desks, would never have guessed that their well-groomed teacher was a rugged adventurer and the sole survivor of a recent shipwreck off the Portuguese coast. Facing the blackboard, Indy said, "Archaeology is the search for *fact* ..." He used a piece of chalk to write the word FACT for emphasis, then turned his gaze to his students and added, "... not truth. If it's truth you're interested in, Dr. Tyree's philosophy class is right down the hall."

Indy's students chuckled at this. When the laughter subsided, most of the female students went back to staring at their handsome professor. Staying focused on his lecture, Indy continued, "So forget any ideas you've got about lost cities, exotic travel, and digging up the world. We do not follow maps to buried treasure, and 'X' never, *ever* marks the spot."

In the corridor outside Indy's classroom, his friend and patron, Marcus Brody, Curator for the National Museum of New York, approached the room's door. Brody was wearing a gray suit with a dark striped tie. When he reached the door, he peered through its window to see Indy before he reached for the doorknob.

"Seventy percent of all archaeology is done in the library," Indy said. "Research. Reading." Indy saw the door open and Brody stepped in. While Brody walked over to stand against a wall beside the first row of tiered desks, Indy continued, "We cannot afford to take mythology at face value."

The bell rang. As the students began filing past his desk and out of the room, Indy announced, "Next week: 'Egyptology.' Starting with the excavation of Naukratis by Flinders Petrie in 1885. I will be in my office, if anybody's got any problems, for the next hour and a half."

After the last student had left, Brody walked over

to Indy. Indy leaned on his desk and said, "Marcus. I did it."

"You've got it?!" Brody said excitedly.

Indy reached into a desk drawer and removed a green cloth bag. He placed the bag on his desk. Brody opened it and gazed upon the Cross of Coronado.

"Oh!" Marcus gasped as he picked up the cross.

Removing his glasses, Indy said, "You know how long I've been looking for that?"

"All your life," Brody said, his eyes riveted to the cross.

"All my life," Indy said. He pocketed his glasses.

"Well done, Indy," Marcus praised. "Very well done indeed. This will find a place of honor in our Spanish collection."

Indy picked up a stack of books and tucked them under his left arm. Turning for the door, he said, "We can discuss my honorarium over dinner and champagne tonight." Before he walked out, he aimed a finger at Brody and added, "Your treat."

"Yes," Marcus said as he continued to admire the cross. "My treat." He remained absorbed by the cross as he followed Indy out of the classroom.

Indy headed for his office, where he anticipated a few students would want to meet with him. But as he opened the door to the reception area outside his office, he was momentarily speechless to find dozens — possibly *all* of his students — crammed into the room. Seeing him, the students began calling out his name trying to get his undivided attention.

"Dr. Jones!" cried a student. "Dr. Jones!"

While some students shouted and held notebooks out for Indy to examine, the few female students who were nearest to him just tilted their heads back to gaze up at him with mute, adoring expressions. The reception room hadn't been designed to accommodate such a crowd, and Indy felt the temperature rise more than a few degrees.

"Shush!" he said to the demanding students. "Shush! Shush!"

"Dr. Jones!" called out another female voice. Indy almost shushed her, too, before he saw the speaker was his secretary, an overwhelmed teaching assistant named Irene. "I am so glad you're back," Irene said frantically. She was holding a stack of papers which she handed to Indy in batches. "Here are your phone messages. This is your appointment schedule, and these term papers *still* haven't been graded."

"Okay," Indy said as he began jostling past the students, who became more desperate and vocal as he neared his office door. "Irene, put everyone's name on a list, in the order they arrived, and I'll see each and every one of them ... *in turn!*"

The students were still clamoring for Indy's attention as he entered his office and shut the door behind him. The door had a frosted glass window, which was supposed to allow the passage of some light as well as maintain privacy, but right now, all it did was display the shadows of the students' outstretched, waving hands. Indy felt as if he were suffocating.

Indy's cramped office was on the ground floor in Hamilton Hall, but given that he shared the space with a large boiler, it may as well have been in the basement. The room's walls were lined with deep shelves loaded with ancient artifacts, most of which Indy had picked up on his travels.

As he sat in the chair behind his desk and set his books and paperwork aside, his eyes flicked to his fedora, which rested on his cluttered desktop. Seeing the hat gave him a pang, a reminder of his life outside the walls of the college. Then his eyes fell on another object on his desk, a small package that was wrapped in brown paper and bound with twine. Inspecting the postmark, he read aloud, "'Venice, Italy.'"

The students began banging their hands against his door.

Indy took one last look at the door. Then grabbed his hat, opened the window, and climbed through it, stepping onto the green lawn outside Hamilton Hall. He shoved the package from Italy into one of his jacket pockets and then began walking away from the building with a brisk, determined stride.

Indy saw some students and faculty milling about outside. Hoping to appear innocuous, he stuck both hands in his pockets and kept his head down as he walked up along the green beside Grove Avenue, practically whistling with relief.

The sun was out. There was a breeze in the air. Indy felt better with every step he took away from the college buildings.

He didn't see the long black Packard sedan that was parked outside Hamilton Hall and was unaware that the sedan's passengers had seen his window exit. He hadn't walked far when the sedan moved off from its parking spot, trailing him just a short distance before a man called from the moving vehicle, "Dr. Jones!"

Indy stopped. So did the car. Three men got out. One of them said, "Dr. Jones?"

Indy kept his hands in his pockets as he eyed the three men. They were all stocky fellows with no-nonsense expressions, and there was nothing flashy about their suits, hats, or shoes. Everything about the men suggested that they were government agents, the kind of men who could be most persuasive when they asked someone to take a ride with them.

Indy didn't like the way the three men had interrupted his escape from Hamilton Hall, but they didn't intimidate him either. The way he figured it, a ride with them would probably prove more interesting than the pile of paperwork waiting back at his office.

He got into their car.

Indy was delivered to a luxury apartment building in New York City, where his caretakers ushered him into a private elevator that carried him up to the penthouse. The next thing Indy knew, the three men were gone, and he was standing alone in a surprisingly large, airy reception room that was elegantly furnished and free of clutter. Tall windows offered sweeping views of the skyline and Central Park. Along one curved bay of windows, a semi-circle of plush white lounge chairs were arranged below a wide skylight. The skylight housed a contemporary crystal chandelier that resembled nothing less than an incredibly expensive arrangement of icicle stalactites. From beyond a set of double doors, Indy heard muffled conversation and music playing in an adjoining room. It sounded like a cocktail party.

Throughout the reception room, streamlined shelves and built-in niches displayed museum-quality artifacts. Indy took the opportunity to examine some of the ancient objects, but he kept his hat on. Although he was curious about the identity of the apartment's owner, he hadn't *asked* to be brought to New York City and didn't feel any need to be polite.

An ivory figure of a recumbent bull caught Indy's eye. At a glance, he pegged it as an Assyrian piece from the ninth or eighth century B.C. The bull's head was turned sharply to its left, and one of its horns was partly missing, but it was still a good find. *You don't see one of those in some-one's home every day*, he thought.

Just then, the double doors swung open to reveal a silver-haired man wearing a black tuxedo. The man had the broad shoulders and trim physique of a young man, but Indy guessed he was probably in his late fifties. As the man pulled the doors closed behind him, he smiled gently at Indy and said, "I trust your trip down was comfortable, Dr. Jones. Uh, my men didn't alarm you, I hope." Crossing the room and extending his right hand to Indy, the man said, "My name is Donovan. Walter Donovan."

Donovan had phrased his name as if it were a question. Indy took the man's hand and shook it. "I know who you are, Mr. Donovan," Indy said. Then Indy, deciding to show some courtesy, removed his hat as he added, "Your contributions to the museum over the years have been extremely generous."

Donovan gave a gratified nod.

Letting his gaze sweep across the room, Indy said, "Some of the pieces in your collection are very impressive."

Donovan beamed. "Well, like yourself, Dr. Jones, I have a *passion* for antiquities." Motioning with his hand for Indy to follow, he stepped over to a circular-topped marble table and said, "Have a look over here." There was a cloth-covered object on the table. As Donovan pulled back the cloth to reveal the object, he said, "This might interest you."

The object was a fragment of a flat stone tablet, which originally might have been about two feet square. The fragment was dominated by the lower half of a symbol of a cross, which was surrounded by engraved text.

Indy placed his hat beside the tablet, removed his glasses from his pocket, and put them on. Leaning over to inspect the tablet more closely, he said, "Well, it's sandstone. Christian symbol. Early Latin text. Mid-twelfth century, I should think."

Indy raised his gaze to Donovan. Donovan said, "That was our assessment as well."

Returning his gaze to the tablet, Indy said, "Where did this come from?"

"My engineers unearthed it in the mountain region north of Ankara while excavating for copper," Donovan said. There was a slight twinkle in his eye when he added, "Can you translate the inscription?"

Translating inscriptions was no easy matter, even for someone as knowledgeable as Indy. He moved his finger along the edge of the tablet as he read aloud, "'. . . who drinks the water I shall give him, says the Lord, will have a . . . spring inside him welling up for . . . eternal life.'"

Eternal life? Indy had his doubts about the authenticity of such words, and he raised his eyebrows and chuckled under his breath. While Donovan stepped over to another table and poured champagne into two fluted glasses that rested on a silver tray, Indy resumed his translation. "'Let them bring me to your holy mountain in the place where you dwell. Across the desert and through the mountain to the Canyon of the Crescent Moon, to the temple where the cup that —'"

Donovan held a glass of champagne in each hand, and he smiled as Indy raised his gaze to meet Donovan's. Indy wore a slightly stunned expression as he recited the remaining text: "'Where the cup that holds the blood of Jesus Christ resides forever.'"

"The Holy Grail, Dr. Jones," Donovan said as he carried the glasses over to Indy. "The chalice used by Christ during the Last Supper. The cup that caught His blood at the crucifixion and was entrusted to Joseph of Arimathaea."

"The Arthur legend," Indy said as he accepted a glass. "I've heard this bedtime story before."

"*Eternal life*, Dr. Jones!" Donovan said brightly. "The gift of youth to whoever drinks from the Grail. Oh, now *that's* a bedtime story I'd like to wake up to!"

"An old man's dream," Indy said as he raised his glass to take a sip.

"Every man's dream," Donovan insisted. "Including your father's, I believe."

The mere mention of his father made Indy go tense, and he nearly choked on the champagne. Regaining his composure, he lowered his glass and said, "Grail lore is his hobby. He's a teacher of medieval literature. The one the students hope they don't *get*."

Just then, the double doors opened again. Indy and Donovan turned to see Donovan's wife, a matronly woman in a black evening gown and a gold necklace. Some other well-dressed people were visible in the room behind her. Smiling sweetly, she said, "Walter, you're neglecting your guests."

"Be along in a moment, dear," Donovan said, stepping over to his wife to kiss her cheek. She looked in Indy's direction, but he had already returned his attention to the stone tablet and had his back to her. Mrs. Donovan left the reception room, closing the doors behind her.

Indy had set his champagne beside the stone tablet.

He dipped his finger into the champagne, and then rubbed his moistened finger over a small area of the tablet's surface to remove a thin layer of dirt. Donovan returned to Indy's side and said, "Hard to resist, isn't it? The Holy Grail's final resting place described in detail!"

"What good is it?" Indy said. "This Grail tablet speaks of deserts and mountains and canyons. Pretty vague. Where do you want to start looking? Maybe if the tablet were intact, you'd have something to go on, but the entire top portion is missing."

"Just the same," Donovan said, "an attempt to recover the Grail is currently underway."

Currently underway? Indy looked at Donovan with a bemused expression. If Donovan had already begun searching for the Grail, Indy had to assume that the man lacked judgment.

But Donovan was very serious. He said, "Let me tell you another 'bedtime story,' Dr. Jones. After the Grail was entrusted to Joseph of Arimathaea, it disappeared, and was lost for a thousand years before it was found again by three knights of the First Crusade. Three brothers, to be exact."

Indy grinned. *That old chestnut*, he thought, *and Donovan actually buys it.* Figuring he'd humor the millionaire just to see what happened, Indy said, "I've heard this one as well. Two of these brothers walked out of the desert one hundred and fifty years after having found the Grail and began the long journey back to France, but only one of them made it. And before dying of *extreme* old age, he supposedly imparted his tale to . . ." Indy tried for a moment to remember the story, and suddenly recalled, "to a Franciscan Friar, I think."

"Not 'supposedly,' Dr. Jones," Donovan said with conviction. He gestured to an ancient leather-bound volume that was set on a curved shelf that hugged the wall. The volume was opened to display Latin text on two illuminated pages that appeared very brittle. Donovan continued, "This is the manuscript in which the friar chronicled the knight's story. It doesn't reveal the location of the Grail, I'm afraid, but the knight promised that two markers that had been left behind *would*."

While Indy studied the displayed pages, Donovan walked back over to the table that supported the stone tablet. Donovan said, "This tablet is one of those markers. It proves the knight's story is true. But as you pointed out . . . it's incomplete. Now, the second marker is entombed with the knight's dead brother. Our project leader believes that tomb to be located within the city of Venice, Italy."

Venice, Italy? Indy had been thinking of Venice recently, maybe even earlier that day, but he couldn't remember just when or why. He looked at the tablet and then back at the ancient volume. Donovan had obviously gone to some effort to gather his information, and Indy wondered if the man might be on to something. Not the Grail, necessarily, but *something*. While Indy carefully turned the volume's right page to examine the preceding spread, Donovan said, "As you can now see, Dr. Jones, we're about to complete a great quest that began almost two thousand years ago. We're only one step away."

"That's usually when the ground falls out from underneath your feet," Indy said, casting a cautionary glance at Donovan.

"You could be more right than you know," Donovan said mysteriously.

"Yes?"

"We've hit a snag," Donovan said, his brow furrowing. "Our project leader has vanished, along with all his research. We received a cable from his colleague, Dr. Schneider, who has no idea of his whereabouts or what's become of him. I want you to pick up the trail where he left off. Find the man, and you will find the Grail."

Indy grinned again. "You've got the wrong Jones, Mr. Donovan," he said as he crossed the room and picked up his hat from the table. "Why don't you try my father?"

"We already have," Donovan said. "Your father is the man who has disappeared."

CHAPTER *THREE*

Your father and I have been friends since time began," Marcus Brody said as he climbed out of the Ford coupe that Indy had parked in the driveway outside a white clapboard house. "I've watched you grow up, Indy," Marcus continued as he followed him from the car and onto the short path that led to the front porch. "I've watched the two of you grow apart. I've never seen you this concerned about him before."

Indy found the front door open. "Dad?" he called out quietly as he walked through the doorway and into the dark hall. Glancing back at Brody, he responded, "He's an academic. A bookworm. He's not a field man." Then Indy called out again. "Dad? Dad?"

Faded green curtains hung over a wide doorway, separating the hall from the sitting room. Indy and Brody reached up to push the curtains aside and found that the sitting room had been ransacked.

Bookshelves and tables had been overturned, and books and papers were lying all over the floor. There was a fireplace on the far side of the room, and the two electric sconces above the mantle had been left on, as had the overhead light and the lamp on the desk to Indy's left. A fan whirred away on the desk, and all of the desk's drawers had been opened and emptied. Beyond the desk, French doors had been thrown open to expose the house's small kitchen. The kitchen lights had been left on too, and the refrigerator door was hanging wide open.

"Dear God," Brody said as Indy stepped into the sitting room. "What has the old fool got himself into now?"

"I don't know," Indy said as he surveyed the damage, "but whatever it is, he's in way over his head." He stepped across the scattered papers, threw open the door to another room, and shouted, "Dad?"

No response. Indy looked back at Brody, who had found a stack of postmarked envelopes that rested on the desk. Brody's brow wrinkled as he picked up the envelopes. "It's today's mail," he said, "and it's been opened."

Indy's mind reeled. *Dad's missing, and someone tears up everything in his house, including today's mail.* Suddenly it hit him. "Mail," he said. "That's it, Marcus." He reached into his jacket pocket and removed the brown paper package he had found earlier that day, on his own desk at

Hamilton Hall. Turning the package over in his hands, he looked at the postmark again and said, "Venice, Italy."

Indy grimaced. During his conversation with Walter Donovan, he had thought Donovan's mention of Venice sounded familiar. According to Donovan, Indy's father had been last seen in Venice, searching for a tomb that somehow served as the second marker to the location of the Holy Grail.

Indy tore open the package and removed a small book. It was covered in brown cow leather. Indy recognized it at once.

"What is it?" Brody asked.

"It's Dad's Grail diary," Indy said as he opened the book and began flipping through the pages. Nearly every page was filled with detailed notations and sketches, all written and drawn by Indy's father. "Every clue he ever followed," Indy said. "Every discovery he made. A complete record of his search for the Holy Grail. This is his whole life. Why would he have sent this to me?"

"I don't know," Brody said, "but someone must want it pretty badly."

Clutching his father's diary, Indy stumbled over to the fireplace. Above the mantle hung a small medieval painting, a depiction of Christ on the cross. Positioned below Christ was the figure of a woman, Ecclesia, who represented the Church, and who sat upon a beast composed of a winged man, a lion, a bull, and an eagle, which represented the Gospel writers, Matthew, Mark, Luke, and John. Blood flowed from Christ's wounds, and Ecclesia captured the blood in a chalice.

Indy turned to Brody and asked, "Do you believe, Marcus?"

Before Brody could reply, Indy noticed a second painting on another wall, to the left of the French doors. The second painting depicted eleventh century knights plummeting to their deaths over a high cliff. One knight, however, appeared to float safely in midair as he "walked" toward the hovering Grail. Turning away from the painting to face Brody, Indy asked, "Do you believe the Grail actually exists?"

"The search for the Cup of Christ is the search for the divine in all of us," Brody said. "But if you want facts, Indy, I've none to give you. At my age, I'm prepared to take a few things on faith."

Indy looked down at his father's desk and was surprised to see his father's face staring back at him. The photo had been taken years ago, when Indy was still a kid, and it showed his father as a dark-haired man, with a thick beard and a mustache that only intensified his brooding features. Some papers were partially covering the photo, and Indy pushed them aside to reveal the image of an unsmiling boy standing beside Henry Jones. The boy was gazing at something to his left, away from Henry Jones and the lens of the camera, and looked like he'd rather be anywhere else than having his picture taken beside that man.

The boy had been Indy. The photograph had been taken when his mother was still alive.

Indy left the photo on the desk but felt his grip tighten on his father's diary. He looked to Brody and said, "Call Donovan, Marcus. Tell him I'll take that ticket to Venice now." Indy headed for the front door.

"I'll tell him we'll take two," Brody said.

A private, twin-engine airliner, adorned with Walter Donovan's corporate logo, waited for Indy and Brody at the airport in New York. They arrived at the airport with Donovan in his limousine. While the airliner's engines revved, the limo's chauffer opened the door and Brody climbed out, but then stopped and turned to face Donovan, who remained on the backseat.

"All right," Brody said anxiously, "tell me what's going to happen when we get to Venice."

"Don't worry," Donovan said with assurance. "Dr. Schneider will be there to meet you."

"Uh, Schneider?" Brody said.

"I maintain an apartment in Venice," Donovan said. "It's at your disposal."

"Oh, well," Brody muttered, "that's good. Thank you." He shook Donovan's hand and then stepped away from the limo.

Indy had been sitting beside Donovan, waiting for Brody to move out of the way so he could climb out, too. As he moved past Donovan, Donovan said, "Dr. Jones . . . good luck." They shook hands, and Donovan added earnestly, "Now, be very careful. Don't trust *anybody*."

Indy nodded and then walked away from the limo. He had never been convinced that the Grail actually existed. Still, there was the matter of finding his father. If Donovan was willing to finance the trip to Venice, Indy was glad to let him pay for it.

Without a word, Indy and Brody boarded the airliner.

The flight from New York to Venice required stops in Newfoundland, the Azores, and Portugal. Indy spent much of the time studying his father's Grail diary. Henry Jones had notes on everything from ancient legends and medieval poetry to the histories of knights and battles, all related to the existence of the Holy Grail. There were also detailed maps, including one of a place called the "mountain road," and sketches of various obstacles that one might encounter before finding the Grail. Henry Jones had even speculated on the spiritual properties of the Grail.

One two-page spread was illustrated with an ink sketch of a detail from a stained-glass window, which showed a knight holding a shield that had a cross on it. The cross's lower half resembled the design of the partial cross on the Grail tablet fragment Indy had seen in Donovan's apartment. Henry Jones had also indicated that the Roman numerals III, VII, and X seemed to have some significance in relation to the stained-glass window or the knight, but Indy couldn't figure the purpose of the numbers, or how they were supposed to add up. A statue of a lion that supported an "upper floor" was also illustrated, and another spread showed a series of sculpted lions perched atop stone columns. The diary also contained a few pieces of folded parchment, including a rubbing of the Grail tablet fragment — a full-size copy of the words and partial cross — no doubt made by Henry Jones himself.

The diary was hardly easy to read, which didn't surprise Indy one bit. No one had ever claimed that Henry Jones was an easy man to understand.

Venice, on the other hand, was something that Indy understood perfectly. He'd visited the city before, and found much to admire about the old architecture, the vast network of canals and countless bridges, and the gondolas that carried passengers from place to place. As Indy and Brody disembarked a water bus onto a boat landing across the canal from Piazza San Marco, Indy sighed and said, "Ah, Venice . . ."

"Yes," Brody said distractedly from under his black bowler hat.

Indy was wearing his fedora. Both men wore pale gray suits, and were followed off the water taxi by a young Italian boy who carried their luggage. While Indy soaked in the sights around him, Brody was focused on more practical matters. "How will we recognize this Dr. Schneider when we see him?"

"I don't know," Indy said as he led Brody and their luggage carrier down a gangplank from the dock to the sidewalk. "Maybe he'll know us."

Just then, from behind Indy and Brody, a woman's voice said, "Dr. Jones?"

Indy, Brody, and the young boy turned to see a woman standing near the end of the gangplank. She wore a dark gray suit and skirt that complimented her long blonde hair.

"Yes?" Indy was surprised he hadn't noticed her when he'd been walking down the gangplank.

"I knew it was you," the woman said with a smile. "You have your father's eyes."

"And my mother's ears," Indy said with brazen charm, "but the rest belongs to you."

The woman smirked and said, "Looks like the best parts have already been spoken for."

Indy thought her accent was Austrian, but he wasn't sure. As he grinned at her, she looked past his shoulder to the man behind him and said, "Marcus Brody?"

"That's right," Brody said, removing his hat.

"Dr. Elsa Schneider," the woman said as she extended her hand to Brody.

"Oh, how do you do?" Brody said, shaking her hand.

Like Brody, Indy had assumed Dr. Schneider would be a man. Indy didn't always like surprises, but this one wasn't so bad.

CHAPTER FOUR

*A*s things turned out, Dr. Elsa Schneider also had a room at Walter Donovan's spacious apartment in Venice. After paying their young porter and leaving their luggage at the apartment, Indy and Brody walked with Elsa along a narrow canal that was lined with buildings on either side. Indy liked the way Elsa walked, like a healthy athlete with a good sense of direction.

"The last time I saw your father," Elsa said to Indy, "we were in the library. He was very close to tracking down the knight's tomb." Then she laughed brightly and added, "I've never seen him so excited. He was as giddy as a schoolboy."

"Who? Attila the Professor?" Indy said. "He was never giddy, even when he was a schoolboy."

They were walking past a street vendor who was selling flowers as they approached a small footbridge that spanned the canal. As Elsa turned to step up onto the bridge, Indy deftly reached out and stole a single flower from the vendor. Brody witnessed Indy's action with some astonishment and glanced back at the oblivious vendor as he followed Elsa and Indy onto the bridge.

Catching up with Elsa on the middle of the bridge, Indy held the flower out to her and said, "*Fräulein,* will you permit me?"

"I usually don't," Elsa said, not breaking her stride.

"I usually don't, either," Indy said.

"In that case, I permit you."

"It would make me very happy," Indy said, and he inserted the flower into the lapel of her jacket as they descended the other side of the bridge.

"But I'm already sad," Elsa said as they headed away from the bridge. "By tomorrow, it will have faded."

"Tomorrow," Indy said, "I'll steal you another."

"I hate to interrupt you," Brody broke in with irritation, "but the reason we're here —"

"Yes," Elsa said. "I have something to show you." Reaching into her jacket pocket, she removed a slip of paper and handed it to Indy. "I left your father working in the library. He sent me to the map section to fetch an ancient plan of the city. When I got back to his table, he'd gone, with all his papers except for that scrap, which I found near his chair."

Indy looked at the scrap, and then held it up for Brody to see. "Roman numerals."

"Here is the library," Elsa said as she led the two men toward a large building that loomed over a wide piazza where people walked about and sat at tables. The building was made of white marble, and its façade had tall columns with ornate capitals. Most of its windows had been bricked over, and there were two empty niches on either side of the arched main doorway.

"That doesn't look much like a library," Indy said.

Brody noticed the empty niches, which had probably once held statues, and added, "Looks like a converted church."

Elsa led the men into the building. "In this case it's the literal truth," she said. "We are on holy ground." Their heels clacked across the marble floor as they passed silent patrons and aisles lined by tall bookshelves, and proceeded into a chamber with a high ceiling. Elsa walked toward a wall that housed a stained-glass window with two massive marble columns on each side of the window. "These columns over here," Elsa added, "were brought back as spoils of war after the sacking of Byzantium during the Crusades."

The stained-glass window depicted several religious figures, and at its center was a knight carrying a shield. Below the window, several brass stands held red cordons to prevent the general public from getting too close to the wall or glass. When Elsa arrived at the cordons, she stopped and turned to Indy and Brody. "Now, please excuse me," she said. "The library's closing in a few moments. I'll arrange for us to stay a little longer."

Elsa walked off, taking the sound of her clacking heels with her, but Indy didn't watch her go. He had noticed the sculpted lions on top of the columns, and now his eyes were riveted on the stained-glass window. Lowering his voice to almost a whisper, Indy said, "Marcus . . . I've seen this window before."

"Where?"

"Right here, in Dad's diary." Indy removed the book from his pocket. Flipping through the pages, he found the two pages he had studied during the flight to Venice. Holding Henry Jones' illustration of the window up for Brody's inspection, he said, "You see?"

Indy and Brody lifted their gaze to the window. "Look, Indy," Brody said. "The Roman numerals."

Indeed, the three Roman numerals that Henry Jones had written on a scrap of paper had been worked into the window's design, set within scrolls that were positioned beneath the central knight and two female figures. "Dad was onto something here."

"Well, now we know the source of the numbers," Brody said, "but we still don't know what they mean."

An increasingly loud clacking sound announced Elsa's approach. Taking advantage of their last few moments alone, Indy faced Brody and spoke gravely. "Dad sent me this diary for a reason. Until we find out why, I suggest we keep it to ourselves." Indy returned the diary to his pocket.

"Find something?" Elsa asked as she drew up beside the men.

"Uh, yes," Brody said, directing Elsa's attention to the stained glass. "Three, seven, and ten. That window seems to be the source of the Roman numerals."

Gazing at the window, Elsa gasped, "My God, I must be blind."

"Dad wasn't looking for a book about the knight's tomb," Indy said, "he was looking for the tomb itself!" Looking from Marcus to Elsa, he continued, "Don't you get it? The tomb is somewhere in the library! You said yourself it used to be a church. Look."

Stepping to the right of the window, Indy directed their gaze to one of the marble columns, on which had been carved *III*.

"Three," Indy said, pointing to the numerals. He looked to the window and pointed to the lower left corner, where a yellow-glass scroll contained three I-shaped strips of lead. "Three," Indy said again.

Then Indy pointed to an engraved column on the left, where he found an engraved *VII*. "Seven," he said, and then quickly redirected his index finger to the window, where the same numerals were set within the glass scroll below the shield-bearing knight. "Seven."

At the bottom right of the window, there was a glass scroll with an *X* in it. "Ten." Indy reached into his pocket to pull out the scrap of paper that Elsa had given him. Seeing the *X* on the paper, Indy said, "And ten." He let his gaze travel to the surrounding walls and bookshelves. "Now where's the ten? Look around for the ten."

While Brody and Elsa stepped away from the cordoned area to inspect the nearby aisles, Indy walked over to inspect the bookshelves on the wall opposite the window, but quickly dismissed them. *These shelves were built for the library, not the church.* He glanced at a wrought iron spiral staircase that traveled to the library's upper level, but figured that the staircase was installed at the same time as the shelves.

The ten is probably set in stone. Clutching the scrap of paper with the Roman numerals on it, he returned his attention to the window and the columns.

"Three and seven," he muttered as he paced beside the cordons. *Could the numerals be a code?* "Seven and seven . . . and ten." Indy froze. He had let his gaze fall from the columns, window, and walls, and was now looking at the floor. He stared at the floor's center, walking backwards to get a better view.

Remembering the staircase, Indy ran over to it and up the steps. When he reached the catwalk on the upper level, Indy gazed down at Elsa and Brody, who had moved back to the center of the room. The floor beneath their feet was an elaborate tile design that contained a huge X that was only clearly discernible from Indy's elevated vantage point.

"Ten," Indy said as he pointed to the floor. Then he shrugged and added wryly, "X marks the spot."

Indy rushed down the staircase and went to the center tile where the two sides of the X intersected. While Brody and Elsa watched, he knelt on the floor and bent over to blow dust out of from the narrow gap that separated the tile from those that surrounded it. Unfortunately, the exposed gap wasn't wide enough for his fingers to grip the tile's edges.

Eager to see what was beneath the tile, and hopeful that he was on the right trail to find his missing father, Indy jumped up and ran over to one of the brass stands that held the cordon below the stained-glass window. After removing the cordon from the brass stand, he carried the stand back to the central tile.

Indy glanced around to make sure only Brody and Elsa were watching. He gripped the upper part of the stand as if it were the handle of a sledgehammer, and then he lifted the stand and swung, bringing its metal base down hard on the edge of the tile.

Elsewhere in the library, at the same moment that the stand struck the tile, an elderly, bespectacled librarian with wavy white hair brought a stamp down upon the back page of a book that lay open beside a stack of books on his desk. The librarian had been stamping books on a daily basis for many years, and this was the first time his action seemed to produce a loud thud that echoed throughout the building. Unaware that an unauthorized archaeological dig was going on in a nearby room, he pressed his stamp on an inkpad before bringing it down on the page of another book. Again, there was a loud thud, and he wondered if something had perhaps finally gone wrong with his hearing. When he stamped a third book and heard yet another thud, he looked at the stamp warily. Then he placed it gingerly on top of the book stack, deciding that perhaps he'd had enough for the day.

Indy didn't know that his three strikes at the floor had coincidentally caused a librarian to seriously question his own ears and contemplate retirement. But he could clearly see that his handiwork had shattered the edge of the tile, leaving a hole that he could get his hand into. Setting the brass stand aside, he bent down to lift the tile up and out of the floor, leaving a two-foot square hole at the center of the *X*.

While Brody hung back a short distance, Elsa knelt beside Indy. Cold air and a wet, rancid smell escaped from the hole. Indy said, "Bingo."

"You don't disappoint, Dr. Jones," Elsa said. "You're a great deal like your father."

"Except *he's* lost, and I'm not." Indy knew Elsa had meant to compliment him, but he didn't like being compared with his father at all.

"Lower me down," Elsa said, swinging her long legs into the hole and raising her arms to Indy.

Indy was impressed and cooperated agreeably. He gripped her wrists and lowered her into the opening. When her feet had safely reached the ground below, he released his grip and stood up beside Brody. He retrieved his father's Grail diary from his pocket and handed it to his friend. "Look after this for me, will you?"

Indy didn't tell Brody, but he'd kept one item from his father's diary in his pocket: the rubbing that his father had made of the Grail tablet, which Indy thought might come in handy. Brody tucked the diary into his own pocket while Indy crouched down and lowered himself through the hole.

When Indy touched down in the subterranean chamber beside Elsa, he was even more impressed with her.

They had arrived in a dank, dark place, and the floor was littered with human skulls and other skeletal fragments. Numerous holes had been carved out of the surrounding walls, and nearly every one contained a leering skull. Plunging into such a horrid, foul-smelling environment would have made most people tremble or even scream, but from the slight smile on Elsa's face, Indy realized she was as eager to explore the place as he was.

There was a steep step just below them. Indy jumped down, and then turned to look up at Elsa and said, "Come on." He helped her down, and they moved away from the step.

Elsa removed a cigarette lighter from her pocket and lit it to illuminate some markings that were carved into a wall. "Pagan symbols," she observed. "Fourth or fifth century."

"Right," Indy said. "Six hundred years before the Crusades." He glanced at the flickering light and noticed that the lighter Elsa held had a four-leaf clover design on it. Then he looked to his left, where shadows indicated the mouth of a dark passageway.

Lifting her gaze to Indy, Elsa said, "The Christians would have dug their own passages and burial chambers centuries later."

"That's right," Indy said, taking the lighter from Elsa. "If there's a Knight of the First Crusade entombed down here, that's where we'll find him." Holding the lighter out in front of him, Indy reached out with his free hand to take Elsa's, and then guided her into the passage.

While Indy and Elsa ventured deeper into the catacombs, Brody remained stationed in the library room. He knelt beside the rectangular hole in the floor, patiently waiting for Indy and Elsa to return. He never heard the three men who made their way down the spiral staircase behind him.

The three men had dark hair and similar mustaches. Identical dark gray suits, silk neckties, and red fezzes only furthered their mutual resemblance. And each one carried a pistol.

One of the men moved silently up behind Brody. The man raised his gun and brought it down hard on the back of Brody's head. Brody gasped, collapsing unconscious beside the hole.

Brody's assailant made a sweeping gesture with his gun toward Brody's body. The man's two accomplices grabbed Brody's wrists and dragged him away from the hole and into one of the book-lined aisles.

*I*ndiana Jones and Elsa Schneider proceeded through the catacombs. Indy held tight to Elsa's lighter as they walked past the decomposing corpses that rested in niches carved into the stone walls, the grotesque skeletal remains with rotting linen stretched across blackened bones. It wasn't until they rounded a dark corner that Indy saw something that made him stop in his tracks.

It was a faded-gold relief, partially covered by cobwebs, which had been carved into the wall. Elsa followed Indy's gaze and leaned closer to the relief to brush away the cobwebs. Gazing at the remains of the image, she said, "What's this one?"

"The Ark of the Covenant," Indy answered tersely.

Elsa's brow wrinkled. "Are you sure?"

"Pretty sure," Indy said. Not seeing any need to go into details, he raised the lighter and moved on. Elsa followed.

They entered another passage. At the end, a wall of

rough stone was almost completely obscured by cobwebs. Indy ran his hand over the stones and felt a slight breeze. He began brushing away the cobwebs, revealing small gaps and cracks between the stones. On one stone, someone had carved the Roman numeral *X*.

"Watch out," Indy said, handing the lighter back to Elsa. Indy took a step back and then rammed his shoulder into the wall. Several stones loosened. Indy struck the wall again, this time with so much force that it collapsed on impact, sending him tumbling into the next chamber.

Indy fell onto a group of rocks that were surrounded by a bubbling, slimy liquid. Curious, Indy dipped his hand into it and rubbed his fingers together. Then he looked back at the hole in the wall behind him, where Elsa stood holding her lighter.

"Petroleum," Indy said, wincing at the smell. "I could sink a well down here and retire." He pushed himself up to his feet. His suit was filthy.

Indy noticed some cloth-covered skeletons in a nearby niche at the edge of the bubbling pool. He reached down and pulled out a strip of cloth and a length of bone, and then quickly fashioned a crude torch. After dipping the cloth end into the oil-slick water, he turned to Elsa. "Give me the lighter."

Elsa handed the lighter to Indy, and he lit the torch. He held it high above the wet floor as they continued their journey into the catacombs. Although they'd tried to stay on the rocks, they soon found themselves wading through ankle-deep water. But that wasn't the worst of it. As they ducked through an arched stone doorway to enter a narrow passage, Indy looked down and said, "Oh, rats."

Elsa gasped.

The place was teeming with rats. Thousands of them. There wasn't enough room for the rodents to move across the stones, so they crawled on one another's backs and thrashed in the water. They were all squealing and squirming.

Indy knew it was best to keep moving. He kicked his legs forward through the rat-infested water. Elsa let out a small scream as the rats darted over her feet. Indy stumbled slightly, and Elsa gasped again as more rats scampered around her.

Indy got his footing and turned to Elsa. He could see she was terrified, and he didn't blame her in the least. "Come on," he said. Holding the torch in his right hand, he leaned over, scooping Elsa up in a fluid motion. He draped her body over his left shoulder and carried her out of the chamber and into the next passage.

The three men who had subdued Marcus Brody did not linger in the library. Carrying flashlights as well as their pistols, they followed Indy and Elsa down into the catacombs.

The men were familiar with the underground passages, and they noticed every sign of trespass. When they saw the rocky debris below the hole that Indy had formed in the crumbling wall and the scattered human bones that rested amidst the bubbling oil-slick water, they knew they were still on the right trail.

Indy had hoped there would be fewer rats in the next passage, but there weren't. Fortunately, Elsa quickly regained her composure and insisted that Indy didn't have to carry her any longer.

The floor of the passage now resembled a long, deep brook of black, briny water. Narrow ledges lined both walls, and the rats scampered along them in a steady stream. Indy climbed up onto one ledge and Elsa took the other. They moved slowly on the opposite ledges, trying not to disturb the rats that squirmed in the crevices at their sides, while stepping over and sometimes on the rats that darted around their ankles.

Indy was wondering whether they were still on the right path to the tomb when the passage's two ledges terminated on either side of an arched doorway. Still holding his torch, he lowered himself into the knee-deep stream of water. He looked back over his shoulder and beckoned Elsa to join him. "Come here."

Elsa placed a hand on Indy's shoulder and stepped down into the water. She followed him through the arched doorway and into a large burial chamber. There were several ancient coffins in the room, some jutting above the water, and others resting in niches. The coffins were made of ornately carved oak, fairly well preserved despite some obvious water damage. Human skulls decorated the chamber's walls.

Surveying the coffins, Indy said, "Look, it . . . it must be one of these."

Elsa waded forward into the chamber. As she moved past the coffins, she gazed at them with admiration. "Look at the artistry of these carvings and the scrollwork."

At the end of the chamber, a single coffin was elevated on a high niche that kept it above the others and out of the water. The coffin's carved sides depicted a group of knights. Steps led up to the coffin, and Elsa climbed them to examine the coffin more closely. Beaming, she proclaimed, "It's this one."

Indy held the torch high as he climbed up beside Elsa. After Elsa blew some dust off the coffin's lid, they gripped the lower edge of the lid and shoved it back. Within the coffin lay the decomposed remains of a knight in armor. The skeletal arms still grasped a sword and shield that rested upon the lower half of the knight's body. A fine layer of dust covered the shield's surface.

"This is it," Indy gasped. "We found it!" Handing the torch to Elsa, he climbed up over the coffin to position himself above the shield. "Look," he said, and then he bent down to blow the dust from the shield, revealing detailed engravings of a large cruciform surrounded by Latin text. "The engraving on the shield, it's the same as on the Grail tablet! The shield is the second marker!"

Indy removed the folded parchment in his pocket. As he began to rapidly unfold the parchment, Elsa looked at it and asked, "What's that?"

"It's a rubbing Dad made of the Grail tablet," Indy answered as he smoothed the parchment over the shield and aligned the two designs. The engravings on the lower half of the shield matched the parchment's rubbing perfectly, and the upper half contained all the text that was missing from Donovan's tablet fragment. Indy retrieved a small drawing stick from his pocket and dragged it back and forth over the parchment. A broad, excited smile creased his face as his action extended the rubbing to include the entire shield.

Seeing how excited Indy was by their discovery, Elsa said, "Just like your father — giddy as a schoolboy. Wouldn't it be wonderful if he were here now to see this?"

Indy chuckled. "He never would have made it past the rats!" he said as he continued to rub the parchment. "He hates rats. He's scared to death of them."

Back at the hole in the wall where Indy had assembled his bone-fragment torch, the man who had knocked out Marcus Brody struck a wooden match along the side of a matchbox. The man smiled at the thought of what he was about to do and then tossed the flaming match onto the oil-slick water.

Indy had just completed his rubbing and was folding up the parchment when he and Elsa heard what sounded like a distant, muffled explosion. Then the noise grew louder, like an incoming roar, accompanied by the panicked shrieks of thousands of rats. A moment later, the rats came stampeding around the corner of the narrow passageway and into the burial chamber.

Indy scrambled down from the coffin and shoved the folded parchment into his pocket. As Elsa gripped the torch and gazed back to the burial chamber's entrance, Indy shouted, "Get back! Back against the wall!"

Elsa stepped away from Indy and placed the torch in a

dry niche while he bent down and shoved the entire coffin over, spilling the remains of the knight into the water below. The overturned coffin bobbed in the water. "Quick! Under it!" Indy shouted. "Air pocket!" As the words left his mouth, a wave of fire blasted into the chamber.

Indy shoved Elsa down under the water then ducked under himself. A moment later, flames filled the chamber and transformed it into a massive oven.

Keeping their bodies submerged, Indy and Elsa gasped as they raised their heads into the air pocket formed within the inverted coffin. Elsa was still catching her breath when Indy said, "Don't wander off."

"What?" Elsa said, turning to Indy as he took a deep inhale. "What?!" she repeated louder and more anxiously, but Indy had already ducked back under the water.

Holding his breath, Indy searched the chamber's lower walls for an escape route. The chamber's walls were brightly illuminated by the inferno from above. The oily water stung Indy's eyes, but he kept them open until he saw what looked like a dark area.

Another passage!

Moving fast, Indy rose back under the inverted coffin. He'd only been gone for a few seconds, but when his head surfaced beside Elsa's, her face was filled with terror.

Rats, desperate to escape the flames, had begun to force their way into the coffin. The ones that didn't swim in from below tore their way through charred and splintered wood. Some had landed on Elsa's head and shoulders.

"I think I've found a way out!" Indy said as he brushed a rat from Elsa's hair. "Deep breath!"

They both took deep breaths, and then dived under the water again. Indy held tight to Elsa's hand and hauled her after him as he swam toward the dark area he'd spotted earlier. It was a broken section of wall. They passed through it and up a long water-filled tunnel. Lungs straining, they saw a faint light above them before they broke the surface.

Indy and Elsa had emerged at the bottom of a storm drain. The light from above was daylight, streaming down in shafts through a circular iron grate. A metal ladder was built into the wall of the shaft. Indy started climbing. Elsa followed.

Pigeons had settled around the top of the iron grate. The pigeons hopped and fluttered away as Indy pushed up against the grate and shoved it aside. He was soaking wet from head to toe as he climbed out of the shaft. As he rose to a standing position beside the open shaft, he bumped a table behind him, and then looked around to see that he had emerged in the middle of the crowded café in the piazza outside the converted library. Well-dressed café customers recoiled at the sight and smell of Indy.

Indy let his gaze sweep over the piazza. Smiling wryly, he said, "Ah, Venice."

Looking down, he saw Elsa coming up the shaft, and he reached down to help her out. Like Indy, her hair and clothes were drenched and stank of petroleum.

There was another loud flurry of pigeons, this time from the entrance to the library. Indy glanced toward the entrance and saw six men wearing gray suits and red fezzes come running out. One of the men sighted Indy and then gestured to the others to run toward the café.

Indy had never seen them before, but he had a hunch that the fire in the catacombs hadn't been an accident. As the six men ran toward him and Elsa, he saw that one had done a lousy job of using a jacket to conceal what appeared to be a machine gun. Indy grabbed Elsa's hand and tugged her after him as he bolted from the astonished café customers.

Hoping to elude their mysterious pursuers, Indy and Elsa fled the piazza and ran down an alley between two old brick buildings. The alley ended at a rocky jetty, where three men were seated and playing a card game in a dry-docked gondola. Three open-topped wooden motorboats were moored in the water beside the pier.

Indy and Elsa ran to one of the motorboats. They released the boat's mooring lines and jumped into the front cockpit. As Indy slid behind the steering wheel and gunned the engine, the three nearby cardplayers looked up from their game in surprise. Elsa glanced back and saw the Turkish men come hurtling out of the alley and onto the jetty.

Indy launched the boat forward, but as it pulled away, one of the men leaped from the jetty and landed on the back of the boat. Both Indy and Elsa heard a *thud* at the man's impact. While Indy accelerated and weaved through the water in an effort to shake off his uninvited passenger, the other five pursuers scrambled into the two remaining boats. The three cardplayers were too stunned to protest.

Indy's boat had a loud, powerful engine. He had it going full speed, racing past some large barges along an industrial pier, when he turned and leaped from the cockpit. Elsa grabbed the steering wheel as Indy flung himself at the man who'd jumped onto the boat's stern. He had hoped to shove the man off, but a moment later, they were engaged in a wrestling match on the back of the boat, and Indy's opponent drew an automatic pistol.

Indy grabbed the man's wrist and tried to angle the gun's barrel away from his body as he fell back against the boat. The man threw his weight on top of Indy, pinning him. But Indy held tight to the man's gun arm as he began squeezing off shots. The first shot went wild, but the next three went past Elsa and blasted holes in the boat's windshield. Elsa threw an angered glare back at the shooter and saw the other two boats coming up fast behind her. There were three men in one boat and two in the other.

Elsa steered the boat hard to port, and Indy's attacker was thrown off balance. Indy rolled out from under the man and pinned his gun arm before throwing two punches at the man's head. Both punches landed square on his jaw. Indy was still grappling with the man when he glanced up to see that Elsa was steering straight toward a gap that ran between two enormous freighters joined together by thick ropes. A tugboat was pressed up against the outer freighter, pushing the two ships closer together.

"Are you crazy?!" Indy shouted to Elsa. "Don't go between them!"

Elsa could barely hear Indy over the noise of the motor. "Go between them?" she shouted back. "Are you crazy?!" Despite her own cautions, she stayed on course, heading for the increasingly narrow gap between the freighters.

Indy pulled his attacker up and belted him so hard that he sent the man flying overboard. A moment later, the sterns of both freighters suddenly loomed up on either side of the motorboat, and then the boat was racing up the gap. Indy's heart pounded as he scrambled up to the helm. Seizing the wheel from Elsa, he shouted, "I said go *around*!"

"You said go *between* them!" Elsa answered with outrage as she slid aside in the seat and Indy lowered himself behind the wheel.

"I said *don't* go between them!" Indy snapped back. The two freighters were closing in like a massive vise, and there was less than a foot of clearance on either side of Indy's stolen motorboat. Indy kept his eyes forward and focused on the strip of water and sky between the freighters' tapered bows.

While the boat that carried two men steered wide of the freighters, Indy's other pursuers increased speed and followed his path. There was an awful scraping sound as the side of Indy's boat struck the lower hull of one freighter, but as he neared the freighters' bows, the passage widened. Indy and Elsa hadn't realized that they were both holding their breaths until their boat cleared the gap. They gasped simultaneously with relief as they sped away from the freighters.

The three who had followed them weren't so lucky. Indy and Elsa had only just cleared the gap when the freighters crushed the speeding motorboat behind them. The boat exploded, and its momentum sent its fiery hull blasting out between the freighters' bows.

Indy and Elsa were still catching their breaths when they heard the report of gunfire from behind. Glancing back, they saw the other boat was still in pursuit. One man was behind the boat's wheel while the other stood up in the cockpit, firing his weapon in Indy's direction.

The gunner was the same man who had knocked out Marcus Brody and ignited the fire in the catacombs. He stared fiercely after Indy as he continued firing.

Bullets slammed into the stern of Indy's boat, splintering the wood. Hoping to protect Elsa, Indy grabbed the back of her neck and shoved her down against the seat. He hoped that none of the bullets had struck the boat's engine, but then smoke began billowing out from the damaged stern.

The gunfire stopped. Indy didn't know whether the gun had run out of bullets, but he didn't wait around to find out. He angled his boat away and tried to accelerate. Despite his evasive maneuver, his damaged, smoking boat began to lose speed. Even worse, his boat was drifting toward the stern of another freighter, a steamer that had giant, rotating propellers at its stern.

Before Indy could think of what to do next, his pursuers rammed the port aft of his boat. Indy and Elsa glanced back to see that the machine gunner had moved behind the wheel and the other man was seated in the open passenger compartment behind the helm. Returning his gaze to the nearby steamer, Indy realized with mounting panic that their pursuers were trying to send him directly into one of the steamer's propellers.

The machine gunner's boat slid alongside Indy's. When the man in the passenger compartment drew a pistol from his jacket, Indy leaped from his boat and smashed into him, slamming his gun arm into the side of the boat and knocking the pistol from his grip. The other stood up behind the wheel and turned to strike, but Indy turned fast and backhanded him.

As Indy fought the two men, Elsa returned to the controls of the damaged boat and sent it into reverse. Grimacing at the thick black smoke that now poured from the boat's stern, she managed to guide the vessel away from the steamers lethal propeller.

Indy kicked one man overboard, and the man immediately began to swim away from the steamer. The other — the machine gunner who had rammed Indy's boat — threw an arm around Indy's neck. Indy flipped him into the boat's rear compartment, but the man lashed back.

As Indy and his attacker exchanged blows, Elsa looked over from her own boat to see that the men were caught in the drift of the churning water behind the steamer. Elsa gasped. Gripping the shattered windshield, she stood up in the cockpit and screamed, "No!"

Unless Indy did something fast, the steamer's propeller would smash the boat and hack him and his opponent to pieces.

*I*ndy saw that the boat he had boarded was drifting toward the steamer's enormous propeller, which chopped the water so loudly that he could hardly hear the impact of his fist against his opponent's jaw. The man's red fez fell from his head. Grabbing the lapels of his gray jacket, Indy hauled the man into the cockpit and slammed him down against the seat so he was facing away from the propeller. A moment later, the propeller began hacking at the boat's stern.

As splintered wood flew in all directions, Indy shouted into the man's face, "Why are you trying to kill us?!"

"Because you're looking for the Holy Grail!" the man yelled back.

"My *father* was looking for the Holy Grail!" Indy snarled. "Did you kill him, too?!"

"No," the man answered loudly, not out of fear or anger, but because the propeller was almost deafening.

"Where is he?!" Indy shouted as the propeller continued to savagely reduce the boat's length. Shaking the man violently, Indy said, "Talk or you're dead!"

The man remained silent and made no effort to escape.

"Tell me!" Indy shouted as larger chunks of wood began tearing from the boat. "Tell me!"

Fixing his eyes on Indy's, the man said, "If you don't let go, Dr. Jones, we'll both die."

"Then we'll die," Indy said. The boat continued to feed into the propeller.

"My soul is prepared," the man answered with great composure. "How's yours?"

The propeller was less than eight feet away from the boat's cockpit. Indy said, "This is your last chance."

"No, Dr. Jones," the man said. "It's yours."

If the man knew what had happened to Henry Jones, Indy needed him alive. Indy pulled the man up from the cockpit just as Elsa brought the other boat beside them. The two men leaped into the passenger compartment behind Elsa, and then she accelerated away from the propeller. The rapidly spinning blades quickly consumed the abandoned boat's remains.

Although the surviving motorboat remained visibly damaged, Elsa was able to guide it away from the industrial area and back toward the quieter canals of Venice.

Behind her, Indy faced his captive and said, "All right. Where's my father?"

"If you let me go," the man replied, "I will tell you where he is."

Staring hard into the man's eyes, Indy rasped, "Who are you?"

"My name is Kazim."

"And why are you trying to kill me?"

"The secret of the Grail has been safe for a thousand years," Kazim replied, "and for all that time, the Brotherhood of the Cruciform Sword have been prepared to do anything to keep it safe." Kazim pulled back the collar of his shirt to reveal a tattoo of a cruciform with a tapered end, like the blade of a broadsword. Except for the tapered end, the symbol was nearly identical to the cross that Indy had seen on the Grail tablet and the Grail Knight's shield.

Kazim looked to his right, then returned his gaze to Indy and said, "Let me off at this jetty."

Elsa moved aside as Indy got behind the wheel and steered the boat over to a wooden dock that stretched out from a tall stone building, where an older man watched their approach. Kazim tossed a mooring line to the man and then stepped off the boat and onto the dock. Turning to gaze down at Indy, he said, "Ask yourself, why do you seek the Cup of Christ? Is it for His glory, or for yours?"

"I didn't come for the Cup of Christ," Indy said severely. "I came to find my *father*."

"In that case, God be with you in your quest," Kazim said as he buttoned his jacket. "Your father is being held in the Castle of Brunwald on the Austrian–German border." Then Kazim turned and walked off.

The old man handed the mooring line back into the boat. Indy looked at Elsa with a weary smile. *Well, maybe we're finally getting somewhere.*

After they got rid of the boat, Indy and Elsa went back to the library and found Marcus Brody, who was fine except for a nasty bump on the back of his head. Then they all returned to the apartment that Walter Donovan kept in Venice. Both Indy and Elsa still reeked from their journey through the catacombs and were more than eager to get cleaned up.

After Indy had taken a bath and then a shower and done his best to rid his flesh of the stench of petroleum, he put on a plush green bathrobe and went into the apartment's sitting room to confer with Brody. Brody was sitting on a couch, holding an ice pack against the back of his head. He sat in front of an expensive Chinese coffee table, upon which he had placed Henry Jones's Grail diary. A light breeze came in from the room's open window.

As Indy sat down in a lounge chair beside Brody, he handed over the folded, water-soaked parchment that held the impression of the Grail Knight's shield. Brody still looked a bit dazed as he took the parchment and began to unfold it.

Indy said, "How's the head?"

"It's better, now I've seen this," Brody said as he spread the parchment over the coffee table. Studying the Latin text, he said, "It's the name of a city. 'Alexandretta?' Hmmm . . ."

Indy leaned forward in his chair. While Brody continued to examine the parchment, Indy said, "The Knights of the First Crusade laid siege to the city of Alexandretta for over a year. The entire city was destroyed."

Brody lowered the ice pack, placed it on the table beside the parchment, and looked at Indy.

Indy continued, "The present city of Iskenderun is built on its ruins. Marcus, you remember what the Grail tablet said: 'Across the desert and through the mountain to the Canyon of the Crescent Moon.'" He looked away, thinking. "But where exactly?"

Brody rubbed his hands together, massaging his fingers. He said, "Your father would know."

He probably would, Indy thought, but he answered Brody's comment with a noncommittal, "Mm."

Suddenly, Brody's eyes widened and he exclaimed, "Your father *did* know. Look. He made a map." Brody picked up the Grail diary and began flipping through the pages until he found a map that Henry Jones had drawn. "He must have pieced it together from clues scattered through the whole history of the Grail quest. A map with no names."

Fascinated, Indy leaned in closer.

Brody continued, "Now, he knew there was a city with an oasis due east, here." Brody tapped the position on the map. "He knew the course turned south through the desert to a river, and the river led into the mountains, here. Straight to the canyon." Brody traced the route with his finger. "He knew everything except where to begin, the name of the city."

Indy smiled. "Alexandretta." Clapping his hand on Brody's arm, he said, "Now we know."

"Yes, now we know." Brody was beaming with excitement.

"Marcus, get hold of Sallah," Indy said as he rose from his chair. "Tell him to meet you in Iskenderun."

Indy's friend Sallah was a professional excavator. Brody had met him before. Looking at Indy, Brody said with some concern, "What about you?"

"I'm going after Dad," he said grimly. He took the

Grail diary from Brody, pushed it into one of his robe's deep pockets, and left the sitting room.

Still in his bathrobe, Indy walked to a vestibule that led to his bedroom door. When he opened the door, he found that the room was not at all as he'd left it. Most of the furniture had been overturned, and the bureau drawers had been emptied. Indy felt a sudden burn of anger. *It's just like Dad's house*, he thought. *All over again!*

He heard the muffled sound of music playing on a phonograph from an adjoining room. Elsa's room was next door. *Elsa!*

It had suddenly hit Indy that the person — or people — who had ransacked his room might still be in the building. Leaving his room, he returned to the vestibule and went to another door, the one that led to Elsa's room. He knocked on the door and said in a deliberately calm tone, "Elsa?" As concerned as he was for Elsa's safety, he was also angered by the work and possible presence of the unknown intruder. He didn't wait for a reply, but opened the door and stepped right in.

Elsa's room was also in shambles. Her bureau was a mess, her clothes were strewn across the floor, and framed pictures dangled at odd angles on the wall.

Elsa's room had its own bathroom. The bathroom door was closed. To Indy's ears, the music sounded as if it were coming from the other side of that door. Stepping over the debris, he went to the bathroom door, rapped twice, and said in his still calm-sounding voice, "Elsa?" The music suddenly blared as he opened the door and said again, "Elsa?"

"Oh!" Elsa gasped, startled as she turned away from a mirror and saw Indy. She was wearing a silk bathrobe and had yet to empty the water from her bathtub. The music was coming from a portable phonograph that rested on a windowsill beside the tub.

Indy wagged his finger at Elsa and then retreated from the bathroom. Without a word, she lifted the phonograph's needle off the spinning record and followed Indy into her bedroom. Her jaw dropped open when she saw the awful mess. She seemed to be in shock as she said, "My room . . ."

"Mine, too," Indy said.

"What were they looking for?"

Indy pulled the Grail diary from his pocket. "This."

Elsa's eyes went wide when she saw the book in Indy's hand. Because she had worked with Henry Jones, she recognized the book. "The Grail diary."

"Uh-huh," Indy said as he walked out of Elsa's bedroom, carrying the diary with him.

"You had it?" Elsa asked, following him into the vestibule. Shaking her head as Indy entered his room, she looked hurt as she said, "You didn't trust me."

Turning to face Elsa, who remained standing outside his doorway, Indy said, "I didn't know you. At least I let you tag along."

"Oh, yes," Elsa said as she stepped into his room. "Give them a flower, and they'll follow you anywhere." She slammed the door shut behind her.

Indy's eyes flicked to the closed door, then he faced Elsa and said, "Knock if off. You're not mad."

"No?"

"No." Indy lifted an upturned table from the floor. "You like the way I do things."

"It's lucky I don't do things the same way," Elsa said petulantly. "You'd still be standing at the Venice pier!"

Elsa stomped her foot. Indy flinched. She turned for the door. He grabbed her arm and spun her around to face him.

"Look," Indy said, "what do you think is going on here? Since I met you, I've nearly been incinerated, shot at, and chopped into fish bait. We're caught in the middle of something sinister here. My guess is Dad found out more than he was looking for. And until I'm sure, I'm going to *continue* to do things the way I think they should be done."

Indy reached for the back of Elsa's neck, pulled her face toward his, and kissed her. Elsa pulled her head back and said with a scowl, "How *dare* you kiss me!" Then she reached up with both hands to grab the back of Indy's head, pulling his face toward hers, and kissed him back.

Indy's eyes rolled. He pulled his face away from hers and said with a deadpan expression, "Leave me alone. I don't like fast women."

Indy buried his nose under Elsa's chin. She replied, "And I hate . . . arrogant men."

From outside Indy's open window came the sound of a gondolier's voice, singing as his gondola carried two passengers along the canal outside the building. Hearing the song echo up from the canal, Indy smiled and said, "Ah, Venice."

*T*he day after Brody left Venice for Iskenderun to meet with Sallah, Indy and Elsa left Venice in Elsa's Mercedes-Benz and drove north for Austria. Indy liked the way the car handled and did most of the driving. The following day, storm clouds blew in overhead as they navigated their way up along the high roads of the Austrian mountains to reach Brunwald Castle.

It was raining hard by the time Indy brought the car to a stop in the driveway outside Brunwald, a large, imposing stone structure with a number of soaring turrets that seemed to pierce the dark sky. Indy wore his leather jacket, fedora, safari shirt, khaki pants, and leather boots. He'd added a necktie to his ensemble for the occasion and had brought his gun along. Elsa wore a gray raincoat over a simple dress and a black beret.

Looking at the castle's walls through the car's

rain-streaked windshield, Indy said, "What do you know about this place?"

"I know the Brunwalds are famous art collectors," Elsa replied.

Indy reached into the back seat and picked up his bullwhip. Elsa's eyes went wide at the sight of the whip. She said, "What are you going to do?"

"Don't know," Indy said, coiling the whip. "I'll think of something." He looked at Elsa's face and then lifted his gaze to her beret.

Elsa realized Indy was staring at her beret and reached up to adjust it. Then Indy told her his plan.

A few minutes later, Elsa knocked on the wooden door that functioned as the service entrance. Elsa was wearing Indy's hat on her head and shrugging into his leather jacket when a tall, bald butler in a black suit opened the door and said sharply, "Yes?"

"And not before time!" Indy said from behind Elsa as he pushed her forward and followed her through the doorway. Elsa's coat was draped over Indy's shoulders and her beret rested on his head. Indy had also adopted a Scottish accent, or at least his attempt at one. "Did you intend to leave us standing on the doorstep all day?" he snarled at the butler as he shook the water from the coat on his back. "We're drenched!" Suddenly, Indy sneezed hard in the butler's face. As the butler recoiled, Indy said, "Now look, I've gone and caught a sniffle." He yanked a white handkerchief from the butler's breast pocket and dabbed at his nose.

Clearly irritated, the butler said, "Are you expected?"

"Do not take that tone with me, my good man. Now buttle off and tell Baron Brunwald that Lord Clarce MacDonald and his lovely assistant . . ." — Indy grabbed Elsa's arm and pulled her beside him — ". . . are here to view the tapestries."

"Tapestries?" said the butler incredulously.

Glancing at Elsa, Indy said, "Dear me, the man is dense." Guiding the butler away from the doorway, Indy gestured at the surrounding walls and said, "This is a *castle*, isn't it? There are tapestries?"

"This *is* a castle," the butler answered curtly, "and we have many tapestries. But if you are a Scottish lord, then I am Mickey Mouse!"

Indy looked back over his shoulder at Elsa and said, "How dare he?" Then he spun back at the butler, launching his fist outward to knock the man out cold with a single slug. The butler fell back against the wall, which happened to be adorned with a rather fine old tapestry.

After tucking the unconscious butler into a cupboard, Indy took his hat and jacket back from Elsa and they began exploring the castle. As they moved cautiously down a wide, vaulted hallway, they heard voices from below their position. Peering over a banister, they looked down to see a room full of Nazi soldiers who were working around a large table with a map on it. It looked like a secret Nazi command center.

Lifting his gaze to Elsa, Indy muttered softly, "Nazis. I hate these guys."

While thunder rumbled outside the castle, Indy and Elsa eased away from the banister and continued down the hallway, searching for any sign of Henry Jones. Indy took his gun out of its holster and patted the coiled whip that hung from his belt. Elsa glanced back over her shoulder, and then followed him over to a closed door.

Indy aimed his thumb at the door. "This one. I think he's in here."

"How do you know?"

"Because it's wired," Indy said and raised his thumb to point to the electrical wire that traveled from the top of the door to a small alarm that was mounted above the doorway.

Indy looked to another closed door, a short distance away on the same side of the hallway. The door didn't appear to be wired. Elsa followed Indy as he walked to the door and rapped on it. There was no response. When Indy twisted the doorknob, he found it was unlocked.

Holding his gun out in front of him, Indy entered a dark, empty room. Light was coming in through a rain-spattered window. Followed by Elsa, Indy holstered his gun as he walked straight to the window and opened it, letting rain into the room. He climbed up onto the wet windowsill, and then he stepped onto a ledge outside the window. He leaned out to peer out at the castle walls and look for a route to the neighboring room. When he found something that looked good, he reached for his bullwhip.

"Indy?" Elsa said, watching with mounting concern as he uncoiled the whip. "Indy!"

"Don't worry . . . this is kid's play," Indy said. "I'll be right back."

Indy threw his bullwhip out so that its end wrapped around some wires protruding from the castle wall above the window to the neighboring room. He gave the whip a forceful tug to make certain it would hold his weight, and then leaped away from his position. He swung through the air and landed on a stone gargoyle that jutted out from a nearby turret.

As he stood atop the gargoyle, Indy looked back to see Elsa leaning out of the window that he'd just left. He shifted his body, angling to swing toward a shuttered window to the right of Elsa. He knew that the room with the alarmed door was on the other side of the shutters.

Gripping his whip tightly, he leaped out again, swinging away from the gargoyle and straight for the shuttered window with his feet extended.

A clap of thunder drowned out the loud crash of Indy's body hurtling through the shutters and window. Wood splintered and glass shattered as he landed inside the room. Rain and cold air whipped through the smashed window behind him. He gasped as he rose from the debris on the floor.

No sooner was Indy on his feet than a large vase came crashing down on top of his head. Although his hat absorbed some of the impact, his skull still took the brunt of it. He fell to his knees with a stunned, dazed expression.

A bespectacled man with a gray beard and mustache stepped out from the shadows behind Indy. The man wore a tweed suit and hat. His brow furrowed as he looked down at Indy. "Junior?"

Jumping to his feet to face his attacker, Indy responded automatically to the sound of his father's voice. "Yes, sir." Indeed, the man who'd struck Indy was Dr. Henry Jones.

Facing his son, Henry smiled. "It *is* you, Junior!"

Indy's shoulders sagged. "Don't call me that, *please*."

The room in which Henry was being held captive was relatively small. Except for some German words engraved in the molding above the wooden doorway, there were few remarkable architectural details and even fewer comforts. The furniture included a wooden desk with a lamp on it, a chair, and a bench built into the wall. As rain continued to pour in through the ruined window, Henry said, "Well, what are you doing here?"

"I came to get you. What do you thi —?"

From outside the window came the sound of voices approaching. Indy threw his arm across Henry's chest, and they both pressed themselves against the wall. As Indy cautiously stepped toward the window to look at the grounds below, Henry lifted his right hand and realized he was still gripping the handle of the vase — or rather the remains of the vase — that he'd brought down on Indy's head. Henry's eyes widened with dismay.

While Indy remained by the window, Henry carried the ruined vase over to the desk and held it under the lamp to examine its broken edges more closely. "Late fourteenth century, Ming Dynasty," he observed with a frown. "Oh, it breaks the heart."

"And the head," Indy said, leaving the window. Rubbing the back of his skull, he added, "You hit me, Dad."

Lifting his gaze from the vase, Henry said, "I'll never forgive myself."

What? Indy could hardly believe his ears. "Don't worry," he said with a smile. "I'm fine."

"Thank God," Henry said and gently reached out to take his son's arm and pull him closer to the desk. Then Henry pointed to the exposed interior of the broken vase and said with a grin, "It's a fake."

Indy had thought that his father had been expressing remorse for clobbering him, but he suddenly realized that his father wasn't concerned about him at all. Indy's smile vanished as he redirected his gaze to the vase.

"See," Henry continued, "you can tell by the cross section."

Indy nodded.

Obviously pleased with himself for having determined that he hadn't destroyed an actual Ming vase, Henry — without any concern about alerting his captors — tossed the damaged vase at the wall.

"No!" Indy shouted, but too late. The vase crashed against the wall, and its pieces clattered against the floor.

"Dad, get your stuff," Indy said. "We've got to get out of here."

Indy knew his father couldn't make it out through the window and that they wouldn't get far if they tried opening the wired door either. While Indy looked for another way out, Henry turned to pick up his umbrella and a leather bag that contained a few other belongings. As Henry sat down in a chair near the window, he said, "Well, I'm sorry about your head, though, but I thought you were one of them."

"Dad, *they* come in through the *doors*."

Henry glanced at the door and laughed, "Heh! Good point. But better safe than sorry."

Indy didn't reply as he examined the room's other doors. All were locked.

"Humph," Henry said, "so I was wrong this time. But, by God, I wasn't wrong when I mailed you my diary." He slid his umbrella through the straps of his bag, which he'd placed on his lap. "You obviously got it."

Walking back to stand beside the desk, Indy looked at his seated father across the room. "I got it, and I used it," Indy said. "We found the entrance to the catacombs."

In a hushed, excited voice, Henry said, "Through the library?"

Indy smiled and nodded. "Right."

Keeping his eyes on Indy, Henry stood up. "I knew it," he said. "And the tomb of Sir Richard?"

Indy nodded again. "Found it."

Carrying his bag and umbrella before him, Henry stepped quietly across the room to stand before his son. "He was actually there? You saw him?"

"Well, what was left of him," Indy said.

Henry's eyes were riveted on Indy's. "And his shield . . ." Henry said, "the inscription on Sir Richard's shield?"

Indy grinned. "Alexandretta."

"Alexandretta!" Henry exclaimed as he dropped his bag on top of the desk. He spun away and walked in a circle as he pulled off his hat. "Of course!" He stopped to face Indy and said, "On the pilgrim trail from the Eastern Empire. Oh . . ." Smiling broadly, Henry sat back down on a wooden bench against the wall, looked up to his son and said, "Junior, you did it."

"No, Dad," Indy said. "You did. Forty years."

Shaking his head, Henry sighed, "Oh, if only I could have been with you."

"There were rats, Dad," Indy said, placing his hand on his father's arm to urge him up from the bench.

"Rats?" Henry said meekly.

"Yeah, big ones," Indy said as he guided his father back to the desk. "What do the Nazis want with you, Dad?"

Placing his hat back on his head, Henry said, "They wanted my diary."

"Yeah?"

Checking his bag, Henry said, "I knew I had to get that book as far away from me as I possibly could."

Indy hadn't imagined or realized that his father *didn't* want the Grail diary returned to him. Turning his head slowly to look away from his father, Indy said, "Yeah," while he thought, *Uh-oh*. But before he could think of whether he should explain to his father that he was carrying the Grail diary in the pocket of his leather jacket at that very moment, there was a sudden *wham* from the doorway as the door was kicked open, followed by a *thud* as it slammed into the wall.

Indy and Henry looked to the open doorway to see a Nazi S.S. officer holding a machine gun. The officer stepped into the room, followed by two Nazi soldiers who also held machine guns.

Indy raised his hands. Henry glanced at Indy and followed his example.

The S.S. officer glared at them. "Dr. Jones."

"Yes?" Indy and Henry answered simultaneously.

The S.S. officer aimed his machine gun at Indy and said, "I will take the book now."

Indy and his father looked at each other, then both replied, "What book?"

Keeping his eyes fixed on Indy, the officer said, "You have the diary in your pocket."

Henry laughed at the officer. "You dolt!" he said. "Do you think my son would be that *stupid* that he would bring my diary all the way back here?" Henry grinned as he turned his head to face Indy, but his grin vanished when he saw Indy's sheepish expression. Henry said, "You didn't, did you? You didn't *bring* it, did you?"

Indy felt his throat go dry. "Well, uh . . ."

"You *did*," Henry said.

Gesturing at the Nazi soldiers, Indy said, "Look, can we discuss this later?"

Glowering, Henry said, "I should have mailed it to the Marx Brothers."

"Will you take it easy?" Indy said, lowering his voice.

"Take it easy?!" Henry roared in return. "Why do you think I sent it home in the first place? So it wouldn't fall into their hands!" He gestured at the Nazi soldiers, who kept their guns trained on him and Indy.

Staring hard at his father, Indy shouted back, "I came here to save you!"

"Oh, yeah?" Henry said, "And who's gonna come to save you, Junior?!"

Indy's eyes blazed and nostrils flared. "I *told* you . . ." Indy snarled with rage, and then interrupted himself by stepping forward to grab the S.S. officer's machine gun. Shoving the officer backwards, Indy slid his finger over the gun's trigger and opened fire on the Nazis. Henry Jones cringed at the noise and gaped in astonishment as the officer and two soldiers went down. Only after the Nazis lay dead on the floor did Indy turn to face his father and complete his sentence: ". . . *don't* call me Junior!"

Indy grabbed his father's arm and tugged him toward the doorway. Still gaping, Henry glanced down at the fallen soldiers. "Look what you did!" He was genuinely aghast. "I can't believe what you did. . . ."

Clutching the machine gun, Indy led his father down the corridor to the next door, which led to room where he had left Elsa. "Elsa?" Indy said as he opened the door and stepped in. "Elsa?" And then he saw her.

Elsa's eyes were wide with fear. A black-uniformed, blue-eyed Nazi colonel named Vogel stood behind Elsa, pinning her arms behind her back with one hand while the other pressed the muzzle of a Luger pistol against her head.

"That's far enough," Vogel said as Henry followed Indy into the room. "Put down the gun, Dr. Jones. Put down the gun, or the fräulein dies."

As Vogel held Elsa in front of him like a shield, Henry glanced at Indy and said, "But she's one of *them*."

Trembling in Vogel's grip, Elsa cried, "Indy, please!"

Henry raised his voice. "She's a Nazi!"

"What?!" Indy snapped, keeping his gaze on Elsa.

"Trust me," Henry said.

Elsa screamed, "Indy, no!"

"I will kill her!" Vogel said as he pressed his pistol's muzzle hard against Elsa's lower jaw.

"Yeah?" Henry said casually. "Go ahead."

"No!" Indy shouted at the colonel. "Don't shoot!"

"Don't worry," Henry said. "He won't."

"Indy, please!" Elsa cried desperately. "Do what he says!"

Henry added, "And don't listen to *her*."

"Enough!" Vogel shouted. "She dies!"

Elsa screamed again.

"Wait!" Indy shouted. Then he lowered his voice and said again, "Wait ..." There was a table to his right. He placed the machine gun on the table and shoved it down toward the colonel.

Vogel re-aimed his pistol at Indy and then pushed Elsa away from him. Elsa was propelled directly into Indy's arms. He held her tightly against him, and then she drew back to look up into his eyes. She whimpered, "I'm sorry."

"No," Indy said, "don't be." He hadn't believed his father's assertion that Elsa was a Nazi, so he could hardly blame her for their situation. He gave her what he hoped was a comforting smile.

And then Elsa looked down to one of Indy's jacket pockets. Indy lowered his head to follow her gaze, then watched with astonishment as she dipped her hand into his pocket and removed the Grail diary.

Stunned speechless, Indy glared at Elsa. Her lips curved into a smile as she backed away from him, taking the diary with her. She said, "But . . . you should have listened to your father." She was still smiling as she returned to Vogel's side. Vogel kept his pistol trained on Indy.

Indy looked away from Elsa. He was still speechless. He kept his gaze averted from his father, too.

olonel Vogel, Elsa, and several armed Nazi soldiers escorted Indy and Henry to a large baronial room within the castle. A long wooden table with benches on either side stretched the length of the room, which was decorated with ancient tapestries, displays of swords, and suits of armor. Old rugs with ornate designs rested on the floor. A giant fireplace, nearly large enough for a man to stand upright within it, dominated one wall, and the fire cast flickering shadows across the walls and ceiling.

The soldiers had taken away Indy's weapons and his father's bag and umbrella, and had tied the two men's hands behind their backs. Inside the baronial room, the soldiers maneuvered their bound captives to stand near one end of the long table.

Carrying the diary, Elsa brazenly brushed past Indy and Henry, and walked toward the fireplace. Indy glanced at his father and muttered, "She ransacked her own room, and I fell for it."

Elsa walked over to a tall, wooden wingback chair that was positioned to face the fireplace. Because of the angle, Indy and Henry could not see who was sitting in the chair, but as Elsa stepped beside the chair and held the diary out, they did see a hand reach up to take the diary.

Looking to his father, Indy said, "How did you know she was a Nazi?"

"Hmm?"

Leaning closer to Henry, Indy repeated, "How did you know she was a Nazi?"

As Indy returned his gaze to Elsa and the mysterious person in the wingback chair, Henry replied, "She talks in her sleep."

Indy gave a slight nod to acknowledge that he'd heard his father, but it took a few seconds longer for that information to sink in. When it did, Indy looked at his father with surprise. Henry smiled sheepishly, looked at the floor for a moment, then returned his gaze to his son and said, "*I* didn't trust her. Why did *you*?"

"Because he *didn't* take my advice," came a man's voice from the wingback chair. And then the man, who wore an expensive gray three-piece suit, rose from the chair. Holding the diary, he turned and walked slowly toward Indy. The man was Walter Donovan.

SUSPENSE!

INTRIGUE!

RISK!

TROUBLE!

TREASURE!

CAN YOU KEEP UP WITH THE JONESES?

"Donovan," Indy said with a scowl. Henry Jones had also had dealings with Donovan and recognized him, too.

Gazing at Indy, Donovan said, "Didn't I warn you not to trust *anybody*, Dr. Jones?"

As Donovan began thumbing through the pages of the diary, Henry said, "I misjudged you, Walter. I knew you'd sell your mother for an Etruscan vase, but I didn't know you would sell your country and your soul . . . to the slime of humanity." Henry fixed his gaze on Elsa and the smirking Colonel Vogel.

"Dr. Schneider!" Donovan said. "There are pages torn out of this."

While Elsa took the book from Donovan and examined it, Indy grinned slightly and exchanged a glance with his father. Henry had no idea that any pages had been removed from his diary and looked baffled.

Elsa looked at Indy. Holding the book up as she walked toward him, she said, "This book contained a map, a map with no names, precise directions from the unknown city to the secret Canyon of the Crescent Moon."

"So it did," Indy said flatly.

From behind Elsa, Donovan said peevishly, "*Where* are these missing pages, this map? We must have these pages back."

Elsa shook her head. Glancing back at Donovan, she said, "You're wasting your breath." Returning her gaze to

Indy, she continued, "He won't tell us, and he doesn't have to. It's perfectly obvious where the pages are. He's given them to Marcus Brody."

"Marcus?" Henry gasped. He and Brody were both members of the University Club and had known each other for years. Glaring at Indy, he said, "You didn't drag poor Marcus along, did you? He's not up to the challenge."

"He sticks out like a sore thumb," Donovan said. "We'll find him."

"Fat chance," Indy said with bravado. "He's got a two-day head start on you, which is more than he needs. Brody's got friends in every town and village from here to the Sudan. He speaks a dozen languages, knows every local custom. He'll blend in, disappear. You'll never see him again. With any luck, he's got the Grail already."

Hearing this, Henry Jones looked amazed and impressed. Either there was much more to Marcus Brody than Henry realized, or his son was talking about a completely different person.

"Does anyone here speak English?" Marcus Brody asked feebly as he waded through the crowd on a Turkish train platform. "Or even ancient Greek?"

He had just disembarked the train in the city of Iskenderun, on the Mediterranean coast of Turkey, and was surrounded by merchants and traders as well as passengers. Wearing a straw hat and pale gray suit and carrying a set of battered luggage, Brody did indeed stick out like a sore thumb.

A man held a water-filled stein out to Brody, who said, "Uh, water? No, thank you, sir." As more goods were shoved in his face by various merchants, he politely but loudly refused everything. "Goodness me. Thank you so much. No, I don't like that. No, I really don't want . . . No, no, thank you very much." When a woman thrust a clucking chicken before him, he replied, "No, thank you, madam. I'm a vegetarian." The chicken fluttered, and Brody's suit and face were suddenly adorned with small feathers.

Dazed by the heat, overwhelmed by everything and everyone around him, Brody came to a stop and muttered, "Does anyone understand a word I'm saying here?"

"Mr. Brody!" said a voice from behind.

Brody turned to face Sallah, who was wearing a red fez and a rumpled white linen suit. Sallah beamed as he embraced Brody.

"Oh, Sallah," Brody sighed as Sallah brushed the feathers from his face and jacket. "What a relief."

"Marcus Brody, sir!" Sallah said brightly as he took Brody's luggage. Then, cocking his head slightly, he added, "But where is Indy?"

"Oh, he's in Austria," Brody replied. "A slight detour."

"You are on your own?"

"Yes, but don't panic," Brody said. "Everything's under control." As they walked out of the busy train station, he said, "Have you . . . have you arranged our supplies?"

"Oh, yes, of course," Sallah answered. "But where are we *going*?"

"Oh, this map will show you," Brody said as he reached for the folded map in his jacket's breast pocket. "It was drawn by, uh . . ."

Brody saw two fair-skinned men approaching them. Both men wore black suits and hats. The man on the right wore dark wire-frame glasses and black leather gloves, and had a matching leather coat draped over his left arm. The second man was in his shirtsleeves and had his jacket slung over his shoulder. Brody quickly tucked the map back into his pocket as the bespectacled man stopped before him.

"Mr. Brody," the man said, clicking his heels together and then bowing quickly. "Welcome to Iskenderun. The director of the Museum of Antiquities has sent a car for you."

"Oh, well . . ." Brody said, removing his hat in an appreciative gesture. "Your servant, sir."

"And I am his," Sallah interjected as he leaned close to Brody.

Baring his teeth in a strained smile, the bespectacled man bowed to Sallah and then said, "Follow me, please."

The two men in black suits turned away from the station and Brody and Sallah began following them. Brody had been so honored to receive an official greeting that he failed to think anything of the bespectacled man's German accent. Smiling smugly, Brody said, "My reputation precedes me."

"There is no museum in Iskenderun," Sallah said under his breath.

But the second man, the one in his shirtsleeves, heard. Turning fast, the second man held out his hand to Sallah and said in an official tone, "Papers, please."

"Papers?" Sallah said. Then he smiled at the two men and said, "Of course." But as he bent down to place Brody's luggage on the ground, he tilted his head slightly to face Brody and said, "Run."

But Brody, still oblivious to the fact that he might be in any danger, said absently, "Yes."

"Papers," Sallah said as he stood up and patted his pockets. "Got it here." He pulled out a folded newspaper and held it up for the men to see. "Just finished reading it myself," he said, laughing. Tossing another glance at Brody, he repeated, "Run."

"Yes," Brody said, even though he still didn't understand what Sallah meant by the word.

Sallah held up the newspaper so that the man in shirtsleeves could see the masthead. Still smiling, Sallah said, "'Egyptian Mail,' morning edition." Gritting his teeth, he barely moved his lips as he glanced at Brody again and desperately muttered, "Run."

Leaning closer to Sallah, Brody said, "Did you say, uh . . ."

"Run!" Sallah shouted as he threw a punch through the raised newspaper to hit the second man. As the man stumbled back and fell over a nearby vendor's table, Sallah grabbed the bespectacled man and hurled him into another table.

A crowd gathered around the fight immediately. Even then, Brody didn't run, but stood at the edge of the crowd, watching Sallah with amazement. Brody probably would have remained there had Sallah not run toward him, grabbed his arm, and pulled him aside.

With Brody in tow, Sallah pushed his way past the fight's spectators and ran a short distance up the crowded street. When Sallah sighted a ramp that led up to a building's dark, curtained doorway, he shouted, "Okay, okay, quick, quick, quick!" He guided Brody onto the ramp and added, "Find the back door! Find the back door!"

As Brody stepped up the ramp, past the curtains, and into the doorway, Sallah — expecting that he and Brody had been followed by the men in dark suits — turned around and raised his fists, ready for another fight. But a moment later, he heard the sound of an engine start and a door slam behind him.

Sallah turned around to face the building just in time to see that it wasn't a building at all, but merely a wide, arched doorway. Two men had raised the ramp, which was actually the rear hatch of a troop truck. On the back of the hatch was a painted swastika.

Sallah bolted after the truck, but it tore off, leaving him in a cloud of dust, and standing in an empty archway. Feeling utterly defeated, Sallah slumped against the archway's inner wall and watched the truck vanish in the distance.

He had lost Marcus Brody to the Nazis.

*B*ack at Brunwald Castle, Indy and Henry's circumstances had hardly improved. They were still in the baronial chamber with the large fireplace, where two soldiers had tied them back-to-back in a pair of chairs. Henry's hands remained tied behind his back, but Indy's wrists had been retied in front of him to prevent the two men from attempting to untie each other's bonds. Even their legs were bound, leaving only their heads with some range of motion. The fire in the fireplace had gone out, leaving a chill in the room.

Elsa Schneider and Walter Donovan stood nearby. They had watched the two soldiers tie up the American captives and now waited for Colonel Vogel to return from the radio room. As the soldiers stepped away from Indy and Henry, Henry muttered out of the side of his mouth, "Intolerable."

The soldiers were walking out of the room just as Vogel returned. Striding toward Elsa, he said, "Dr. Schneider. Message from Berlin. You must return immediately. A rally at the Institute of Aryan Culture."

Neither impressed nor intrigued, Elsa said, "So?"

"Your presence on the platform is requested . . . at the highest level."

Addressing Vogel by his Army rank, Elsa said, "Thank you, Herr Oberst." Then she turned to Donovan and said, "I will meet you at Iskenderun."

Donovan handed the Grail diary to Elsa. "Take this diary to the Reich Museum in Berlin. It will show them our progress, ahead of schedule. Without a map, I'm afraid it's no better than a souvenir."

Vogel eyed Indy and Henry, bound and helpless just a short distance away, then glanced at Donovan and Elsa and said, "Let me kill them now."

"No," Elsa said. "If we fail to recover the pages from Brody, we'll need them alive."

Donovan shrugged. "Always do what the doctor orders." Then Donovan walked out of the room with Vogel at his heels, leaving Elsa alone with Indy and Henry.

From his chair, Indy stared hard at Elsa. He was angry at himself, but was even angrier with *her*. She had misled him from the beginning and betrayed him with ease.

She was obviously intelligent, brave, and beautiful, but there was no getting around the fact that she was far more dangerous than any snake Indy had ever encountered.

And Indy hated snakes.

Elsa looked at Indy, bound to his chair, and felt the burn in his gaze. "Don't look at me like that," she said. "We both wanted the Grail. I would have done anything to get it." Holding the Grail diary out as if it were a trophy she had earned fairly, she smiled as she added, "You would have done the same."

"I'm sorry you think so."

Stung by Indy's words, Elsa's smile vanished and she drew back. But then she smiled again and bent forward to run her hand down the side of Indy's face. As Indy strained against his ropes, trying to pull away from her, she whispered into his ear, "I can't forget . . . how wonderful you are."

Because Henry and Indy remained seated back-to-back, and because their heads were only a short distance apart, Henry heard Elsa's whispered words. Thinking she was speaking to him, Henry replied, "Thank you."

Surprised by his father's response, Indy began to twist his head to look at Henry, but Elsa grabbed Indy's chin and kissed him. Henry sensed the sudden quiet behind him and turned his head slightly to see Elsa kissing his son. With some disappointment, Henry winced as he turned his head back to face forward.

Just then, Vogel returned to the room to remind Elsa of her appointment in Berlin. Vogel saw Elsa kissing Indy and said curtly, "Oh, Dr. Schneider. Your car is waiting."

Elsa dragged out the kiss a moment longer, and then pulled away from Indy's face. Standing before him with a satisfied smile, she said, "That's how Austrians say good-bye." Then she walked off, taking the Grail diary with her.

As Elsa left the room, Vogel stepped in front of Indy and looked down at the bound man. With an evil leer, Vogel said, "And this is how we say good-bye in Germany, Dr. Jones."

Vogel punched Indy in the jaw. It was a hard and vicious jab that snapped Indy's head back and to the side. His head struck Henry's, who gasped, "Oh!"

Vogel followed Elsa out of the room. Indy shook his head clear. "Ooooh . . ." he groaned. "I liked the Austrian way better."

"So did I," Henry admitted.

"Let's try and get these ropes loose," Indy said as he began wiggling his fingers against his bonds. "We've got to get to Marcus before the Nazis do!"

Confused, Henry said, "You said he had two days' start. That he would blend in. Disappear!"

"Are you kidding?" Indy said. "I made that up. You know Marcus. He got lost once in his own museum."

"Oh . . ." Henry sighed as he lowered his head with dismay.

Squirming in his seat, Indy said, "Can you try and reach into my left jacket pocket?" Then both men were squirming, struggling against the ropes, until Henry was able to wiggle his hand toward Indy's coat pocket.

Henry said, "What am I looking for?

"My lucky charm."

Removing a small, metallic object from Indy's pocket, Henry said, "Feels like a cigarette lighter."

In fact, it was Elsa's lighter, the one with the four-leaf clover design. Indy had hung onto it since Elsa had let him use it in the catacombs in Venice. Indy said, "Try and burn through the ropes."

"Very good," Henry said. Because of the way that the ropes pinned his upper arms to his torso, he couldn't actually see the lighter in his hand, but his fingers managed to open the lighter and ignite the flame. Unfortunately, as he tried to angle the flame towards the ropes, the flame met his flesh. "Oh!" he yelped as his fingers reflexively dropped the lighter, which fell on the rug, just in front of his right shoe.

It was bad enough that Henry had dropped the lighter on the old rug, but even worse, it continued to burn. While Indy kept trying to loosen the ropes, Henry tried to kick the lighter away from his foot, which wasn't exactly easy — his legs were bound, too. Unable to reach the lighter with the tip of his shoe, he tilted his chin down and began blowing at the flames. Although Henry Jones was a highly intelligent man, he did not stop to think that this action might actually fan the flames and cause them to spread across the old rug, which was exactly what happened.

Henry watched with dread as the flames spread from the rug to the nearby wooden table and bench. Behind him, Indy remained oblivious to the blaze. As the table and bench ignited, Henry said over his shoulder, "I ought to tell you something."

"Don't get sentimental now, Dad," Indy said, still unaware that half the room was on fire. "Save it 'til we get out of here."

"The floor's on fire," Henry said. "See?"

"What?" Indy said as he craned his neck to confirm that the floor in front of Henry was blazing.

"*And* the chair," Henry added.

"Move!" Indy shouted as he began jerking his body to his right. "Move it out of here! Go!" Henry echoed Indy's movement, rocking the legs of their chairs to inch away from the flames and off the burning carpet.

"It's scorching the table," Henry observed.

"Move!" Indy commanded.

"Okay!" Henry said, eager to comply.

Outside the castle, a moment after Elsa was driven away in a black sedan, Vogel opened the rear door of another waiting car and Donovan stepped past him and climbed in. A moment after Vogel closed the door, a Nazi lieutenant walked up beside the door. "*Etwas wichtig, mein Herr,*" the lieutenant said as he handed a written message through the door's open window to Donovan.

Still standing outside the car, Vogel leaned down beside the open window as Donovan read the message. "Well, we have Marcus Brody," Donovan said. "But more important, we have the map."

As the lieutenant returned inside the castle, a radio operator stepped up to Donovan's car with yet another message. "*Aus Berlin, mein Herr.*"

Donovan took the message and read aloud, "'By the personal command of the Führer. Secrecy essential to success. Eliminate the American conspirators.'" Lowering the message, Donovan said to Vogel, "Germany has declared war on the Jones boys." Then Donovan caught his driver's eye in the car's rear view mirror and said, "*Los fahren.*"

As Donovan's car pulled away from the castle, Vogel grinned. He had been looking forward to eliminating the Americans, especially the younger one, and now he could do it on the Führer's orders.

Vogel turned and walked straight back into the castle.

The baronial room was rapidly becoming a wall-to-wall inferno. The hanging tapestries and most of the wooden furniture were blazing away, launching cinders in all directions. Still tied back-to-back, Indy and Henry maneuvered their chairs away from the flames. Indy looked to his right and saw that one of the few areas *not* on fire was inside the large fireplace.

"Dad!" Indy shouted.

"What?" Henry replied and turned his head to his left.

But Indy, thinking his father hadn't heard him over the roaring fire, turned his own head in the opposite direction and shouted again, "Dad!"

Turning the other way, Henry shouted louder, "What?"

"Dad!" shouted Indy, turning again.

"What?"

When he and his father were finally looking in the same direction, Indy yelled, "Head for the fireplace!"

"Oh," Henry said.

Banging, rocking, and hopping their chairs, they

worked their way into the fireplace. As Indy looked down at his bound wrists and wiggled his fingers, he said, "I think I can get these ropes off." But as he struggled to free his hands, his foot kicked out and accidentally hit the nearest andiron. Indy didn't know it, but this particular andiron did more than hold logs within the fireplace. As he hit the andiron again, there was a clicking sound, and then the fireplace floor began to rotate like a carousel.

Indy said, "Whoops!"

Moving counter-clockwise, the rotating floor carried Indy and Henry around in a tight circle and revealed that the baronial chamber adjoined a Nazi radio room that was without windows. It was a different room from the one Indy had seen earlier, shortly after he had entered the castle with Elsa, but like that room, there was a table with a map on it. As the fireplace floor rotated, Indy quickly counted five people in the room, including a radioman wearing headphones who sat at an elaborate panel of dials, switches, and meters, and a woman who monitored the map on a table. Speaking in German, the woman appeared to be plotting coordinates for other soldiers. All of the Nazis had their backs turned to the fireplace and failed to notice Indy or Henry, who remained silent as the carousel carried them a full 360 degrees. When the carousel came to a stop, Indy and Henry had been returned to the blazing chamber.

"Our situation has not improved," Henry said grimly.

"Listen, Dad," Indy said, "I'm almost free." But as Indy continued to loosen the ropes at his wrists, his leg accidentally struck the andiron again, but just a single time. As the fireplace floor began to rotate, Indy suddenly realized that the andiron was the mechanism that activated the carousel. But because he had only hit the andiron once this time, the carousel did not turn completely on its axis, but instead carried Henry and Indy around to face the radio room before it came to an abrupt stop.

Indy and Henry sat very still, but their intrusion did not go unnoticed by the woman who stood beside the map on the table. While the men in the room continued to focus on their controls, the woman, who'd felt a wave of heat travel from the wall behind her, turned her head slowly to face the two Americans. She gazed at them with a surprised, puzzled expression.

Knowing they were completely vulnerable, Indy and Henry smiled sheepishly at the woman. A slightly nervous smile crept across her face, and then she screamed at the top of her lungs, "Alarm!"

The four radiomen jumped as they turned to see Henry and Indy. Suddenly, an alarm began ringing loudly. The woman yelled, "*Schnell!*"

As two of the radiomen reached for their holstered pistols, Indy deliberately threw the side of his leg against the andiron, and the fireplace floor began to rotate again. The radiomen fired several rounds at Indy and Henry, but they missed and the bullets pinged off against the closing door.

When the carousel came to a stop, Indy and Henry were delivered back to the baronial chamber. Every piece of furniture was ablaze, and the flames that reached up to the ceiling had transformed the room into a massive broiler. Henry grumbled loudly, "This is intolerable!"

Just then, Indy pulled his wrists free from the ropes and declared, "I'm out, Dad!"

"Well done, boy!" Henry said.

Meanwhile, in the radio room, all four radiomen had their guns drawn. Their female counterpart motioned them to stand near the secret door before she drew her own pistol. One of the men activated the mechanism to open the secret door, and it swiveled open halfway, so that the dividing wall stopped at a perpendicular angle within the fireplace.

Three radiomen and the woman moved cautiously through the open passage and into the burning room. On the floor in front of the fireplace, they found two overturned chairs and a few small piles of rope. They squinted at the flames, but couldn't see any sign of the escaped Americans.

Indy and Henry had not even attempted to flee through the inferno, but had concealed themselves within the chimney above the fireplace. They both dropped down at the same time, landing behind the radiomen, who continued to face the opposite direction, searching the burning room. Indy and Henry were about to jump back into the radio room when Indy was tackled by the lone radioman who had not entered the burning chamber.

The man locked his arm around Indy's neck, and Indy reached down to slam the andiron mechanism forward. As the rotating floor turned, leaving a frightened-looking Henry temporarily behind, Indy knocked out his attacker with a single punch and left the man slumped against the dividing wall. A moment later, the carousel carried Henry around to Indy's side, and the knocked-out radioman was delivered to his allies.

In the radio room with his father, Indy heard a clicking sound and realized the radiomen were trying to activate the secret door again. The radiomen had already tried to shoot him and Henry, and he wasn't about to give them another chance. Thinking quickly, he reached for the nearest object he could grab, a small bust of Adolf Hitler that rested on top of a shelf. Indy shoved the bust forward to jam the rotating wall in place, sealing the Nazis inside the burning chamber.

On a table in the radio room, Indy found his whip, the sack that contained his gun, and his father's bag and umbrella. Indy grabbed his things and shoved the other stuff at his father. "Come on, Dad!"

The radio room had only one exit, and they took it. They ran through an L-shaped corridor that led them straight into an empty room with a vaulted ceiling. Daylight seeped in through a few small, barred windows, but the windows were so covered with grime that Indy couldn't see outside. His eyes swept the room and found it was without any doors.

"Dead end," Indy said. He knew it was only a matter of time before more soldiers came in response to the alarm from the radio room. Searching frantically for an exit, he said, "There's got to be a . . . a secret door or a . . . passageway or something."

In the middle of the room, Henry walked around in a circle as he followed Indy's movement. While Indy ran his hands over the walls and tried to find anything resembling a concealed passage, Henry noticed a chair that rested near a circular arrangement of inlaid stones in the floor. Indy had just set foot on the stones when Henry eased himself down onto the chair and said, "I find that if I just sit down and think . . ."

As Henry sat, the chair tilted back with a creak and a click. Suddenly, the stones beneath Indy's feet slid downwards and transformed into a spiral staircase. Indy tried to right himself but tumbled down the stone steps and hollered, "Dad!"

Still seated in the chair, Henry saw his son fall down the staircase that had appeared. Staring in amazement at the staircase, Henry completed his thought with some satisfaction: "... the solution presents itself." He got up from the chair and climbed down the steps after his son.

Indy had only suffered a few bruises from the staircase, which delivered him and his father to a cavern beneath the mountain on which the castle was built. The cavern opened to the edge of a river, where the Nazis had set up a boat dock for receiving supplies.

The previous day's storm had passed, and the sky was almost as blue as the three supply boats moored beside the dock. Remembering his recent chase through the canals of Venice, Indy muttered, "Great. More boats."

He quickly inspected several large crates that rested on the dock and then jumped into one of the boats. As Indy started the boat's outboard engine, Henry walked to the edge of the dock. "You say this has been just another typical day for you, huh?" He tossed his bag to Indy.

"Oof!" Indy gasped as he caught the heavy bag. Throwing it back at his father, he answered, "No! But better than most." Indy left the boat's engine running as he jumped back onto the dock. After bending down to release the boat's mooring line, he turned and moved quickly down the dock. "Come on, Dad," he urged. "Come on!"

"What about the boat?" Henry said as the empty boat began moving away from the dock. "We're not going on the boat?" Baffled, he followed his son.

Colonel Vogel had failed to reach the castle's baronial room or the concealed radio room before Henry Jones and his arrogant son had escaped, but Vogel knew the castle's layout well enough to know that they only had one way out: the spiral staircase, if they could find it. As he led a squad of soldiers out of the radio room and into the adjoining room with the vaulted ceiling, he nearly seethed when he saw the hidden staircase had been accessed.

Vogel and his men descended the staircase and ran out onto the riverside loading dock. Seeing that one of the motorboats had left the dock and was traveling up the river, he turned to the six soldiers behind him and barked, "*Sie alle ins boat! Schnell!*"

Following Vogel's command, the six soldiers scrambled into one of the remaining boats. None of them even glanced at any of the large crates on the dock. Just as Vogel leaped into the back of the boat, the side of one of the larger crates fell open to reveal its contents: a motorbike with a sidecar, as well as the two escapees.

Indy was already seated on the motorbike and his father was in the sidecar that was mounted on the bike's right side. Indy gunned the engine and they raced across the dock. Vogel turned and saw them, and then howled with rage. As the motorbike roared past the dock and through a small tunnel, two Nazi soldiers jumped out in front of the tunnel. Indy rammed them, sending them falling into the river, and then accelerated onto a dirt road.

Indy glanced back and saw that Vogel had jumped off the boat and was shouting orders from the dock. Indy exclaimed, "Ha!" as he and his father raced away from the castle. He grinned as he looked at his father beside him, but when he saw Henry Jones's worried expression, he returned his gaze to the tree-lined road ahead.

A moment after Indy rounded a bend in the road, he and his father heard loud engines approaching from behind. Glancing back over their shoulders, they saw four Nazi soldiers on motorcycles in hot pursuit. The soldiers had machine guns slung over their shoulders.

Henry gasped as Indy twisted the throttle, throwing their vehicle forward even faster.

*A*s Indy increased speed and tore off down the dirt road, the four motorcycle-mounted Nazi soldiers behind him simultaneously reached up to their helmets and pulled their goggles down over their eyes before they accelerated, too. There was a fork in the road ahead, with a smaller road that led down a hill to the left and a slightly wider road that ascended to the right.

During his journey to the castle with Elsa, Indy had studied a map of the area. He wasn't sure which fork to take, but he had to go somewhere, so he turned left down the hill. Three of the soldiers raced after him, but the fourth took the high road.

Henry nearly lost his grip on his bag when Indy weaved around a sharp corner. As Indy glanced back at the three soldiers behind him, his motorbike began to drift to the left side of the road. Henry's hand darted up to grab the right handlebar, setting the motorbike straight with a jerk, and Indy returned his gaze forward.

Indy saw a road station with two barricades up ahead. The barricades were wide, wooden gates that stretched across the road. A guard was stationed beside the first barricade, and when he saw their approach, he ran from his post and waved his arms, trying to signal them to stop. Indy ignored the guard, and Henry cringed and ducked as Indy sent the motorbike straight at the barricade.

"Halt! Halt!" the guard shouted after Indy as his motorbike and sidecar smashed through the wooden barrier. Knowing that three Nazi soldiers were still right behind him, Indy kept the bike at full speed as he headed for the second barricade. But just then, the barrier shattered at the impact of the motorcycle ridden by the fourth Nazi soldier, the one who had taken the high road — and, apparently, a short cut — so he could approach Indy from the opposite direction.

A flagpole was embedded in the ground at the side of road to Indy's left. Indy grabbed the pole as he drove past it, snapping it free from its base. While the oncoming Nazi soldier unshouldered his machine gun, Indy shifted the broken flagpole in his left arm and held it out like a lance.

There was a loud crack as the tip of the flagpole met the torso of the Nazi soldier, knocking him clear off his motorcycle. Part of the flagpole broke off, but Indy held tight to the remaining portion. Henry Jones knew all about jousting competitions from his history books, but he had never expected his own son to show such mettle.

As Henry gazed at his son with some admiration, the felled soldier's motorcycle continued to hurtle toward the first shattered barricade . . . just as the three other Nazi soldiers were racing past the guard's station. The riderless motorcycle collided with two of the soldiers, who crashed and rolled across the ground.

The one remaining Nazi soldier maneuvered his motorcycle around his fallen comrades and continued the chase. Indy saw the soldier coming up fast behind him and accelerate around a curve. Although the sidecar's weight helped stabilize Indy's motorbike, it also made his vehicle slower than his pursuer's.

The soldier twisted his motorcycle's throttle and jerked back on the handlebars, lifting his front wheel up off the road. Balancing on his rear wheel, he raced up behind Indy and dropped his front tire upon the back of the sidecar, nearly hitting Henry. Indy swerved away and the soldier's wheel slid off the sidecar and returned to the road.

Keeping both wheels on the ground, the soldier accelerated and came up fast on Indy's left. As the soldier reached for his machine gun and prepared to fire, Indy quickly extended the remaining length of the flagpole and rammed it through the spokes of the soldier's front wheel. The soldier's motorcycle flipped over the jammed wheel and somersaulted through the air before landing with a horrid crash.

Indy glanced back at the demolished bike and grinned. He thought his father would look happy, too, or at least relieved, but his father merely offered a slight grimace before removing his pocket watch from his jacket to check the time.

Facing forward, Indy saw a wooden sign at a crossroad. At the top of the sign, arrows pointed in opposite directions for Berlin and Venedig. As Indy started down the road for Venedig, Henry said, "Stop."

"What?"

"Stop! Stop!" Henry bellowed.

Indy brought the motorbike to a stop.

"You're going the wrong way," Henry said over the idling engine. "We have to get to Berlin."

Pointing toward Venedig, Indy said, "Brody's *this* way."

"My diary's in Berlin."

"We don't *need* the diary, Dad," Indy said sternly as he looked down at his father in the sidecar. "Marcus has the map!"

"There is more in the diary than just the map."

Indy turned off the engine. "All right, Dad. Tell me."

"Well," Henry said cagily, "he who finds the Grail must face the final challenge."

"What final challenge?"

Holding up three fingers, Henry said, "Three devices of such lethal cunning."

"Booby traps?"

"Oh, yes," Henry replied with glee. "But I found the clues that will safely take us through, in the Chronicles of St. Anselm."

"Well, what are they?"

Henry's lower lip quivered, and then he squinted as he lowered his gaze from Indy.

Getting angry as well as impatient, Indy said, "Can't you *remember*?"

Henry took off his hat and answered, "I wrote them down in my diary so that I wouldn't *have* to remember."

Pointing to the road behind them, Indy scowled and said, "Half the German army's on our tail, and you want me to go to Berlin? Into the lion's den?"

"Yes!" Henry said. "The only thing that matters is the Grail."

"What about Marcus?"

"Marcus would agree with me."

Looking away from his father, Indy muttered, "Two selfless martyrs." Then he returned his gaze to his father, shook his head, and exclaimed, "Jesus Christ!"

Henry slapped his son across the face. Indy gasped and his whole body shuddered. As tough as he was, he had not been prepared for his father's strike, not on any level.

"That's for blasphemy," Henry said.

Indy looked away and stared at the ground in front of the motorbike. His left cheek still stung from the slap.

In a grave tone, Henry continued, "The quest for the Grail is not archaeology. It's a race against evil. If it is captured by the Nazis, the armies of darkness will march all over the face of the Earth. Do you understand me?"

Indy's eyes burned with anger as he turned his head to face his father. Aiming a finger at Henry, he said, "This is an *obsession*, Dad. I *never* understood it. *Never.*" Looking away from his father, he added, "Neither did Mom."

Henry's body stiffened in the sidecar. "Oh, yes, she did," he said. "Only too well." Lowering his voice to almost a whisper, he said, "Unfortunately, she kept her illness from me until all I could do was mourn her."

Still looking away from his father, Indy thought about his mother. Anna Jones had contracted scarlet fever and died in 1912, not long after the Jones family ended a two-year tour of the world and returned to America.

Both Indy and his father had been devastated by her loss. Unfortunately, Henry Jones had not known how to put his grief into words and had done little to console his son. Shortly after Anna's death, Henry and Indy moved to Utah, where the emotional gulf between father and son only grew.

Indy lifted his gaze to the wooden sign at the cross-road. He stared hard at the word *Berlin*, and wondered if his mother really had understood his father.

Indy restarted the motorbike and drove off with his father in the sidecar.

Night had fallen on Berlin, where the Nazis were holding a massive rally in the city square in front of the Institute of Aryan Culture, a wide Neoclassical building with a peaked roof and a façade of monolithic columns. At the center of the square, a book-burning was in progress. The Nazis were delighted to destroy any and all books that they regarded as decadent or insignificant, books that did not glorify the German people or their leader. The mound of burning books was ten feet tall and growing by the minute as college students and Nazi brownshirts tossed more books onto the fire. As the flames rose higher and martial music filled the night air, a parade

of soldiers marched around the square, carrying banners
that displayed the swastika.

The Nazi revelers were so absorbed by the rally that
they did not notice when two men arrived by a motorbike
with a sidecar, which they parked at the edge of the square.
Fortunately for Indiana Jones and his father, there were so
many Nazi soldiers in the vicinity that it would take them
some time to discover that one was missing.

Indy had found a Nazi officer who was about his size
and build. The officer had been standing alone near some
parked cars when Indy knocked him out and then hastily removed the man's gray uniform and hat. After
disguising himself in the Nazi uniform, Indy stuffed his
own clothes and gear into his father's bag and placed
them in their stolen motorbike's sidecar. Then he walked
slowly over to his father, who stood silently as he watched
the book-burning from a distance. Even though they
were over fifty feet away from the flames, Indy could feel
the heat.

"My boy," Henry said, "we are pilgrims in an
unholy land."

Henry directed Indy's gaze to a podium in front of the
Institute, which was decorated with enormous Nazi banners. High-ranking officers of the Third Reich stood upon
the podium, and at the center was their leader, Adolf

Hitler. And just a few feet away from Hitler stood Dr. Elsa Schneider.

Despite the distance, Indy saw that Elsa appeared uncomfortable, possibly even troubled. She kept looking toward the burning books, then averting her gaze, and then looking toward the flames again. But because Elsa had betrayed him and his father, Indy could not have cared less whether she was even slightly disturbed by the sight of some books being destroyed. If things went his way, he was about to make her life a whole lot more miserable.

The Nazi rally was still going strong when Elsa left the podium. She was alone, walking past the shadows of the Institute's columns and heading back to her car, when Indy slunk out from the darkness behind her. "Fräulein Doctor." As she turned, he gripped her arm and growled, "Where is it?"

Elsa was startled by the sight of Indy. Not just because he was wearing a Nazi officer's uniform, but because he was alive at all. She gasped, "How did you get here?"

"Where is it?" Indy repeated. "I want it." He pushed her back up against a column and began to search her clothing. He found his father's diary in one of her pockets and pulled it out.

"You came back for the *book*?" Elsa said, trembling. She seemed almost disappointed, like she had hoped Indy had come all the way to Berlin for her. With a pained expression, she asked, "*Why?*"

"My father didn't want it incinerated." Indy released her and began walking away.

Realizing that Indy was referring to the book-burning that was still going on in the square, Elsa reacted as if he had slapped her. Walking fast, she stepped in front of him to stop him and said, "Is that what you think of me? I believe in the Grail, *not* the swastika."

Through clenched teeth, Indy snarled, "Yet you stood up to be counted with the enemy of everything the Grail stands for. Who cares what you think?!"

"*You* do," Elsa said quickly and desperately.

Now it was Indy's turn to feel smacked. He'd made a mistake when he'd fallen for Elsa, and he wasn't the sort of man who liked to make the same mistake twice. As sincere as she sounded, Indy knew she had a talent for faking sincerity. His left hand flew to her neck and he locked his thumb around her throat. He said, "All I have to do is squeeze."

Keeping her eyes on Indy's, Elsa answered sadly, "All I have to do is scream."

While the martial music continued to blare from the city square, Indy and Elsa just stood there for a moment, staring at each other. It was a standoff. Indy knew he wasn't capable of strangling Elsa, and she knew it, too. And the same went for screaming. There were dozens of Nazis within earshot, and even though a single scream would alert them to Indy's position, Elsa just couldn't do it.

Indy removed his hand from her neck and backed away. Elsa looked even more pained as he walked off, not because he was taking the Grail diary with him, but because she had realized that mistakes had been made. *Her* mistakes. She had failed to recognize the evils of the Nazi party, and she had never planned on falling in love with Indiana Jones.

Henry Jones was standing among a crowd of people at the bottom of a flight of steps outside the Institute. As the disguised Indy descended the steps to rejoin his father, he held the diary up and said, "I've got it. Let's get out of here."

Indy and Henry had barely taken two steps when they were suddenly thrust apart by a wave of frenzied people, all shouting and eager to catch a glimpse of the Nazi party's leader. Indy held tight to the diary but was unable to resist the force of the mob, and was shoved backwards as the crowd swept him toward the marchers in the square. When he came to a sudden stop, he turned and found himself face-to-face with Adolf Hitler.

Indy gasped as his eyes met Hitler's. He was so surprised that he almost forgot that he was wearing a Nazi officer's uniform. Hitler had been moving through the crowd with his Nazi entourage and was surrounded by numerous spectators who held out autograph books, hoping to get Hitler's signature.

Hitler's eyes flicked to the leather-bound book that Indy held in one upraised hand. Remembering that he was in disguise, Indy stopped gaping and straightened his back to stand at attention. He stood in stunned silence as Hitler reached out and took the Grail diary from him, and then took a pen from a nearby aide.

Indy held his breath as Hitler opened the diary to the first page and began to sign it. He wondered if Hitler could read English and if he might spot any mention of the Holy Grail or Henry Jones's name. But a moment later, Hitler completed his signature and handed the diary back to Indy.

Indy grinned as Hitler and his entourage moved on. As much as the Nazis had wanted to get their hands on the Grail diary, their leader had literally let it slip through his fingers.

Working his way through the crowd, Indy found his father. A Nazi S.S. officer wearing a long black overcoat spotted them as they approached the stolen motorbike and sidecar. Noticing Indy's uniform and believing him to be a Nazi soldier, the S.S. officer loudly ordered him to return to his post. Indy silenced the man with his fist and relieved him of his overcoat.

As Henry climbed into the sidecar, it did cross Indy's mind that Elsa might alert the Nazis that he and his father had recovered the diary in Berlin. He didn't know whether she would rat him out, had no reason to trust that she wouldn't, and didn't really care. If she brought more trouble, he would just have to deal with it.

*A*fter hiding out in Berlin for the night, Indy and his father rode to the airport, where they abandoned their motorbike and sidecar. Indy also got rid of his officer's uniform, but kept the pilfered overcoat, which he put on over his own clothes before he and Henry entered the terminal building.

Inside the terminal, Nazi agents in black coats distributed leaflets bearing Henry Jones's photograph to soldiers stationed throughout the building. While Indy went to a ticket booth, Henry kept out of sight by standing beside a doorway behind some men who, like himself, were reading newspapers. Henry held his own newspaper up high so no one could see his face.

Indy turned up the collar of his overcoat and did his best to look casual as he walked past some soldiers and returned to his father. Henry tucked his newspaper under his arm as he stepped away from his hiding spot and followed Indy toward the boarding gates. Seeing the tickets in his son's hands, Henry said, "What did you get?"

"I don't know," Indy admitted. "The first available flight out of Germany."

"Good," Henry said.

They showed their tickets to the boarding guards and then got into line with a group of passengers who were moving toward a moored zeppelin. At a glance, Indy guessed the aircraft was ten stories tall and longer than two football fields. He also noticed that it had a biplane secured to its underside. Henry took a look at the tickets and informed his son that the zeppelin was bound for Athens.

They boarded the massive aircraft and made their way to a small dining table beside a wide-open louvered window in the luxurious passenger compartment. Outside the window, men were loading luggage and supplies onto the zeppelin. As Indy and Henry took their seats and Henry opened his newspaper, Indy smiled broadly and said in a hushed voice, "Well, we made it."

Lowering his paper to look at his son, Henry said, "When we're airborne, with Germany behind us, *then* I'll share that sentiment." He returned to his newspaper, holding it up so no one could see his face.

"Relax," Indy said. But then Indy looked out the

window to his left, and what he saw made him realize his father had had every reason to be concerned. Colonel Vogel and a black uniformed Gestapo agent were rushing across the tarmac, heading toward the zeppelin's gangplank.

"*Nicht zumachen!*" Vogel yelled to someone Indy couldn't see. "*Wir steigen ein!*"

They're coming aboard, Indy realized. He was about to say something to his father when a steward, an older man with gray hair who wore a white jacket and hat, stepped over and placed a bowl of nuts on their table. As the steward turned and walked down the aisle past other passengers, Indy quietly got up from his seat and followed the steward, who was a few inches shorter than him. When Indy caught up with the steward in the foyer outside the passenger compartment, he put his arm around the man's shoulder and addressed him in a low, confidential tone as he led him up a flight of stairs.

A moment after Indy left with the steward, Vogel entered the passenger compartment. Vogel carried a walking stick, and as he moved down the aisle, he raised the stick to push down at the top of a newspaper that had been obscuring a male passenger's face. There were three other people seated at the table with the man, and they all looked up at Vogel as he held up a photograph of Henry Jones and said, "*Haben sie disen Mann gesehen?*"

The passengers did not recognize the man in the photo. They shook their heads and said, "*Nein.*"

While the zeppelin remained moored, Vogel moved on to another group of passengers, from whom he received the same response. As he noticed yet another person concealed behind a raised newspaper, Indy emerged from a nearby doorway. Indy was wearing the white jacket and hat that he had just appropriated from the steward. The hat fit well enough, but the jacket was more than a little snug. Indy saw Vogel, turned to face a seated passenger, and asked the passenger for his ticket: "*Fahrscheine, bitte.*"

The passenger answered, "*Ich habe ihn nicht gesehen.*"

With mounting tension, Indy watched Vogel move toward the table where Henry was concealed behind his newspaper. Indy stepped over to the seated passengers that Vogel had just left and said in a low voice, "Tickets, please." Only when no one responded did he realize that he'd spoken in English. He glanced down to a female passenger and said, "*Fahrscheine meine Dame. Bitte.*"

As the passengers beside Indy slowly reached for their tickets, Vogel slowly brought his walking stick down on top of the newspaper in Henry's hands. Henry looked at the tip of the walking stick, then lifted his gaze to Vogel.

Henry had removed his spectacles. He squinted at the man who had interrupted his reading and then went suddenly tense when he realized who it was. Vogel smiled menacingly and said, "*Guten Tag, Herr Jones.*"

Indy moved behind Vogel and said, "*Fahrscheine meine Herr.*"

Keeping his eyes fixed on Henry, Vogel said over his shoulder, "*Weg.*"

Indy said, "Tickets, please."

Henry squinted at the steward who stood behind Vogel. Henry wondered if something were wrong with his hearing. He could have sworn the steward sounded just like his own son.

With mild annoyance, Vogel said, "*Was?*" He turned to face the white-jacketed man behind him. And then he recognized Indy.

Indy threw his right fist into Vogel's jaw. Vogel stumbled past Henry's table and fell against the sill of the open window. As frightened passengers gasped and recoiled, Indy grabbed the back of Vogel's jacket and belt and heaved him out of the zeppelin. Vogel fell over twenty feet before he crashed down upon a large pile of luggage.

The fight had happened so fast, most of the shocked passengers blinked in bewilderment as Indy stepped away from the open window. Indy faced the gawking passengers and aimed a thumb at the open window. "No ticket."

All of the passengers gaped at Indy for a second, and then there was a sudden flurry of activity as hands dipped quickly into pockets and purses to produce tickets. A moment later, everyone was holding up their tickets for Indy to see.

Below the zeppelin, Vogel crawled out from the pile of luggage just as the massive aircraft began to rise into the sky. Standing amidst the luggage, he shook his fist and shouted, "*Du wirst nochmal boren von mir!*"

Indy had slipped out of the steward's white jacket and hat and back into his own clothes. Indy wasn't too concerned that the crew would figure out an SS officer had been thrown overboard because, while no one had been looking, he had disabled the zeppelin's radio. Later, as the airship traveled over a mountain range, he couldn't help looking a bit smug while he had a drink with his father in the passenger compartment's dining lounge.

Henry was cleaning his spectacles with a handkerchief when he looked across the small table to Indy, who was wearing his leather jacket. Henry said, "You know, sharing your adventures is an interesting experience."

Henry's Grail diary was on the table. As he opened the diary and began flipping through the pages, Indy said, "Do you remember the last time we had a quiet drink? I had a milkshake."

"Hmm?" Henry said without looking up from his diary. "What did we talk about?"

"We didn't talk," Indy said, staring down at the drink in front of him. "We never talked."

A moment later, Henry said, "Do I detect a rebuke?"

"A regret," Indy admitted. "It was just the two of us, Dad. It was a lonely way to grow up. For you, too. If you had been an ordinary, average father like the other guys' dads, you'd have understood that."

Still looking at his diary, Henry shook his head and smiled. "Actually, I was a wonderful father."

"When?"

Henry's brow furrowed as he lifted his gaze to his son. "Did I ever tell you to eat up?" he said sharply. "Go to bed? Wash your ears? Do your homework? No. I respected your privacy, and I taught you self-reliance."

Indy leaned forward with his elbows braced upon the table. "What you taught me was that I was less important to you than people who'd been dead for five hundred years in another country," he said bitterly. "And I learned it so well that we've hardly spoken for twenty years."

"You *left*," Henry said emphatically, "just when you were becoming *interesting*."

"Unbelievable," Indy muttered as he rocked back in his chair. "Dad, how can you —?"

"Very well," Henry interrupted. "I'm here. Now . . ." He closed his journal and sat erect, staring at Indy. "What do you want to talk about? Hmm?"

"Well, I . . ." Indy exhaled, flustered. "Uh . . ." He glanced away from his father, and then looked back. Henry just sat there staring at him. Indy shook his head and laughed. "I can't think of anything."

Holding his arms out at his sides, Henry exclaimed, "Then what are you *complaining* about? Look, we have *work* to do!" Holding the back of his chair, he made a series of small hops to shift his chair over closer to Indy. Then he opened his diary again so Indy could see the pages he had been reading, and said, "When we get to Alexandretta, we will face three challenges. The first, 'The Breath of God, only the penitent man will pass.'"

Indy got out his own eyeglasses, put them on, and saw his father was reciting handwritten notes. Henry had also drawn a picture of the Holy Grail, an undecorated goblet with lines radiating out around it. Beneath the drawing, Henry had written, *The cup of a carpenter.*

"Second," Henry continued, "'The Word of God, only in the footsteps of God will he proceed.' Third, 'The Path of God, only in the leap from the lion's head will he prove his worth.'"

Indy read the words to himself as Henry said them aloud, but then he looked at his father with a blank expression and asked, "What does that *mean*?"

Henry shrugged and chuckled. "I don't know." Then he nudged his son and added gleefully, "We'll find out!"

Indy smiled, too. But a moment later, as he removed his eyeglasses, he noticed that the shadows cast by the drinking glasses on their table had begun to move counterclockwise, and then he heard the zeppelin's engines whine. As the sunlight pouring in through the compartment's windows shifted suddenly across the walls, Indy looked up and said with grim certainty, "We're turning around. They're taking us back to Germany."

Mere minutes after the zeppelin had swung around over the mountain and began heading back to Berlin, Indy and his father snuck into the belly of the zeppelin, where the aircraft's elaborate metal framework was exposed. Indy carried his father's umbrella and leather bag, and both men had their hats on. Although Indy had no intention of starting a gunfight inside the highly-flammable zeppelin, he had taken the precaution of sticking his revolver down into his belt.

As Indy led his father down an aluminum ladder to a long, narrow catwalk, he grumbled, "Well, I thought it would take them a lot longer to figure out the radio was dead. Come on, Dad. Move!"

Their shoes made clacking sounds as they ran the length of the catwalk until they arrived at an open hatch in the floor. A ladder went down the hatch. As Indy began scampering down the ladder, he shouted, "Come on, Dad. Come on!"

They felt a great rush of wind as they went down the ladder, for it descended out of the zeppelin and into the open air, straight into the open cockpit of the biplane that was suspended from the zeppelin by a hook and crane device. Right behind the pilot's seat was a mounted machine gun. As Indy lowered himself behind the pilot's controls and his father climbed into the tail gunner's seat, Henry slapped the back of Indy's leather jacket and said with delight, "I didn't know you could fly a plane!"

"Fly — yes!" Indy said, shouting over the wind, but quickly added, "Land — no!" He started the biplane's engine and released the mechanism that secured it to the zeppelin. A moment later, the biplane fell from the zeppelin's belly, and Indy and his father were flying across the great blue sky. Indy didn't know exactly where they were, but he knew they were over Turkey, not far from the Mediterranean coast.

As the zeppelin receded into the distance, Indy turned around to see his father grinning as he gazed down at the ground below. Elsa had been wrong about a lot of things, but Indy figured she had made at least one good call: his father really *did* look as giddy as a schoolboy sometimes. *A big, old, bearded schoolboy,* Indy thought with some amusement.

Indy smiled at his father and gave him the thumbs-up signal. Henry smiled back, but then they both became aware of a strange sound in the skies behind them, a sound that was a cross between a roar and a wail. Both men gazed past the biplane's rear stabilizer to see two fighter planes racing toward them. The planes were painted with German Air Force colors.

One of the Nazi fighters opened fire on the biplane. A moment later, the fighter screamed past the biplane and began circling back. Indy knew there was no way he could outrun the Nazi fighters, and he severely doubted he could outmaneuver them, at least not at their current altitude. As he guided the biplane into a dive, he shouted back, "Dad, you're gonna have to use the machine gun! Get it ready!"

Henry wore a perplexed expression as he turned and gripped the machine gun.

"Eleven o'clock!" Indy shouted as he aimed his left arm toward the upper left area of the sky in front of the biplane. "Dad, eleven o'clock!"

Henry took his hands off the machine gun and removed his pocket watch from his jacket. After examining his watch, he put it back in his pocket and turned around to his son. "What happens at eleven o'clock?"

Frustrated beyond belief, and thinking he would have been better off with an *actual* schoolboy in the gunner's seat, Indy raised his left arm again to demonstrate that he was referring to a direction and not a time. He chopped at the air, moving his arm counter-clockwise as he shouted "Twelve, eleven, ten!" Then he pointed at the incoming fighter and shouted, "Eleven o'clock! Fire!"

Henry got the idea. He swung the machine gun around and fired high and to the left over the biplane's upper wing, aiming for the speeding fighter. The machine gun shuddered in his hands with such violence that he was afraid he'd be shaken out of his seat, but he held tight to the trigger and continued firing at the fighter as it whizzed past the biplane.

Indy was amazed that they hadn't taken even one hit, and then he realized that the biplane's slow speed and small size were actually working to their advantage. The Nazi fighters flew *so* fast that they continually overshot the biplane and then were forced to make wide turns before they could take aim again. Indy knew his only chance was to fly even lower, close over the hills and trees below, where the fighter planes would be even less maneuverable.

As Indy guided the biplane down over a small forest, Henry took aim at one of the fighters and opened fire. The fighter banked hard to the left, but Henry swung the machine gun around, kept the fighter in his sights, and continued firing. He kept firing as the fighter tore off and away from the biplane, but failed to hold his fire as his machine gun swung toward the biplane's rear stabilizer. An instant later, Henry had inadvertently blasted through the stabilizer, completely destroying it.

Indy had not seen his father's accidental action, but he knew something bad had happened by the way the biplane suddenly dropped altitude. As Henry gaped at the ruined stabilizer, Indy shouted over his shoulder, "Dad, are we hit?"

"More or less," Henry replied. "Son, I'm sorry."

As Indy turned his head to see the missing tail section, his father added, "They got us."

The biplane's engine sputtered, and then it began to go down.

CHAPTER TWELVE

*I*ndy struggled with the biplane's controls, trying to slow its descent. "Hang on, Dad!" he shouted. "We're going in!"

The terrain was mountainous. Henry saw they were descending toward a shrub-covered hill. He fearfully ducked and braced himself in the gunner's seat. A moment later, the biplane's wheels crashed down on the ground, sending the plane skidding out of control toward a rickety corral of goats. A cloud of dust trailed behind the biplane as Indy tried to kill the dying engine. As he neared the corral, the goats panicked and stampeded through a wooden fence. A moment later, both the biplane and its propeller came to a sudden stop when it slammed into the side of the adjacent barn.

"Nice landing," Henry said sarcastically.

"Thanks," Indy said as he pulled himself out of the cockpit, taking his father's bag and umbrella with him. Henry scrambled out after his son.

The Nazi pilots sighted the crashed biplane and swooped down toward the farm. Indy and Henry heard the fighters coming and ran away from the barn and across an open field. One of the fighters opened fire, and bullets slammed into the ground behind the running men.

There was a low retaining wall at the edge of the field, and Henry and Indy jumped down to hug the side of the wall as the fighter soared over their position. Outraged, Henry gasped, "Those people are trying to kill us!"

"I *know*, Dad!" Indy roared.

"Well," Henry said meekly. "It's a new experience for me."

"It happens to me all the time," Indy said. He shoved the bag and umbrella into his father's arms, and then ran from the retaining wall. Henry followed.

Nearby, alongside a gravel road, an old man was repairing one of the rear tires of his car, a Citröen Traction Avant convertible. The old man was about to place a hubcap over the jacked-up rear wheel when he heard two planes whine overhead. After he watched the fighters pass, he picked up the hubcap and moved it into position beside the wheel. But before he could set the hubcap in place, his car's engine started and the entire vehicle rolled away, right off the jacks.

In the car's passenger seat, Henry looked nervous as Indy gripped the steering wheel and stomped on the accelerator. Henry didn't like the fact that they'd just stolen an old man's car, but he liked the idea of getting shot down by Nazi fighters even less. Indy was just glad that the car had front-wheel drive, or their getaway wouldn't have been nearly so easy.

Then Indy glanced to the car's side mirror and saw the reflection of one of the fighters. It was flying low, coming up fast behind them. As Indy sent the car faster down the mountain road, the fighter's pilot opened fire, sending twin streams of bullets into the road behind the stolen Citröen.

"This is intolerable!" Henry cried.

Indy saw the road curve up ahead and said, "This could be close."

Indy took the curve fast and drove straight into a tunnel that cut through the steep mountainside. A moment after the car entered the tunnel, the low-flying fighter wrapped around the curve. The pilot was unable to pull up in time, and his fighter slammed into the mouth of the tunnel. The wings sheared off at the impact, but the fuselage continued to rocket through the tunnel like a bullet down the muzzle of a gun. Sparks flew as its belly scraped against the pavement and the tunnel's rough-hewn sides.

Indy and Henry glanced back over their shoulders to see that the wingless fuselage had been transformed into a racing fireball. Even worse, the fuselage had maintained its velocity and was rapidly gaining on them.

Glancing at his son, Henry urged, "Faster, boy! Faster!"

But Indy couldn't go any faster, not without losing control of the car. Maintaining speed, he steered the car so that he was traveling as close as he dared along the right wall of the cave. A moment later, the flaming fuselage cruised past the left side of the Citröen, so close that Indy and Henry could see the stunned German pilot gaping at them before he hurtled ahead.

As the fuselage exited the cave, it exploded in all directions. Indy and Henry ducked their heads as they made their own exit and drove straight through the wall of flames and over the scattered debris that covered the road. Indy held tight to the wheel, and when Henry looked back, he was amazed to see they had cleared the burning wreckage.

"Well," Henry chuckled, "they don't come much closer than that!"

At that very moment, the remaining fighter plane released a bomb that fell to the road directly in front of the Citröen. The bomb exploded, missing the car by only several feet and instantly creating a deep, wide crater in the road. Indy was unable to stop the car from nosing straight into it.

Dust and dirt were everywhere. Indy scrambled out of the car and bounded up to the side of the road, which overlooked a steep hill that stretched down to the

Mediterranean Sea. Glancing around, Indy saw they were completely exposed. Henry had already extricated himself from the car, but Indy turned and gestured at the fighter as he said impatiently, "Dad, he's coming back."

Clutching his bag and umbrella, Henry trotted off after Indy and followed him down the hill, which led to a wide beach. Indy had hoped to find some kind of protective cover along the beach, but except for some distant rocks, there was nothing.

Overhead, the Nazi fighter began to circle back toward them.

Indy remembered his revolver and pulled it from his belt. Had anyone ever used a handgun to shoot a fighter plane out of the sky? Indy had no idea, but he would give it his best shot.

But then Indy remembered something else. He opened the revolver's chamber and saw it was empty. In all the excitement, he'd forgotten to load his gun.

We're dead.

While Indy just stood there, Henry gazed down the stretch of beach between them and the approaching fighter. Without a word, he thrust his leather bag into Indy's arms and then drew his umbrella out from straps at the top of the bag. Indy noticed that his father had removed the umbrella with a slight flourish, like a knight unsheathing his sword.

Then, even more unexpectedly, Henry left Indy's side and began running down the beach. As he ran, he made clucking noises as he rapidly opened and closed his umbrella. Only then did Indy notice that his father was heading for a large flock of seagulls that had gathered along the shore.

At Henry's approach, the seagulls became agitated and took to the wing. Indy watched with wonderment as thousands of birds suddenly rose up into the sky, just as the fighter swooped down from above.

Before the pilot could take evasive action, his fighter collided with the unfortunate birds. Some gulls were shredded by the whirling propeller blades. Others smashed straight into the cockpit with such impact that they cracked the glass. The pilot screamed as he fired blind into the sky. A moment later, his out-of-control fighter slammed into a high rocky wall that loomed above the beach.

Slightly stunned, Indy pocketed his revolver and turned to see his father walking back up the beach. Henry casually held his open umbrella over his shoulder, shielding his face from the sun. As he returned to his son's side, Henry said, "I suddenly remembered my Charlemagne. 'Let my armies be the rocks and the trees and the birds in the sky.'" Then, like a schoolboy, Henry chuckled.

Indy knew that if it hadn't been for Henry's quick

thinking and action, both of them probably would have been shot dead. As Henry walked past him, Indy felt slightly ashamed that he had been treating his father like excess baggage. He also felt something else for his father that he hadn't before: pride.

In the Republic of Hatay, a Sultan received a group of visitors to his palace in Iskenderun. The Sultan wore a red fez and an ornate gold tunic. His visitors included Walter Donovan, Colonel Vogel, a few Nazi soldiers, and the captive, Marcus Brody.

In a palace courtyard, Donovan and Vogel walked alongside the Sultan, followed by Brody, an armed Nazi soldier, some Turkish soldiers, and the Sultan's various minions. Donovan clutched the Grail diary's missing pages, and Brody couldn't help but wince at the sight. As they walked, Donovan held the pages out before the Sultan and said, "These pages are taken from Professor Jones's diary, Your Highness. And they include a map that pinpoints the exact location of the Grail. As you can see, the Grail is all but in our hands."

The Sultan gave the map a cursory glance, but showed no real interest in it.

"However, Your Highness," Donovan continued, "we would not think of crossing your soil without your permission, nor of removing the Grail from your borders without suitable compensation."

The Sultan stopped walking, and everyone else stopped, too. Glancing at Donovan, the Sultan got straight to the point and said, "What have you brought?"

In response, Vogel looked over to two nearby Nazi soldiers and snapped, "Bring *den Schatz!*"

The two soldiers brought forward a large steamer trunk. They placed it on the ground in front of the Sultan and then pulled its lid open. The trunk was filled with gold and silver objects of every description. Vogel dipped his walking stick into the trunk to lift a gold pitcher for the Sultan's inspection.

"Precious valuables, Your Highness," Donovan said, "donated by some of the finest families in all of Germany."

But Donovan had lost the Sultan before he'd even said the word "donated." Apparently, the Sultan had little use for these expensive trinkets, for he stepped away from Donovan and the offered treasure and moved to the center of the courtyard, where he'd seen something else that had taken his fancy.

"Ah!" exclaimed the Sultan as he opened his arms to the gleaming black Nazi staff car that had delivered the foreigners to his palace. "Rolls-Royce Phantom Two," the Sultan declared. Then, glancing at Donovan while he made sweeping gestures at the car, the Sultan rattled off the car's specifications from memory. "Four-point-three liter, thirty horsepower, six cylinder engine, with Stromberg downdraft carburetor. Can go from zero to one hundred kilometers an hour in twelve-point-five seconds. And I even like the color."

Donovan smiled as he removed his hat with an almost bowing gesture and said, "The keys are in the ignition, Your Highness."

Stepping away from the Rolls-Royce, the Sultan said, "You shall have camels, horses, an armed escort, provisions, desert vehicles — and tanks!"

"You're welcome," Donovan said.

The Sultan led Donovan and Vogel past a man who happened to be a spy at the palace. Like the Sultan, the man wore a red fez. As Donovan and Vogel passed him, the spy turned his head and eyed them carefully. The spy was Kazim, agent of the Brotherhood of the Cruciform Sword.

A short while later, after completing their negotiations with the Sultan, Donovan and Vogel were walking through a corridor at the palace when they saw a blonde woman wearing a trim dress suit and sunhat coming down a stairway.

"We have no time to lose," Dr. Elsa Schneider said as she approached the two men. "Indiana Jones and his father have escaped."

*I*ndy and Henry wasted no time traveling to Iskenderun. There, they were greeted by Sallah, who led them to an open car. Indy climbed into the front seat beside Sallah, and Henry got in back. As Sallah drove them through the crowded streets, he explained how Marcus Brody had been abducted by the Nazis. Listening to Sallah's account, Indy and Henry scowled.

There were many pedestrians, carpet sellers, and goats in the street. "We go this way," Sallah said as he blasted the car's horn and weaved through the crowd. Steering onto a narrow street, they came up fast behind a man herding three camels. Sallah hit his horn again and shouted, "Get that camel out of the way!"

Indy said, "What happened to Marcus, Sallah?"

"Ah, they set out across the desert this afternoon. I believe they took Mister Brody with them."

Henry removed his hat and whacked the back of Indy's

jacket with it. "Now they have the map!" Henry said angrily. Leaning forward from the backseat, he added, "And in this sort of race, there's no silver medal for finishing second."

The Sultan had supplied Donovan with all he needed for an expedition across the rocky desert: staff cars, troop carriers, supply trucks, riding camels, spare horses, and Turkish soldiers to serve alongside their German counterparts. As promised, he had also let them borrow his prized tank, a modified British type from the Great War. Equipped with a large turret-mounted primary cannon and two side cannons, the thirty-six-feet long treaded tank was a massive war machine. It was operated by a driver and side gunner, who had been instructed to obey Colonel Vogel's commands. Vogel was proud to have the tank lead Donovan's procession across the rocky desert.

To allow those on foot to keep up, the drivers kept their vehicles at a relatively low speed as they moved along through the ramble of a box canyon. In the front seat of an open car directly behind the tank, Donovan, wearing a pith helmet and a tailored safari jacket, sat beside the driver. In the back seat were Elsa and Brody. Elsa wore a white shirt with black pants and matching black gloves and leather boots; she had pushed her hair up under a German soldier's cap and wore field goggles to keep the dust out of her eyes. Brody wore the same suit he'd been wearing since his arrival and abduction in Iskenderun; he looked rumpled, exhausted, and miserable.

Donovan handed a canteen back to Brody and said, "Care to wet your whistle, Marcus?"

"I'd rather spit in your face," Brody replied. "But as I haven't got any spit . . ." He took the canteen, but before he could open it and raise it to his parched lips, Vogel walked up alongside the moving car, stepped on its running board, and plucked the canteen from Brody's hands.

Holding the canteen, Vogel stepped down from the running board and continued to walk beside the vehicle. As he opened the canteen, he said to Donovan, "Must be within three or four miles. Otherwise we are off the map." Vogel handed the pages torn from the Grail diary to Elsa and then drank from the canteen.

Brody glanced at the pages in Elsa's hand. She was studying the map that Henry Jones had made. Knowing that he had allowed the Nazis to take possession of the map made Brody feel ill.

Donovan removed his pith helmet and said, "Well, Marcus, we are on the brink of the recovery of the greatest artifact in the history of mankind."

As Donovan took the canteen from Vogel and raised it to his own lips, Brody said, "You're meddling with powers you cannot possibly comprehend."

"Ah," Indy said. "I see Brody. He seems okay."

Indy was stretched out on the ground, peering through binoculars from atop a high, rocky hill that overlooked Donovan's caravan. Because of the distance, he did not recognize Elsa as the goggled person who sat beside Brody in the open car.

Henry and Sallah had crouched down behind some boulders a short distance behind Indy. Beyond the boulders was a dirt road, where Sallah had parked their supply-laden car.

Indy pushed himself up from the ground and stood upright before the boulders. "They've got a tank," he said as he readjusted his binoculars. Looking at the tank's main cannon, he commented, "Six-pound gun."

Unfortunately, the bright sunlight reflected off of Indy's binoculars. In the canyon below, Donovan glanced up from his car to see a bright light flash in the upper hills.

From his hiding place behind a boulder, Henry glared at Indy and said in a loud whisper. "What do you think you're doing?! Get down!"

Turning to face his father, Indy said with some annoyance, "Dad, we're *well* out of range."

Indy's sentence was punctuated by a loud blast from the canyon floor. Indy cringed as he glanced back to see a large puff of smoke in front of the tank's main cannon and heard the fired shell tear through the air in his direction. As the shell whistled overhead, Indy dove down beside the nearby boulders, and both Henry and Sallah moved fast to take cover beside him. A split second later, the shell smashed into their parked car, blowing it to smithereens.

The three men covered their heads as automobile fragments rained down upon them. A flaming tire bounced and rolled away from the explosion. As the tire blazed past Sallah he gasped, "That car belonged to my brother-in-law."

Crouching low, Indy gestured at his father and Sallah to follow him and shouted, "Come on, come on!"

Down in the canyon, beside the tank, Vogel peered through binoculars to confirm that the fired shell had destroyed an automobile. Lowering his binoculars, he walked over to Donovan's car and said, "I can't see anyone up there."

Donovan said, "Maybe it wasn't even Jones."

"No," Elsa said. "It's him all right." She stood up in the back of the car, glanced at the surrounding hills and added, "He's here somewhere."

Donovan stepped out of the car and looked to Vogel. "Put Brody in the tank."

While Vogel escorted Brody to the tank, Donovan's party was unaware that they were surrounded by white-robed men who had concealed themselves in the hills around their position. The men were agents of the Brotherhood of the Cruciform Sword, and Kazim was among them. From his hiding place behind a rock, Kazim readied his rifle as he peered at the group below.

Elsa stepped away from Donovan's car and walked over to stand beside Donovan. While Elsa reached up to massage the back of her travel-weary neck, Donovan said, "Well, in this sun, without transportation, they're as good as dead."

Suddenly, the concealed Brotherhood opened fire on the soldiers and vehicles below. A Nazi soldier fell from the top of the tank as bullets hammered into the vehicle's armor. Elsa and Donovan ran and dived for cover beside Donovan's car. Donovan muttered, "It's Jones, all right."

But Indy was as surprised by all the gunfire as Donovan. Indy was leading his father and Sallah down the hill to the tank and parked vehicles when shots rang out from all around them. Indy and Sallah ducked down behind some rocks, but Henry stood straight up, gestured at the men in white robes who were shooting at the Nazi and Turkish soldiers, and exclaimed, "Now, who are all *these* people?"

"Who cares?" Indy said as he pulled his father down beside him. "As long as they're keeping Donovan busy." Seeing that his father looked winded, he said, "Dad, you stay here while Sallah and I organize some transportation."

Indy and Sallah snuck off, leaving Henry behind, sitting on a rock. Henry was brushing the dust from his jacket when a bullet hit the other side of the rock he was sitting on. He ducked down fast.

Donovan's party responded to their attackers with a vengeance. While two Nazi soldiers threw hand grenades into the cliffs, others opened fire with machine guns. The grenades exploded, launching dirt and white-robed men into the air. One of the men was killed instantly, and after his body rolled to a stop, a Nazi soldier bent down to see the man's exposed sternum bore a tattoo of a cruciform sword.

Indy and Sallah crouched down behind a wide rock and watched men on both sides of the battle run amongst the camels and horses. Indy said, "I'm going after those horses."

"I'll take the camels," Sallah said.

Staring hard at Sallah, Indy said, "I don't need camels."

"But, Indy —"

"No camels!" Indy insisted.

Indy moved off, heading for a hill just beyond the horses. He saw several dead men on the ground, but had no idea that Kazim had participated in the attack on Donovan's party, or that Kazim had been mortally wounded.

Kazim lay on the ground, face-up with his arms stretched out by his sides. Lifting his head slightly, he looked up to see Elsa staring down at him with a sad expression. Donovan stepped over beside Elsa, looked at the dying man before him, and said to Elsa, "Who is he?"

"A messenger from God," Kazim gasped. "For the unrighteous, the Cup of Life holds everlasting damnation."

Hearing this, Elsa trembled. Donovan glanced at her, sneered, and walked away. Elsa wondered whether Donovan held disdain for the man's words or her reaction to them, but realized it didn't matter. A moment later, as Elsa watched, Kazim lowered his head and died.

A moment after Kazim drew his last breath, Indy leaped from the hillside to tackle a mounted soldier. The soldier went down along with his horse. Indy belted the soldier as he scrambled onto the horse's saddle, and then grabbed the reins to urge the horse up from the ground. As the horse got up with Indy on its back, another soldier came running at Indy. Indy backhanded the man and galloped off.

Indy had assumed that his father would stay put and did not see Henry leave his hiding place and head for the tank. Henry had seen the Nazis put Brody inside the tank, and he was hoping to be of some aid to his old friend. He snuck up to the tank and climbed on top of it, discovering that its hatch was open.

There were just a few metal steps that led down into the tank's hatch. Henry stepped down them and found Brody seated inside the tank. Brody had his back to the hatch and looked more miserable than ever. The tank's goggled driver and side gunner were peering out through the front viewing port, and did not hear Henry's entrance.

Henry reached out and tapped Brody's shoulder as he said in loud whisper, "Marcus!"

"Arghhh!" Brody nearly jumped out of his skin. Turning around, he saw Henry crouched below the hatch and exclaimed, "Oh!"

The two men launched into the traditional University Club toast by swinging their arms at one another and deliberately missing. Then Henry flapped his arms and tugged his ears and recited, "'Genius of the Restoration —'"

Brody tugged his ears, flapped his arms, and touched his head as he responded, "'— aid our own resuscitation!'"

Then they shook hands and Brody said, "Henry! What are you doing here?"

"It's a rescue, old boy! Come on." Henry was about to get up when shadows appeared above the hatch, and then two Nazi soldiers came down fast into the tank, their Luger pistols drawn. One soldier grabbed Henry and held his gun to his head while the other aimed his own gun at Brody. Then a third Nazi stepped down into the tank. It was Vogel.

"Search him," said Vogel, his icy-blue eyes boring in on Henry's. As the soldier patted down Henry's pockets, Vogel reached to his own right hand and removed his leather glove. "What is in this book?" he said. "That miserable little diary of yours."

Before Henry could even think to respond, Vogel slapped his glove across Henry's face. Henry's head jerked to the side, and he reached up to touch his wounded cheek.

"We have the map," Vogel continued. "The book is useless, and yet you come all the way back to Berlin to get it. Why?" He slapped Henry again, and again Henry's head jerked aside.

"What are you hiding?" Vogel said. "What does the diary tell you that it doesn't tell us?!" He was about to slap Henry again when Henry, despite the pistol aimed at his head, reached up fast to catch and stop Vogel's wrist.

Barely restraining his rage, Henry growled, "It tells me that goose-stepping morons like yourself should try reading books instead of burning them!" He shoved Vogel's hand away.

Vogel's face went red with anger. Before he could strike Henry again, Donovan poked his head over the hatch and shouted down, "Colonel? Jones is getting away!"

Gesturing to Henry Jones, Vogel replied, "I think not, Herr Donovan."

"Not that Jones, the other Jones!" Donovan shouted as he gestured away from the tank and pointed to Indy.

Indy was mounted on one horse and was holding tight to the reins of three others, leading them away from the tank and soldiers. Vogel raised his head up through the hatch just in time to see the back of Indy's fedora and leather jacket as he rode off with the horses. Seething with fury, Vogel pushed his hand past Donovan to grab the inner handle on the hatch's lid, then pulled the lid shut.

Indy brought the horses around a bend in the canyon, where he caught up with Sallah, who was also mounted on a horse. But much to Indy's dismay, Sallah had acquired not more horses but the beasts that Indy had forbidden.

"Sallah, I said no camels!" Indy shouted. "That's five camels. Can't you count?!"

"Compensation for my brother-in-law's car," Sallah said defensively. "Indy, your father and Brody —"

Instantly losing all interest in the camels, Indy said, "Where's my father?"

"They have them," Sallah said, tilting his head back in the direction he and Indy had come from. "In the belly of that steel beast."

Indy clenched his jaw and looked away from Sallah. Already, he could hear the sound of the approaching tank. He gazed forward, shouted, "Hyah!" and then charged off with the horses in one direction while Sallah took off with the camels in another.

The tank, Donovan's car, and supply trucks followed Indy and Sallah around the bend in the canyon. Inside the tank, Vogel peered out through a slot, saw his quarry with the horses, and directed the tank's driver to go after Indiana Jones.

But as the tank headed off after Indy, Donovan instructed his driver to take him and Elsa in a different direction. As they veered away from the caravan, Elsa once again examined the map from Henry's diary.

The moment Indy realized that the tank and other vehicles had focused on him and not Sallah, he cut the other horses loose and rode off. As he headed for some rocky dunes, the tank increased speed and raced after him.

"Fire!" Vogel commanded the tank's driver and side gunner. Before Indy could reach the cover of the dunes, the tank fired and the nearest dune exploded into a high plume of desert dust. Indy guided his horse fast to the left and toward another dune, but then the tank fired again and it exploded, too. Inside the tank, Henry and Brody held their hands over their ears and watched helplessly as the emptied artillery shells fell to the floor.

Indy knew he had to keep the horse moving. Moving away from the dunes, he zigged and zagged over a wide-open area, forcing the tank to keep changing direction and preventing its crew from getting a bead on him. Glancing back over his shoulder, he saw the other vehicles emerge from around the dunes, and then he looked at the tank. He noticed that the tank's armored ports allowed limited visibility for the driver and that the side guns could only pivot so far, and saw an opportunity for action.

Indy guided his horse in front of the tank and then made a rapid 180 degree turn. As expected, the tank followed. But as the tank completed its full wrap-around turn, Vogel peered through the viewing port to see the oncoming German caravan. Indy had herded the tank into a head-on collision with a Kubelwagon, a German military sedan, and there was no way to avoid it.

Vogel screamed, and then the Kubelwagon smashed into the front of the tank. Everyone inside the tank was slammed against the hard-metal interior. The Kubelwagon flipped over and the tank's six-pound cannon drove straight through the sedan's roof. The force of the impact made the tank rock back on its treads, but it kept moving with the Kubelwagon now affixed over and in front of the turret, blocking not only the tank's front viewing ports but the use of its main cannon.

Still riding at full gallop, Indy shot a glance toward the tank to see that his maneuver had worked even better than expected. He laughed and then rode on ahead of the impaired tank.

One of the tank's side cannons fired. Indy was keeping his horse out of range, and the shell exploded into a dune over forty feet behind him. As he galloped onward, he saw a stone on the ground, slightly larger than a baseball. Clutching the reigns with his left hand, he leaned out from his saddle and stretched out his right arm to scoop up the stone. The horse never even broke its stride.

Incredibly, not all of the Kubelwagon's occupants had died when it collided with the tank. But as the survivors struggled to free themselves from their inverted, ruptured vehicle, Vogel decided that killing Indiana Jones was a higher priority than liberating the trapped Nazis. Turning to the gunner, Vogel ordered, *"Der Kubelwagon sprengen!"*

The gunner put a shell into the large gun and then fired, blasting the Kubelwagon straight off of the tank. The Kubelwagon sailed through the air and crashed in front of the tank. The tank never stopped moving, but drove through the smoke and dust and rolled over the Kubelwagon, crushing it.

As the tank left the flattened sedan behind, Indy guided his horse up along the left side of the tank. He held out the stone that he'd plucked from the ground, and then jammed it down the barrel of the side cannon. When the rock was firmly lodged, he rode away from the tank, steering his horse directly in range of that cannon.

Inside the tank, Henry moved over beside one of the viewing ports and peered out. One of the Nazi soldiers shoved him aside and snapped, "*Keine Bewegung.*"

Henry stumbled back and landed on a bare metal bench beside Brody. The soldier aimed his Luger pistol at them and repeated, "*Keine Bewegung.*"

The tank's side gunner had moved behind the trigger of the tank's left side cannon when he sighted Indy. The gunner grinned as he took aim and fired, but the cannon, blocked by the stone, backfired, killing the gunner instantly and filling the tank with smoke. Henry, Brody, and the Nazi soldiers began to choke and cough.

Indy saw smoke pouring out through the tank's ports. He guided his horse back alongside the tank so he was a short distance from the ruined cannon, which appeared to have blossomed into a flower of twisted metal. Turning his head to face the tank, Indy shouted, "Dad! Dad! Dad!"

Despite the noise inside the rumbling tank and that Henry's ears were still ringing from the cannon backfire, Henry heard his son's cry. The soldier who had shoved Henry away from the port still had his Luger out, but Henry shouted in return, "Junior! Junior! Junior!"

Incensed by Henry's shouting, the soldier lashed out with his gun hand, punching Henry in the jaw. Henry rocked back on the bench and glared at the soldier.

Indy had maneuvered his horse back behind the tank when Vogel popped open the hatch above the turret, releasing the smoke from within. Vogel coughed and felt his eyes tearing as the smoke billowed out and around him. And then he turned his head and saw Indy, and he reached for his pistol.

Indy knew that it was no easy trick to shoot from horseback at full gallop, but he'd had some experience. He drew his own revolver, took aim at Vogel, and fired. There was a bright flash as the bullet ricocheted off the turret, causing Vogel to duck, but Vogel quickly returned fire. The bullet tore past Indy, who kept his gun arm steady and fired more rounds at the turret.

Realizing that Indy was a much better shot and fearing for his life, Vogel ducked back down into the turret. Just as Vogel ducked, Indy tried to squeeze off another shot and was disappointed when his revolver's hammer only produced a loud *click*.

Indy jammed his revolver back down into his belt. As he kept after the tank, he thought, *How am I going to stop that thing?* The tank headed onto a trail that ran alongside a rocky slope. Thinking fast, Indy steered his horse up the slope to a parallel trail that carried him above the tank's position. When he was about twelve feet higher than the moving tank, Indy lifted both of his legs up, planted his boots on the saddle, and leaped from the horse.

Stretching out his arms and legs, Indy landed hard atop the trundling tank. He felt the wind get knocked out of him, but he refused to think of the pain. As the rapidly moving treads kicked up dust on either side, he thought only of his father, still trapped inside.

Indy pushed himself up from the back of the tank just as Vogel resurfaced through the hatch. Indy was about to reach for his bullwhip when he felt the wind knocked out of him again, this time because someone tackled him from the side.

The tank had veered away from the rocky wall, allowing a troop truck with five German soldiers in the back to draw up along the tank's left side. One of the soldiers had leaped from the troop carrier and knocked Indy down. The two men grappled as they rolled down the middle of the back of the tank and tried to avoid the treads whipping past them on either side. The soldier had drawn his

Luger, but Indy pinned his arm and belted him across the jaw.

Indy grabbed the gun from his opponent as two more soldiers leaped from the troop carrier to the tank. The first soldier, now deprived of his pistol, jumped up and was about to try and shove the American off the tank when Indy raised the Luger and fired. The bullet not only tore through the first soldier, but the two who had just moved directly behind him. As the three soldiers collapsed dead onto the back of the tank, Indy stared at the gun in disbelief.

But the fight wasn't over. A fourth soldier, wielding a combat knife, leaped from the truck and landed in front of Indy. Indy grabbed the soldier's wrist, but before Indy could raise the Luger, the soldier seized Indy's gun hand. Both men were struggling to keep their balance when Indy landed a punch across the man's jaw, then hurled himself against the man, knocking him back onto a cargo net behind the turret. The knife went flying out of the soldier's grip. Indy rolled away from the soldier and rose fast to stand beside the turret, and that's when Vogel made his move.

CHAPTER FOURTEEN

Vogel stepped out of the turret and picked up a metal chain that was rattling against the turret's side. While Indy's back was turned, Vogel clutched both ends of the chain as he threw it over Indy's head and pulled back hard. Indy felt the chain bite into his neck as he stumbled back into Vogel.

Indy and Vogel teetered atop the moving tank. As the soldier who had lost his knife began to get up from the cargo net where Indy had left him, Vogel twisted the chain and Indy suddenly found himself staring down into the turret's open hatch. Despite the chain that was choking him, Indy managed to shout, "Dad!"

Indy was still clutching the Luger in his right hand, and he was holding it in front of him when Vogel slammed him against the hatch. Indy's right wrist hit the hatch's metal rim and the Luger flew out of his hand and landed inside the tank.

"Dad!" Indy shouted again. "Dad! Get it!" He tensed his neck muscles as Vogel tugged him away from the hatch.

Inside the tank, Henry saw the Luger fall. But because a soldier inside the tank still had his own Luger aimed at Henry and Brody, all Henry could do was keep an eye on the fallen pistol and hope that none of the other soldiers noticed it.

As Vogel pulled Indy away from the hatch, Indy saw the other soldier — the one who had tried to stab him — step up and help Vogel. With the chain still around his neck and Vogel at his back, Indy swung out with his right arm and belted the soldier, knocking him onto the tank tread. The soldier screamed as the moving tread carried him forward and dropped him in front of the tank, which immediately rolled over him.

Indy threw all his weight backward against Vogel, who landed on the cargo net behind the turret. Inside the tank, Henry eyed the fallen Luger again and then glanced through a viewing port to see another troop truck speeding toward the tank. As he looked away from the port, the soldiers within the tank shifted positions. While one soldier kept his pistol aimed at Henry, the other went to a periscope, lowered its metal handgrips, and adjusted the scope to observe the action outside.

Outside the tank, the periscope rose up near Indy's

outstretched legs. Peering through the scope, the soldier saw Indy lying on top of Vogel but facing skyward, with the chain pulled taut across his throat. Indy lifted his feet and lunged forward toward the periscope, pulling Vogel with him.

Indy's face hit the lens of the periscope, causing the soldier who was watching him from below to flinch. Then the soldier — realizing what a great view he had — grinned and returned his eyes to the scope. A moment later, Vogel pulled back hard, yanking Indy back on top of him.

Down below, the soldier removed his hands from the periscope and turned to face his ally who was guarding Henry and Brody. The scope-operator laughed and said, "*Diese Amerikane. Sie Kampfen wie Weiber.*"

Up above, Indy's legs kicked out. His right boot smacked the periscope so hard that it spun. Below, the scope's metal handgrips spun as well, and whacked the scope-operator in the back of the head so hard that he collapsed against the other soldier, who stumbled back.

The periscope-struck soldier landed on Henry, but Henry shoved him aside and accidentally onto Marcus, and then Henry moved fast for the fallen Luger. But no sooner had Henry wrapped his left hand around the gun than the other soldier jumped at Henry and grabbed his wrist. The soldier maneuvered himself behind Henry, who managed to twist the gun's muzzle back toward his attacker before he realized that he was more likely to shoot his own head off if he pulled the trigger.

While Henry struggled with the soldier, Vogel rolled Indy off him and tried to push Indy's head down onto the treads. Indy felt the treads brush against the side of his face. Vogel was stronger than he looked. Vogel pressed harder and the treads scraped flesh from Indy's left cheek.

Within the tank, the soldier was still behind Henry when he managed to get hold of Henry's Luger. With his left hand, Henry grabbed the soldier's wrist and tried to angle the gun's muzzle away from his body. As Henry felt his grip begin to slip, he reached into his vest pocket with his right hand and removed his fountain pen. Henry lifted the pen and squirted ink back over his left shoulder and directly into the soldier's eyes.

The soldier grimaced and squeezed his eyes shut, and Henry pushed himself back against the man, slamming his wrist into a metal bar and his head against the wall of the tank. The Luger instantly fell from his hand and clattered on the floor.

As the soldier collapsed behind Henry, Brody scrambled up from under the other soldier and said, "Henry, the pen ..."

"What?" Henry said with a startled expression.

"But don't you see?" Brody said with a delighted grin. "The pen is mightier than the sword!"

Henry jumped up from the floor. The tank's driver was staring out the front viewing port, unaware that Henry and Brody were no longer under guard. Henry glanced out a port to see that the troop truck he'd glimpsed earlier was now drawing even with the tank's right side. Henry moved behind the tank's right side cannon, slipped his finger around the trigger, and fired at almost point-blank range straight at the troop truck.

The truck was knocked off its wheels as it exploded, launching soldiers high into the air. The power of the blast threw Vogel off of Indy, sending both men onto the tank's left tread, with Indy in the lead on a trip to the font of the tank. To avoid being dragged under the treads, Indy rolled his body hard over the side. He grabbed onto the shredded cannon — the one he had jammed the stone into — that protruded from the tank's side.

With his left cheek hurting like blazes from the gashes made by tank tread, Indy clung to the damaged cannon. The tank was traveling parallel to a wall of rock at Indy's left, so close that the cannon's erupted muzzle nearly brushed against it. Indy hoped that Vogel had failed to roll off of the tread, but a moment later, he glanced up to see Vogel standing atop the tank once again. Evidently, Vogel had rolled in the other direction.

Indy reached up to the edge of the tank to pull himself back up. Vogel moved closer to the edge and stomped on Indy's fingers. Indy wrapped both arms around the cannon and hung on for dear life.

Vogel could have drawn his pistol and shot Indy, but that would have given him little satisfaction. From the tank's cargo net, Vogel removed a long-handled metal shovel. He returned to the edge of the tank and brought the shovel down on Indy's hands. Indy groaned in pain, but held tight to the cannon.

Within the tank, Henry returned his pen to his vest pocket as he stepped away from the right side cannon. Brody gazed from the cannon to Henry in astonishment and said, "Look what you did!"

"It's war!" Henry said, without pleasure. Motioning Brody to the steps that led out of the hatch, he added, "Didn't I tell you it was a rescue, huh?" But just as Henry began climbing up after Brody, he felt powerful arms grab at the back of his jacket and yank him back down into the tank. He was under attack by the soldier that he thought had been knocked unconscious — the one whose face was stained by the ink from Henry's pen.

While Henry resumed his fight with the soldier, Vogel brought the shovel down on Indy's fingers yet again. Indy grimaced, his injured hands losing their grip. But instead of falling to the rocky ground, he stopped short. His bag's shoulder strap had become tangled around the end of the damaged side cannon. His legs dragged below him, kicking up dirt and dust — but he was alive.

The tank veered closer to the parallel wall, and the cannon's broken end began dragging against the rock, spilling dirt and stones down on top of Indy. He gasped and tried to wriggle free of his shoulder strap, but could not. Desperate to escape, he began tugging on the strap, trying to break it, but the only effect was that he felt the strap jerk sharply under his right arm. Dangling beside the tank, he turned to look up ahead and saw that the wall beside the tank ended at a rocky outcrop, which jutted out from the wall at almost a right angle.

Vogel saw the outcrop too. He moved over to crouch beside the turret and shouted a command to the driver. In response, the driver laughed and steered even closer to the rocky wall on the left, narrowing the gap between Indy and the wall.

Indy realized the driver was trying to crush him and he twisted his body sideways. He howled as heavier stones began raining down. His eyes went wide with fear as he watched the outcrop coming up fast. He had no reason to doubt that his death was only seconds away.

While the tank's driver focused on his target, he remained unaware of the battle raging only a few feet behind him. The ink-stained soldier wrestled Henry to the floor, and then both men saw the Luger that Henry had knocked from the soldier's hand earlier — the same weapon that Indy had dropped through the hatch.

The soldier reached for the Luger first. He was about to pull the trigger when he saw something stir in the corner of his vision. Turning his head, he saw Brody kneeling on the steps below the open hatch, holding a cylindrical artillery shell. Before the soldier could react, Brody brought it down hard over his head.

Still clutching the Luger, the stunned soldier fell backwards, and as he fell, he discharged the gun at the tank's ceiling. Sparks flew as the bullet ricocheted several times through the tank's interior, until it finally pinged off the metal above the front port and slammed into the driver's head. Blood flowed from under the driver's hat, and his body slumped forward.

As the dead driver's body depressed the steering levers, the tank veered sharply to the right. Vogel was unprepared for the sudden turn that sent the tank away from the rocky outcrop, and he was thrown down in front of the turret, onto an expanse of metal just below the main cannon.

Indy felt a brief but incredible sense of relief as the tank veered away from the outcrop — but the relief was quickly replaced by overwhelming rage. He grunted as he pulled himself up onto the cannon, worked his bag's strap free from the barrel, and hauled himself back onto the tank. Vogel was just rising from the area in front of the turret when Indy seized him by his jacket and launched his fist right into Vogel's face. Vogel fell backward and vanished over the side.

Leaning over the turret's hatch, Indy shouted, "Dad?"

Henry popped his head up through the hatch. He laughed and said sarcastically, "You call this archaeology?"

"Get out of there, Dad!" Indy said, tugging his father up through the hatch. And then they helped Brody out, so that all three men were standing on the back of the tank. That was when Vogel rematerialized.

Vogel had not fallen off the tank, only down in front of the turret again. After recovering himself, he grabbed the long-handled shovel and scrambled over the turret. Indy saw Vogel coming and barely dodged the Nazi's vicious swing. The shovel made a whooshing sound as it whipped past Indy's stomach.

Vogel swung at Indy's head, but Indy ducked and caught the shovel with his left hand. Behind Indy, Brody said, "How does one get off this thing?"

Brody got his answer when Indy wound back his right arm and his elbow knocked Brody off the back of the tank and onto the ground. Then Indy sent his fist into Vogel's jaw. Vogel stumbled back and fell over the turret's hatch. His hat fell off his head and landed somewhere within the tank.

Henry had not seen Brody's departure. He turned to Indy, looked around, and said, "Where's Marcus?"

Before Indy could reply, Vogel pushed himself away from the turret and swung the shovel at Indy. Indy ducked. The shovel hit Henry, and Henry fell over onto the left tread. Henry howled as his body bounced along the tread, heading for the front of the tank.

Moving with lightning speed, Indy reached for his bullwhip at his side, backhanded Vogel, then lashed out with his whip. The end of the whip wrapped around Henry's right ankle, and Henry yelped again.

Holding tight to the whip with both hands while his father bounced on the tread like a rag doll, Indy shouted, "Hang on, Dad!"

Henry yelled again. And then, while Indy struggled to save his father, Vogel came up behind Indy and punched him in the back. Indy gritted his teeth, but refused to let go of the whip.

Suddenly, a mounted figure came riding up fast behind the tank. It was Sallah on the horse he had taken from Donovan's caravan. As Sallah drew up along the left side of the tank, he tipped his fez to Henry and shouted, "Father of Indy, give me your hand!"

Vogel slid one arm around Indy's neck and struck him again in the back with the other. Indy shouted, "Sallah! Get Dad!"

"Give me your hand!" Sallah shouted again. As Henry reached out and Sallah grabbed hold of him, Indy flung his whip aside. Years of excavation work had made Sallah extremely strong, and he had no difficulty holding Henry aloft until his horse carried them away from the tank.

Vogel tried to choke Indy, but now that he had both hands free, Indy didn't hesitate to use them. He drove his elbow into Vogel's stomach and twisted Vogel's left arm up behind his back. Then Indy turned Vogel to face the back of the turret and slammed his head into it. Then he did it again. And again.

Indy was still unleashing his rage when he felt a strange shift in the air pressure. He lifted his gaze and looked ahead, only to see that the land appeared to fall away in front of them. The tank was heading straight for the edge of a high cliff.

Indy saw that Sallah had stopped his horse near the cliff's edge, and that his father was all right. And then a strong wind blew Indy's hat right off his head, and his face filled with horror as he realized he might have missed his last chance to jump off the tank.

Leaving Vogel draped over the turret, Indy's arms flailed as he threw himself backwards and rolled down the back of the tank, just as the front began to dip over the edge. The tank trundled over the cliff and plummeted.

Vogel clung tight to the turret and screamed his head off until the tank met the rocks far, far below.

Brody had just caught up with Henry and Sallah when they saw the tank vanish at the edge of the high plateau, and then they heard the crash. Sallah climbed down from his horse, and then all three men were running to the cliff's edge. Henry got there first.

"Junior?!" Henry shouted.

The tank exploded.

"Indy!" Sallah cried.

Smoke billowed from the tank as it continued to roll down the base of the cliff.

Henry scanned the ground below, searching for any sign of his son, but then his face fell with a sudden realization. "Oh, God," he gasped. "I've lost him." Henry's lower lip trembled. "And I never told him anything." He tried to look at Brody, but couldn't tear his gaze from the burning tank. "I just wasn't ready, Marcus. Five minutes would have been enough."

Just a short distance away, a tangle of dried-out roots shifted in the dirt at the cliff's edge. Hatless and battered, but otherwise breathing, Indiana Jones pulled himself up and over onto relatively firm ground. Rising to his feet, he turned to see his father and two friends standing dangerously close to the edge of the cliff, gazing down at something. Dazed and bewildered, he staggered up behind them, came to a stop beside his father, and followed their gaze to the wrecked tank far below. Nodding his head at the wreck, Indy gasped and caught his breath.

It took a moment for Henry to realize that it wasn't Sallah or Brody who had moved up beside him. Henry turned, saw Indy, and his mouth fell open. And then he threw his arms around his son and murmured, "I thought I'd lost you, boy!"

Indy's head began to clear, and he became aware of his father's embrace. Indy couldn't remember the last time his father had ever held him like that, if ever. But it touched him and he put his arms around his father, patted his back, and replied, "I thought you had too, sir."

Sallah and Brody watched silently as Henry and Indy embraced. Sallah knew it was a very special moment, and not just because Indy had survived. While Sallah beamed with happy appreciation and felt proud to be a witness to Indy's reconciliation with Henry, Brody looked from Indy to the tank and then back to Indy again, trying to sort out how Indy could be standing in front of them at all.

Pulling away from Indy and regaining mastery of his emotions, Henry said, "Well . . ." He clapped Indy's upper arms and finished, "Well done. Come on." Henry stepped away from the exhausted Indy, who promptly collapsed in a barely upright position.

Brody and Sallah followed Henry away from the edge

of the cliff and back to Sallah's horse. As Henry walked, he added, "Let's go, then." But then he stopped, turned to see that Indy wasn't walking with them, and he shouted back, "Why are you sitting there resting when we're so near the end?! Come on, let's go!"

Indy thought he would just sit there a while longer, but then a sudden gust of wind delivered his fedora from out of nowhere. As his hat rolled to a stop in front of his knees, Indy thought, *Maybe it* is *time to get moving.*

CHAPTER FIFTEEN

*W*alter Donovan and Elsa Schneider stood beside their open car, which was parked atop a high plateau overlooking a wide desert. Shortly after Colonel Vogel had taken the tank to pursue Indiana Jones, Donovan and Elsa had driven off in another direction along with the remains of their caravan and did their best to follow the map from Henry Jones' diary. While the German and Turkish soldiers kept watch nearby, Donovan peered through binoculars to view the upper rim of a narrow canyon; from his perspective, it looked like a C-shaped gorge that curved across the desert floor.

Lowering the binoculars, Donovan wore an astonished expression as he continued gazing at the gorge and said, "The Canyon of the Crescent Moon."

Elsa took the binoculars and peered through them. Indeed, it appeared that Donovan had found the legendary canyon. And if the ancient text on the Grail tablet was correct, the canyon would lead them to the temple where they would find the Holy Grail itself.

Sallah had rounded up the horses that Indy had been forced to release earlier, including the horse that had carried Indy to the tank. Hoping to recover the camels later, Sallah joined Indy, Henry, and Brody as they continued on horseback, making their way to the Canyon of the Crescent Moon.

Indy reached to the upper left side of his cheek and felt the wounds he had gained from the tank tread. He'd stopped bleeding and the pain wasn't too bad. He never wanted to add more scars to his collection, but the way he figured things, a few more scars were nothing compared to outright death.

Although Henry had never been to the Canyon of the Crescent Moon, he remembered the details of his map well enough to lead the way. Soon, the four men found Donovan's car and other vehicles abandoned at the mouth of a gorge that traveled through mountainous sandstone rocks, too narrow for the vehicles to enter. Henry and Indy went first, maneuvering their horses slowly along the shadowy floor of the gorge. Sallah and Brody followed.

Eventually, the gorge delivered them to an open area that faced a towering wall of rock illuminated by a broad shaft of sunlight. Carved directly into the sandstone cliff was a spectacular architectural façade, the remains of a hidden city, which displayed obvious Grecian influence. The men gaped at the sight of the colossal columns that lined the façade's entrance. Indy guessed the entire structure was around 150 feet tall.

The men dismounted, leaving their horses behind as they walked toward the structure. They climbed a flight of wide stone steps to arrive before a dark, rectangular doorway. Indy had reloaded his revolver, and Sallah also carried a pistol. Indy got his gun out and entered the doorway first. The other men followed silently.

They crept through a twisting, shadowy passage with rough-hewn walls until they heard a voice up ahead, someone speaking in German. They paused for a moment and then moved forward to peek around a corner that offered a view into a large chamber. It was a temple, with a broad stone floor embedded with a metal seal, and reliefs carved into the high walls. Standing in the temple was Donovan with about a dozen Turkish soldiers and just a few Nazis, all of whom were looking away from Indy's group, facing a stairway that led up into another passage. The stairway was bracketed by stone statues of knights and a pair of monstrous lions.

Indy, Henry, Sallah, and Brody lowered themselves behind some rocks that offered some protective cover as they watched Donovan's men. From what Indy could see, the men were all focused on one Turkish soldier in particular; the Turk held his sword out in front of him and had just begun moving cautiously up the steps to the next passage. At the bottom of the steps, a Nazi soldier held a pistol out, but Indy couldn't tell whether the pistol was aimed at the passage's entrance or the ascending Turk's back.

The Turkish soldier was nervous and sweating hard as he walked slowly into the passage. The passage's walls were dark and lined with thick cobwebs. When he glanced down at the floor, he saw one of his fellow soldiers lying on the ground; the soldier's eyes were closed and his mouth agape. Because the passage was so dark, it took a moment for the walking Turk to realize that the fallen soldier's head was lying *beside* his body, which had been neatly decapitated.

The walking Turk gasped, but held tight to his sword and stepped forward. He knew that if he turned back, the Nazi soldier would shoot him. His eyes were wide with terror when he heard what sounded like a distant beast's roar, and then the roar became louder. A sudden rush of air traveled toward him, making the cobwebs shiver, and then there was a whooshing sound. The last thing that the soldier heard was a clang as something struck his sword's blade.

Even from his hiding place, Indy had felt the surge of air that blew out from the upper passage, but he could only imagine what had happened to the Turkish soldier. A moment later, Indy had his answer when the Turk's head tumbled out of the passage and rolled past Donovan and the other soldiers. It was then, as a white-shirted figure near Donovan turned with a horrified expression, that Indy saw Elsa's face. The Turk's head didn't stop rolling until it thudded against the base of the rock that concealed Indy. Indy kept his own head low.

Donovan turned to the pistol-wielding Nazi soldier and said, "Helmut, another volunteer."

Helmut and a fellow Nazi grabbed another Turk and shoved him toward the passage's entrance. As the Turk protested and struggled, Brody cringed and looked away from the sight, only to face a group of Nazi soldiers who had snuck up behind him. The soldiers surged forward, leveling their guns at Indy and each member of his party.

Indy raised his hands. The Nazis took his gun and Sallah's pistol.

Donovan heard the commotion from behind, and signaled the Nazi soldiers to release the "volunteer." The other Nazis escorted Indy, Henry, Sallah, and Brody to stand before Donovan.

Elsa stepped past Donovan to face Indy. "I never expected to see you again."

"I'm like a bad penny," Indy said with a sneer. "I always turn up."

"Step back now, Dr. Schneider," Donovan said. "Give Dr. Jones some room. He's going to recover the Grail for us."

Indy laughed in Donovan's face.

"Impossible?" Donovan said, eyeing Indy cagily. "What do you say, Jones? Ready to go down in history?"

"As what?" Indy said. "A Nazi stooge, like you?"

Wincing with distaste, Donovan answered him scornfully. "Nazis?! Is that the limit of your vision? The Nazis want to write themselves into the Grail legend . . . take on the world. Well, they're welcome. But I want the Grail itself."

Indy and his father were standing beside each other, and they exchanged glances to confirm they were both thinking the same thing: Donovan was a lunatic.

"The cup that gives everlasting life," Donovan continued. "Hitler can have the world, but he can't take it with him. I'm going to be drinking my own health when he's gone the way of the dodo."

Donovan drew a small pistol from his pocket and aimed it at Indy as he backed away slowly, putting some distance between them. "The Grail is mine," Donovan said, "and you're going to get it for me."

Staring hard into Donovan's eyes, Indy said, "Shooting me won't get you anywhere."

"You know something, Dr. Jones? You're absolutely right." Donovan shifted his aim just slightly, pulled the trigger, and shot Henry. The bullet entered Henry's side, just below the ribs. Henry gasped and clutched at his side as his body pivoted to face his son.

"Dad?" Indy said, gripping his father's shoulders. "Dad?!"

"Junior . . ." Henry rasped out, and then fell forward against Indy.

"No!" Elsa shouted with concern as she moved toward Indy and Henry.

"Get back!" Donovan shouted to Elsa as she stepped in front of him. Elsa stopped in her tracks.

Brody and Sallah rushed over to help Indy lower Henry to the floor. Blood was flowing from the wound. Indy unbuttoned and pushed back his father's shirt, then grabbed a handkerchief from Sallah and pressed it against the wound to stanch the flow.

And then the rage overcame Indy. With murder in his eyes, he rose fast and spun toward Donovan, but saw that Donovan once again had the gun leveled at him.

"You can't save him when you're dead," Donovan said. "The healing power of the Grail is the only thing that can save your father now. It's time to ask yourself what you believe."

Indy had seen some incredible things in his lifetime, but he still wasn't convinced that the Grail existed, let alone that it possessed the power to save his father. However, there was one thing he believed with utmost certainty: If he didn't at least try to go after the Grail, Donovan would probably shoot Sallah and Brody, too — or try to send them into the passage.

Indy couldn't let that happen.

All the soldiers who surrounded Indy and his allies now stepped back, leaving a clear path between Indy and the steps that led past the monstrous lion statues to the upper passage. Indy carried his father's Grail diary as he walked slowly toward the passage's entrance. He also carried his whip, which dangled at his side. At least the Nazis had left him with that.

As he climbed the steps, he opened the diary to the pages his father had shown him when they had been on the zeppelin. In a low whisper, he read aloud, "'The Breath of God . . . only the penitent man will pass.'"

He lifted his gaze from the diary as he continued up the steps. Struggling to find the meaning of the words, he repeated, "'The penitent man will pass.'"

At the top of the steps, Indy stopped and glanced back into the chamber. He looked at his father, saw that he was still breathing, and then turned to proceed into the passage.

"The penitent man will pass," Indy whispered again to himself. "The penitent man ..." He looked down and saw the bodies of the two decapitated Turks who had preceded him.

In the temple chamber behind Indy, Henry lay on the floor, looking up at the ceiling as he contemplated the words he remembered from his diary. Unintentionally echoing his son, Henry rasped, "'Only the penitent man will pass. Only the penitent man will pass.'"

In the passage, Indy's eyes flicked to the passage's cobweb-covered walls. "The penitent man will pass," he repeated again. Holding the diary out in front of him to push the cobwebs aside, he muttered, "The penitent, penitent ... The penitent man ..." His eyes and ears were alert for the slightest movement, and he repeated the words without thinking about them, as if they might be a mantra that would lead him to enlightenment, or at least allow him to keep his head affixed to his neck. And out of this rhythm of words evolved a slight variation, as Indy said aloud, "The penitent man is humble before God. Penitent man is humble ..."

Then the passage seemed to breathe, and Indy saw the cobwebs begin to move.

"... kneels before God."

As Indy was hit by a rush of wind, he shouted, "Kneel!"

Obeying his own command, Indy dropped to his knees and instinctively rolled forward. There was an immediate grinding sound from overhead and behind him. When he came to a stop, he sat up beside an ancient gear mechanism made of wooden wheels. Somehow, he had activated the wheels, which were still moving. A length of rope dangled from the wall, and he looped it around one of the spinning wheels, jamming the mechanism.

Indy looked back to see a pair of large, rotating discs of metal with razor-sharp edges: one traveled out at an angle from a concealed slot in the wall, and the other pushed up through a similar slot in the floor. Because he had jammed the wooden mechanism, both circular blades stopped turning.

Catching his breath, Indy shouted back through the passage, "I'm through!"

In the outer chamber, Donovan and Elsa heard Indy's cry. Donovan said, "We're through."

Brody and Sallah heard, too, and they smiled with relief. Sallah was holding Henry, and looked down at him and said, "He's all right."

But Henry shook his head and said, "No."

Unaware of his father's negative response, Indy stood a short distance from the disabled blades as he consulted the diary again. "The second challenge: 'The Word of God. Only in the footsteps of God will he proceed.'" Brushing a layer of sticky cobwebs off the brim of his hat, he turned slowly and began to proceed deeper into the passage.

"The Word of God..." Indy repeated. "The Word of..."

He arrived before a thick curtain of cobwebs. Pulling them aside with his hand, he looked down to see that the passage floor extended with a cobblestone path. Each cobble was engraved with a letter. Turning the words of the second challenge over in his mind, Indy said, "Proceed in the footsteps of the Word."

While Indy examined the cobblestones, Brody and Sallah watched as Henry lifted his head painfully and said, "'The Word of God...'"

Thinking Henry was delirious, Brody said, "No, Henry. Try not to talk."

Henry lowered his head, which Sallah cradled carefully with his hands. Looking again at the chamber's ceiling, Henry rasped, "The name of God."

The words came to Indy at the same time. "The name of God..." he said, his gaze sweeping over the cobblestones. "Jehovah."

Unfortunately, Indy could not hear his father's coincidental caution, which Henry muttered out: "But in the Latin alphabet, 'Jehovah' begins with an 'I.'"

Hovering beside Henry, Sallah and Brody looked at each other with concern. They were both now convinced that Henry was just rambling.

In the passage, Indy said aloud, "J," and took a step forward onto a cobblestone that bore that letter. Immediately, the stone broke away and Indy crashed down through a hole in the floor. His arms shot out and he clutched the edges of the hole. For a moment, his legs dangled over a deep pit, but he grunted and pulled himself up through the hole. Incredibly, he had managed to hang onto the Grail diary.

"Idiot!" Indy cursed himself, and then muttered, "In Latin, 'Jehovah' starts with an 'I.'" He found the cobblestone that he was looking for and said aloud as he stepped onto it, "I." Then he moved to a stone at his left and said, "E." He moved to "H" without difficulty, but when he landed on "O," he found himself saying, "Oh!" as the stone behind him pivoted slightly, nearly knocking him off balance. He proceeded. "V ... A."

With some relief at having passed the second challenge, Indy arrived before a passage that was so narrow that he had to move sideways to walk its length. As he moved through it, he saw the silhouette of a carved lion's head that jutted out from one of the walls above him.

The passage ended at a sheer drop into a chasm that receded into darkness and which faced another wall of rock that appeared to be about a hundred feet away. Indy wouldn't even try to guess the chasm's depth. It looked bottomless, and he couldn't see any way to reach the opposite wall.

"'The Path of God,'" he said aloud. Strangely, there was something familiar about the chasm. He peered back into the passage, looked up at the lion's head, and then he remembered the medieval painting he'd seen in his father's home, the one that depicted a knight walking on thin air between two cliffs. He also recalled that his father had done a pen-and-ink sketch of that painting in his diary. Indy thumbed through the diary until he found the sketch, and he recited from memory, "'Only in the leap from the lion's head will he prove his worth.'"

Indy looked down and around his position again. "Impossible," he said. "Nobody can jump this."

Just then, he heard a distant cry of pain echo up from the passage behind him. A moment later, Brody's voice called out, "Indy! Indy, you must hurry! Come quickly!"

Indy knew his father was dying, and he wanted to run back through the passage and return to his father's side, but then he thought, *What if the Grail really can save Dad?*

And that's when it all hit him. Gazing forward at the empty air that stretched out between him and the far wall, he said, "It's a leap of faith." But then he glanced down again and said, "Oh, geez . . ."

While Indy tried to think around and through his situation, Henry gasped out from the temple chamber, "You must believe, boy. You must . . . believe."

Indy put his hand over his heart, took a few deep breaths, and closed his eyes. When he opened his eyes again, he felt almost relaxed with the idea of what he was about to do. And then he did it: He lifted his left foot and fell forward.

*I*ndy's arms went out at his sides, as if he might catch himself somehow before he plummeted to the rocks below, but then his left foot landed on something hard. It felt like a stone floor — an invisible stone floor — and then his right foot landed beside his left. Astonished, and wondering what exactly he was standing on, Indy held still for a moment, but then he shifted his head slightly to realize he was standing on a painted pathway. And then he figured out how.

Ingeniously, the first Crusaders had painted the surface of a stone bridge to create an illusion that aligned the bridge with the rocks below. The illusion only worked if one were standing below the lion's head at the end of the passage, and as Indy moved forward, the forced-perspective painting on the bridge became more obvious. Because the bridge was only about three feet wide and without railings, he moved very carefully.

After Indy crossed the "invisible" bridge, he saw some loose sand lying at the edge of the far wall. He bent down, scooped up a handful of sand, and then turned and tossed it out across the bridge. The scattered sand revealed the bridge's surface area, which would allow him to return safely.

The passage at the other end was so small that he had to crawl through it. He got down on his hands and knees and moved through until he emerged within a chamber illuminated by numerous torches. The torches cast a golden glow throughout the chamber, which had an altar displaying a vast array of chalices. The chalices were in different shapes and sizes, from small metal cups to large goblets, and most appeared to be made of gold or silver. There were possibly more than a hundred chalices in all.

But to Indy, the most amazing thing in the chamber was the knight.

The knight knelt before the altar, his back to Indy. He wore a cowl and gloves that were made of chain mail, and a gray cape covered his back. An ancient book was spread open on a stone bench in front of him, and his head was lowered over it. A shining sword rested against the edge of the bench beside his right hand, and he didn't move as Indy stepped up behind him. For a moment, Indy wondered if the knight's armor housed a skeleton or if it were merely empty.

But then the knight slowly raised his head.

Indy was speechless. Remembering his father's condition, he glanced at the chalices and wondered, *Why are there so many?*

Without warning, the knight reached for the sword as he stood up, and then swung the blade at Indy. Indy easily dodged the sword, which the knight then raised high over his head as he prepared to strike again. The knight's face was visible then, and Indy saw that he was a very old man with a white beard and mustache.

But the knight's attack ended there. Holding the sword overhead, he gasped at his effort, and then the sword's weight carried him backwards so that he fell on top of the stone bench behind him, right beside the book he had been reading.

"Oh," moaned the knight as Indy stepped over to help him up to a sitting position on the bench. The knight looked up at Indy and then smiled. In a deep voice, he said, "I knew you'd come . . ." Then the knight shook his head and finished, ". . . but my strength has left me."

Seeing the knight up close, Indy saw that his flesh, like his armor and cape, was gray, as if all color had been drained from him. Indy said, "Who are you?"

"The last of the three brothers who swore an oath to find the Grail and to guard it."

Indy's mind reeled. He said, "That was seven hundred years ago."

"A long time to wait," the knight said with a solemn nod. Still seated, he reached up to touch Indy's hat and said, "You're strangely dressed . . . for a knight."

As the knight examined Indy's bullwhip, Indy said, "I'm not exactly . . ." Catching himself, Indy said, "A knight? What do you mean?"

"I was chosen because I was the bravest, the most worthy. The honor was mine until another came to challenge me to single combat." Lifting his sword and holding it out to Indy, the knight said, "I pass it to you who vanquished me."

Indy gulped, then shook his head slightly. "Listen," he said, "I don't have time to explain, but —"

Indy was interrupted by a shuffling sound from behind. He turned, and then both he and the knight directed their gazes to the chamber's small opening. Donovan, clutching his gun in his right hand, came through first. He was followed by Elsa.

Indy stayed close to the knight. Both Donovan and Elsa gave the knight a cursory glance before their eyes fell upon the display of chalices. Dumbstruck by the sight, they moved forward toward the altar, searching for the Holy Grail amongst the gleaming cups and goblets that reflected the dancing light of the surrounding torches.

After gazing at the chalices for several seconds, Donovan turned with a perplexed expression to look directly at the knight and ask, "Which one is it?"

"You must choose," the knight replied. A moment later, he added, "But choose wisely. For as the true Grail will bring you life, the false Grail will take it from you."

"I'm not a historian," Donovan said as he surveyed the chalices. "I have no idea what it looks like. Which one is it?"

Moving behind Donovan, Elsa said, "Let me choose."

"Thank you, Doctor," Donovan said. Elsa smiled at him, and then she turned her attention to the chalices.

The knight looked to Indy, and Indy returned his gaze. Both were curious about whether Elsa would find the Grail, but Indy was more curious about what would happen if she didn't.

Elsa reached out with her black-gloved hands to pick up a solid gold goblet encrusted with emeralds. Still smiling, she handed it to Donovan, who took it and sighed, "Oh, yes." Holding the goblet out before him, he marveled at it and remarked, "It's more beautiful than I'd ever imagined!"

Elsa continued to smile, but then she glanced at Indy and her smile melted away. Indy caught something in her gaze, a certain look that told him that maybe, just maybe, she really had learned something from her mistakes, and that she had just done something to try and make amends — or was it to further her own ends?

A large basin of water was on a table across from the altar. As Donovan carried the goblet to the basin, he said, "This certainly is the cup of the King of Kings." He dipped the goblet into the basin, filled it with water, raised it as if making a toast, and said, "Eternal life." And then he raised the goblet to his lips, closed his eyes, and drank the water.

Donovan's eyes were still closed as he slowly lowered the goblet from his face. He sighed with satisfaction at his accomplishment, but a moment later, his eyes opened and he gasped again as he bent forward over the water-filled basin in a painful convulsion. Staring into the basin, he saw his face reflected in the water and saw that his skin appeared to be sagging below his eyes.

Donovan turned away from the basin and looked at the backs of his hands, where liver spots and wrinkles had suddenly formed. Trembling, he raised his gaze to Elsa and rasped, "What . . . is happening . . . to me?" He lurched forward and grabbed Elsa by her shoulders.

Elsa gasped and screamed as Donovan began to age rapidly in front of her. A moment after he gripped her shoulders, his silver hair suddenly sprouted, growing long, gray, and brittle. Donovan shouted, "Tell me, what . . . is . . . happening?!"

Indy froze, horrified by the sight of Donovan's transformation. Beside him, the seated knight barely stirred.

Elsa shrieked as Donovan's skin turned brown and leathery, stretching across his bones until it cracked and split. His eyeballs shrank back into his skull as he raised his boney hands to Elsa's throat and tried to choke her.

Indy rushed forward and pulled Elsa toward him as he pushed Donovan's fury-driven remains away. Donovan's skeleton fell back against the wall and shattered, exploding into dust. Elsa clung to Indy and kept right on screaming.

Indy stared at the heap of bones and dust on the floor. A sudden wind whipped through the chamber and blew back the dust beside what was left of Donovan's skull. The dust shifted to reveal a small metal pin with a black swastika in the middle of it. Evidently, Donovan — for all his claims otherwise — had been a member of the Nazi party after all.

The knight looked to Indy and Elsa and said, "He chose ... poorly."

Indy held the knight's gaze for a moment, but then he moved to the altar and looked at all the ornate chalices. Elsa followed him and said, "It would not be made out of gold."

Indy's eyes came to rest on a simple earthenware cup

that sat behind some metal chalices that appeared to be far more valuable. "That's the cup of a carpenter." Elsa looked at it doubtfully, but Indy was determined, and said, "There's only one way to find out."

Indy glanced at the knight as he walked over to the water basin. He filled the cup, but paused for a moment as he remembered what had become of Donovan. But then Indy thought of his father, and it was with that thought that he raised the cup to his lips and took several large swallows.

Indy turned fast and looked at the knight. As he turned, Indy felt a strange sensation at his upper left cheek. Reaching up to the side of his face, he touched the place where the tank tread had cut into his flesh. But instead of touching wounds, he felt smooth skin above the whiskers along his jaw. Indy's wounds had been healed.

The knight said, "You have chosen wisely. But the Grail cannot pass beyond the Great Seal. That is the boundary and the price of immortality."

Indy remembered the metal seal as he refilled the Grail, and Elsa followed him as he left the knight behind and carried the Grail back to the chamber where he'd left his father. Brody and Sallah were still with Henry, trying to comfort him, but his flesh had assumed a deathly pallor from all the blood he'd lost. The soldiers stepped aside as Indy returned. Henry's eyes were closed, and he had been about to breathe his last when Indy lowered the Grail to his lips.

Henry drank from the Grail, but some of the water ran down the corners of his mouth. Sallah tilted Henry's head forward so the water would flow more easily. After Henry had gulped some down, Indy moved the Grail over the wound on his father's side and poured the remaining water directly onto it. Henry winced and steam rose from his flesh, but then, to everyone's astonishment, the blood washed away and the wound disappeared.

Looking to his father's face, Indy saw the pallor had left and his color had returned. Henry's eyes opened, and he gazed up at the ceiling for a moment as if he were trying to remember where he was. Then, he noticed Indy. Seeing his son, Henry beamed. And then Henry saw the cup in his son's hands.

Henry reached up and touched the Grail. He looked at Indy with questioning eyes, and from Indy's smile he knew the answer. *Yes, it's the Holy Grail, Dad.*

Henry took the Grail and held it. It felt so much lighter than he'd imagined, and he could barely believe that he was actually holding the object that he had spent most of his life searching for.

Elsa stood just a short distance away, staring at the Grail with wonder. The Turkish soldiers were awestruck by the sight of the Grail and Henry's recovery, and they threw down their weapons and fled from the temple. Sallah snatched up a fallen rifle and leveled it at the Nazis. "Drop your weapons," Sallah said. "Please."

The remaining soldiers dropped their weapons and raised their hands in surrender.

Indy was still kneeling beside his father. "Dad, come on. Get to your feet." As he helped his father up, Henry left the Grail on the floor.

Elsa bent down and picked up the Grail. Indy noticed Elsa's action, and then Henry saw her, too. She took a few steps across the chamber, and then turned to Indy and said, "We have got it! Come on!" She started to back up, moving across the metal seal in the floor toward the passage that led back outside.

"Elsa!" Indy said and took a cautious step forward. "Elsa, don't move!"

"It's ours, Indy," Elsa said, holding the Grail out in front of her. "Yours and mine." She took another couple of step backwards, and there came a rumbling sound from all around the temple as she arrived at the seal's center.

"Elsa, don't cross the seal," Indy said firmly. "The knight warned us not to take the Grail from here."

The rumbling continued, and Elsa looked around nervously. Indy looked toward the chamber walls, and then dust and dirt suddenly rained down from the ceiling. The floor began quaking, and Elsa was knocked off balance. As she fell upon the seal, the Grail bounced away from her grasp and rolled across the floor. A crack opened up in the stone floor directly below the Grail, and then the crack became a split. Elsa scrambled up from the floor and lunged for the Grail.

Elsa landed on top of the split, but the broken floor to her left rose suddenly, and the split widened, throwing her off balance again. The tips of her gloved fingers bumped into the Grail, knocking it into the crevasse. The Grail landed on a small, rocky ledge below, and Elsa found herself slipping off the edge of the broken, rising floor.

The temple was in chaos. Sallah and Brody felt the floor beneath them tilt back at a steep angle. The remaining soldiers leaped across the chasm and dodged falling rocks in a desperate effort to escape. Henry stumbled, and Indy grabbed him and picked him up.

Elsa clung to the upper edge of the widening crevasse and screamed. She lost her grip, slipped down to a shallow ledge, and kicked off, hurling herself across the gap to land on her stomach on the opposite floor. But that floor began to tip up, too, and Elsa's legs kicked at empty air as she began to slide off the edge.

Seeing Elsa's position, Indy dived away from his father's side and slid headfirst down the inclined stone floor, skidding across the small, loose stones that now shifted and bounced across the upended floor's surface. Spreading his legs out behind him, he launched his arms forward and caught Elsa's hands in his just as she fell away from the floor.

Elsa's eyes were wide with fear as she clutched at Indy's wrists and her body swung out over the dark abyss. Above and behind Indy, Henry shouted, "Junior! Junior!"

Elsa turned her head to see the Grail resting on the nearby ledge. Indy knew what she was thinking. Muscles straining, he gasped, "Elsa —"

Too late. She jerked her left hand free of his grip and extended her arm out, reaching for the Grail. Indy's suddenly empty right hand flew beside his left to clamp onto Elsa's right gloved hand.

Elsa swayed slightly as she tried to grab the Grail. It was only a few inches beyond her grasp. Above her, Indy said, "Elsa, don't. Elsa . . ."

But she kept trying for it.

"Elsa . . ." Indy said, trying to keep his voice calm. "Give me your other hand, honey." Feeling her gloved hand begin to slip through his grasp, his voice grew louder with mounting panic as he said, "I can't hold you!"

"I can reach it," Elsa said, keeping her eyes obsessively fixed on the Grail. "I can reach it."

Her right hand slid slightly out of her glove. Indy clamped his fingers even more tightly around hers, but he could feel he was losing her.

"Elsa, give me your hand. Give me your other hand!"

But Elsa kept her left hand extended toward the Grail. And then her right hand slipped again.

"Elsa!"

She screamed as she plummeted into the chasm, falling past the jagged walls of rock to her death far below. Before Indy could pull himself back, the stone that he lay upon crumbled and broke apart. He threw his arms out as he tumbled over the edge, just as Henry moved fast to grab Indy's right hand.

Indy found himself in the same position that Elsa had been. He looked to his left and saw the Grail on the ledge.

"Junior, give me your other hand," Henry said. "I can't hold on!"

"I can get it," Indy said in a harsh whisper. He stretched out his left arm as far as he could. "I can almost reach it, Dad." One of his fingers actually brushed against the side of the Grail.

"Indiana . . ." Henry said, keeping his voice calm, just as Indy had done when he had tried to lure Elsa away from the Grail. "Indiana . . ."

Indy had never heard his father call him "Indiana"

before. His left arm went slack against his side, and he turned his head to look up into his father's eyes. Henry said, "Let it go."

Indy realized his father was straining at the effort to hang onto him. And although his father hadn't said it in so many words, he realized that his father cared more about him than he did for the Holy Grail.

Indy threw his left arm up to his father. Henry grabbed it and hauled Indy up over the edge. Sallah and Brody had been braced against a nearby wall, and now that Indy and Henry were all right, they edged toward the exit. As the ground went on rumbling and rocks continued to fall, Henry was about to head for a way out when he saw a shadowy figure looming at the top of the stairway between the lion statues. The figure was the Grail's ages-old guardian.

The knight gazed through the falling debris to Henry.

More stones began to fall, and Indy rushed to Brody and Sallah, steering them toward safety. Then Indy saw that his father had stopped walking and was staring back at the upper passage. "Dad . . ." Indy said, and then followed his father's gaze to see the knight.

The knight raised his right arm, saluting Henry across the temple chamber.

"Please, Dad," Indy said.

Henry looked at the knight for just a moment longer

before he turned and ran with Indy. They didn't look back at the knight, who continued to stand there with his hand raised, watching the men run away. As Indy and Henry hurtled out of the temple, a stone column crashed down behind them, sealing off the temple and leaving the knight to his fate.

*I*ndy and Henry bolted down the steps outside the ancient, palatial entrance to the temple. From behind, they heard the roar of walls caving in, and a high cloud of dust rolled out from the large, rectangular doorway and then crashed like a wave onto the ground outside. Ahead of them, they saw Sallah and Brody had already reached the horses that they'd left outside. There was no sign of the surviving soldiers.

When they reached a safe distance from the temple's entrance, Indy stopped and turned to face it. The rumbling had ceased, and the dust appeared to be settling. Indy gazed at the temple's façade and thought of Elsa.

He really had cared for her.

Henry looked at Indy, then walked up beside him and said, "Elsa never really believed in the Grail. She thought she'd found a prize."

Turning to face his father, Indy said, "What did *you* find, Dad?"

"Me?" Henry said. His eyes flicked to the façade and back to Indy as he mulled over the question, and then he answered, "Illumination."

Sallah and Brody had already mounted their horses. As Henry and Indy climbed onto their own, Henry looked to his son and said, "And what did you find, Junior?"

"'*Junior?*'" Indy snapped. "Dad . . ." He raised his hand and aimed an accusatory finger at his father.

"Please," Sallah interrupted, looking at Indy. "What does it always mean, this . . . this 'Junior?'"

"That's his name," Henry informed Sallah. "Henry Jones, Junior."

"I *like* Indiana," Indy muttered as he averted his gaze to the sandstone wall in front of him.

Leaning out from his saddle to scowl at his son, Henry said, "We named the *dog* Indiana."

Brody interrupted, "May we go home now, please?"

Sallah stared at Indy and bellowed, "The *dog*?!" Sallah chuckled. "You are named after the dog?" And then Sallah roared with laughter.

Keeping his eyes on the sandstone, Indy said, "I've got a lot of fond memories of that dog." Then he turned his head to face his father and Sallah, as if daring them to challenge him on the subject. While Sallah continued to laugh, Henry removed a handkerchief from his pocket, draped it over his head, and then wrapped and tied his bowtie around his head to fashion an improvised *keffiyeh*. When his father was done tying off the bowtie, Indy said, "Ready?"

"Ready," Henry replied.

"Indy! Henry!" Brody exclaimed. "Follow me! I know the way!" To his horse, he cried out, "Haaa!"

Brody had a tight grip on the reigns, but he nearly fell off his horse's back as it launched off into the narrow gorge that led back to the high desert. From their own horses, Sallah, Henry, and Indy watched Brody's departure with some amusement.

Turning to his son, Henry said, "Got lost in his own museum, huh?"

"Uh-huh," Indy said.

Henry gestured toward the gorge and said, "After you, Junior."

"Yes, sir," Indy said. He jerked his horse's reigns and shouted, "Haaa!"

Indy rode off after Brody. Sallah and Henry followed. They rode at full gallop, weaving through and out of the Canyon of the Crescent Moon. It wasn't until they exited the canyon and arrived at the edge of the wide-open desert plain that Indy finally caught up with Brody and helped the man right himself on his horse.

The four men rode off, heading off across the desert toward the setting sun. Indy cast one last glance back toward the Canyon of the Crescent Moon. This might have been his grandest adventure yet, but he was sure it wouldn't be his last.